PAINFUL LOVE

T ASHLEIGH

ADDISON BECK

To all those who feel just a little different.
Bunk's got you.

CONTENTS AND TRIGGERS

Trigger/Content Warnings

Be advised this story is written with some 'slang' and broken dialect to authenticate and give a well-rounded representation of the characters.

This book contains very dark themes/references and is meant for readers eighteen and older.

Underage Drinking

Drug Use

Underage Smoking

Gang Affiliations

Distribution of Drugs

Past Deceased Parents

Past Parental Violence

Past Murder-Suicide

Murder

Past Parental Neglect

Blood Kink

Toxic Relationships

Physical Violence

Profanity

Untreated Mental Illness
Undiagnosed Mental Illness
Unsafe Kink Practices
PTSD
Torture
Mutilation
Degradation
Suicidal Thoughts
18+ Sexual Scenes

INTRODUCTION

Painful Love is book two in the Kings of Aces series. This interconnected series can be read as standalones, as each book revolves around a different couple. However, reading them in order is recommended due to world building and background information you learn over the course of the series.

Be advised this story is written with some 'slang' and broken dialect to authenticate and give a well-rounded representation of the characters.

SYNOPSIS

Whaley

My life has been a series of one nightmare after another. Every day is a fight to be stronger as I try to outrun the past that refuses to give me peace. Somehow, I managed to keep myself under control...

Until Bunky messed it all up.

His soul screams to mine in a way that awakens every part of me, even the parts I've tried to keep buried. We're a jagged fit, a match made in Hell, but I can't have him because together we'd burn the world to the ground.

Bunky doesn't see that. He'd rather fuel the toxic fire of obsession than give up, and I don't know how much longer I can hold out before I cave to the demon that everyone should fear.

Including him.

Bunky

I'm not what most people would consider normal.

Everything in my life is touched by darkness and shaped by my past. Living life constantly on the brink of being swallowed up by the monster that wants to consume me is exhausting, so I drowned myself in vices to try and smother the memories.

Until I realized all I needed was my missing piece.

Whaley flipped a switch in my brain, making me see he was meant to be mine, but he's not letting us be together like we were made to. He's too worried we'll destroy everything in our path if we give in to the connection that tethers us together.

Good thing I have no problem watching the world burn if it means I get him.

Painful Love is an age-gap, dark obsessive romance that centers around a guarded man and his little psycho. Mix in some toxic vibes, looking pasts, and deep connections, and Painful Love will have you itching for more.

PLAYLIST

Painful Love - playlist by AddisonBeckRomance | Spotify

PROLOGUE

Whaley
25 Years Old

I sit back on the couch, sweat-slicked and sated for the first time in weeks. I grab my pack of smokes off the table, take one out, and light up. I close my eyes as the taste of tobacco coats my tongue, the smoke relaxing me as it fills my lungs. The nicotine buzz mixed with the dopamine from my recent orgasm, along with remnants of the line I snorted, sends me fucking soaring. I'm so high on endorphins that I sail past the moon.

I release a sly chuckle and take another puff of my smoke, trying to blank out my mind for this very small window I allow.

It's *that* Saturday again. My once-a-month getaway to unwind and regroup to stay sane.

"That was good," the girl whose name I don't remember says, pulling my attention back to her.

Damn, through my haze I forgot she was even here. I should probably thank her for making the trip worth it, but I don't have the energy. I'd rather enjoy the jelly-like feeling that's settled in my limbs.

I watch as she redresses, sliding on her risqué nightgown and too-high heels before she hits me with a saucy wink and smile. "If you're ever back, ask for me. I wouldn't mind a second round."

I don't bother telling her that it's never going to happen. The reason I use this particular sex service is for their discretion, and even though she sucks cock like a Hoover, obeys, and breaks apart beautifully when she comes, I'll never want a second go. It's not her fault, it's just not my thing. I keep my fucks anonymous, using paid women to quench my desires. It's been working fine for the last few years, and I have no reason to change it now.

After a few moments of silence where we stare at each other, her eyes hopeful and me ready for her to fucking go, her smile wavers and she finally relents. After placing a card with what I assume is her contact info down, she leaves me to my peaceful nirvana.

Well, peaceful for all of five-fucking-minutes until my phone blares. My eyes snap open, and I lean forward, snatching it off the table. When I see *Badge* across the screen, I know it's serious. He's my right-hand and knows how important these R&R weekends are for me, so if he's calling that means some shit's going down.

I slide right to answer, hearing his uneven pants of breath through the line instantly and... screams?

Who the fuck is that?

"Badge?" I dab out my smoke, unable to hold back the worry in my tone. The cries grow louder, and I can hear the muffled sounds of Badge as he tries to calm whoever that is. "Badge?"

When he doesn't answer me again, I hop up from the couch, pull on my discarded clothes, and gather all my shit from around the room. I don't know what's happening, but if the sounds are anything to go by, it's fucked.

"Badge!" I bark out, sliding on my jacket and heading for the door.

"Whaley."

The broken way he says my name has me pausing briefly in surprise before I run down the motel steps. "Badge?"

"Whaley, I need your help."

It's five words. Five words that, unbeknownst to me, just set the course for the rest of my life.

Half an hour later, I'm stepping off my bike, and I spot Badge and Pike waiting for me in front of a run-down apartment building.

"Where is Ellen?" I take note of Badge's sad eyes and Pike's downcast stare.

"4B," Badge mutters.

Pike gives his arm a little squeeze before finally looking at me. "She's dead."

Badge met Ellen at a bar a few months back. They hit it off, and he'd been seeing her ever since. I've met her a few times and thought she was a good fit for him. Sadly, tonight proves how little we actually knew her.

From what I gathered during Badge's frantic explanation on the phone, her stalking, abusive ex-husband was still in the picture. I note the crimson splotches on Badge's arms, along with an assortment of cuts and scratches he now carries like battle wounds. I don't know if it's his blood or hers, or what *exactly* happened before I got here, considering I could hardly understand him through his freak-out, but as I had suspected earlier, the whole situation is fucked.

I give his shoulder a comforting pat, doing my best to make sure he knows I'm here. "You good if I go in?" I need to see what I'm dealing with.

"Go ahead," he whispers, sounding nothing like the burly, strong guy I know. "I'll come with you."

I'm about to tell him it's fine, but his hard look deters me. He's stubborn like me, and in order to move on he needs to handle the rest of his *business*.

I inhale deeply, nodding to them both before making my way into the complex and down the hall. It's a shitty building with water-stained ceiling tiles, blinking fluorescents that look close to dying any second, and yellow-tinted walls from years worth of cigarette smoke and grime. It's nothing like I'd expect for Ellen, but I guess it's just one more thing we didn't know about her.

I fight the urge to look back at Badge, not wanting him to think I'm judging. Some people have demons and way too many skeletons in their closet to ever recover from. Sadly, I think Ellen fell victim to her fucked-up past and circumstance.

I can relate.

My eyes scan the numbers on each door, and I stop when I come to 4B. I don't hesitate in grabbing the handle and twisting it open. The door creaks loudly, drawing me in with a deafening finality. I follow its call, stepping into the apartment and holding back the rising bile that threatens to spew past my lips as I'm assaulted by the acrid smell of piss, smoke, and liquor. My eyes dart around the space, taking in the array of empty bottles and trash littering the floor before settling on the needle, lighter, and spoon on the coffee table.

"I didn't know," Badge whispers as if reading my mind. "She didn't give off this vibe at all."

"It's not your fault," I try to assure him. "And honestly, we don't know the whole story, so who's to say any of this was hers."

He sighs, reaching up and fisting his messy curls. "I didn't ask enough questions. It's so fucked now. We were together for months, and I never saw her place, always just brought her back to mine. I never pushed about her bruises or why she sometimes looked way too tired. The red lights were flashin' so brightly and I missed them all. I was stupid."

He was lonely.

That's what it comes down to. He was starved for attention and thought he found the one in Ellen. He jumped in headfirst and asked questions later, missing all the red flags, and it ultimately fucked him up. Fucked *us* all up, but it'll be okay.

I already called my clean-up crew to get this settled.

I don't have to ask where the bodies are, not when I see the spattering of blood leading down the hall like some fucked-up treasure trail. I follow it, grimacing slightly at the feel of the sticky, crusted carpet under my boots. I didn't know it was possible for a carpet to be either of those things, but apparently it is.

The hall is short, and soon enough I'm pushing open the door to the bedroom, taking in the torn-apart space with splatters of blood up the walls. I see what I assume is Ellen's dead ex in the center of the dirty mattress, now saturated in blood.

"You did this?" I motion to the mutilated body behind me as I look at Badge.

"Yeah, stabbed him four times. I didn't bring my silencer, or it'd have been less messy. Sorry about that." He looks past my shoulder, glaring at the dead body on the bed. "Well, not too sorry. I should have stabbed him more. He deserved it."

I nod, having no doubt that's true. Badge is older than me, more like a dad than my old man ever was, and despite the fact that he has literal blood on his hands, he follows a code. We all do when it comes to this kind of shit.

"Where is she?"

"Just there, the bathroom." His whole body changes, shoulders dropping as he shuffles on his feet, pain-filled eyes flicking to the closed door beside me. "I have to warn you, this is where everythin' gets fucked-up."

5

He's hesitant, which makes my hackles rise. Badge is usually very direct, he doesn't sugarcoat shit, and by his lack of conversation on the phone and inability to hold my gaze, I'm wondering how screwed up this is going to be. I turn to look at Pike lingering at the end of the hall, but he doesn't meet my eyes.

I quirk a brow, unable to hold back my unease. "More fucked-up than two dead bodies?"

"More fucked-up than that," he confirms.

Unable to take the suspense any longer, I give the door handle a twist, pushing it open slowly and methodically, as if I'm somehow schooling myself for the scene that awaits me on the other side.

Honestly, it doesn't matter, because I don't think *actually* knowing could have prepared me for this.

"Badge!" I gasp, my heart pounding and sweat beading across my forehead as I take in the scene.

Ellen is beaten past the point of being recognizable. She's lying in a pool of blood, her body twisted in a weird shape and her head is busted open. It's a typical murder scene, one I've seen a hundred times, but the small boy huddled near the tub in dirty clothes, covered in Ellen's blood, is what has me almost dropping to my knees.

He's shaking, his little arms wrapped tightly around his drawn-up legs as he rocks back and forth in a daze. He's young, probably eight or so. Looks around the same age as Silas if I had to guess. His dark hair is matted, caked with God knows what, reminding me a little of a young *Tarzan*. I take a tentative step into the bathroom, and as if he just real-ized I was there, the boy lurches, coming up onto his haunches, dirty fists raised as if he's prepared to fight.

My heart sinks.

The things this kid must have gone through.

I hold my hands up, prepared to tell him I mean him no

harm when his gaze meets mine. The biggest, doe-like green eyes I've ever seen.

The ghost of my old self.

A mirage of my past.

A cautionary tale.

Then the room tilts and I really do drop to my knees.

Her tear-streaked face, busted eye, tousled hair.

Mommy.

"Charlie, hide. I need you to hide, baby."

Scared.

My legs running, sprinting through the house trying to find a spot.

Down there.

Shut the door quietly and race down the stairs.

It's dark. So dark. Ouch. I busted my knee because I can't see.

Crawling. Need to hide.

Panting.

Shaking… It's cold in the basement.

How long have I been down here?

I'm hungry.

Lights.

"He's over here."

Fight, fight, fight!

"Don't touch me."

A wail, a punch, both from me.

"The bitch is dead."

"Mommy. Mommy, please, wake up."

Her cold, dead body… Hands, my tiny hands, shaking her.

Blood. So much blood.

Flashlights, police, loud voices.

A gunshot.

He's dead too.

Red, blue, red, blue.

Sirens.

Loud sirens, too loud.

"What's your name, kiddo?"
My name?
"Charles Whalen."
"Whaley!"

I inhale sharply, my chest shuddering as I regain my senses. My hand flies to my throat as I gasp for air.

Fuck, did I stop breathing?

My panicked eyes dart around the room as sweat coats my skin. Those long ago suppressed feelings of abandonment and fear crash over me, making me turn my neck and vomit on the blood-covered floor. Thank God I'm already on my knees because the woozy, lightheaded feeling has my peripheral dimming. I think I'm going to pass out. It's been so long since I thought about that shit. *That time.* I always try to pretend it didn't happen at all.

"Whaley!"

A sharp sting to my cheek has me blinking roughly, refocusing on the bathroom. No, not the bathroom, the curious, yet terrified-looking boy directly across from me.

"Sorry, fuck, I didn't mean to hit you, but you were spacin'. I need you to focus, man."

Shit, that's Badge, but I don't care about him right now. I only care about the kid whose eyes hold the same insecurity, the same level of pain that I'm all too familiar with.

It's like looking into the same dejected eyes I see every morning in the mirror.

"What the fuck, Badge?" I mutter, wiping my spit-covered chin with the back of my hand. I want to scream. I don't though, not wanting to alarm the skittish boy.

"I know, I know. I just—I told you it was all messed up."

"That doesn't even scratch the surface," I whisper, my voice sounding gargled.

What the hell am I supposed to do about this? I can't call the cops because Badge killed the asshole lying in the next room, and I don't have an in with anyone at CPS, so...

What the fuck do I do?

I pull out my phone, my mind racing with a thousand unanswered thoughts, and I do the only thing that makes sense.

ME:

Can you grab some of Silas' clothes and meet me at my trailer in thirty? I need your help. Will explain in a bit.

The response comes quickly, as expected, and I read it feeling a bit more at ease.

DONNA:

I got you.

Tucking my phone away, I look at the wide-eyed boy once more. He's untrusting, that much is obvious, and I hold my hands up once again, wanting to appear unthreatening.

"I'm Whaley. Do you have a name?"

The kid eyes me, not saying a thing, so I nod and don't press him any further. As careful as I possibly can, I shift forward, trying not to touch Ellen's body, but grimacing slightly at the feeling of cooling blood seeping through the knees of my jeans. I don't want to stand and freak him out more. At least like this, I'm on his level.

"Be careful. Kid's got nails like razors and a surprisingly good left hook," Badge warns, pulling my attention to him, and it's only now that I notice the bruise blossoming on his chin.

Despite the situation, my lip quirks as I look back at the kid. "You good at fightin', huh?"

He still doesn't speak, and I move a little closer, being as slow as possible so he doesn't go apeshit.

"You see this?" I ask him, tapping the Kings of Aces patch on the right side of my leather jacket. "I'm an Aces. Doubt you know what that means, but basically, I got a code. I don't wanna hurt you, kid, but I do need to get you outta here." He jerks back, his hand shooting out at my words, and if it wasn't for my reflexes, he'd have clocked me in the jaw. Badge wasn't lying. "Hey, hey. None of that," I utter, trying to calm him. "I mean it, I won't hurt you, won't even touch you."

That causes him to relent, his body slackening from his defensive pose. "Really, you won't?"

My heart threatens to crack at his raspy, worry-filled, broken words. It sounds like each utterance costs him something. I wonder if he's thirsty or just hasn't talked in some time.

Neither option is good.

"I promise."

"Don't trust you," he whispers, his eyes flicking down to Ellen's body before zeroing back on me. "Mama said don't trust strangers."

"Your mama is a very smart lady." My tone wavers a fraction, the mix of emotions I'm trying to keep at bay surfacing so quickly it's beginning to suffocate me.

"*Was*. She's gone now." He doesn't sound as sad as expected. If anything, he sounds resigned, like this was a long time coming.

An old soul.

A kid with the mentality of a grown-ass man.

"I know." I understand his reaction completely.

"Whaley, the crew's here. We need to get goin'," Badge says, but I don't acknowledge him, not wanting to lose the ground I've made with...

"What's your name?" I try again, but he still doesn't waver. Instead, his eyes drill into mine, refusing to give me an inch. "What about this?" I reach my hand into my pocket and pull out my knife. It's my lucky one. I've had it since I was initiated, and I'm hoping it'll give me the luck I need right now to get this kid out of here unnoticed. I flip it open before placing it down on the bloody floor, then shuffle back to give him space to take it. "That's yours. If anyone tries to touch you, I want you to stab them, okay?"

"Whaley…" Badge inquires with a shocked voice, but I raise my hand to shut him up. This is no doubt the stupidest thing I've ever done, but I'm desperate. The longer we're here, the greater the chance of getting caught, and that's the last thing I need.

The kid is skeptical, his eyes bouncing between me and the knife before making his decision. He grabs it quickly, slicing it through the air experimentally.

"Stab you," he mumbles, his eyes challenging. "Because I can?"

"Then you'd be bitin' the hand that feeds you. That's not somethin' we do. It's against our code," I tell him firmly, hoping to convey how serious those words are to me.

"Code? You keep saying that. Don't get it."

"How about this?" I stand and shoot a thumb behind me. "We go back to my car, I take you to get cleaned up, and afterward, I'll tell you all about it."

He bites on his bottom lip, the knife still pointed outward as his eyes briefly fall down to Ellen before flickering back up to me. "Touch me, I will *stab*. Not scared."

"You'd be warranted to stab me if I broke my word. It's my bond."

I can tell he doesn't know what that means either, but he reluctantly stands on shaking legs. He's smaller than I originally thought, and his body is covered in dirt and blood. What the hell happened to him to make him look like this? And more importantly, how in the hell am I going to get him out of here unnoticed?

Without a thought, I tug off my jacket and place it on the bathroom sink before taking a small step back into the hallway. "Can you put that on? It's cold and you're—"

"Gross," he finishes, stepping over his mom's body, bare

feet sliding a bit in her blood. "I know, always dirty. I'm picked on a lot."

He grabs my jacket, eyes never leaving me as he slides it on quickly, doing his best to keep his blade extended. My jacket drowns him, but it'll have to do.

"Come on, kid." I motion for him to follow, hoping like hell he actually does, or better yet, hoping he doesn't fucking run for the hills once we're outside. I really don't want to have to chase him down, but I will for a number of reasons. I don't need this kid running to the cops, but I also feel the need to help him.

Like the Aces helped me all those years ago.

Badge and Pike are both looking at me like I've lost it, and they're not wrong to assume that. I have no clue what's possessed me to act so recklessly, aside from the fact that the kid reminds me of *me*.

"Keys." I hold my hand out to Badge, knowing he drove his truck. No way I'm carting this kid on the back of my bike.

He pulls them out, pausing a second as if he's still contemplating my sanity before letting out a long breath and nodding. We exchange keys, another thing that's not like me. No one drives my bike, but tonight is proving to be an episode straight from *The Twilight Zone*.

I head down the hall, passing my clean-up crew who nods, eyes shifting before widening at the bloodied-up boy who I'm guessing decided to follow behind me, knife likely on full display.

"No one touches him." My tone is stern, loud enough for them all to hear, and the collective hums of understanding meet my ears in return.

We get to the truck easily enough, and I'm thankful to the universe the kid didn't try to escape. Maybe the knife gave him the security he needed to follow me, and I'm grateful as fuck for that.

I take out my smokes, lighting one up before reversing

from my spot and heading home. I try one more time to get him to tell me his name, but it falls on deaf ears. He doesn't say a peep the entire way to the trailer park, just keeps his back to the door, knife tilted up as he watches me.

I pull up in front of my place and park, glad that it's so early, or late depending on who you ask, so there's no one here to witness this. I don't want the kid to be alarmed by too many people right now.

"Kid, you see that lady over there?" I point to Donna, who's standing on the bottom step of my trailer, looking curiously at me with a grocery bag full of clothes dangling in her hand. "She's gonna get you cleaned up, okay? Even has some stuff for you."

"Who?" he questions, his eyes softening a bit when he takes her in. "Looks nice."

"She's very nice," I confirm. "You wanna meet her?"

He nods once, hesitantly opening the door before sliding out.

I have to hand it to Donna, she doesn't flip out. Her eyes only widen for a brief moment before she schools her features and kneels down to take him in with a big smile planted on her lips. "Hey, sweetie, I'm Donna. What's your name?"

He still doesn't answer, only looking at her curiously. Damn it, I really need to know his name because I can't keep calling him kid.

"Kid, you wanna shower? Donna will take you inside and get you squared away."

I look at Donna, conveying with my eyes how much I need her help, and she doesn't hesitate, not that I thought she would. It's why I asked her to come over to begin with. "Come on, let's get you inside. I'll set these clothes out for you, and while you shower, I'll make you something to eat."

"Starving," he blurts, nervous eyes bouncing between us before settling on me. "Knife?"

"You can keep it," I find myself saying before I can think it over.

He looks toward Donna. "Won't touch me?"

Donna doesn't miss a beat as she walks up the steps and opens my door. "I won't touch you. I'll just set the shower up and leave you to get clean."

He mulls it over, practically chewing a hole through his bottom lip before he nods. "Okay. Lots of food? Really hungry."

Damn, his hopeful tone hits my soul. When's the last time he ate?

She agrees, waving at him to follow her, which he does apprehensively. "I'll make you anythin' you want. Do you have a favorite food—"

Her voice is cut off by my trailer door closing and that's when I let out the breath I didn't know I was holding. I do a slow spin, my fingers lacing to grip the back of my neck as I try to calm my racing mind.

I hear the motorcycles approaching and spin around just in time to see Badge and Pike hop off the bikes. Badge's face is full of worry and uneasiness, and even though I want to knock his fucking teeth in for not giving me a warning about the boy, I can't. His head's already full of fucked-up shit because of Ellen, and I don't need to add to it.

"What are we goin' to do?" he asks, coming to stand in front of me.

I thought it over the whole way here, trying to figure every possible avenue to go down, but ultimately, there's only one option.

"He's ours now."

There's no way I'm letting that kid out into the world by himself. Not when there's a possibility he could go straight into the system. The same system that—

Stop!

Badge and Pike both agree, probably figuring that was the

case. It wouldn't be the first time we brought someone in, it's just the first time it was a circumstance like this one.

"I can take him. I'll raise him with Fox like he's my own." Badge looks lost as he tries to make sense of it all. "She met my kid so many times, I can't believe she never mentioned she had one."

I nod, unsure of what to make of his confession, but thankful Badge is taking responsibility because there's no way I could do it. A kid on my plate is the last fucking thing I need.

"I hate to ask because I know this is all shitty, but can you dig up some information on Ellen? Find out about her family, her past? Need to know if someone will be looking for them. I need the boy's birth certificate so I can learn his name. Then, I need to do some tweakin' to make it all legal."

They both give me understanding looks, then we go back-and-forth for a few moments, making plans for the next few days.

After we're finished, Pike motions toward his trailer. "Sounds good. I'm headin' home. Yell if you need me."

Once he's gone, I turn back to Badge, taking in his reserved expression. I know this has all got to be a shock and not at all what he expected his day to go like, it sure as fuck isn't what I was expecting either. "You're good with this? Takin' in the kid? I'm sure Donna would—"

"I'm positive," Badge cuts me off, eyes full of determination. "The kid's been through a lot. I want to help him if I can. Try to show him how things could be. I dunno." He sighs and shakes his head. "It was bad, Whaley. The scene I walked in on... Him watchin' that guy beat Ellen. I dunno if that was his dad or what. The whole thing was a literal nightmare."

The thought makes my stomach sick.

Too fucking close to home.

"He's gonna need some work," I agree, thinking about all I've done to make myself better. "But you can help him."

"I'll do some research tomorrow, figure out what I can." He shrugs with all the tiredness of the world. "I'll do my best."

I reach up and give his shoulder a quick squeeze. "I know you will. You'll get it. For now, go home and rest. Gonna have Donna watch him tonight."

He doesn't argue, only giving me a long look before heading home. Then I spin around, looking up my steps with a daunting feeling settling in my bones. It's all stemming from my fucked-up past and things I've spent years suppressing. I can't brush them away now. The thoughts are lingering. The flashes of lights, sounds of screams, and rivulets of blood dances in the back of my mind—taunting me.

It takes everything I can muster to march up the steps, but I do in the end, knowing I can't put it off any longer. I need to check on the kid.

To face the monster who was born today. The one who will reside in the back of the boy's mind. The one who will manifest and turn into a demon.

A demon he will never outrun.

A demon who looks so much like my own.

Our rebirth comes at the cost of our souls, and now the devil will forever chase.

ONE

Bunky

10 years later

It all started on a Tuesday.

I wince as I get out of my car, every muscle and bone in my body screaming at me to go home and fall into bed, but I can't. I already ditched the shop yesterday after fucking away the weekend with Gunnar's sister. Besides that, all I remember is a bottle of vodka, a tattoo gun, and more weed than I should have smoked.

I look down at my arm, smiling at the new ink. A bear fighting a biker, fucking badass if you ask me. I hope the guy was paid well for it, and I wish I had been sober enough to remember to get his name for my next tattoo.

I tug out my pack of smokes, hoping the nicotine buzz will dull the pain a bit. I light up and inhale deeply as I head toward the shop. My dead phone feels like a lead weight in my pocket, no doubt filled with hundreds of missed calls and texts. I should feel bad making my friends and family worry, but honestly, I don't have it in me to care. Not with all the energy I've spent trying to numb the rumbling in my skull.

Crack.

Pop.

Squish.

I slap the side of my head before shaking it, as if that'll do anything to drown out the noise, but it doesn't work. It never fucking does.

I spot Raid and Silas through the window of the shop, and already know I'm about to get my ass handed to me as soon as I step through the door. They're always on me about how I disappear, but if they understood what the fuck was happening inside my mind, I'd bet they'd give me a break.

Finishing off my smoke, I stomp it out before rolling my shoulders to release some tension, then snatch the door open to head inside. They both turn to look in my direction, eyes narrowed when they take me in. Yeah, I know I look like shit with the dark circles under my eyes, split lip, a busted eye, and wrinkled clothes that have been in the back of my truck forever.

I do my thing though, plastering on a smile and walking to them like it's a normal day. "What's up, guys?"

"What do you mean?" Silas barks, rounding the counter to close the space between us. "Where the fuck have you been?"

"Just out." I shrug, reaching up and toying with the buttons on his coveralls, a little smirk playing on my lips. "Why? Did you miss me?

He bats my hands away, his eyes filled with annoyance. "Can you at least send us a text, asshole? Thought you were dead."

"Nah, not yet," I taunt, pushing past him and heading over to Raid. "You know I plan on goin' out in a Viking's death. Valhalla awaits." I pump my fist in the air and let out a little warrior cry for effect.

"Badge should really not let you watch the Discovery Channel." Raid sighs, shaking his head and looking back at his clipboard.

"Anythin' interestin' happen?" I attempt to jump up onto the counter, but my entire body protests in pain and I stumble into it instead. "Shit."

Raid's gaze jerks back up, his eyes filled with worry as he takes me in. "You good?"

"Nothin' to worry about." I wave him off, trying to appear unbothered even though my insides are screaming in pain.

He looks like he doesn't believe me, but doesn't press, just gives me that disapproving look of his before motioning behind me to where I'm sure Silas is drilling a hole in my back. "Silas was tellin' me about how he ran into the golden boy this mornin'."

That has my ears perking and I clap my hands in excitement. I have my own bullshit but I *live* for other people's drama. "Where?" I can't help the elated note in my voice. "Tell me all the details." I'm also thankful for the subject change because it keeps the heat off of me, and Blaine is the perfect way to make that happen.

"Fuckin' school," Silas grumbles, his mood shifting from being pissed at me to being pissed at Blaine, and I love it. "The dick nearly knocked me over tryin' to get to the other jock. Swear, I hate that guy."

"Uh-huh," Raid mumbles while scribbling away, acting like he doesn't give a shit, but I know he's just as nosey as I am. "Couldn't make it through the first day of senior year without pickin' a fight, could you?"

Oh shit.

I missed the first day of school. Badge is going to be pissed at me again. Jesus Christ, I've been fucking up lately, haven't I? Between all the shit that I'm doing and now ditching school, it's a wonder he hasn't thrown my ass out yet. I wouldn't even blame him if he did. It's not his fault he fucked the wrong woman and got stuck with a kid. Bet he regrets ever meeting her.

Crack.

Pop.

Squish.

"Bunk? You listenin' to me?" Silas' growly tone has me snapping back to the present, and I turn in time to catch what he throws my way. "Put this shit on. We've got work to do."

I shake my head, jiggling everything back in place, and throw him a two-finger salute. "Gotta piss first."

"Fine, but hurry up, and Bunk? I swear, if there's blood in your piss, we're takin' you to the damn hospital!" Silas calls to my retreating form.

I cackle, only wincing when I'm out of sight, not wanting them to know just how much pain I'm in.

I push into the bathroom to take care of business before trying to clean myself up. I'm surprised the guys didn't give me more hell over the dried blood still staining my face but take it as a small win. Bracing myself against the sink, I stare at my own reflection, trying to recognize myself in the mirror.

I tip my head to the side, noting the deep cut on my chin and the split in my upper lip, then I take a step back and raise my shirt up, smiling at the deep bruises that cover my torso. God, that last bar fight did a number on me. I don't know what I was thinking, challenging three huge guys to take me on, but I guess that's the point. I wasn't thinking, just feeling.

Feeling anything but…

Crack.

Pop.

Squish.

The laugh tears past my lips before I have a chance to stop it. I'm insane, aren't I? I'm completely batshit, only getting worse every day. The violent thoughts, the suffocating nightmares, and the volatile mood swings are getting stronger. I used to be able to go about my day without too many problems, but now I'm in a constant state of battle with myself.

"You've got this, Bunky," I say, bouncing on my toes to hype myself up while giving my hands a little shake. "You've got this shit."

Then I give myself a wink, making sure that it comes off as somewhat convincing before stepping into my coveralls. Fuck, maybe I more than just bruised my ribs because this really hurts. I think about the pills I have stashed in my room under the bed, wondering if I have time to sneak out and grab them before getting started, but I know Silas would track my ass down and haul me back so he wouldn't have to do all the work himself.

It takes everything in me to walk out of the bathroom with a smile planted on my lips, but I do, knowing I can't put this shit off any longer. I have no clue how I'm going to work a whole shift, let alone bend over cars to do oil changes, but I guess I'll figure it out.

I'm only three steps out of the bathroom when I spot Whaley leaning against the wall, arms and ankles crossed. His jaw is tense—hell, his whole body is—and I feel bad for whoever pissed him off. I'm thankful that, despite all my shit, Whaley pretty much leaves me alone. Even when I fuck up, his 'scoldings' are very minimal and I think it might be because he has bigger fish to fry. Why the fuck would he really fuss over me when he's the leader of the Aces?

I walk past, choosing not to acknowledge him, or at least that's my plan until—

"Bunky."

His sharp tone has me pausing, and I spin around to look at him in confusion. He's standing fully now, staring at me like he doesn't know if he wants to help me or strangle me.

What the fuck?

"Um, yeah? What's up?" I question, not understanding what he needs.

"My office. Right now." He doesn't wait for me to respond, just leaves me standing there, my mouth opening and closing several times as words fail me.

Wait? Was he waiting on *me*?

I follow behind him, unable to hold back my unease. I don't know why but this feels more ominous than anything I'm used to with Whaley. I step into his office, closing the door softly behind me before parking my ass in the first chair I come to, unable to hold back the relieved sigh now that I'm no longer standing.

"So…" I twiddle with my thumbs and gulp when he sits down. "What's up?"

He braces his elbows on the desk, fingers steepled as he assesses me. "Is that all you have to say?"

I rack my brain and spit out the first thing that comes to mind.

"Um, it looks like we'll get rain later?" He doesn't say anything, only drills me with his unamused stare, making me squirm a bit in my seat. "No? Did you get a haircut?"

"Cut the shit, Bunky," he barks, hands falling to his desk in a fist, and I watch the way his tattoos flex from the movement.

Yeah, he's really fucking mad this time. Now I'm buzzing with nerves because I've seen Whaley angry, and I don't want to be on the receiving end of his wrath.

"What shit?" My tone is pitched, and I anxiously scratch the back of my neck before shrugging a shoulder. "I don't know what you want from me. Can I go now?"

He ignores the question, not missing a beat as he continues. "Where were you?"

Isn't that a loaded question? "I dunno."

"Bunk!"

"Seriously, I dunno. Somewhere West? Maybe North? It was still hot so I couldn't have been anywhere outside of

Georgia." Well, I guess everywhere is still kind of warm right now, but he's got me lost on what *exactly* he wants.

"You're not funny," he says dryly.

Lovely, he thinks I'm dicking around. I'm really not. I'm just scrambling with what to say. "I wasn't tryin' to be. Can you tell me what's goin' on?"

"You were gone for three days. *Three days.* No call, no text, no note. Do you know Badge was goin' crazy lookin' for you?"

I purse my lips, trying to think over my words carefully. This wouldn't be the first time I've disappeared needing an escape, so why is he acting like it is?

"I'll apologize to Badge the next time I see him." I go to stand, but his fist slams down on his desk again, causing me to plop right back down in fear.

"It's not that easy. This ain't the first time this shit's happened, but it's gonna be the last," he tells me, his teeth grinding as his stare pins me in place. "I've let you do this for far too long. You're done now."

I snap my head back, looking at him like I've never seen him before. I'm sorry, but what the fuck did he say? What is he talking about? Done with what exactly? This doesn't make any sense.

I'm growing frustrated and angry and confused and holy shit I need some pills. I begin to rub my temples as I let out a breath and think 'happy' thoughts.

Snickerdoodles. Dinosaurs with tiny hats. Silas pissed off.

"What do you mean?" I ask once I'm feeling relatively okay. Then I quickly look down at myself, trying to see what he does, before letting out an annoyed huff. "I'm alive, ain't I?"

"Alive?" he fires back, his brows raised as he throws his hands in the air. "Look at you. You can't even sit without fuckin' wincin'. I should cart your ass to the hospital to make sure you don't have internal bleedin'."

"Nah, I'm fine. Just got a little roughed up. No big deal." I give him my best smile, but he doesn't so much as blink, his eyes filled with disbelief.

After a moment, he pinches the bridge of his nose and sighs. "You're done with all of this."

I wrinkle my brows in confusion, the words not registering. "Done with?"

"No more pills. No more fightin'. No more leavin' for days without sayin' shit to anyone." His tone is definitive and he looks at me like I'm an idiot as he cocks his head to the side. "Seriously, Bunky? What the fuck were you thinkin'?"

I'm stunned, and my brain feels like I'm on a bad acid trip. Is this all really happening? I pinch the skin on my hand, expecting to wake up from this weird-ass dream, but nothing happens. Whaley is still sitting there, staring at me, waiting for me to agree to his insane terms.

"I'm sorry, alright? Won't happen again." Holding my hands up placatingly, I expect that to be the end of it, but he keeps going, hitting me with another jab.

"You need to actually try. Can't just say it. What would Badge do if he lost you, huh? Or your brother? What about Raid and Silas?"

The frustrated scoff leaves me before I can hold it in.

Now he's just pissing me off. It's so fucking easy for everyone to tell me what to do, but no one knows what it's like inside my head, all the messed up shit that crosses my mind on the daily. They don't know how miserable it is to be fine one second and angry the next, to go to bed happy to being ripped out of slumber in the middle of the night by a sick as fuck flashback from the past. No one fucking gets me and I'm sick of it.

"I said I got it," I yell at Whaley, no longer giving a fuck. "Can everybody hop off my dick? I'm tired of this shit."

He shoots up from his chair, eyes dark, jaw locked, and I

feel the room growing hotter as he glares at me. "You watch how you fuckin' speak to me."

I gulp, eyes widening as I take him in, and my whole body flushes with heat while I try to wrap my head around my emotional whiplash. Oh damn. Did he just growl? I don't think I've ever heard that tone from him before, and I think I kind of like it.

"Shit, Whaley," I breathe out, not understanding why I suddenly feel warm in places I definitely shouldn't. "You've never been like this with me."

He rounds the desk, his hands squeezing my shoulders in a vise grip like he's trying to shake some sense into my head, but I don't move, barely react because I feel like I'm spiraling.

"I've been too fuckin' lenient with you." He stops shaking me but doesn't let me go, only holds my gaze as he grits out the next words through clenched teeth. "You need to get your shit together, Bunk. I'm done with all of this. If you don't, you'll be dealin' with me."

I... Why... Wait... What the fuck is happening and why the hell do I like it so much?

My throat feels tight and my Adam's apple works to swallow. He's lingering above me, face pinched as he waits for me to say something, so I blurt out the first thing I can. "Okay."

We stay in some weird limbo, with him glaring and me just staring at his face, realizing for the first time how great his bone structure is. Like if I pulled out my knife and cut the skin away, he'd be Hollywood-perfect beneath the layers.

Oh, blood. I bet he'd look nice covered in blood.

I let out a little grunt and his hands tighten as I fight the urge to grab him, and it's like my noise shocks him awake. His hands fall away and his body snaps straight as he looks down at me with confusion before it morphs to shock, then worry.

"Shit, sorry, fuck. I shouldn't have grabbed you like that."

He frowns, taking a step back. "Look, we worry about you because we care. That's all. Just make better choices."

My mind comes to a screeching halt, and I'm pretty sure my heart does too. Did he say…

"You—You care about me?"

"Of course I care about you." His brows furrow in confusion once more before he sighs, reaching forward and gently patting my shoulder. "You have a lot to offer. Just gotta keep your…"

I don't hear what he says after that. My brain is set on a loop, his words repeating over and over in my head like a scratched record as the feel of his hand on my skin electrifies me.

We care.

We care.

I care.

And that's all I focus on for the rest of the conversation.

When I leave his office and stumble through work, his words linger in my mind. They stay there long after the shop closes and long after I'm home and Badge grills my ass for being gone. They keep repeating, keep lingering, manifesting even. I can't stop thinking about it.

About him.

I think about things in a new light. The way his eyes aren't just brown, but dark and depthless, like looking into a pool of stars during the night. I think about the presence he carries, so authoritative and commanding. I've always respected him, and I realize now it's because he's someone worth following.

Bits and pieces of Whaley combine like a mosaic in front of me. All the little things I've missed before coming full circle. My obsession grew after that. Stronger and fiercer as the days passed. Those words became the sole focus of my existence. Poor Whaley. His future was sealed with those simple words, because he'll be mine and I'll make sure of that.

Whether he likes it or not.

TWO

Whaley

He's staring again.

The itch that sparks across my skin and the tingle that pulses at the base of my spine lets me know it's true.

I fight all my instincts to look up from the car I'm currently working on to search out the threat, because that's exactly what this feels like. It's as if I'm a hunk of flesh and Bunky's the tiger ready for a feast. Only, I'm not some unknowing victim about to be hunted, the opposite really. I'm the monster that lurks in the dark, ready to break free and terrorize all your peaceful dreams.

I feel his penetrating stare so deep that it makes my nerves burn hot. It's as if he's trying to look past every layer of my skin and peek at my insides. He should be really fucking careful though. I'm tainted, soiled beneath the surface. My soul is tarnished, heart empty, and my head? Well, that's where the darkness lies. It festers away, growling, scratching, chomping at the bit to snap its restraints and come forward once again.

I won't let that happen. I stopped letting him win a long time ago, stopped letting the plague of pain and shadows from my past be in control. I fought tooth and nail, clawed my way from the deepest dimensions of Hell and managed to come out alive. I take pride in knowing that nothing was powerful enough to break me.

It never fucking will.

Bunky seems to be searching for something inside me though. That much I'm certain, even if I don't know what it is or why he's doing it now. I just know that I see it every time our eyes catch. There's a sparkle in his green depths, one that's never been there before. A hint of something he's trying to convey with just his looks alone. I would like to say I'm not bothered by it, or that I thought his intentions were harmless, but that'd make me a liar.

It's unsettling the way he stirs something inside me. It's not a good feeling but an ominous one. It doesn't make sense, but it feels equivalent to two hunters preparing to rip each other apart. I don't get where that's coming from though, and I'd rather pretend it's not happening at all because I don't want to deal with it. So that's what I do.

He stares and I ignore. He talks to me and I'm evasive. He taunts and jokes around while I remain stoic and serious. All of it is so damn unusual, and I don't know what the hell to do. I've thought about talking to Badge but thought better of it. What if this shit is really just in my head? What if I'm over-thinking things that aren't really happening?

I look over my shoulder, eyes bouncing around the garage, searching for the source of my discomfort, and *boom*. Green eyes that are a swirl of the deepest forest lock with mine. No, not only a forest. His eyes are too clear, almost like an emerald. There are words lingering in them. I can see them calling to me… but what are they saying?

They want us to play.

I jerk my gaze away, my heart thudding hard inside my chest as that noise rumbles in the recesses of my brain. Yeah, it's definitely *not* in my head. I'll have to keep doing what I've been doing. I have to be distant and avoid this shit until it goes away because it has to eventually.

It fucking better.

I go back to work and focus on all the cars I have lined up today. I'm overbooked so it's easy to ignore him and keep busy. Hours slip by so quickly that I don't even realize it's over until Badge claps me on the shoulder.

"You good? Been a long time since I've seen you work a shift," he says, looking me over with concern.

He's not wrong. I typically do drop-ins, only helping out when needed.

"Yeah, all good," I tell him, straightening and reaching for a rag to wipe my oil-covered hands. "Had time, saw it was really packed, so figured I'd help out."

He nods as he pulls off his coveralls before throwing it in the bin. "What are you doin' after? Wanna get a beer?"

I hate telling Badge no, but I'm not feeling it. I haven't been sleeping much lately. Between runs, work, and the nightmares, which made a surprise appearance for the first time in a long time, I need some sleep.

I shake my head and put the rag down. "I'm gonna head home. Feelin' like I could sleep for days."

His lips turn down a bit. "It's not even six."

I crack a smile, heading over to the sink to wash the remaining oil off my hands. "Rain check?"

"I'm holding you to this one. You've said that the last three times I've asked." I can tell by his tone he's joking around, but it does make me stop and think.

When was the last time I went out for fun? A long damn time. Even at our parties in the lot behind the trailer park, I've been MIA.

I need to do better.

I wipe my hands before turning back to Badge. "Next time. You have my word."

"Good."

"What are you talkin' about?"

My hackles rise, but I keep my face neutral when we both turn to see Bunky approaching us, nothing but devious intention in his eyes. Badge might not see it with the way he smiles so easily at his son, but I do. Bunky wants something, or else he wouldn't be pushing his way into the conversation. I take a small step back, barely moving before he bumps into me, clearly trying to get a rise out of me.

"Nothin' important," Badge tells him. "Ready to go?"

"In a minute." Bunky's eyes flick to me briefly before going back to Badge. "I was wantin' to talk to Whaley about a part I need for the bike."

Badge hums under his breath. "You do that. I need to go check with Silas about these last two invoices. Come find me when you're done."

He turns to leave and I'm about to protest. I can take the clipboard and talk to Silas myself, but Bunky's hand shoots out, locking around my wrist, halting my ability to move. I look down at his oil-stained hand wrapped around my tattooed wrist and stare with fascination. His palm is hot, so hot that it makes my skin flame. It feels like a volt of electricity has shot through my arm, lighting up every cell inside me.

I jerk my gaze, our eyes clashing for a moment, and my brain fails. We're locked in this trance. With him latching onto my tattered soul and me suffocating in his emerald stare.

Come on, let's go play.

I rip my hand from his hold, my jaw clenching. "Don't fuckin' grab me again."

Those words mixed with my tone would make any man fold, but not Bunky. If anything, it looks like he got the response he wanted with the way a smile splits across his face.

"You don't like it when I touch you?" His head tilts to the side as his gaze runs over me. I'm wearing a black T-shirt and old jeans covered in grease stains, but by the way that pierced tongue of his snakes out to wet his bottom lip, you'd think I was naked.

"I don't like bein' touched in general." It isn't a lie. Even when I fuck, I keep things as distant as possible. The only touching I need is my cock in a tight hole, everything else isn't necessary.

"Hmm." He fiddles with his piercing, one shoulder lifting in a shrug. "Shame. We could have fun."

My head snaps back. What the hell did he say? I look around, making sure no one overheard his remark. The last thing I need is anyone thinking something is going on between us.

I lower my voice, fists clenched at my sides. "I don't know what your deal is—"

"No deal," he says 'oh so innocently' as he motions behind him. "Can you come look at my bike and tell me what part I'm missin'? It's still not runnin' and I feel like I've done everythin'."

Normally, I'd take a look, but I'm ready to put some distance between me and whatever thoughts are happening inside his head. "I'll look tomorrow. Ready to go home."

I spin to leave but his voice stops me. "Please, I've been workin' on this thing forever. Badge is lettin' me do it on my own, and I'm almost done, but I can't figure out what the final issue is."

He's pleading with me, and fuck, is it working? If it were anyone else, it wouldn't, that's life after all, but I feel compelled for some reason I can't explain. Despite my reservations, I agree, keeping several feet between us as I follow him to his bike.

My eyes widen when I take it in. I don't know what he was talking about because this thing isn't close to being done. There are pieces scattered everywhere, some parts not even attached, and he's missing basic shit too like the hand clutch.

"The hell?" I examine the disaster in front of me, squatting to look it over quickly, unable to hold back my irritated grunt as I shoot him a glare. "I thought you said you were almost done?"

"I may have been exaggeratin'..." He bends down and snags the front fork from the ground before turning to me once more. "...Just a little."

"The fuck?" I bark, not finding this shit funny at all. He's lost his damn mind, and he's wasting my time. Does he not know who I am? I've stabbed people for less.

"Oh, lighten up," he singsongs, waving a dismissive hand at me. "It's no big deal."

I grit my teeth. "My time is a pretty big deal."

"Right." He nods, his green eyes flicking up at me through his thick lashes, then he licks his lips again, making a show of waving his hands around. "Sorry, I forgot. You're the all-powerful Wizard of Oz."

I'm losing my patience with him and his taunting, and growing more frustrated as he laughs. "Bunky—"

"No! Batman, right?" He snaps his fingers, giggling like a maniac under his breath, finding himself so hilarious. "Should I get the bat signal?"

Before I even know it, I'm snatching him up off the floor, my hand gripping his throat and nails digging into his tattooed skin. I try to shake some sense into him, but it ends up smashing the front fork between us in the process.

I ignore the stab of pain and speak through clenched teeth. "You watch your damn mouth."

There must be something wrong with me. I *never* act this way with my people. Hell, I never lay my hands on them if not absolutely necessary. That's not the kind of leader I am, but something about this moment with Bunky is working me up.

His eyes glaze over as his breaths stutter from my tight hold on his throat. "Oh, fuck. I like this. Can you squeeze just a little harder?"

For fuck's sake, he can't be serious? I was aiming for threatening, and he's... what? Turned on?

"I squeeze any harder and I'll pop your eyeballs out," I growl, despite the way my hand tightens around him.

"Shit," he whispers, eyes falling closed as he wiggles under my hand. "That tone, the way you're handlin' me... Gonna make me nut if you keep it up."

Wouldn't let you come. Would edge the fuck out of you for having such a smart-ass mouth.

I drop him like a hot coil, springing back like I've been soaked with a bucket of ice water. No, like I've been shot through the middle with a rifle.

What the fuck am I thinking?

I open my mouth to tell him off, but he lets out a little wince as he opens his eyes and looks at his hand. I do the same, noting the blood staining the side of his pointer finger.

"The fuckin' part got me," he grumbles, tilting his hand to get a better look.

"Come on, let's go get you cleaned up," I tell him, even though I just want to get away from him and all the shit he's doing to my head.

He gives me a baffled expression before shaking his head in confusion. "Why, it's not deep? Just a little cut. Nothin' I can't handle."

Then he brings his finger to his mouth, licking the blood away.

I stand there frozen, eyes glued on him. It's entirely too sensual watching his tongue ring come out to play and the way his blood glides across his lip, making it a pretty shade of red. He closes his eyes again, like he's enjoying himself, and I feel the zing of lust shoot straight to my dick.

What the actual fuck?

"Mmm," he moans, his eyes opening to refocus on me. "I love that shit."

I gulp, my mouth feeling dry as the air between us begins to heat. "Cuttin' yourself?" I ask, even though I already know what he means. I know because I feel the same way.

Blood.

He says it at the same time I think it. "There's just something about it, you know? Do you like blood?" His penetrating stare makes me feel so damn exposed. It's as if he's managed to worm his way into my head and read my thoughts. "I do," he continues when I don't answer. His tone is husky, and his eyes gleam as they hold mine. Then he takes a step toward me, licking his skin again. "It's heady, has that metallic taste, but also there's a little sweetness too." He holds out his hand for me, but I stay rooted in place, unsure of what to do next. "Wanna taste me, Whaley? I'd let you."

My heart is pounding, sweat coating my skin as I look at his offering. It'd be so easy to take. So tempting.

Yes.

There it is. That fucking voice again. The demon that lives inside trying to break free. I should just accept him now. He's always showing up at the most fucked of times.

I smack his hand away, already taking several steps back while shaking my head.

"No, and don't do that shit again. Any of this," I bark, needing some fucking distance, needing *something*. "I ain't fuckin' playin'."

I spin around and hightail it out of there, ignoring his call as I go. I practically run to my truck, desperate to get away, to be alone.

The ride home is quick but uncomfortable with the way my dick digs into my zipper the whole time.

Fuck, I can't believe I'm this turned on.

But the blood… just the sight of it. That's all it was. That's why I'm reacting this way. It has nothing to do with the one who was offering it.

As soon as I'm inside my trailer, all bets are off. I'm fumbling with my belt, shoving my hand inside my pants to grip my aching dick, not even locking the door behind me as I sag against the wood.

This is going to be fast. I'm too keyed up, and it's been too long.

I close my eyes, trying to think of the last woman I was with. Her taut body and perky tits, the wet heat I sunk into, and her sweet cries for mercy, but it does nothing. My mind and body want only one thing.

Bunky.

The way his neck felt under my hand. The way his eyes closed as he offered himself to me. The way his chest stuttered at my touch. Fuck, he's like a wet dream come to life. Every single dirty and twisted desire I've ever had played out in front of me.

Do you like blood?

I fucking love it.

My hand pumps faster, images of him sucking his finger flashing in my mind.

"Wanna taste me, Whaley?"

I want to taste him, rip out my knife and knick his skin. Suck on his flesh and—

"Fuck!" I groan, my body vibrating as my orgasm crashes into me, and I soak my hand with spurt after spurt of cum. My knees feel weak, and I have to brace myself against the door to not fall on my ass.

My chest is heaving, eyes feeling heavy as endorphins wash over me. I don't know the last time I came so hard. My body is humming, and I wobble to my couch, plopping down onto the seat as I try to wrap my head around what I've done.

I just got off thinking about Bunky.

With that last thought in my head, the demon that's been locked up tight bursts free from his cage, wanting one thing and one thing alone.

Our newest obsession.

THREE

Whaley

He knows exactly how to get under my skin.

My jaw ticks, and I take another gulp from my beer, trying to ignore the loud vibrato of Bunky's laughter several feet away. I swear he doesn't usually laugh like that, only being extra obnoxious to gain some attention—my attention. Ever since our talk a couple of months ago, that's all he's tried to do. The constant flirting, dirty talk, lust-filled stares, and late night, filthy text messages has me ready to snap.

He's manipulated me in every sense of the word. He's made himself the star of *my* fucking show, jabbed himself under my skin, and nestled his way inside my brain, and it's become impossible to escape.

But I don't want to.

And that's the problem.

I try to focus on Badge and Pike as they talk about the Vipers, which is an important as fuck conversation that I really need to be involved in. Only, of course, Bunky's voice cuts through the air, filling my ears again.

Despite how hard I try, I can't fight the pull I feel toward him, and my head involuntarily swivels until I can see where he's standing with all his friends around the old burn barrel. His head is thrown back, that mop of dyed blond hair tousled, eyes squinted, and cheeks flushed as if whatever the fuck he just heard is the most hilarious thing ever.

As if sensing my gaze, he turns and locks eyes with me. Again, like it always does when our gazes clash, I feel the tightening in my stomach and the rush of heat to my skin. He doesn't seem shocked by my stare. If anything, it's like he achieved his ultimate goal. He tosses me a wink before looking back to his friends, brushing me off. I hate that he does that. He draws me in and then acts so dismissive when I know for a fact he wants me.

He keeps playing these games and keeps asking for things he doesn't even understand. I would gobble him up, eat him alive, do things he so desperately craves, and introduce him to things he doesn't even know he needs. I'd ruin him from ever having anyone else, and even though it's always so fucking tempting to snatch him up and drag him off to fuck some respect into him, I won't.

I can't.

I'm too old for him and he's too fragile. He deserves someone better and that's not me. I'd only drag him under the water, hold him there until he choked, and make him join me in misery and Hell.

I turn back to Badge and Pike, trying to add to the conversation, but it's no use. The object of my darkest obsessions, my most depraved thoughts, and regular late-night fantasies is too close to me, going out of his way to make sure I'm hyper-aware of his lingering presence.

"Be back," I tell the guys, not waiting for a response before heading in the direction I know, deep down, I shouldn't.

My eyes track over the group of teens as my mind tries to come up with what the fuck I'm going to say when I get over there. The answer comes easily enough when I spot Blaine,

Silas' boyfriend. I haven't officially met him yet, so this is as good an excuse as any.

Raid sees me approaching and greets me like he always does, causing all attention to snap in my direction. I nod back, refusing to look where I know Bunky is drilling me with his eyes. I can practically feel the heat of his laser-focused stare.

"This your guy?" I ask Silas, motioning to Blaine who's sitting on his lap.

Poor Blaine looks like a deer caught in headlights with his spine snapped straight, eyes huge, and mouth open. He tried to shoot out of Silas' lap, but the kid is possessive as hell. He holds Blaine down while rubbing his back, trying to soothe him as he gives me a proud smile.

"Yeah. Whaley, this is Blaine. Blaine, this is Whaley."

"Hello, sir," Blaine chokes out, and I can't help but chuckle because no one calls me that.

"Don't gotta call me sir. Whaley's fine."

"Right, Whales." His cheeks flush as he stares at me with embarrassment. "Shit, no, Whaley. I knew that."

"My guy's a bit nervous to meet you," Silas says, and although his voice is a bit teasing, the affection in his eyes is clear.

I wave him off, not wanting Blaine to be scared of me. While I know I have a reputation, I'd never step out of line unless necessary. "Not gonna hurt you. Not as long as you keep your mouth shut and treat Silas well."

I can tell Blaine wants to say something, but he's interrupted by the little shit who's practically chomping at the bit to get my attention.

"Whaley!" Bunky shouts, almost directly beside me now. I jerk my gaze to see him bouncing slightly before he does some weird arching shit with his back. It makes my way too fucked-up head conjure images of him it has no business thinking. "Want to see me be all bendy? I can do a great doggy style."

Oh, for fuck's sake.

My jaw works as I do my best not to react. He said that shit on purpose. No way it's called that.

Blaine's friend, I'm assuming based on his jacket, bursts out laughing, confirming my thoughts. "I think it's called downward dog."

I take a hard look at Bunky, who seems a bit dazed as he straightens. I don't miss the telltale signs that he's buzzed. His cheeks are flushed red, pupils blown, and he has a little twitch in his fingers while his signature, manic-ass smile is locked in place across his lips. Yeah, he's definitely feeling it.

"What's he had?" I ask Raid in exasperation.

"A Red Bull, three shots of vodka, all of *my* joint—fuck you very much, Bunk—and some other shit he snorted," Raid tells me, ticking off a finger as he does.

"Alright," I start, huffing as I tug up the sleeves of my leather jacket. "Time to go."

Bunky shoots me a look, eyes wide as he drops his jaw and whines. "I don't want to go. I'm *fine.*"

"You don't look it," Silas chimes in. "Listen to him for once."

Bunky narrows his gaze at him before he stares dead at me. At first, he tries the big watery eyes, turning his lips down into a pout, looking every bit the innocent little lamb he's not. When he sees that doesn't work, he grows frustrated, hands clenching at his sides. He looks high, but not gone. That won't last long though if I let him stay.

"No." He shakes his head challengingly, as if that's really going to stop me from putting an end to his night. I run the show here, even though he likes to pretend otherwise.

I take a second, chewing the inside of my cheek, knowing exactly what I have to do. "Fine. I see we'll have to do this the hard way."

"The hard way? What are you— Hey! Put me down! Let go of me!"

I flip him over my shoulder, ignoring the way he protests and smacks my back. Oh, *please* fucking hit me. Make this shit worth it.

I dare you.

I say my goodbyes before spinning around and heading toward the trailers. Bunky doesn't relent the whole way to his house, flailing around and talking all kinds of shit the further away we get from the party. He's moving so much that I'm about to drop him, so I reach up and smack his ass hard, hearing the pop ricocheting in the air.

He stops moving instantly, a loud gasp leaving his mouth at my assault. Of course he's only stunned for a second, that teasing tone of his meeting my ears a moment later.

"You know, if you wanted to touch my ass, Whaley, all you had to do was ask. I like it rough."

I let out an amused grunt as I adjust his weight, carrying him easier now that he's no longer fighting. "If that was rough, then you'd never be able to handle me."

"Oh, fuck off," he snaps, but there's a laugh in his tone that does stupid shit to my chest. "I could handle you just fine, Whaley. I'd be the best you ever had."

No, I'd be the best you ever had, and you'd never be able to escape me then. Be careful what you wish for, Bunk.

You can only tempt a man so much before he takes what he wants.

And the things I want to do…

I continue toward his trailer, not bothering to say anything else. He's in his I-have-to-have-the-final-word mood, and I don't have the energy to argue. Not to mention my jeans are getting tight at the thought of turning his plump ass red and showing him just how rough I can be.

"Oh, what? No response?" he probes to no avail as I reach the stairs of his trailer. I grab the handle to open it, only to find it's locked.

Damn it.

"Gimme your keys."

"Don't got them," he says petulantly, and I'm damn near close to giving him a rough pat down that we'd both likely enjoy too much.

Instead, I set him on his feet before holding out my hand. "Don't got time for your shit, Bunk. Keys."

He eyes my hand, his lips pursed before he finally digs into his pocket and hands them over. "Ugh, you're no fuckin' fun. Would it kill you to crack a smile every once in a while?" Reaching forward, he jabs a finger into my cheek, giving it a drilling twist as he pouts. "You gotta nice smile, but you never let me see it. I hate that, you know?"

Our gazes collide, and I spot the devilish gleam in his eyes right before his fingers drag down to glide through my trimmed beard.

I hate to admit that I let him do it for several seconds, taking enjoyment in having his hands on me. My breath hitches because, damn, his touch feels so good. The soft caress sends my blood soaring, electricity crackling and racing through me, but when his face splits into a grin, I realize I must look like a happy pup being rubbed down by its owner, so I smack his hand away.

He frowns, swinging his hands back and forth while singing his next words. "Aw, I almost had you purring."

"Fuck off," I bite out, annoyed at myself for letting him, once again, get to me. I don't need his hands on me. Want them, yes, but I won't play this game.

The problem is that he's gotten way too comfortable with me. It's like he flipped a switch since our big talk, making me his main vice where he channels all his bullshit. I should be glad it's that instead of fighting and all the other things he was doing before. And I am, but all the shit he's doing to me is making it harder to stay in control.

I fiddle with the keys before unlocking his place and pushing open the door. Then I grab his arm to tug him inside.

He follows, muttering under his breath the whole time, but I ignore him as I walk him down the hall, never letting go of his arm while we head to his room. When we get there, I flip around, motioning for him to get inside.

He folds his arms over his chest, breaking my hold. "I'm buzzin'. There's no way I can sleep."

"Then watch a damn movie," I spit out, needing to put some space between us.

"What the fuck? Am I bein' grounded? I don't think so." He spins, heading away from his bedroom door. "I'm goin' back to the party because you're killin' my buzz."

He. Doesn't. Ever. Listen.

My aggravation and frustration finally boils over as I think of Bunky being a goddamn tease, about my lack of mental control, and about the fact that this fucking eighteen-year-old is calling the shots.

His hand is on the front door handle, about to tug it open, and I pounce. I press my hand between his shoulder blades and smash him up against the door. He releases a grunt, his cheek planted into the wood as my front becomes flush with his back. I'm tempted, so fucking tempted to bury my nose in his hair and inhale, to move my hand up and take hold of his neck, squeezing it harshly and showing him just how in control *I* actually am.

I don't though, because while I know he enjoys riling me up, there's a part of me that isn't sure if he's only trying to provoke me, and I refuse to cross that line.

"You're not goin' anywhere," I growl. "Take your ass back to your room."

The little shit snickers before he pushes back into me, his perky bubble butt rubbing against my crotch. "But why? This is so much more fun."

Goddamn it.

I step back quickly. He's testing every bit of patience I have left. He flips around, his chest heaving and eyes filled with so many things it's making my head spin. Fuck, I wish he wouldn't look at me like that. Like he wants to be devoured. Like he wants to be completely owned by me. Both things I could do easily, but it'd be the start of our demise.

"You're drivin' me up the wall. Fuckin' with my head," I hiss, my teeth clenching at every single emotion rushing me. "You like that, huh? Makin' me crazy?"

"I'd rather do that by ridin' your dick," he tosses back, dropping his gaze down my body, that wicked smirk of his in place.

I drop my hands, fisting them at my sides to prevent me from reaching out and snatching him up. "Bunky—"

"I think about it a lot, you know?" he rasps, his hand coming up to his chest to rub there for a moment as his eyes continue to greedily run over my body. "Think about how you'd look naked." Tucking his lip between his teeth, his hand begins to slowly run down his stomach, the siren call I've been trying to avoid. "I wonder how big your cock is. I bet it's huge. You look like you're packin'."

He moans, his eyes falling shut briefly, and his hand stops at the band of his jeans. I don't say anything as shaky breaths escape me. I can't because I'm lost in the trance that is *Bunky* as he gives me the show I've been dreaming of lately.

"Are you cut or not?" He fiddles with his belt, getting it open before working on his jeans. "Do you keep yourself clean-shaven or do you have some hair? God, I hope you have hair, Whaley. I bet it'd smell so fuckin' good." He shoves his hand inside his pants, letting out a groan and arching up when he reaches his prize. *My prize.* He's touching himself for me. Touching himself while thinking about me. "I'd worship your cock. Kiss it like it's never been kissed. Suck it like it's never been sucked. Take my time, drivin' you fuckin' wild."

I gulp as sweat coats my neck. "Bunk…"

He peeks at me through hooded lids, his hand moving faster now. "You want me."

It's not a question. Hell, for once he's not even teasing. It's just a statement, a true as fuck fact, and all I can do is nod, because right now, I'm pretty damn sure I'd give up anything to have him one time.

"Why you always fightin' it, Whaley? Always playin' hard to get?" He licks his lips, eyes pleading with me to do something. "I'm gettin' tired of finger fuckin' my ass pretendin' it's you. Please, put me out of my misery already. I'm beggin' you."

In a flash, I'm there, my control slipping and mind warring as I wrap my hand around his throat, pressing him further into the wall, and he lets out a gasp that quickly turns into a moan.

"Fuck, yeah! Please," he cries out, the plea beautiful to my ears. "*Whaley.*"

"You need to be really fuckin' sure about this," I tell him, my eyes looking over every inch of his face. "I mean it. This ain't a game. I'm not one of those other guys you've fucked in the past. I like it rough, I like to be in control, and I will own every inch of your damn body. So if you want to back out, you need to tell me now because once we get started, I ain't gonna stop. This is it, your *one* chance to escape."

I feel his throat working under my hand, and I watch his eyes glaze more with every word that leaves my lips. A second later, I feel a tug and look down and note his pants are around his ankles. His hands are working on my belt, then they move to my jeans but he doesn't push them down. Instead, his fingers glide up the fabric of my shirt before they run down my arm to grip my wrist. I look at his eyes once more, never releasing my hold on his throat, and his mouth turns up in a manic smile.

"Do your worst," he whispers, his eyes filled with delight, and the demon in my head lets out an animalistic roar.

Game on, Bunky. Game fucking on.

I slam my lips against his, eating his moan before fucking

his mouth. He flicks his tongue against mine, letting me feel the metal bar there, and he tastes just like I've imagined, sweet with a hint of tobacco. Addictive in the best possible way. A drug I'm going to hit every time to chase a higher high.

Damn it, I want to eat him alive. I want to tear him apart. I want to be his salvation, his glory, and his fucking demise.

His hands work to push off my jacket before he grabs my shirt, tugging it off. I growl at the momentary separation of our mouths, hauling him back to me and diving in again. This is intoxicating; the feel of his soft lips, his teasing tongue ring, his body against mine like this.

Fuck, I need to be inside him.

Ripping my mouth off his, I strip him the rest of the way, taking a moment to appreciate the way his body looks. His heaving chest is covered in tattoos, and my eyes widen when I realize he has a replica of one of mine splayed over his pec. What the fuck? When did he get this? I knew Bunky was into tattoos but had no idea about this. I should find this strange, too fucking creepy, but the territorial side of me really likes it. It's like he's marked himself with my stamp, proving to everyone who he belongs to.

Unable to stop myself, I lean in and trace the ink with my tongue before sinking my teeth into his flesh. He hisses, hands coming up to hold my head and pull me closer. He's keeping me in place, not wanting me to let go, so I get to work indulging him, nipping at his skin and dragging my teeth along his flesh. His tattoos make it impossible to see the hickeys I'm leaving, but not the bite marks. Those are obvious little dents in his skin, and I hate knowing they'll soon fade.

I'll just have to keep biting him while I fuck him, so at least they'll be there as he's being thoroughly railed. I suck on his neck before working my way up to his jaw, taking in every gasp, moan, and sigh that leaves his lips, recording it to my memory.

"Want me to fuck you?" I question, biting his lobe and rolling the stud with my tongue.

"If you don't soon, I'm gonna fuckin' die, or fuckin' come," he pants, his body writhing and pleading. "You have me so keyed up. I don't think I've ever been this turned on before."

You and me both.

"Good." Then I stand straight, flipping him around and pressing his chest to the wood. Damn, I nearly lose my words at seeing that pert ass in front of me, two beautiful full globes that I want sullied by my touch. I'm practically salivating, wanting a taste, but that can come later. "Lube?"

While I want this to be depraved, hard, and dirty as a punishment for what he's been doing to me—I don't want to hurt him. Well, that's not true. I want to hurt him very fucking badly, but only in ways he'll enjoy.

"To hell with lube. Just spit on my hole and fuck me already. I wanna feel it." He moans and pushes his ass back into my jean-covered cock. "I want it to hurt so fuckin' bad."

"You sure?" I ask, though he clearly knows what he wants, and who am I to deprive him?

"Fuck, yeah. I already fingered myself earlier thinkin' of you. I'll still be nice and soft."

I groan, my lip peeling back from my teeth in a half-snarl. Part of me hates the fact that he prepped. I want to be the one to stretch him out, to be the only one inside him, but waiting another second sounds much worse.

Next time, I'll be sure to drag it out.

"God, so fuckin' big," Bunky carries on in my silence. "You should be glad I'm horny right now, else I'd be suckin' the life outta your cock. Do it so good you'd never be able to be with anyone else."

He's still so damn confident and bratty even though he's the one naked, bent over, and about to get pounded into a door. I spit on my hand and slather my cock before prying open Bunky's cheeks, indulging in how soft and pink he looks inside. It's still tight, but loose enough that my piercing won't rip him up.

Though the little shit would probably love that.

Bunky slams his fist against the door impatiently, the muscles in his back straining as he arches. "What's the damn hold up?"

"Just thinkin' of how my piercings could tear you up," I manage through gritted teeth, barely keeping my composure. "How pretty you could bleed for me."

Suddenly, he shudders, groaning loudly. "*Fuck*. Your dick's pierced? Oh, hell yeah, I ain't missin' that."

Before I have a chance to react, he's pulling off me, spinning, and dropping down to his knees. His eyes widen as he looks at my cock, then he brings his hands up in prayer, closing his lids while letting out a happy sigh. "Lord, thank you so much for blessin' Whaley with this monster of a cock, and thank you for givin' me the opportunity to worship it. I swear, I won't forget this service."

I can't help it, I laugh. Nobody's prayed over my dick before, but I kind of like it.

"What the fuck, Bunk?" Because honestly, what else can I say?

"This is a masterpiece," he moans, his face filled with wonder as he leans in and takes ahold of my cock. Then he drags his tongue across the first, second, and third bar resting on the underside of my shaft, ripping all the laughter from my lungs and shifting the mood back to where it was moments before.

He gives me a few licks, teasing the metal, and the feeling of his piercing dragging along mine is going to make me combust. I've never had anybody play with my piercings before, everyone was too nervous or intimidated to bother. But Bunky? Bunky's licking my dick like it's ice cream on a summer day, as if it's the best treat he's ever tasted.

I take hold of his face, spreading my legs a bit to get a better angle. "Open your mouth."

He does quickly, his jaw dropping and tongue flattening as he lets me shove inside. I'm not easy, and I don't fucking hesitate in rocking my hips back and forth. I expect him to gag, but of course he doesn't, only stares up at me with challenge.

Well, challenge fucking accepted.

I let loose, pulling my hips back before snapping forward and pushing as much of me as I can into his hot mouth. He relaxes his throat, letting me fuck into him. His eyes water, but he never breaks our connection.

He's a sight. Nothing like I've ever seen before. A beautiful fucking mess, aching to be ripped apart and soiled with my filth.

"You take my cock so damn good, Bunk," I rasp, moving a hand up to run through the soft strands of his hair. He hums, eyes falling closed at my touch and letting his guard down momentarily, which causes him to gag. The feeling shoots straight to my balls, and I gasp, pulling out and pushing back in harder. "That's good. Make my dick nice and wet. Get me ready to fuck your ass."

His eyes snap open, and it's like the whole world stills. Nothing else matters, nothing else exists besides this. I pull out of his mouth, the urge to come slamming into me at rapid speed, and I pinch the base of my dick to stop the orgasm from rushing forward.

"Goddamn, that mouth," I grit out, clenching my jaw and motioning for him to spin around. "Hands and knees."

His cheeks are flushed, chest heaving, but it doesn't stop him from flipping over and baring himself to me. He's fucking perfection as he spreads his cheeks, giving me a nice long look at his hole. I press against it with my thumbs, pulling it open to spit into him. The way he whines makes me do it again and again until he's squirming. "God I can feel it, Whaley. Yeah, like that. Don't need fingers, want you."

"Be patient."

He pushes back, throwing me a glare over his shoulder. "I've been patient. Months and months of fuckin' patience. Now I'm done. Give me your cock."

"Shut it, Bunk." I slap his ass, and he moans. I chuckle as the power I'm feeling races through me and heats my blood. I would be inside him already if he shut his mouth. I'm being petty, dragging it out just 'cause he's begging for it.

I am the one in control.

Only me.

"That ain't your dick," he teases and I slap his ass once more, wanting to hear all his sounds. "Yeah, God, do that. Please, do it again."

Fuck it, I'll be here all night if I wait for him to stop being a brat.

I line my cock up but don't push inside yet. Instead, I lean over his back, hooking my hand around his throat and squeezing gently. "You ain't runnin' this fuckin' show, remember? I'm the one who calls the shots. Always *me*."

Then I push forward, giving him every inch of my cock in one thrust.

He screams, actually fucking screams, and it's music to my ears. "Damn, you're splittin' me in half. Feels so good. Own my ass, Whaley. Fuck me like you mean it."

"With pleasure."

I place a kiss on the back of his neck before sitting up and taking hold of his hips, no longer able to hold back. I pull out, then slam forward and give him what he asked for. Again and again and again. I fuck into him, ruthless in my pace, desperate in my determination to make this the best he's ever had.

The best either of us have ever had.

I want to be so permanently seared in his head that there's no escaping me.

"You feel so fuckin' good, Bunk," I groan as his tight heat overwhelms me. I already know his ass could be my vice. If he lets me, I'll be in it twenty-four-seven, keeping him so sore he'll never walk straight again. "You like this?"

"Yes," he whines, trying to push back on my cock, but the grip I have on his hips prevents him from doing so. He cries out, twitching and writhing in such a beautifully distressed way. "Whaley, you're ruinin' me."

Good. That's exactly what I want.

When I slap his ass and he turns his head, there are tears in his eyes. When I pull out all the way and slam back in, his breath gets caught in his throat. When I take one hand and anchor it in his hair, he purrs.

He's so fucking responsive, and I'm certain he'll be my ruin too.

"Shit, can't last any longer," I huff, draping my entire body over his, our sweat-slicked skin sliding against each other. "Bunky, gotta come."

"Yes, please," he moans, pushing back against me more. "Want you to fuck the come outta me."

That dirty mouth. Maybe *that's* what will be the end of me instead.

I take his cock in my hand, reveling in its silky texture for only a brief moment before pumping hard and fast. When his ass tightens around my cock and I start wringing the cum out of him, I lose it.

I collapse on top of him, running my hands up and down his naked back, easing his shudders. Then I regretfully slip out and sit back so I can admire the view. "Push out."

"Kinky." He snickers but does what I ask. I sit mesmerized as my cum pulses out of him, chuckling when he wags his ass playfully. "Wanna fuck it back into me?"

So damn perfect for me.

I would, but my body's now registering how tired it really is. Plus, I've got a run I need to do early tomorrow morning. So instead, I stand and pull up my jeans. "Not tonight. Get to bed."

He turns, splaying on his back and stretching out like a cat, once again tempting me to say fuck it to my run and have him again and again until neither of us can move.

"You wanna stay with me?" he teases, running his tattooed hands across his stomach. "Wanna cuddle?"

I know he probably only meant it as a joke, but it makes me clam up. It's like I'm hit by a freight train, reality crashing in and knocking me on my ass.

I fucked Bunky.

I fucked Bunky in the living room of Badge's trailer when my right-hand could have come home at any time.

Shit.

I shouldn't have done this. No matter how much I wanted it, this was so wrong.

"I gotta go," I rush out, zipping up my jeans with clumsy fingers and practically rushing out of there. He's saying something else, wanting to have the last word like always, but I'm not there to hear it.

I'm too busy freaking out over the fact I just fucked the one person I know I can't have.

FOUR

Bunky

Jesus Christ, I've never been happier.

As I lazily stretch, holding my arms over my head and arching my back, I revel in the soreness I feel. Damn, Whaley did a number on me last night, and I'm not mad in the slightest.

I want him to pound me like that every day of my life.

It's not even the fact that I got laid which is making me so deliriously cheerful. It's because it's *Whaley*. All my late-night fantasies and wishes to the gods didn't prepare me for how fucking awesome it would be. I can still feel him—the ache deep inside from his piercing. Can still taste him, can still sense his cum leaking out of my ass.

Well, since I didn't clean up afterward, that doesn't surprise me. Seriously though? Who can blame me? I'm not wasting any of Whaley's magic spunk. I want to collect it all, slather it over my skin, and make my own lotion so I can mark myself with him whenever I want.

If people knew how much I think about him or the way I watch him when he's not looking, they'd be concerned. Not to mention my collection of Whaley treasures I hide in my closet. All the pictures I've taken of him when he wasn't watching and my fan fiction *might* come off a tiny bit obsessive, but it's all out of severe like for him, I swear.

I'm not crazy.

Superficially, he's hot as hell. Tall, broad, with tattoos covering ninety percent of his body, which I know thanks to the times I've caught him shirtless at the shop. He's got scars on his back that tell a story I want to listen to. He's got thick, dark hair that almost reaches his shoulders, and I drool every time I see it in a man bun.

There's also something on a biological level that appeals to me, all those skeletons dancing around his closet are like bait and a hook, and the mystique he carries, so formidable and aloof, is such a turn-on.

It's not only that.

He's caring, and wants to take care of everybody. When he looks at me with those dark, smoldering eyes, I soar.

I think back to the moment we shared the first day of my senior year when my obsession began. The way he talked to me, the way he cared for me, and the way he looked at me. There's nothing he could ask me for that I wouldn't give him, nothing I wouldn't sacrifice, because I know he'd do the same.

I know I tease, I know I joke, and I know I push, but I never imagined that something like last night would happen. I always thought my deep dark obsession with Whaley was one-sided, and well, maybe it is. But the more I remember the territorial dig of his nails against my hips and the way he growled through his orgasm, I'm starting to think maybe it's not so one-sided after all.

I reach for my phone, biting the corner of my lip to hide my smile as I scroll through my contacts.

ME:

> God, my ass misses you. It wants your dick back, pretty please.

I give Whaley a beat, but my lips turn down when I don't get a reply after a few minutes. I shouldn't be surprised, because in the last several months of me sending him teasing messages, he hardly ever responded, but I was hoping things would be different now. Maybe he's caught up because he's on a run. I shrug it off and push away the discomfort twisting in my gut before getting dressed.

I light a joint, perching it between my lips as I grab a ratty T-shirt and a pair of ripped jeans. Snatching up my leather jacket, I leave my trailer and head to my car. It's Saturday and a little past noon—yeah, I'm not necessarily an early riser—so everybody should be at the shop for their shift.

When I step inside the open garage door, Raid and Silas are already there, both in their coveralls and hunched over an old Chevy. Silas is the one who notices me first, scowling like usual the second he sees me. "Finally. We're goddamn swamped here, asshole."

I laugh, taking the last hit on my joint before tossing the butt outside. "Oh, fuck off, Silas. Can't handle a little work?"

"Shut it," he hisses. "We got three tire rotations and four oil changes to get through before we close up."

"Plenty of time." I take off my jacket and put it behind the reception desk before grabbing some coveralls. "It'll be fine."

Raid snickers as he pushes his wire-rimmed glasses up his nose with an oily finger. "He's all wound up because he's got a date with his *baby* tonight."

I cackle at the look Silas gives Raid. Then he leans over the open hood of the car to punch Raid's shoulder. "Stop bein' a dick."

Even though Silas being in a committed relationship isn't surprising, the fact that it's Blaine is what threw us all for a loop. You wouldn't think those two would work together, but they fit. They're adorable. Always touching and cuddling and kissing. It makes me want to throw up, but in a fun way, you know?

"Oh, come on," I coo, saddling up beside him and flinging my arm over his shoulders. "It's okay. You're just in *love*. It's fuckin' hot. Wanna jack off to the two of you."

His eyes narrow as he shrugs me off, wondering if I'm being honest. He must decide I'm only joking because he shoves a wrench into my hand before manhandling me to his place. "You finish this shit up. Gotta text Blaine."

"Tell him we love him too!" I shout at his retreating form. Blaine's got nice teeth. Maybe if I suck up enough, I can get the number for his guy. I want mine so shiny and white that Whaley gets a chubber just from looking at them.

Raid and I work silently on the car like two well-oiled machines until he reaches into his coveralls. I glance up, only to find him staring at his phone with a dopey smile on his face as his fingers fly across the screen.

He catches me staring and frowns. "What?"

"What do you mean 'what?'" I fire back. "You look like you just got your first pube. Who are you textin' that's got you like that?"

He scoffs before setting his phone down on the car so he can wipe his hands. "Nobody— Bunk!"

He's too late. I already have his phone, and my swoony-teen heart *dies* when I see who he's texting. "Landon?" I howl, jumping up and down, unable to contain my excitement as he reaches around me trying to get it back. "Oh shit. You're fuckin' with me, right? The jock?"

"So what?" he counters with obvious discomfort on his face as he eyes his phone in my hand, preparing to snatch it back. "Blaine's a jock."

"So, you ain't denyin' this is a thing."

He angrily snatches back his phone and shoves it into his

coveralls. "It ain't a thing, Bunk! We're *friends*. Can't two guys just like talkin' to each other? Huh? That so weird?"

"Well, that depends. What were you talkin' about?" I should have read the messages but I was too preoccupied with the fact that they were texting at all.

This is where he blushes, his face all red and his eyes seeming a bit sketchy as he looks away. Ha! Got him. I want to tease him more, but the coward stalks away, probably going to the bathroom to send Landon a dick pic or something.

Speaking of dick pics.

ME:

Wanna feel those piercings in my hole again.
You free tonight?

After a few minutes of no response, Silas and Raid come back, but I barely notice them or what I'm doing as we continue to work. I'm also a bit distracted, caught in a doubtful web as stray thoughts filter through my mind. I start going through all the possibilities in my head. If he's not texting me back, he better be dead, or else I'll kill him myself.

Joking.

But seriously, I'm a goddamn snack. I'm young, hot, and bendy as hell thanks to all the Tai Chi. There should be absolutely no reason he wouldn't want me, especially not after what we shared last night. I *know* I felt it—that magic fucking spark reserved for one of Raid's cheesy romance movies.

ME:

Are you dead or something? Answer me.

ME:

I'm not gonna stop.

ME:

> Pretty please, I'll suck your dick real good if you answer.

Is it desperate? Yes. Do I care? No, I don't.

"Bunky, calm the fuck down."

I snap my head up, wrinkling my nose as I look at an annoyed Silas. "What?"

"You've been clickin' your tongue for the last five minutes," Raid says, wiping the sweat off his forehead with the back of his hand. "It's irritatin'."

I stop toying with my barbell, realizing he's right. "Hey, Silas, question."

"What?" he drones, no longer looking at me as he checks the engine.

"So, hypothetically, let's say Blaine isn't textin' you back."

This gets his attention. His head snaps up, murder mixed with concern in his eyes as he glares at me. "Why wouldn't Blaine text me back?"

My eyes widen and I try to explain but he keeps cutting me off. "It was just a hypothetical—"

"My guy always texts me back."

"I know. But what if—"

"You sayin' somethin's goin' on?"

Oh my God. He's so possessive. Maybe I shouldn't have gone this route. "What? No. I'm just—"

"I'm gonna text him again," he grumbles, angrily stomping away. I look at him, baffled at his reaction, but I shouldn't be. That guy is crazy protective when it comes to Blaine.

"You can't do that shit," Raid chastises, shaking his head. "What's with the question anyway?"

"What if Landon didn't text *you* back?" I ask, searching for some clarity. "What would that mean?"

"Nothin', considerin' Landon and I are *just friends*," he says slowly, but damn, he's flushed again. I make a mental note to pick at him later about this. I need all the details too. "Seriously, you ain't gonna tell me what's goin' on?" he pulls me from my thoughts, wiping his hands on a rag after checking the oil level. "Not like you, Bunk. You once texted me at three in the morning to tell me about an impressive shit you took."

Oh, well, that thing was a beauty.

I open my mouth, ready to tell him everything about Whaley, but then I close it and hold back. There's... No, it's not guilt. I don't feel at all guilty about what happened between us, but is it that doubt again that I felt earlier? Do I not want to say anything because saying it out loud would make it real and make Whaley's rejection sting even more than it is now?

No, Whaley isn't rejecting me. He's busy.

That's what I tell myself the rest of the day as we work on the cars. When Silas leaves to pick up Blaine, *nothing*. When Raid tells me he's going to hang out with Landon, *nothing*.

ME:

Whaley, text me back. I mean it!

Nothing!

"You good, Bunk?" Raid questions, sending me a worried look as he takes off his coveralls. "You know, you can come hang with Landon and me. We're just gonna shoot the shit down at the diner."

While that does sound like a good time, considering Jerry spikes the soda there with whiskey after seven, I shake my head. "Nah, I'm good. Gotta close, remember?"

He nods but looks a little relieved, which would offend me if I weren't otherwise distracted. "Suit yourself. Text me later, yeah? We'll chill."

"Sounds good, man." He claps my shoulder before leaving. I'm not alone for long though, because after a few minutes, bodies start to filter into the shop and my heart feels like it's going to fall out of my ass.

Whaley.

I jump up, watching as some of the older members walk in. They all look tired and worn down, probably from riding all day to get back home before dark. When Badge comes through the garage door, he's tired too but perks up when he sees me.

"Hey, Bunk." He smiles wide and brings me into a hug. "How'd it go today, kid?"

I love Badge, I really do, but I can't focus on him or his question when I realize someone's missing. "Where's Whaley?"

Badge furrows his brows as he steps back, then looks behind him before shrugging. "Guess he went home? Didn't want to join us for drinks."

"Oh," I say, and although my voice comes out even, my insides churn.

"You okay?" Badge asks, looking at me warily. When I don't answer, he nudges my shoulder. "Bunk?"

All I see is red.

How fucking dare he ignore me?!

I push past Badge, still in my coveralls, and stalk out of the garage. I'm sure I'll have to answer to him later, but I don't care about that right now.

I want to rampage.

I've always been like this. A switch flicks at any minor inconvenience. Any little thing, any threat of an insult gets me going. I've always had a darkness, something waiting to be unleashed, banging against the cage, wanting every opportunity to break free—

Crack.

Squish.

Pop.

My vision blurs as thoughts rush back to me. The sounds… They were so loud.

"Snap out of it!" I scold, slapping myself across the face, my eyes widening with the impact. The pain sends a sharp thrill of awareness through me, immediately clearing my head.

Coping mechanisms for the win.

Who the fuck does Whaley think he is? Fucking me and then abandoning me? He can't abandon me. He can't leave me alone after what we shared. He can't just toss me aside and forget about me.

I won't fucking let him.

FIVE

Whaley

BUNKY:

Whaley, fucking text me back. I mean it.

I flop back on my bed, my mind racing as I stare at the ceiling, my phone burning in my palm. I don't want to look at it anymore. Don't want to see the thirty-plus messages I've left on read. Bunky doesn't fucking give up, but I should have expected this, especially with how we left things last night.

Really, how *I* left things.

I still can't believe I fucked him, that I let my inhibitions down and put aside my carefully constructed level of control. Maybe if I was a stronger man I could have resisted, but I can only do so much. He was taunting me. Literally jacking his dick, while he told me all the shit that was happening in that wickedly devious head of his.

I close my eyes, still able to feel his skin against my fingertips and the way his tongue ring flicked in my mouth as we tried to eat each other alive. God, and the way his ass strangled my cock...

I'm close to reaching down and palming it to relieve some tension, but my phone vibrates in my hand, stopping my wandering thoughts. My eyes snap open, and even though I already know it's Bunky, I open my messages immediately to see.

BUNKY:

> I'm going to set your fucking shop on fire if you don't answer my texts.

"Fuckin' lovely," I grit out, knowing he wouldn't actually do that, then I toss my phone beside me on the bed and fling my arm over my face. He's going to go apeshit soon—assuming he's not already there. By that message, I think it's safe to say I need to do damage control, and soon.

I sit up as my mind runs through a thousand scenarios of how to let him down easy. Not gonna lie, I got nothing. What should I say outside of the obvious, 'We can't do that shit again' and 'I'm too old for you'? Knowing Bunky, he'll hit me with the 'Why' and the 'That's not good enough.' I bet if I gave him a mile-long list, he still wouldn't care. He likes to tap dance on the morally gray line, and being with me? I may as well supply him some yellow caution tape and a one-way ticket straight to Hell. Maybe even a flashing red light so other people know to steer clear of the chaos.

Because that's all we'd be.

We're like a lit match and lighter fluid, which is fine separately, but the second they come together, it creates a fire that spreads, burning everything in its path.

We'd burn the fucking world to the ground. His demons mixed with mine would be noxious. We'd destroy each other, leaving nothing left but broken shells once it was all said and done.

I grab my smokes from the nightstand, lighting one up and taking a long drag. I'll finish this, head to the shop, and—

Bang, bang, bang.

"Whaley, open the damn door!"

I don't know whether to groan at the fact that I won't get to finish my cigarette before dealing with Bunky or be grateful that I can go ahead and get this conversation over with.

Bang, bang, bang.

"Whaley, I know how to pick a lock. Hell, you got a big-ass glass ashtray on your step. Pretty sure it's heavy enough to knock out your window. If you don't open up, I'm goin' to start smashin' shit!"

I grit my teeth and put out my smoke before stomping to the door, ready to wring the little bastard's neck. Apparently, he thinks letting me screw him means he can act however the hell he wants.

Oh, please. He acts that way with you every-damn-day and you let him.

"Fuck off," I mutter to that aggravating as hell voice that lives in the back of my head rent-free. It's the prime example as to why I never let anyone in. Who would deal with all the messed up parts of me? Who *could?* Definitely not Bunky. He has his own demons that linger in the forefront, ready to break through and suffocate him any minute.

Bang, ban—

I snatch open the door, making Bunky stumble in and onto his hands and knees from the force. He glares up at me, and I'm tempted to drag him to my room and spank his ass red while he chokes on my cock for being such a brat.

"I'm surprised you answered," he growls, sounding about as ferocious as a kitten.

"What do you want?" I sigh, already exhausted, and I don't even have the door closed yet.

He stands and dusts his pants off, eyes drilling into me. "You've been avoidin' my calls and texts."

I would say ignoring, not avoiding. "I never respond to your calls and texts."

"Whaley!" He scoffs as he pushes past me to come inside.

I shut the door, trying to remember that even though he's technically an adult, he doesn't always act like one. I've been telling myself this a lot lately, every time he steps out of line so I don't either stab him or fuck him.

Clearly, I didn't do that last night.

"Bunky—"

He spins around, slashing his hand in the air to cut me off, a wide smile spread across his face. I know that look well, and I'm mentally preparing for a fight. He's angry, but there's something else mixed in with it. Something temptingly dangerous. Intoxicating even.

"Wait, wait. Let me guess what you're about to say." Tilting his head, his eyes roam over me. A normal person would find this terrifying but I'm far from normal, and Bunky at his most unhinged doesn't make me flinch. Until recently, it didn't really make me feel anything but sympathy. "We can't do this again, Bunky. You're too young, Bunky. *Yada yada yada.*" He gives his hand a little wave. "Forever the saint, ain't you, Whaley?"

My jaw ticks, body tensing more at the blatant disrespect in his voice. "You tryin' to piss me off?"

His eyes sparkle with delight as he claps his hands in excitement. "Is it workin'?"

Is it working?

I fist my hands at my sides and start to take a small step toward him but stop myself. I won't do this. I've already let him get under my skin once, and he achieved what he wanted.

Not again.

"Go home," I push out, fury burning in my stomach. "I ain't dealin' with your shit right now."

I turn around, about to open the door and tell him to fuck off when I hear it. The subtle click of a blade opening, a blade that I know all too well. I whip around at the same time

Bunky advances and slams me against the door. He fists the front of my shirt with one hand while the other presses the pocketknife I gave him years ago to my throat. My heated skin registers the cool blade immediately and my body jumps to high alert.

Bunky's not Bunky right now. He's a predator, and somehow, he's made me his prey.

I don't hate it as much as I should. In fact, I feel the buzzing start in my head as my monster threatens to snap forward to nip at his.

Make him see who's the real threat here.

"You can't run me off," he hisses, his expression filled with anger and those emerald-green eyes of his are almost black. "You think you can fuck me and leave me?"

He bares down a little harder, letting me feel the bite of the knife against my skin.

"You mad, Bunk?" I taunt, not caring that he could drag the blade and cut me. God, I kind of want him to. I want to feel the heat of the liquid as it pours from my neck, and by the way he's staring at me with that hooded expression, I think he wants that too.

"I'm past mad, Whaley." He pushes a little harder. "I want to jab this knife in your fuckin' neck and watch you bleed out. You think you can just toss me aside? That ain't happenin'. You fucked me, now you're mine."

I'm panting, my dick's hard, and though this type of power switch is not something I do, for Bunky, I'll allow it this once.

The hold on his knife never lets up as he stares into my eyes with so much intensity. It's like he's looking into my soul, trying to search for all my hidden secrets and the shit I keep locked away.

"You gonna cut me, Bunky?" My tone is husky, and a little groan escapes me when he rubs against my aching cock.

"Fuck, you're hard," he moans, eyes falling shut, cutting off his deep depths from me.

Even though it's so depraved, so insane, I want it back. I want that darkness that lingers beneath his skin. I want us to unleash every twisted part of ourselves, every wicked thought, and just... I don't know, screw until we can't breathe. The chaos, the adrenaline, the overwhelming need to revel in the madness is so alluring.

And that's the terrifying thought that breaks my trance.

He's rocking against me, lost to the lust, and it's almost enough of a distraction for me to unarm him but I fail. His eyes snap open and he fights me, resulting in a little nick to my throat. I can feel the sting, but it's harmless. I've been slashed plenty of times, and this is basically a paper cut in comparison. Bunky's eyes widen as he watches the warm blood dribble from the small cut.

"Shit. Didn't mean to do that. Here, lemme make it better."

I don't understand what he means until he leans forward with lightning speed and licks one solid stripe up my neck.

Fuck, yes!

I thought his ass was good, but this? This is even better. Bunky's actually *tasting* my blood, savoring the evidence of his beautiful violence, sharing my DNA, and it's the best thing I've ever felt. It's like I'm a part of him now, soaked into him, and for a man like me, that power goes straight to my brain.

I don't think as I palm the back of his head, keeping his mouth trapped against my skin. He doesn't care or complain, just continues to give me those sweet little licks. I know I should stop him, but if this is the last time I let his mouth on me, I'm going to enjoy it.

When he pulls back, I drop my hand and note how wrecked he looks. Even more than the other night when I was inside of him. He flicks his tongue out, that silver ball gliding across his lips. "God, Whaley, you taste so good. I want more."

I don't think there's any blood there now, but that doesn't stop Bunky from leaning in again and lapping at the cut. My breath hitches when his hand rushes down my chest, tugging at my belt, and before I know it, he's got his hand down my pants and wrapped around my hard cock. "Gonna suck your blood while I drain your cock."

I feel another nick, but this one's on my wrist. He moves from my neck, tucking his knife away before he grabs my wrist and brings it up to his mouth like a bloodthirsty vampire. He's still stroking my cock, his fingers teasing my piercings as he hums against my skin. "You need to come for me," he whispers, then drags his tongue up and down, his barbell chilling me. His hand speeds up, jacking me harder and faster. "You're gonna come so quick, ain't you? You can't help yourself." I'm so close, almost there. He looks up at me with that devious grin, his green eyes hungry, and my stomach tightens. "Gimme what I want."

His husky tone, longing look, and his buzzing body has me ready to snap and break all the rules I made about staying away from him and never doing this again.

God, why did I make those stupid rules anyway?

I wonder what he tastes like…

What if I cut him too? What if I drag that blade against his sensitive, pale skin, and carved myself into him? Made my mark so that every other fucker knows this guy belongs to me, body and soul?

I'd burn the world down for him. Torch it. I want to keep him locked in my room, gagged and chained and—

No!

I grit my teeth, trying like hell to stave off the pleasure. This is exactly what I meant. The thoughts I have are dangerous. We can't be together like this. We can't give in. We can't let everything else in our lives disappear because we're so entranced in each other to give a damn about anything else.

"You're so thick in my hand, Whaley. Can't wait to feel you inside me again."

I'm two seconds from coming, but I manage to get myself from his grasp, and he stumbles from my swift movement. I drag my fingers through my hair, chest heaving as my urges boil over. I need to get him away from me. I need some space. I said I was going to go easy on him, but that shit's flown out the window. I'm desperate now, barely hanging on by a thread.

"Get out!" I snap, feeling the flip begin.

Bunky's eyes widen before he licks his blood-tinged lips and shakes his head. "What? No—"

"I said, get the fuck out!" I roar, grabbing him by his jacket and trying to get him to leave. He fights me the entire time, scratching at me as he attempts to break my hold.

"You're kiddin' me!" he yells back, escaping my grasp and planting his hands on his hips. "Give me one good reason! Just one!"

"I don't want you!" It's a lie, a blatant one, but I need to say something, anything to get him out.

Unfortunately, he doesn't look like he believes it when he rolls his eyes. "You weren't sayin' that when my hand was wrapped around your dick. Come on. Just let me finish—"

"Don't you get it?" I don't want to say it, but I feel like I have no other choice. "The way you're actin' is pathetic, Bunk," I spit out, trying to school my features into disgust, and it works from the way his face falls. "Get it through your thick head that I don't want this shit with you."

His face falls, but not for long. His stubborn jaw sets as he glares. "You're lyin'."

"I'm not."

"Yes, you are! Don't fuckin' lie to me! I hate it when people lie!" He snatches the glass ashtray from the coffee table and throws it against the wall, causing it to shatter. He's enraged, chest heaving.

"But fine," he spits through clenched teeth, getting all up in my space. "If that's how you wanna play this, I'll go fuck myself!"

He turns to yank the door open and storms out of my trailer. I want to say he's fine, but I know Bunky. I know him far too well. Beneath his anger, beneath his violence, beneath his offense, there's sadness.

"Damn it!" I yell, pacing the length of my living room as a molten hot feeling explodes in my gut. I spot a tumbler that's sitting on my coffee table and follow Bunky's lead, chucking it against the wall, my vision darkening as my wrath consumes me.

I need to get out of here. I need to hit something. I need to forget this damn night ever happened.

Grabbing my keys, I head out to my bike to blow off some steam. I don't know where I'm going and I don't know what I'm going to do, but anything has to be better than this.

SIX

Bunky

Life sucks.

Normally, I can look on the bright side despite my messed up head.

Friends? Check.

Weed? Check.

Tai Chi? Check.

These last few weeks have really fucked me up despite all of that. Silas getting locked up really threw everything for a loop, especially for something we all know he didn't do. Thankfully, now that he's out and the sheriff is gone, things are looking up.

Well, at least that situation is.

I know I'm the one that stormed out weeks ago when Whaley tried to convince me he didn't want me, but damn, what do I need to do to get some fucking attention? He's been so busy lately that I think even if he was all about us, he wouldn't have time to spend with me.

The thing is, I know he wants me. I can see it in his eyes. I saw it when he called me pathetic. I know I should still be pissed—a part of me is—but he didn't mean the things he said. I *know* he didn't. He's stubborn and won't let us have our version of a fairy-tale happily ever after, so I guess I have to be the bigger person and let his comment slide.

Before, when my obsession was unconsummated, I was able to mostly ignore the longing I felt for him. I still did everything I could to get his attention, but it was never this painful. Now that I've tasted his lips, tasted his *blood*, I can't think of anything else. He haunts me every day, and the little glimpses I've gotten of him these past few weeks aren't enough.

I roll off my bed, crawl toward my dingy closet, and fish out the cardboard box tucked in the back. I'm like a dragon appreciating its hoard, little scraps of Whaley I've managed to sneak away laid out in front of me.

It's not creepy, it's sweet, and I don't care if people say otherwise.

I start with his comb that he left in his office one day, rubbing it against my cheek, wanting to feel my fingers threading through his hair.

"He loves me."

I toss the comb behind me and grab his underwear next. I had to do some sneaky shit to get these, but I swear to God they still smell like him.

"He loves me not."

His old headphones, a dirty T-shirt, a hoodie he once lent me, his toothbrush—

Okay, maybe that one's a *bit* creepy.

"He loves me, he loves me not. He loves me, he loves me not," I mumble again and again as I rifle through my treasure. After the day in his office, when my obsession bloomed and I started stealing his shit, I told myself that one day I wouldn't need little pieces of him, that I'd have him as a whole. As someone who would love and never leave me.

If he keeps up his lie, this is all I'll ever have, stolen items to obsess and sniff and worship because they're as close to the real thing as I can get. I'll just spend the rest of my life miserable and alone, wanting the only thing I can't have.

Probably die of a broken heart too.

"What the fuck are you doin'?"

I turn with a start, my hand automatically going to my pocketknife, but I relax when I see the last person I expected.

"Fox? What the fuck?" I yell happily, springing to my feet and throwing myself at him. "When did you get back?"

"This mornin'," he tells me, clapping me on my back as we pull apart. "Damn, bro. You've grown up. Only been gone a few months."

Yeah, five long fucking months.

Whaley had sent Fox over to the Aces' Vegas branch to help them through a rough patch. I've missed him so much. As my adoptive brother, life's been a little less cool without him hanging around all the time like he used to. I know some people hate their siblings, or at least pretend to, but I have no problem saying I have hero-worship for Fox.

Every time I woke up in the middle of the night, when the memories were too strong, Fox was there to help me back to sleep. He taught me how to use the pocketknife Whaley gave me when he and Badge realized I was dead set on carrying it around everywhere. He even tried doing normal brotherly shit with me like Thursday diner nights and occasional arcade days.

"Forget about me," I tell him, ushering him over to the bed. "What's been goin' on with you? How was Vegas?"

The smile on his face dims a little and the edge to his tone spikes my curiosity. "It was fine."

"*Fine?* What kind of things did they have you doin'?" I question as I lie back in the bed, lighting a cigarette. "Did you do any sketchy stuff— Ooo!" I shoot up as my thoughts spin. "Were you a secret spy we sent to infiltrate their lair? Is this a 'If I tell you, I have to kill you' scenario?"

He chuckles at that. "No espionage shit. They were just in a tough spot and needed some extra hands, that's all."

I pout, flopping back again. "Well, that ain't interestin'."

"I never said it was." He looks over at me, lips twisting back into a smile. "I wanna talk about you."

There's a lingering discomfort in his eyes, and I'd be clueless to miss the way he conveniently changes the subject three seconds into the conversation. "What about me?"

"Wanna start with whatever the fuck this shit is?" He gestures to my Whaley pile. "Or the fact that Raid told me you've been actin' weird?"

I sit up and narrow my eyes, annoyed at my friend for ratting me out. "Raid's got a big mouth. What'd he say?"

"Just said you've been off the last couple of days. Very…" He stops, brows furrowing and jaw ticking.

I sigh, giving my free hand a dismissive wave. "Lemme guess, he used the word *psycho*?"

Sigh, don't they all?

"You know I don't like sayin' that word," he snaps, crossing his arms over his chest like the overprotective brother he is. "Nearly smacked him."

"He doesn't mean it in a bad way," I say, scratching my chin as I think over Fox's words. "I guess I can admit I've been more erratic lately."

He lets out an unamused grunt. "He said you released the lab rats in biology yesterday."

The damn snitch. "Well, Susan needed to get back to her side piece."

"And you've been ditchin' your shifts at the shop."

"It's not like they need me," I mutter bitterly, thoughts circling back to Whaley like they always do.

"Are you goin' to tell me what's goin' on?" he asks, cocking a brow. "Or am I gonna have to pry it out of you?"

I reach into my pocket for my joint. Fuck the cigarette, I need something stronger for this. "It's nothin'."

He watches as I drop my cigarette in the ashtray and light up the joint. The smell of weed quickly envelops the room, but Fox doesn't even ask for a hit. He just stares at me, eyes calculating. One would think he hates me with the way he's trying to break me down.

Finally, he sighs. "So, Whaley?"

All the blood drains from my face, and I take a long toke. "Dunno what you're talkin' about."

"Bunk, it's me." He nudges my leg. "When have you kept secrets?"

I want to point out that he's obviously keeping a secret about Vegas, but I don't because he's just being typical Fox. Nothing gets past him. Hell, I never even tried keeping shit from him when I was younger. Like the time I accidentally got my dick stuck in a makeshift fleshlight I created, and I happily swung myself all the way to Fox's room, interrupting one of his hookups. There was also the instance where I thought dying my pubes was a good idea. Yeah. That hurt. I had a lot of explaining to do on our way to the hospital.

There's absolutely nothing that's off-limits when it comes to him, just the way brothers should be.

But still, Whaley is something different.

Speaking of which…

"Wait?" I shoot up, nearly knocking him in the forehead, and burning myself with my joint. "How the fuck do you know about Whaley?"

He rolls his eyes. "You don't think the pictures of him in your closet kind of tip it off?"

I blanch and follow his gaze to where my clothes on the hangers are parted enough to see my Whaley collage. It's not like they're anything bad. Whaley just doesn't like getting his picture taken, so I've had to resort to taking them when he isn't paying attention.

My favorite is the one of him leaving the shower that I

managed to get through his trailer window. I promise it's not as weird as it sounds.

"I can explain," I rush out, scrambling off the bed, setting my joint in the ashtray and try to hide the evidence of Whaley. "It's nothin'."

"Sure, because I have a stalker board up in my room too." His tone is serious but I don't miss the way his lip lifts, as if he expects this type of shit from me.

"It's not a stalker board," I hiss after slamming my closet door shut. "It's just—"

"Proof that you've got an unhealthy obsession with the guy?" he finishes, head tilted as he waits for me to confirm.

My teeth fiddle with the barbell through my tongue. I haven't told any of the guys about Whaley, especially not with the shit that's been going down with Silas, but I don't know if I even would have. It's embarrassing, a little pathetic —just like Whaley called me—and I'm not ready for people to know that I got rejected by the one person I want most in the world.

Fox may not be blood, but he's my brother, and now that the cat's out of the bag, I don't see a reason not to tell him. I know he'll keep his mouth shut anyway because he's loyal like that. It might even help me figure out what to do about the situation.

"Fine." I lean heavily against the now closed door, all the fight leaving me. "We hooked up a couple of weeks ago."

His brows hit his hairline at my admission. "You what?" he chokes out, a little cough leaving him.

I twiddle with my fingers as I think about how good he felt inside me. "It was after a hang out. He made me go home and one thing led to another—"

"And you fucked?"

"Jesus," I moan, flopping back on the bed. "Fucked me so good, I—"

"Nope," he snaps, waving his hand in the air to stop me. "Don't want to hear that shit. But seriously, *Whaley*?"

"What's so wrong with Whaley?" I counter, unable to hide the offense in my voice. "He's perfect."

"Perfect?" He looks taken aback, like he can't believe I said those words. He scoffs. "I respect the man, but he's far from perfect, and nearly two decades older than you."

"One and a half," I mutter, looking at my closet again like I can see the pictures through the door. "And?"

"… You don't find that weird?"

"There are plenty of couples with large age gaps. Lots of romance novels about it too." I fold my arms petulantly. There is nothing wrong with our ages, and I'll die on that hill.

"This ain't like one of your romance novels." He pinches the bridge of his nose. "Whaley… Guy's messed up, Bunk. Got a lot of skeletons in his closet. Again, I respect him, but I don't think you know what you're gettin' into."

"Apparently nothing at the moment," I fire back, and snag my joint again. "Claims he doesn't want me. But he just won't give in."

Fox nods, humming to himself as I smoke away.

After a few minutes of silent contemplation on his part and me getting higher and higher with every toke on my joint, he finally speaks. "Can you tell me what you like about him?"

Is that a rhetorical question?

"I don't *like* him," I clarify, sitting up quickly to look at him in astonishment. 'Like' seems so insignificant in the face of what my true feelings are. "I *love* him."

"Love, huh? That's a pretty big word." He smiles at me like he did when I told him I was going to beat the living crap out of him when I was nine. When I growl at him, he rolls his eyes and holds his hands up in surrender. "Right, sorry. Okay, tell me."

My eyes drop down to my lap and I suddenly feel vulnerable. There aren't words to describe what I feel for Whaley, but I'll try my best to make Fox understand. "He's just... He's everythin', Fox."

All the poetry and love songs pale in comparison to my feelings for him. They're so overwhelming, so deeply ingrained in my soul—what's left of it anyway. The way he walks, the way he thinks, the way he smells... He's it for me.

"So you're obsessed with him?"

No, it's love. Seems less stalkery if you ask me. It's not like I—

Okay, we'll settle with love and a sprinkle of obsession.

"Did you ever consider that's *why* you shouldn't be together?"

I wrinkle my nose before hopping off the bed and waving my hands in the air, nearly burning Fox in my haste. "What do you mean?"

"Fuck, be careful," he grunts, eyes narrowed at my joint. I give him an apologetic smile and he only sighs, tilting his head as he thinks over his next words. It's like he's trying to explain to an addict why drugs are bad. I can see the gears churning in his head as he chooses his words carefully.

"You're both fucked," he explains, wisely scooching back when I crush the lit joint in my fist, not even blinking as it burns my skin. "Damn, calm down. Not tryin' to be a dick. He's got shit in his past, and you..."

We both gulp at the same time. My friends don't know about my past—my origin story, as I so villainously put it— but Fox does. I'm pretty sure Badge told him, or maybe I did when I got too toasted one night, either way, he's in the know.

But that doesn't mean either of us like bringing it up.

Crack.

Squish.

Pop.

Is that what a brain looks like?

"Bunk!" Fox's shout snaps me out of my own mind.

He's staring at me cautiously, a hint of nerves in his steel-like complexion, and that's when I realize I've subconsciously whipped out my pocketknife.

"I…" *Toasted marshmallows. Sparkly unicorns. Whaley's dick.* "I'm fine."

He raises one brow as he juts his chin toward the pocketknife. "Yeah?"

"Yeah," I confirm, smiling as I give a little cackle and slice the knife in the air. *"Let's put a smile on that face."*

"Jesus." Fox's body relaxes and he releases a little chuckle.

I shrug before begrudgingly putting away the pocketknife, even though cosplaying supervillains would be so cool right now. "You love me."

He nods, face once again serious. "Enough to know you need someone good. Whaley ain't it."

I gape at him. Is he serious? "He *is* good! Do you know how much he's done for the people around here?"

"Fine," he relents. "Healthy for *you* then."

I snort. "That shit's borin' as fuck."

Silas and Blaine might want that whole domesticated shit, but I'm good on that. I don't need someone who wants to tame me, or make me go to see a shrink—Badge *severely* regretted suggesting that once—or turn me into someone I'm not. I want someone who wants me just the way I am. Crazy thoughts, devious impulses, sporadic moods—everything.

I need a ride or die, not a white picket fence.

Whaley could be that. He could love me the way I want to be loved. He's the only one who's never called me crazy even once, and he's always the first to jump to my defense when people call me unhinged.

Now if he'd just get his dick back inside me…

"This is really tearin' you up, ain't it?" Fox asks, snapping his fingers in front of my face to regain my attention. "Damn it, couldn't you have lit up after we had this talk?"

"Nope," I say, groaning when I realize I went all Mr.

Incredible on my last joint. "Got any other brotherly advice you want to give about love?"

Something passes over his features before his head drops and he twists his fingers together as he thinks.

"Fallin' in love… Shit, it's the worst. It's like you're givin' your all to someone and forgettin' about the fact that you're a person too." He looks pissed, but it can't be at me, which confirms my earlier thoughts.

Something definitely happened in Vegas.

"Fox?"

"A broken heart sucks, but you gotta pick yourself up," he continues, almost like he's talking to himself now. "Ain't no point lettin' yourself break for someone. Ain't no reason to let anyone have that much control over you."

Something inside me twists up and I'm torn between being worried about my brother and worried over his words. "But what if it's meant to be?"

"Come on, man. You know that shit don't exist. Love is nothin' but trouble. It'll ruin you."

Whaley's love would be the most beautiful ruin.

I go to open my mouth and tell him that his pessimistic outlook on the universe is dumb, but I'm stopped when Badge walks in, a proud smile on his face as he looks at us.

"Damn, you know I love seein' my boys together."

"Hey, Pops," Fox greets, snapping out of whatever the fuck was happening inside his head.

"What are you boys up to?"

"Shootin' the shit," he says with a shrug but turns to wink at me before ruffling my hair. "Bunk's about to wax poetic about the universe. Wanna join?"

My cheeks flush as I shove him off with a scoff. "Asshole."

"It's good to have you two together again." Badge laughs before cupping his hands and rubbing them together. "Wanna go for a ride? It stopped rainin'."

Fox thinks it over. "Where?"

"It don't matter." Badge shrugs, eagerness and excitement shining in his eyes. "Hell, we can go anywhere."

"What do you say, Bunk? Wanna run away with us?"

What I *want* is to snort a line and find some shit to get up to, but I relent because running away with two of my favorite people sounds like exactly what I need.

SEVEN

Whaley

I grit my teeth, staring at my seemingly nervous distributor, Tony. He's refusing to meet my eyes as he shifts from side to side. His hands are strumming the table between us, and I track the movement of a bead of sweat as it glides down his temple.

It's all the signs he's about to give me some bullshit excuse that's going to make me lose my shit. I *really* don't like excuses. It's a cop-out. Instead of owning up to the fact that he fucked up somewhere, he's going to try to save his ass with whatever he can come up with. Honestly, I'd respect Tony just a *smidge* if he told me whatever the fuck he did instead of looking like a terrified lamb being brought to slaughter.

I eye the table, noting the product—lack of product more like —and give Tony an unamused look.

"Where's the rest of my shit?" My jaw is tense, hands clenched, and body vibrating with a mix of anger and annoyance.

I see Tony twice a month when I need to stock up, and

lately, I've noticed a decline in his supply. It's just some coke, but when I pay for quality shit, that's what I expect. Now, not only do I have low-grade product, but I also have half the amount I paid for.

"Well?" I press when he doesn't answer, slamming my fist down on the table to make him flinch.

This is the last damn thing I need to deal with today, especially after everything with—

Nope.

Tony's fearful eyes settle on me as he stumbles over his words. "It's— Well— You see…"

"You should start explainin'," Badge chimes in, pulling my attention to where he stands next to the entrance of the warehouse.

Fox smirks next to Badge, looking so much like his old man as he casually toys with his knife. "Sooner rather than later if you value your fingers."

I turn back to Tony and watch as his face flickers through a dozen emotions before he releases a forced chuckle, as if we're friends or something. Then he holds up his hands placatingly. "There was a little misunderstanding."

"Really?" I say, my voice calm despite my irritation.

"Yes." The dumbass nods so hard and fast you could almost mistake him for a bobblehead. He doesn't elaborate though, just goes back to being quiet, as if the matter isn't pressing.

I look up at the ceiling, trying like hell to remind myself that everything is fine. It's only a little shift in my schedule, just a minor inconvenience, nothing to get worked up over, but that's not what the demon buried in the back of my brain says as he swipes his claws, demanding to be released from his cage.

Usually, I do a good job at keeping him at bay, but Bunky had to go and fuck that up.

More. More. More.

I shake the words out of my head. This is the proof of why Bunky and I can't be together. I'm starting to lose my shit because of him. If we explored this connection between us—if I gave in and caved to his wishes, he'd destroy me. My demon would break free, tearing everything up in its path that isn't its obsession.

I can't have that. I'm not just a man, I'm a leader. I have people depending on me to keep my cool, my reason, and my fucking sanity. Bunky doesn't want me to see reason, just wants me to join him in the madness.

Fuck, but how incredible that madness would be.

Badge says something to Tony, pulling me from my thoughts and reminding me that I need to deal with the issue at hand before anything else.

I dig around in my pocket and pull out my pack of smokes. That shitty little bump I tested didn't come close to giving me the calm needed to deal with this dumbass. I swap the pack for my Zippo, lighting up.

"You see, Tony," I start, flicking my Zippo open and closed a few times before stuffing it back into my pocket. "I have a hard time gettin' how this could be a misunderstandin', considerin' this is the same amount of product I've bought from you the first and third Tuesday of every month for the last year."

And the year before that.

"Has it been that long?" He chuckles, a squeaky sound, his round belly jiggling with his movements.

Unable to control myself any longer, my hand snaps out, grabbing his head and slamming it down on the table. I hear the crunch of bone mixed with the sound of his scream, and when I allow him back up, all I see is crimson pouring from his nose.

Good.

My blood pulses in triumph, eyes closing for a split

second in relief as the irritation subsides. I like causing pain, I like doling out punishment, and I like feeling in control.

"I think you broke my nose!" Tony whines, hands cupping his busted face, and my demon sighs in sick satisfaction at the sight.

"You're gonna have a lot more than that broken if you don't tell us where the fuck Whaley's product is," Badge interjects, chuckling when Tony only cries out again. "Oh, come on. Stop actin' like a bitch. He barely did anythin' to you."

"There was a little mix-up," Tony tries to reason, only fueling the fire that I had begun to quelch. "It ain't a big deal."

"Not a big deal?" I growl, flipping the table and advancing on him as he steps back, not having far to go before his back meets the wall. "It's my business, my time, my money, and you're tellin' me that ain't a big deal?" I grab his chin roughly, forcing him to look at me. "Tony," I whisper, my voice venomous, "All I think you're doin' is wastin' my fuckin' time."

"I'm not, I swear. It's not like that," he pleads, but again, still doesn't explain where my stuff is. I should already be back on my bike, product tucked into the back of Badge's truck as we make our way home, but instead, I'm dealing with this asswipe, keeping me from getting back to Bun—

I jab my fist into Tony's stomach to stop my running thoughts and he slides to the ground with a groan, clutching himself. He's taking the brunt of my rage today, but he's not undeserving. I bend down, pulling his head back by his hair, and he wails, hands coming up to grab my wrist, but I smack his hold off with my free hand.

Brave man.

He looks fucked-up, his face crusted with dried blood, already bruising, and I love it. I want to do more but I refrain, reminding myself it won't be good for business if I kill the bastard, no matter how badly I want to right now.

"You have until the end of the week to get me what I'm owed, or else you'll have to deal with me." Tony gulps and nods his head fast, his face looking worse somehow than moments ago. "Go," I bark at him, slapping his face one more time for good measure, hoping it drives my point home.

Tony scrams, running away and stumbling as he does. Badge chuckles as he watches him go, then comes up to me with a rag. "Here."

I take it from him, wiping Tony's drying blood from my knuckles. "Think he'll actually follow through and get me my shit?"

"Dunno." Badge shrugs. "I can have Fox call his boss and figure out what's up."

I spin to Fox, motioning to where Tony just left. "Yeah, also let him know how fucked my delivery was. Tell him he should fix his runner before I do it for him."

"Will do." Fox is a good guy and is great at what he does. We've missed him these last few months while he's been away.

When the head of the Aces over in Vegas asked for some help with a problem, I knew Fox was the man for the job. He's smart, aware of his surroundings, and careful with what he says and does. If there's somebody more calculating and thoughtful than me, it's him. The leader, Hinge, told me he did a great job and was sad to see him go, but it was time for Fox to come home.

"If he doesn't get us our shit, make sure you take a little memento with you," I tell him, knowing that Fox has more bloodlust than he lets on.

He nods, smiling at the idea. "Anything you say, boss."

"For fuck's sake," Badge grits out, and we turn to see him staring at his phone while pinching the bridge of his nose.

"What's up, Pops?" Fox asks, going to peep over Badge's

shoulder. When he sees what Badge is looking at, he chuckles dryly. "Should have known it'd be Bunky…"

My hackles rise, but I do my best to keep my tone level. "What'd he do now?"

"Ran off a customer," Badge explains, quickly typing a reply. "Told the guy he'd castrate him for suggesting we overcharge for our tire rotations."

My lip lifts despite myself. "Did he pull out his pocketknife?" I can practically see the whole thing unfold as if I was right there.

"Dunno. Just said he was clockin' out from the shop to work on his bike instead." He shoves his phone away, one shoulder lifting. "I dunno what to do with that kid sometimes."

"Not a kid," I snap before I can think better of it. Badge and Fox shoot me questioning looks and I look down briefly, grabbing out another smoke and lighting up—having lost my other one during that bullshit with Tony. "I just mean, you know he's talkin' about doin' runs and helpin' out more."

"Right," Badge says, giving me a confused smile. "Well, he's still young at heart. He's goin' to prom, you know?"

I know. I overheard him talking to Raid and Silas about it the other day. It's not that I don't want him to go off and have fun, but I feel like it's a stark reminder of the reasons we can't be together. He's young and he should be able to enjoy things like prom and the end of high school without having to be weighed down with my shit. Shit he hasn't experienced yet, but that he will if we were to get together.

We've created a mess. Something that's so inescapable where it feels like we won't be able to extract ourselves from the twisted web.

So, let this be it. Let me gather every ounce of self-control I possess. Let this be the moment where it's the end of us.

Permanently.

EIGHT

Bunky

I can't believe Whaley and his extremely irritating self-control. Now that we've graduated and it's summer, I have nothing to do but stew think about why the fuck he's not talking to me. I see Whaley everywhere, but he comes nowhere near me. Even when I'm working at the shop, he'll only pass information through Silas or Raid. Silas is leaving soon with Blaine to Connecticut, so at least one of Whaley's avenues of avoidance will be cut off.

Now about Raid…

See? Plotting about a way to get my best friend out of the picture means I've totally lost it, but can you blame me?

I. Want. Whaley.

I want to gouge my eyes out with the level of frustration this is causing. It's driving me even more batshit than I already am. It's like I'm a jumble of frantic energy, bouncing off the walls. I've had shit sleep in the last month, the nightmares constantly waking me up. If Whaley wasn't so strict about being high as fuck while working, I'd already be teetering on reality. Oh, there's a thought, maybe if I do get high, it'll grab Whaley's attention.

God, I need an escape right now, but I can't put my finger on why. Well, besides the obvious.

"*Raid*," I whine, waving my hands in front of the computer screen. "Let's go do somethin'."

He slaps my hands away and shoots me a glare. "We're in the middle of work. We can't bail. Gotta get this done for Whaley."

Ugh, Whaley. Always about fucking Whaley.

I shift on the balls of my feet as thoughts race through my head, destructive and wrathful. The tires hanging on the hooks by the back look tempting, and I want to slash them. I could pour out all the oil containers and roll around in the mess, just bask in the chaos. Oh, that'd be fun!

No. Bad Bunky.

"Pay attention to me," I snap, rounding the counter and hopping on the counter in front of him. I know I'm acting out of my mind, but Raid should be used to my sporadic mood swings by now. After a second, I tip my head to the side. "How's Landon?"

His eyes widen briefly before his lip curls in irritation. "How am I supposed to know?"

"I heard he broke up with Maybelline," I gossip, planting my chin in my propped hands as I try to gauge his reaction. "That's good, right?"

"I wouldn't know anythin' about that," he says quickly, trying to look around my body at the computer, but then he stops and wrinkles his nose, looking at me again. "How do *you* even know about that?"

"She wouldn't stop goin' on about it in the diner the other night," I tell him. "So? I want the details."

He rolls his eyes and lets out an unamused snort. "You don't care about their relationship, Bunk. You're just bored."

I let out a petulant huff. "Is that not a good enough excuse?"

"Go away," he shoos me away. "You got an oil change to do."

"I. Need. Attention." I throw my head back and release a screech, balling my fists at my sides and pounding on the counter with each word.

"Oh my fuckin' God," he mutters, flipping me off. "Find it somewhere else. What is wrong with you? You're actin' more batshit than usual."

I growl as I jump off the counter and swipe everything off in the process. It's an automatic reaction. I know Raid doesn't mean anything by it, but when it's the wrong place and the wrong time, I flip.

"Fuck you!" I fire back, waving my hands in the air. "I'm batshit then?"

"Yeah." His jaw clenches in a tight line, but he doesn't rise to my temper.

What is wrong with everybody? Why are they all so perfect? Why do they never break?

"How about *this* for batshit?"

I take out my pocketknife, walk over to a car he's been detailing for Whaley, and drag my knife through the side, leaving behind a very noticeable scratch.

"Bunk!" he shouts, shooting up out of his seat. "Why the hell did you do that? It's gonna take me ages to fix!"

"What can I say? I'm just a fuckin' lunatic!" I throw back, pocketing my knife and trying not to feel guilty as he rushes around the counter to look at the damage I've caused.

That's when Silas walks in, hand in hand with Blaine, both of them looking thoroughly confused as their gazes bounce back and forth between us.

"What the fuck?" Silas asks, letting go of Blaine's hand. "What's goin' on?"

"Life fuckin' *sucks*!" I yell, digging my hands into my hair as I stomp my feet.

Then I march my ass outside, ignoring the guys as they try to grab my attention. Damn it, I want to get stabby, and fucking with that car was not enough. I know I'm acting like a child, but Jesus Christ, I can't help it. I'm strumming on the edge, fighting against myself, so entirely unhinged.

I need something to get this excess energy out of my system. If I didn't have to work I'd leave right this fucking minute to find some shit to get into. I need to before I lose it completely.

I take a deep breath, reach for a cigarette, and try to collect myself.

Sugar cookies. Donna's lemonade. Chai tea lattes.
Whaley's dick.

It's working, for the most part, and I'm about to head back into the shop when my phone dings. I take it out and check it, nearly crushing my cigarette when I do.

CODE RED

Oh shit. Maybe that's why I'm in such a terrible mood. I drill the back of my head against the side of the shop. I have this notification in my calendar, and it always sends me spiraling when I see it. I swear, I must really love the pain because there's no other reason I would need a constant reminder of this.

Tomorrow is the day Whaley's leaving for his R&R weekend.

It's the weekend that Whaley holds sacred where he disappears for forty-eight hours and buries himself in whatever paid whore he can find. He resorts to paying for sex to get his rocks off. I only know this because Badge got a little too drunk one night and told me all about it. Jesus, I wanted to break every single thing in our trailer when I heard that. Since then, I've religiously kept track of every weekend, committing them to memory, telling myself I'd make Whaley pay for every single hour he let someone who wasn't me touch him.

It's beyond irritating that he's fighting us. He'd get a free pass to do whatever the fuck he wants with my body and my soul. He could kill me and tear my heart out and I'd thank him for it. Want to cut me? I'll give him the knife. Want to bruise me? I'll happily wear the marks. Want me to suffer? I'm no stranger to that.

I go back into the shop in an angry huff, ignoring the annoyed glare Raid shoots me, the amused smirk on Silas' lips, and Blaine's concerned expression. If they knew about my feelings for Whaley, they'd be a total buzzkill. I don't need their judgment. That's why I haven't said anything, but if they did know, they'd understand why I'm so worked up. The love of my fucking life is going to go off this weekend to bang some random slut.

It should be me!

"Done?" Raid asks, motioning to the car I fucked with. "Are you gonna help me now?"

Fuck, I feel like shit. More so now than before. Why can't I just be normal?

I scratch the back of my neck as I walk up to him. "Yeah, sorry, Raid."

He holds that pissed off expression for only a second before it morphs into a sympathetic one. "Come on. Let's get this done."

We work quietly, ignoring when Silas and Blaine basically start fucking on the counter, but the day passes by slowly. I rack my brain the entire time to figure out what I can do to keep Whaley here this weekend. I'm not putting up with this anymore. I'm putting my foot down. I'm panting at the mouth like a dog in heat. I'll fucking pee on him if I have to.

Ooo, kinky.

Maybe I can stab someone? Yeah, that would make Whaley stay. He'd be like 'Oh shit' and I'd be all 'Oh yeah' and then we'd fuck in some blood and cuddle after. Would Whaley cuddle? He doesn't seem like the type, but I'd make him. Wrap him up in a koala bear hold so he could never escape me. Or I could show up at his trailer naked as the day I was born, shaking my ass in the air until he took mercy and pounded the brat out of me. That wouldn't work either though. He wouldn't buy it no matter how badly I wish he would.

I'm still thinking through the possibilities when Raid's voice cuts through my nefarious plotting.

"You good, Bunk?" He powers down the computer, throwing me a curious glance.

I'm done with my tantrum, but I don't tell him that. Instead, I huff and raise a shoulder as I dramatically palm my heart. "I dunno. You finally ready to tell me what's goin' on with you and Landon?"

He reacts as I expect him to, annoyed beyond belief, but he eventually, after the longest minute ever, laughs it off. "I swear, Bunk. Don't know what the fuck happens in that head of yours."

He wouldn't want to know. I barely want to and it's *my* own head. "Hey, I'm sorry again about…"

He holds a hand up to stop me, sympathy coating his features once more. "It's alright. You don't have to explain it to me. I know it's just…"

He can't finish his sentence because he doesn't actually know. Nobody but Whaley, Badge, and the other members that were there the night my dad beat my mama to death know about what happened. Even after all these years of friendship, I haven't told him or Silas. I don't want to burden them with such grotesque and violent realities.

He does know that there's *something* wrong with me though. Everybody does. How could they not? You don't need to know all the details to see it written all over me.

Defective. Dangerous. Destructive.

All the D's, just not my favorite one.

"Wanna go for a drink?" he asks after a minute, shrugging on his jacket. "Blaine and Silas already left to go to the bar. Gotta sell some shit tonight. You in?"

I shake my head. No, I have to keep Whaley here somehow, and I need time to think. I need a clear head, well, *clearish* to get that shit done.

"Go ahead without me." I grab some scattered parts to put away. "I'll meet up with you later."

He looks like he wants to argue but doesn't, only gives me one last look before leaving. I linger, trying not to act too suspicious as the older members start filtering out. Once it's just me, I pace around for a bit, fisting my hair.

He's mine.

Whaley's mine.

My man. My cock. My soulmate. Nobody else's.

I scream at the top of my lungs, burning my throat as I flip over the metal table in the back, kicking at it once it slams to the ground. I'm too unhinged, too wild, too unmanageable. I don't have any drugs on me to make me chill out. It's all at my trailer, and I refuse to leave before I figure this out.

Stop!

Please, don't!

That sets me off. That young, airy voice. That memory.

Crack.

Squish.

Pop.

I pound my fists against the wall and the pain tethers me but only a little bit. I need something else—crave something else. I don't quite know what that is, but I know that this isn't enough.

Focus on Whaley. Focus on his whores. Focus on what I'm going to do to keep him here.

I look around, trying to see if the answer will magically dawn on me, and it does.

His bike.

Whaley's precious Harley Davidson Fat Boy. It's his pride and joy. He doesn't let *anyone* touch it, and he keeps it locked up in the shop instead of the trailer park because he's that paranoid. It's what he takes every weekend, even though he has a perfectly good truck.

The devious thought blooms, grows, twines like vines in my brain and suffocates me.

I'll toy with his bike.

I do a little villainous cackle as I make my way to it. It's locked behind a special garage door that only he has the pass-code to. Well, him and me. I totally stalked him one day to get it, and I'm glad I did because the perfect opportunity has presented itself.

If this doesn't show how serious about him I am, then I don't know what will.

I get through the door and kneel beside his bike. I loosen this, tighten that, and remove one or two things. It's not like it's going to kill him or anything, but I do want to make it inconvenient enough that he decides he needs to fix it instead of going on his R&R. I even hide the parts and scatter them across the garage, running to each corner and clapping mani-cally when I find the right spot.

I'm about to see if I should take out something else when a booming voice stops me. "What the *fuck* do you think you're doin'?"

I freeze.

Oh, shit.

I turn to Whaley very slowly, surprised at being caught. I'm not scared, not really, but I am now second-guessing my decision-making process when I see the red-hot fury on his face. The logical, sane part of me tells me I should run and hide. I unleashed his rage and messing with Whaley is never smart.

Good thing I'm not always the tightest whip in the kink-shed.

The other side of me, the wild beast is ready. I can feel myself hardening at his anger. He's so fucking edible, I swear. I could slather him in chocolate and have a feast. I'm momentarily caught off guard by the fact that he's wearing nothing more than a white tank and a pair of jeans, showcasing all his beautiful tattoos and those thick thighs I want to wrap my legs around while he plows into me.

"I can explain," I say softly, but the need to poke at him is too strong. "I've been very *very* bad."

"Bunky…" he growls, stalking toward me, and even though he looks murderous, I preen at finally having his attention. "You don't fuck with a man's bike."

I gasp when he grips the back of my head, then I shamelessly moan when he digs his hand into my hair, hard. Fuck, yes. My hips rock in the air, seeking some sort of friction. "Punish me then."

Do your absolute worst.

NINE

Whaley

I stare at the small bag that's sitting on my bed, trying to force myself to pack it with what I'll need for the next two days for my R&R weekend, but I can't make my feet move to go collect my shit.

It's been a month since everything went down with Bunky. More accurately, since I lost my damn mind and dove off the deep end and made all kinds of fucked-up decisions that changed everything.

Which is one of the main reasons I *need* to go and have my fun. Badge is all set to oversee things while I'm away, I've already booked my room, and I've been trying to convince myself all day that it's going to be fine. That fucking someone else will put an end to my obsession and I can move on. I could let *him* move on.

Convincing myself hasn't worked though. If anything, it's only caused my focus to shift to Bunky more, something I didn't know was even possible considering he's always on my mind. I've worked hard to put some distance between us, but he still comes on to me when he gets the chance. He's always flirting and randomly popping up around me to be seen. I've somehow remained impassive, keeping our relationship only work-related and not letting myself cross that line like I did the night we fucked.

He makes me stupid, reckless, and out of control. He makes me feel dangerous. Being with him *is* dangerous.

Yet I still want him. Before, I was able to keep him at bay, but now that I've had him, been inside him, and know what he sounds like when he comes, it's been impossible. I've come so close to snapping and dragging his teasing ass somewhere to spank, but I've resisted. Choosing to angrily jack off instead, as if to prove to myself that I don't need him.

That's been a lie. I do need him. I need him so damn bad, but I can't have him, and that's more torturous than the demon I fight on the daily. That's saying something because that fucker's constantly leaving me in agony.

My phone dings on my nightstand and I snag it, realizing it's my alarm for the shop. Clicking open my app, I scroll through the feed, trying to figure out where the 'suspicious activity' is when I come to a dead stop. I squint, zooming in to take in the figure leaning over my bike.

It takes my brain a minute to catch on, but when I do, all bets are off.

Blinding fury mixed with fiery irritation ignites within me, zipping through every nerve in my body, threatening to completely consume and take over. I'm sure that I'm dreaming—stuck in some nightmare of a fantasy world—because no way in hell am I watching Bunky tear apart my bike through the security camera.

My goddamn baby.

I'm at my truck before I can think it over. My focus is solely on stopping the person who clearly has a death wish. I drive like a crazed man to my shop, where I'm positive I'm about to commit murder. The urge to wrap my fingers around

Bunky's throat and literally strangle him are warring with the parts of me that stay lucid and in control.

I'm surprised I make it in one piece considering how fast I was driving. Let's just say I'm not exactly being rational right now, spiraling with every ticking second that passes.

My tires screech when I pull in, and I throw my truck in park while simultaneously opening the door and hopping out. I don't even bother shutting it behind me, the thoughts consuming as I try to figure out why the hell Bunky would be doing this. Pushing past the front door is easy enough since the jackass inside didn't lock it. What the fuck was he thinking? He's going to get my place robbed, which only further adds to the inferno raging inside me.

I storm to the back, and I'm sure I should take a breather, but I don't. It's too fucking late for the calm Whaley. The one who lets Bunky get away with everything, the one who is reasonable, the one who is filled with guilt and a level of understanding.

He's long gone and I have no idea who I am now, which is a scary thought.

When I reach the back, I halt, taking in Bunky where he leans over my baby. Yeah, I'm past fury. I'm lost to the rage, lost to the world as my vision dims and my peripheral fades, and all I see is him.

"What the fuck do you think you're doin'?"

The words leave me in a roar, so loud it reverberates off all the concrete walls and sounds like a demon awakening.

Pretty accurate actually.

Bunky spins around, eyes wide, but I can still see the stubbornness lingering there.

The challenge.

Oh, you don't want to do this, Bunky. I'm not the guy you're used to right now. There's no logic looming over me. I'm past that point, and all I want is to taste blood.

Bunky's blood.

"I can explain," he whispers, and I watch as his tongue dips out to lick his bottom lip before he says, "I've been *very* bad."

You have got to be kidding.

"Bunky…" His name flies past my lips like venom, and the next thing I know I'm halfway across the shop, stalking toward him, preparing to literally wring his neck. "You don't fuck with a man's bike."

That's the number one rule. The most sacred of them all.

I grab his hair, fisting it, jerking his head back so harshly I can practically feel the dyed strands breaking off into my hand. He winces, but instead of crying out in pain, the little shit moans before rocking his hips into me like some sex fiend.

"Punish me then," he begs.

I clench my teeth, gripping his hair harder, wanting him to see how serious I am, but it doesn't have the desired response. He just moans again, his eyes fluttering closed as he relaxes in my hold like he's being taken to his very own nirvana.

I have him pinned against the wall, holding him up by his hair and my hips, and he's letting me.

"You need to start speakin'," I bite out through my teeth. "I want to know what you were doin'."

His eyes flick open, and I don't see the usual vibrant green depths staring back at me. No, all I see is deep, shadowy pupils, blown so wide he looks like he's high, lust-drunk even. His chest is heaving as ragged pants leave his lips. He's flushed, a deep pink hue to his cheeks, making him appear sun-kissed.

"Whaley." The breathy whisper causes goose bumps to break across my skin. It's some fucked-up type of call, like his demon is reaching through Bunky's body to try and talk to mine.

"Tell me now!" I roar, letting go of his hair to fist his shirt, jerking his body upright and giving him a rough shake. "I want to know what the hell you were thinkin'."

His drunk look fades at my assault, hands coming up to grip my forearms so hard I can feel the bite of his nails as he holds onto me.

"Whaley..." He says my name again but this time it's different, more like his old self. His teasing undertone has me ready to burn the whole shop down with both of us inside.

"This is not the time for your games. Do you realize how serious this is?" I nod my head to the side, motioning toward my Harley. "This crosses the line."

"You care about your bike more than me?" he pouts, and I'm really considering calling a mental hospital to come cart his ass away.

He isn't taking me seriously, and I'm about to go apeshit.

"Are you listenin' to me at all? Is somethin' not clickin?" I unball one of my fists, drilling a finger into his temple, needing to get my point across. "You fucked up! What would've happened had I driven away? Broke down in the middle of nowhere? What if I had gotten in an accident? I could have fuckin' died!"

He lets out a little noise, that stubborn lip of his wobbling as my words hit him. "No—"

"Is that what you want? You mad at me for not comin' back to fuck you?"

"Whaley—"

"That's it, huh?" I cut him off, fisting his shirt again and slamming him into the wall, hoping to knock some sense into him. "You wanna hurt me?"

He's shaking his head and looking at me with wide, sad eyes. "No, I would never—"

"Don't you fuckin' lie," I growl, spit flying past my lips and covering his own mouth. I'm close, so fucking close to him that I can make out every dotted freckle that covers his nose and the small scar through his eyebrow from where he had his piercing ripped out years back.

"I'm not lyin'," he bites out, hands tightening around my wrists as his eyes ping back and forth between mine. "Whaley, I'd never do that to you. I'd never—"

"Then what else is it? You actin' out?" I practically snarl.

"No, I'm—"

I don't let him speak because I'm too goddamn angry. I don't think there's anything he can say to make me stop. I'm too far gone, lost in the slithering wrath that's coiled itself around me and suffocating my brain with every spiraling thought.

"I want to fuckin' hurt you!"

His glazed eyes still have that worry lingering but it's fading, replaced with raw desire. "Please."

That single word is what gets me.

He wants me to hurt him? Gladly.

I'll destroy him.

With my nostrils flaring and my blood roaring, I spin us around and bend him roughly over the back of my bike. I reach over and tear at his fly, cursing when I'm met with an array of zippers and buttons. Fucking complicated-ass jeans.

I don't have time for this.

His eyes widen as he looks over his shoulder, eyes flickering with aroused fear as I pull out my knife. "Whaley..."

"Shut the hell up," I growl as I cut his pants straight down the seam of his ass. I toss the knife behind me so I can pull apart his torn jeans, exposing those perfect round globes as I fish out my cock.

Bunky squirms, rubbing himself against my crotch as he reaches into his pocket, bringing out a small packet. He waves it at me with an impish smirk. Of course. Should have known the little shit would be carrying lube around. It's like he was expecting this, maybe not now, but he wanted to be prepared for the moment I cracked.

And I'm way beyond that now.

"You like torturin' me," I snarl, ripping the packet from his grip and tearing it open with my teeth. I squeeze the contents directly onto his hole, smearing it with my fingers. "Little fuckin' shit. You think you can get whatever the fuck you want."

"You're here, ain't you?" He chuckles, and in a move that's far too sexy to describe, he lifts one leg and props his knee on the bike seat before reaching back to pull his cheeks apart. "Punish me, Whaley. Do it."

"I'm gonna do more than punish you," I hiss, shoving my fingers inside him without care. I don't have the patience for proper prep, and knowing the kinky little fucker, he doesn't either. It's a courtesy that he doesn't fucking deserve right now. So I only stretch him out as much as my two fingers allow, scissoring them enough that he won't tear. "Gonna fucking obliterate you."

"*Yes*," he moans, throwing his head back when I unintentionally graze his prostate. "Oh my fuck. Yes."

Enough of that.

I pull out my fingers and line my cock up with his hole. I don't press gently, don't let him adjust—I'm too consumed with irritation and anger for that—I just plunge in all at once, rocking my bike and Bunky forward with my thrust.

I start with a brutal pace, fucking him roughly and thoroughly, mesmerized by the way my cock stretches him so fucking good. Right now, despite logic and reasoning, I feel like an idiot for thinking this would never happen again.

Not when it's this good. Not when it's this right.

I anchor myself to him by his shoulders, tucking my arms under his armpits and draping myself over him. I growl into his neck, grazing my teeth against his sensitive pulse before biting hard, causing him to cry out in a beautiful mix of pain and pleasure.

He wanted this. He wants me to hurt him, to own him.

So that's exactly what I do.

"You satisfied?" I seethe, reaching a hand around to wrap around his throat and squeeze. "You were bein' a brat. You wanted my attention. Well, you fuckin' got it. How does it feel?"

"Feels incredible," he whines, gripping the bike for dear life. "Should fuck with your bike more often."

I slap his ass, rough tap to get my point across. "You fuck with my bike again, you're goin' over my knee until your ass is blistered and raw."

"You think that's a deterrent?" He chuckles, the sound tapering off into a long groan.

Of course it's not. All those devious thoughts I have, he also shares. I marvel at the fact we really are a perfect match, but anguish builds when I remember the reason that this can't happen again.

That doesn't mean I can't enjoy it while it lasts.

I stand up straight, pressing him down by his lower back as I dominate his ass, unforgiving and cruel, wanting him to feel me for days. My mouth works before my mind can tell it to shut the fuck up, spilling all the secrets I should keep to myself. "You're so perfect, Bunk. Takin' my cock like a champ. God, your ass was made for me, wasn't it?"

"All for you," he agrees, words coming out slurred. "It's your hole, Whaley. It belongs to you. No one else."

That's right. Only mine.

"Wanna fill you with my cum," I tell him, already feeling the signs that I'm close. "Gonna mark that ass. Should fuckin' bite it."

"P–Please… Whaley… Yes! I can't… I'm gonna—"

He tightens and clenches around me, and when I realize he came untouched, that does it. With a roar so loud and one brutal slap to his ass, I fill him. There's so much cum that it drips out of his abused hole, soiling his already ruined jeans.

"Jesus Christ," he mutters, groaning as he tries to stand,

but ultimately, he gives up and flops forward onto the bike. "You fucked me so good. Gimme five minutes and we'll go again."

I shake my head even though he can't see. We're not doing this shit again. I messed up once by doing this after the bonfire and now I've done it again by letting my anger get the best of me.

I can't keep letting this happen. I'm trapped in this vicious circle of want and denial and overwhelming need. I let go and indulge my baser instincts, only for them to bite me in the ass later.

"You need to go home, Bunk," I mumble, reaching into the cabinet beside us for a spare pair of sweats. I toss them at him, flinching when I see the confused look on his face. "But—"

"No," I say, firmly but not filled with rage. I'm resigned because if this keeps happening, I don't know how much longer I can hold out.

Bunky looks at me, but I don't wait to see what he's going to say. Anymore from him, and I'll give in completely.

Fight it. Be strong. He's not what you need.

But I have a feeling he's exactly that, and the thought alone is enough for a restless sleep.

TEN

Bunky

I'm trapped in a hell of my own making.

He fucked me, then he left me. He wanted me, then he dismissed me. He's obsessed with me, then he forgot me.

These thoughts of mine have been going on since the last time Whaley and I last had sex. Bright side, he didn't go on his R&R trip after all, but I think I messed up by screwing with his bike. Once again, I'm getting nothing from him, and I'm pretty sure it's my own damn fault. What's that saying? You can bring a horse to water, but you can't make it drink? Well, I pried its fucking jaw open and poured vodka down its throat.

I keep telling myself this is what I want. Normally, I want it all and I want it *now*, but I can play the long game. I can wait no matter how much I hate it, because Whaley is worth it. Every break in his resolve gets me closer. I've just got to keep playing the game, keep torturing him, keep ruining him.

And then he'll be all mine.

I put out my cigarette as I approach the shop. Raid's gone and fucked off somewhere, so I had to cover his sales this morning. I had told him to get Silas to do it, but apparently, he's taking Blaine camping or some shit. Seriously, he's dick-whipped. Silas doesn't camp.

I suggested sending Fox, even asked him myself, but he told me with all the love in the world that I could fuck off. So that left me.

Today wasn't too bad though. I managed to make two hundred bucks, so it's a job well done in my book. Now I have to head back to the shop for my afternoon shift. I know we're slammed with work, and I'm already dreading the amount of effort I'm going to have to put into it. I don't hate hard work, I'd just rather not do it if I had the choice.

I walk in through the open garage door, running a hand through my sweaty hair, and smile when I see Whaley. God, he always makes my heart throw up glitter. He's so fucking edible, wearing a white tank top and dark jeans that make his legs look like tree trunks. All his beautiful tattoos are on display, and I bite my lip at the idea of getting another tattoo that matches his. That thick, dark hair he keeps in that man bun... Jesus Christ, I want to tug on it.

I put on my best hip sway as I approach him, subtly checking my breath to make sure the fast food I ate didn't linger, but I stop in my tracks when he turns to a customer. I frown, about to turn around and come back later to bug him, but when that bitch puts her hand on his arm and Whaley looks down at it and smiles...

I fucking lose it.

"What the hell!" I screech, causing both of them to whip their heads in my direction. I don't even care that some of the older members are looking at me like I'm insane. I'm blood-thirsty now and ready to fucking slit that woman's throat. "Are you kiddin' me?!"

Whaley springs into action, ignoring the woman and her perplexed look as he rounds the counter. I'm already prepared to pounce at her, hand reaching for my pocketknife, but Whaley binds me with his arms and pulls me away.

"Let me go!" I shout, kicking and screaming as he drags me into his office. "Let me at her."

"Bunky, you need to calm down," he demands, letting me go so abruptly that I stumble into his desk.

"I can't believe you," I spit out, my hands ball into fists at my sides, torn between fury and pain. "How could you?"

He cocks his head in confusion. "What are you goin' on about?"

"You fucked me, but now you're gonna fuck her?" I argue, angry tears springing in my eyes.

He looks at me with astonishment. "How the hell did you get to that conclusion? I ain't gonna fuck her and you can't act like this at work."

"I'll act however I want," I yell, and in my moment of blind fury, I rampage. I start throwing his shit everywhere. I'm screaming the entire time, unintelligible words that I'm sure he doesn't understand either.

Whaley is *mine*.

"Bunk!" Whaley's voice booms and he grabs me before I can toss his desk chair. "Stop it!"

"No," I snap back, taking a fistful of his shirt in my grip. "I'm gonna kill her!"

He narrows his eyes, holding on to my flailing form. "You ain't gonna do shit. You're actin' like…"

"Like *what*?"

"Like a fuckin' psycho!"

I can't help but reel back as if he'd slapped me. The words wash over me like a crushing wave. Whaley's never called me that before. In fact, he's scolded anyone who has. I always figured that to him, it was the worst insult anyone could give me. He's been so careful to make it known that there's nothing wrong with me, so I never expected him to say that shit.

Something that looks a lot like regret flickers across his face. "Shit, Bunk, I didn't—"

"Say it again." When he stays silent, I push his chest. "Again!"

"No." He shakes his head, eyes full of guilt and remorse, and normally that'd make me fold, but not now. Not when he just broke something inside me. "I got caught up—"

"But I *am* a psycho," I argue, feeling blistering tears in my eyes as I hit him once more. "Tell me again. Say it like you fucking mean it!"

He keeps quiet, and I keep hitting him, the pain of his words consuming me. Maybe I'm just a glutton for punishment, needing to hear those words from the person who means the most to me. It's like everything I knew shatters, my perception of Whaley as someone who'd never hurt me like that is dissolving before my eyes.

"Say somethin'," I shout, thrashing in his arms as he tries to hold me in place.

He swallows thickly, fingers twitching as he reaches for my wrists and wraps his hands around them. He presses his forehead against mine, and I can feel the deep, heavy puffs of breath he lets out against my lips. I'm still fighting against him, but his hold is too tight. "You're— Fuck, Bunk. You're my little psycho."

I freeze, blinking at him as my brain resets.

My little psycho.

People can say what they want to about me, and Hell, they *do*, but the only opinion that matters is Whaley's. Others are scared, wary, nervous around me, but not this man. Others want to shove me aside, fit me in a box of their molding, explain away my behavior, but not him. He sees me exactly as I am and… *likes* what he sees?

My little psycho.

My anger and resentment fades, my tears slow, and my body slackens. His words wash over me, and it feels like there's a shift in the air. I don't know what to do about it, I don't know the "proper" way to react, so I do what comes naturally and drop to my knees. My head's a muddled mess, but I want to reward him. My shaking fingers go to the button of his jeans but before I have a chance to tear them open Whaley stops me.

"What are you doin'?"

"Wanna please you," I mumble, batting his hand away, trying once more to no avail. My eyes shoot to his, rejection settling in my gut like a brick. "You don't want me?"

"Not like this." His fingers graze my cheek, featherlight and strangely gentle. "You're cryin'."

I inhale sharply through my nose, drawing the tears back as I shrug a shoulder and wipe at my eyes. "It's nothin'."

"Bunky..." He sighs, leaning forward to help me stand, despite my protests. "I made you cry, and I shouldn't have."

My lips kick into an easy smile, and I reach up to rub down his chest. "You like my tears."

I'm aiming for our usual banter, wanting the emotions of the last few moments to disappear and no longer be, but I can tell by his expression that he isn't having it.

His hand splays over mine, lacing our fingers together, and I revel in the warmth radiating from his palm. "I don't want your tears like *that*, Bunk. I don't ever want to hurt you in that way."

His tone is soft, softer than I've ever heard and I hate the regret I see lingering in his gaze. It's not needed. I don't want him to feel bad. It was a mistake. I know that.

I know he didn't mean it.

"Whaley—"

"No." He shakes his head, sadness plaguing his face. "I fucked up. I've been fuckin' up."

I already know what's coming before it does. His eyes close and his hold on me tightens almost to the point of pain before he drops my hand.

Here we go again.

"We're never goin' to happen are we? You're really never goin' to give in." My voice cracks a bit on the last word, as I'm rushed with a sense of finality. I don't know why but this feels different than any time before. The push and pull—all the games…

This truly feels like the end.

But why? Because I cried? Because he hurt me?

"Can you tell me why?" I ask quietly, dropping my gaze to the floor, taking a step back. "I think I deserve to know why."

He's silent for a brief moment before I feel the tips of his fingers brush my chin. "Look at me, little psycho." I obey. "You already know."

I do, and ultimately regret it when I take in his seriousness once more.

"You know I ain't perfect—"

"You're perfect to me," I cut him off, needing him to know how true that is. I don't care about the past, whatever he's hiding, I just want him.

I *need* him.

`"Bunk…" he continues on as if I hadn't spoke. "If I let myself fall into *us*, everything that ain't you would cease to matter."

My heart flutters, not understanding the issue. That sounds like everything I've ever wanted. "And that's a problem because?"

"I can't give myself to you and still be whole," he says clearly, his thumb brushing against my pierced nose. "If we start this shit, we would be a nightmare. Obsessive, posses-sive, psychotic—"

"But that sounds fuckin' awesome to me," I argue, still not seeing the issue. "Wanna lose myself in you."

"That's exactly it. I can't be losin' myself when I've got

people to take care of. Got a gang to lead. Got to keep my head straight. You… Bunk…"

"Yeah?" I question, and press my nose against his. "What about me, Whaley?"

"We're both fucked-up. I can't think when I'm around you. I do the wrong stuff, say the wrong things… I'd hurt you more than I just did. I'd hurt everyone. Fuck, I wouldn't be able to live with myself if I did that to you again."

I want to argue, but I can't because I know what he's saying is true. While it sounds wonderful to me, objectively I know it's not. We're not going to have the fairy-tale ending like Blaine and Silas. So, I just kiss him. I bring our lips together and he swallows my small whimper. His tongue plays with mine, lapping and trying to inhale my essence. It's like he's trying to suck the little bit of soul I have left from me, wanting to tuck it into his pocket for safekeeping, leaving me a hollow mess.

He's kissing me like it's the last time.

"We good?" he asks me after we both pull away. "You get me?"

I nod. "I get you."

I'm not willing to give up on him—on us—but at the same time…

Jesus, I don't know what to do. I know what I want, I know what I need, but I also know what he needs too.

Maybe the best way to love him is to not have him at all.

Maybe that fate worse than death is my lot in life

ELEVEN

Bunky

"You alright, Bunky?"

"I'm fine. Just sunbathin'." I sigh, stretching my arms over my head. I just wanted a few minutes to myself to clear my head, but I guess that's not going to happen.

Silas lets out an amused grunt. "Exactly. It's cloudy as fuck."

I open my eyes and flip up my sunglasses, coming face-to-face with Silas, Blaine, Raid, and Landon. They're all staring down at me with a creepy intensity that makes my skin crawl.

I sit up, the urge to flee growing the longer they stare. "What's up?"

"What's up?" Silas mimics, shaking his head as he pinches the bridge of his nose. "Seriously?"

"Wasn't a difficult question," I grit out, rolling my eyes. "What do you want?"

"We're worried about you, Bunky," Blaine says, fiddling with his fingers as he frowns. "You're acting a bit strange—"

"—er than usual," Raid finishes as he pulls a cigarette out of his pocket. "Get off the ground, Bunk."

I groan, the urge to leave still in my head but I refuse to abandon my little cocoon. They have no idea how much time it took to build my pillow fortress in front of my trailer.

"What's he doin' here?" I ask, jutting my chin at Landon. "If this is some sort of intervention, I don't care what he has to say."

Raid narrows his gaze, practically fuming at my disregard for... well, whatever the fuck they are. "He's with me," he spits the words out like venom, and I fight the urge to roll my eyes again. "We got plans after this."

"So this *is* an intervention." I cackle, throwing my head back as I put my sunglasses back in place. "No, thank you."

"Fine," Silas barks out, turning to walk away, but Blaine stops him and gives him a pointed look. Silas sighs in response before running his hand over his mouth as he curses. "Jesus Christ, okay. Look, Bunk, we're your friends and you need to tell us what the fuck is wrong with you."

"You're depressed," Blaine so helpfully states.

I don't know what to say and my gaze bounces between all my friends before I settle on Landon. He looks like a deer caught in headlights. It takes him a moment but he eventually drops his gaze, snapping his fingers, and a huge smile blooms across his lips when he reaches into his pocket and produces a candy bar. "Chocolate?"

Wonderful. This Bunky-vention is off to a fabulous start. Fucking trainwreck, if you ask me. Got to give it to him though, Landon's adorable.

Declining his candy offer, I look back at everyone again. "I appreciate what you're all *tryin'* to do, but there ain't anythin' to talk about," I tell them, begrudgingly getting out of my fort, tired of them looming over me. "Things are okay."

"No, they ain't. You almost cried when you accidentally squished a ladybug yesterday," Silas points out. "And when Blaine accidentally called a bimbo a dildo, you didn't crack *one* joke. You didn't even smile."

Blaine pouts, folding his arms over his chest before glaring at Silas. "My mouth was full, asshole."

Raid pushes up his glasses, eyes fixed on me, and I note the calculation there. "You're really not gonna tell us? You might as well fess up."

"To what?" I throw back, even though my face blooms with worried heat. Then I narrow my eyes at him, trying to read his mind. "You can't know..."

That makes him smirk. "Don't I?"

Raid's like freaky smart, but I've been so careful. I think...

After a second, I break our stare off with a scoff. "You don't know."

"What doesn't he know?" Landon asks like an adorably lost puppy as he looks between us. "Raid?"

He looks at Landon for a beat before turning back to me, face impassive. "Fine. If I need to be the villain, so be it."

Silas wrinkles his nose in confusion. "What does that mean?"

"It means that I've got to be the one to say that Whaley and Bunky are fuckin'."

"What?"

"Wait..."

Silas and Blaine speak at the same time, but I can't look at them. I'm too pissed off and preparing to wring Raid's neck.

"Oh shit!" I look at Landon when he speaks, because what the fuck does he have an opinion for? He doesn't even know Whaley. He turns beet red, shrinking and hiding behind Raid's shoulder when he gets my sole attention. "Sorry."

"Raid!" I hiss, advancing on him, but he dodges me. "Why the fuck did you say that? How the fuck do you even know?"

Blaine gasps. "So it's true?"

I ignore him in favor of trying to strangle Raid. Luckily for him, he's a slippery fuck that just slides out of my grasp. "Between you and Silas, I don't know who's more clueless."

"Asshole," Silas snaps, thumping Raid on the back of his

head. I'd have rather he chopped him in the throat but that works too. "Got a lot on my mind these last few months. I was in *jail*, or did everyone forget?"

"Cry me a river," Raid retorts with a roll of his eyes before focusing back on me. "Look, I'm not tryin' to be a dick. I'm bein' real. Whaley is what's got you lookin' like you wanna torch yourself. If that's the case, we gotta put an end to that shit. It ain't a good look, Bunk."

The fact that he cares is the only reason I unclench my fists and relax my shoulders. Can't beat his ass when he's only looking out for me...

I guess.

"Did he hurt you?" Blaine innocently asks, and I don't blame him. All he knows about Whaley is his reputation, not the man he actually is.

And I also can't miss the chance to fuck with him. "Only when I beg for it."

"Ew, I don't want any of those details." Raid shakes his head. "So, if you're fuckin', what's the problem?"

I let out a deep breath. I didn't want to talk about this, but now I have no choice. My friends would likely chase me down and demand the answers anyway, so what's the point?

Where do I even start this story? I'd have to tell them everything for them to get the full picture, but there are details I want to keep to myself. I have no problem admitting that Whaley and I fucked, but those deep, intimate moments we've shared are for the two of us.

It'd feel like betraying Whaley to let anyone else in our heads.

"We just don't work," is all I say with a sad shrug. "Whaley knows it, I know it, and I bet you all know it too."

"Won't lie, it's weird to think about," Silas mumbles, hooking his arm around Blaine's shoulder. "Don't mean I ain't sorry."

"It is what it is," I murmur, feeling like I need to hug myself. Actually, maybe Blaine will hug me.

"Oomph!" Blaine grunts when I wrap my arms around him. Yeah, I knew he'd give nice hugs.

"You're so warm," I tell Blaine as I snuggle into his chest. "Ugh, this is exactly what I needed."

"You have three seconds to get off my guy before *I'm* the reason you're in pain," Silas growls, reaching out to try and pluck me off.

Blaine rolls his eyes, patting my back supportively while knocking Silas away with his free hand. "Don't worry about him. I'm here for you, Bunky. We can hug it out."

"One… Two…"

"Fine," I mutter sadly, breaking away from Blaine and flipping Silas off. "When you need cuddles, don't come cryin' to me."

Silas laughs humorlessly. "Don't hold your breath."

"Are we really lettin' him deflect?" Raid asks, reverting the conversation back in true Raid fashion. Damn it. I was hoping the distraction would work. "We're talkin' about him and Whaley."

"No, we're not," I insist. "I said what I said. There's no hope for us, no future. What's the point of lovin' someone you can never really be with?"

"Love?" Landon's eyes widen as he takes in my words. "You love him?"

"Yeah," I admit, deciding to let it all out in the open. "I think about him all the time, keep all his shit, follow him around. I even got a shrine in my closet."

It's quiet for a moment as I stare at my friends, taking in their mix of expressions. Silas and Raid don't really look surprised, but Blaine and Landon look ready to run for the hills.

"Would we…" Blaine starts, hesitating as he thinks of the right words to use. "Would we call that love?"

"More like obsession," Silas tells him.

"Same thing. You should know." I throw Silas a pointed look. "I think that's all I need to say. I want him, but I can't have him. He wants me, but he refuses to take me. That's the end of it."

"It might be for the best." Raid shrugs, passing me his cigarette. "You need someone good for you, Bunk. Someone that's gonna even out all the"—he waves his hands around my head—"*that*. Whaley seems like he's got his own stuff."

"You sound like Fox," I point out, thinking maybe the popular opinion is the right one, even though I hate it. "He said the same thing."

"Wait…" He scowls before snatching his cigarette back. "You told *Fox* before you told *us*?"

"Duh," I deadpan. "He's my brother."

"Hey, dumbass, so are we," Silas counters, face pinched in something that looks like hurt.

"I know but—"

"All of you shut up!"

We all snap our heads at Landon, who's been quiet for the last few minutes. He's standing there, slack-jawed and looking like he just had a come-to-Jesus moment.

"Landon?" Raid asks, placing a hand on his shoulder. "You good, man?"

Landon ignores him, slapping his hand away and marching up to me. Then he grabs me by my forearms, shaking me hard until I see stars. I don't think he means to be rough, he's just got the body of a truck.

"It's not that I don't like whatever this is… but what's happenin'?"

He stops shaking me, but his hold stays firm. "You got to try again."

I blink repeatedly, eyeing over his shoulder to where our friends are looking at him like he's lost it. "What now?"

"Love, man. That's the end goal, right? *True love*. That

doesn't come about all the time, you know? If you love him, if he's it for you, you *have* to try," he tells me, and it's the most serious I've ever seen him.

Raid chuckles. "Landon, you've been watchin' too many rom-coms. We're puttin' on a horror movie tonight."

"It's not that!" Landon argues, still giving me his sole focus. "I mean it, Bunky. Life is too short to be miserable. It's too short not to act on what you want. I'm not callin' you a coward—please don't hurt me—but you can't be afraid to go after your dreams."

Holy shit.

So much cheese they should grate him on some spaghetti.

He has a point though. He actually has a very great point.

Fuck it, he's one-hundred-percent right.

I know that everyone is looking out for me—Blaine, Silas, Raid, Fox—but Landon's telling me to take a leap. Life is too short to give up. I never really wanted to do that to begin with, but I had talked myself into thinking it was for the best.

Fuck. That.

Thank God, I've never been known to do the *smart* thing.

"Landon, you beautiful himbo," I cheer, slapping two kisses on each of his cheeks as I spring back. "You're right! Fuck it!"

"Yes!" Landon yells back while slamming his fists against his chest. "Let's fucking go, man!"

"Oh, Jesus," Raid groans, dropping his head with a sigh. "What have you done?"

"He's a keeper, Raidy," I tease as I pinch Raid's cheeks. "You all suck. Landon's my new favorite."

"Hell yeah," Landon laughs, looking at Raid. "You hear that?"

"Loud and clear," Raid grumbles, tugging on Landon's jacket. "Let's go, man. *The Exorcist* it is."

"But I don't like scary movies!"

"Tough shit."

I cackle madly as Raid drags Landon away, probably trying to stop him from causing any more damage to our friend group. Bless that amazing jock. He's going to make a great boyfriend to Raid. Raid needs someone to slap some fun into him, and I can't wait to see it.

Well, once Raid grows some balls and actually makes a move.

Silas and Blaine look at me curiously, probably wondering what I'm going to do next. I answer them before they can ask their question. "Anyone got a black turtleneck?"

Time to shoot my final shot.

TWELVE

Whaley

I crack my knuckles as I stare at my desk.

People got issues, people got problems, and they all expect me to fix them.

The matter I'm dealing with right now has been months in the making. Those fucking Vipers, they can't seem to stay in their lane. They're getting ballsier, bolder, and the guys are all worked up about it. It's not that I'm not concerned, I'm always thinking of the good of the gang, but it doesn't seem like something I need to get involved with at the moment. So I tell Pike that very thing.

"We're just gonna let them do what they want?" Pike argues, his face growing a bit frustrated as he paces before me. "They're takin' our customers."

"They're *failin'*," I clarify, cracking my knuckles again. Pike's a loyal member. Steady, but I'm starting to lose my patience. "I told you once and I don't like repeatin' myself. We leave it alone for now."

"How can you say that?" he asks, throwing his hands in

the air. "You know Raid got pushed out of the club over in Clairmont? Vipers were already there, scopin' out the scene."

"Watch your tone," Badge snaps from where he stands by my office door.

I breathe through my nose and count down from three. My restraint is being tested, but I hold back my frustration. "Raid was late goin' in that night. Should have been there earlier. Either way, *like I said*, we're keepin' our distance for now."

"But—"

That's it. I tried to keep it cool because I respect Pike, but I'm done now. I shoot up, slapping my hands against the table, jaw clenched and seething as I approach him. "You think I'm fuckin' stupid?"

Finally, Pike realizes what his big mouth has gotten him into. He takes a step back in what I'm guessing is fear, but I'm there, seizing the collar of his jacket and yanking him back to me. "Whaley—"

"Answer the question," I say slowly, using the voice that chills men to their very bones. "Do you think I'm fuckin' stupid?"

"No, course not—"

"Then why are you questionin' me?" I snap, shaking him as I drill a finger against his temple. "You don't question me. You sure as hell don't barge into my office, scream up a storm, and disrespect me."

His eyes widen and he shakes his head. "I'd never—"

"He's not done," Badge chimes in, walking up behind Pike, caging him between our bodies. "You know what happened last time someone pissed Whaley off?"

Pike nods rapidly. "Yeah…"

The way he trails off isn't satisfying to me, but Badge reads my mind and thumps the back of Pike's head. "Tell us. Fuckin' say what happened."

"Well?" I press after a moment of silence. "You need me to jog your memory?"

"They…" Pike trails off again and gulps audibly. "Let's just say, they couldn't question anythin' for a while after that."

"Exactly," I spit out before pushing Pike back into Badge's arms, and Badge tosses him onto the ground.

I don't like using physical force against my own men, but Pike's been asking what I'll do with the Vipers for weeks, and he doesn't get that I've got it taken care of. I'm not an idiot, I'm not weak, and I'm not cowardly. What he doesn't know is that I'm biding my time and waiting for the perfect moment to strike back. If we're going to start something with the Vipers, it has to be worth it.

"I'm sorry," Pike says, standing up. "Whaley, I didn't mean anythin' by my question."

"I respect you," I start, sighing as I clap his shoulder. "So that's why I'm not beatin' the livin' shit out of you. My word is law, but you gotta trust me. I'm in charge for a fuckin' reason." Pike has regret plaguing his face, and I feel a headache starting to bloom. "Go. You got shit to do right now at the bar."

Pike smiles, something akin to gratitude laced with fear in his expression. Badge doesn't let him get too far before he speaks up. "Oh and, Pike? Next time you piss Whaley off, don't think he's gonna be as forgivin'."

I nod at Badge when Pike rushes out of my office. Some might think Badge's comments are disrespectful, but he gets me. We make a good team, have since the beginning, and he's really good at finishing my thoughts.

That's why a pang of guilt hits me at what I've been doing with his son behind his back. Fucking Bunky. Damn it. I want to say I regret all the things we've done in the dark, but I can't. Not when it feels so right, not when it feels like a universal truth, and not when it makes me feel alive. Badge is another reason, a small reason, but a reason nonetheless as to why I have to cut things off with Bunky. I would never want to disrespect him more than I already have.

"You good?" he asks, cocking his head to the side as I reach for a cigarette. "Seem a bit testy."

That's a fucking understatement. Ever since I explained to Bunky why we couldn't be together, I've started questioning myself. My will grows weaker and weaker every day that I can't touch him and kiss him and be with him. I'm so far gone, too deep in my obsession, and it's starting to cloud my judgment.

I'm trying to be strong. He's kept his distance after that talk, surprisingly, and I should be grateful for it because I don't know what I would do if he pushed a bit more.

"I'm fine," I tell him, doing my best to smile. "Just tired."

His eyes are filled with so many questions, as if not believing my words, but he doesn't say anything. He wouldn't. He respects me too much for that. He's always been able to read me though, so I know he can tell there's something I'm keeping from him.

"You head home." Badge slaps my shoulder when I walk past him. "I'll lock up tonight."

"Thanks," I mumble, taking a deep drag of my cigarette as I avoid his eyes. Damn, I really am the worst. I can't even look at him without picturing all the dirty, depraved things I've done with his son.

My brain begins to spiral as images and words assault me, striking at my knees, and my legs almost give out.

Bunky, the look of hope on his face when I told him he'd become my everything if we got together.

Bunky, the way he clutched my chest when I told him I had people to take care of.

Bunky, his big, watery green eyes when I told him we were fucked-up.

Stay strong. You have to.

I manage to get through the rest of my day, but only with my obsession securely planted in my mind.

Not being with Bunky... This shit's going to be harder than I thought.

It's late by the time I stagger up the steps to my trailer, fighting back a yawn.

I'm dirty, tired, and ready to smoke a joint, shower, and go to bed. If I can even sleep tonight that is. I've been restless, tossing and turning most nights because my mind refuses to settle. It's not like I don't know why, but still, I wish for some damn reprieve.

I use my key to let myself in and begin stripping as I head toward my bathroom. I trip over my jeans in the process and stumble into the wall, further proving how badly I'm lagging.

Don't think about him. Don't think about him. Don't think about him.

But I do just that the entire time I go through my nightly routine. I think about him in the shower as I touch myself to the memory of his slutty moans. I think about his surprisingly soft hands as I towel myself off. I think about his fucking eyes as I tug on my boxers before lying down to try to sleep.

My mind is plagued with him.

I can finally feel myself drifting off into a restless slumber when a loud crashing sound has me jerking awake. I shoot up from my bed, flicking on my lamp before snagging my knife off my nightstand, prepared to filet whoever the fuck broke into my trailer when I come face-to-face with Bunky.

"Jesus Christ, you've gotta be kiddin'," I scold, my hand coming to press against my chest as I look up at my ceiling. I inhale deeply, trying to ground myself before looking back at him. He's wearing all black—black turtleneck, black jeans, black beanie, and even has black war paint on his cheeks.

He's got a wide smile spread across his face as he holds up a brown paper bag. Has he lost it? "What the fuck are you doin'?"

He doesn't so much as flinch at my biting tone, just comes to plop down in my bed, in the spot where I was almost sleeping peacefully moments before.

"Still warm," he says with a sigh, his eyes closing for a brief second before giving the bag a little shake in my direction. "Bagel?" he questions, eyes running over my almost naked body.

"Where did you get bagels at"—I look at the clock on my nightstand and fight the groan wanting to escape—"one in the mornin'?" I put my knife away, realizing there's no harm.

He shrugs, opening the bag and pulling out a bright pink one with some kind of sprinkly shit on top. Is that even a bagel? "I got a guy."

He...

"Seriously, Bunk?" I reach up, fisting my hair in exasperation. "What are you doin' here? We've talked about this."

He shrugs again before taking a bite of his food. "We did. I know you have your reasons, and I know they're valid, but Landon said—"

"Who the fuck is Landon?" I bite out in frustration. "Who the fuck you tellin' our business to?"

"You don't gotta worry. He's harmless." He waves me off, breaking off a piece of the bagel and holding it out to me. When I only stare at him, he sighs and shoves it into his mouth. "Either way, he told me I needed to try again, and I realized I do. If you're not willin' to fight, then I gotta get my knuckles bloodied for the two of us."

I pinch the bridge of my nose, trying not to hunt down some kid I don't even know and beat him to death with this bag of fucking bagels.

"Bunk..."

He cuts me off with a wave of his hand again, putting his

food away before setting the bag on my nightstand. "You talked last time, now it's my turn." He gives me a pointed look, patting the spot beside him. "You're gonna let me talk. Stay quiet until the end and I may suck your dick."

I want to argue. I want to tell him to go, because nothing he says is going to change my mind, but this is Bunky. I know him, and he's not going to relent until he says whatever the hell it is he needs to say. So I humor him.

"Go ahead." I sit down too. "The floor is yours."

"You and I belong together," he blurts, serious eyes holding mine. "I know it and you know it. This push and pull between us is great and all but, Whaley, I'm bored of it. I'm ready for it to be over. I'm ready for you." He reaches forward, grabbing one of my hands. "All your reasons are good reasons. You're right that we would be so wrong for each other, but I don't fuckin' care. I feel like I'm suffocatin'. I can't think without you. I can't even be myself without you."

"You're young." I give his hand a quick squeeze, trying to make him see reason. "You don't know what you're talkin' about."

His eyes harden as he looks at me with disbelief. "I might be eighteen, but I've seen shit. You know it. I know enough to realize that life is too fuckin' short, that life can gut you at any moment, and that if you find somethin' good, you gotta fuckin' take it."

There's so much I want to say. I know he's been through a lot. It's one of the main reasons I want him to steer clear of me. He's been through enough and deserves so much more than anything I could offer. He must see the war conflicting in my eyes because he slides forward, his face coming to rest on my shoulder as he nestles against my skin. "You make me feel alive. You make me feel seen. You make me feel accepted. Don't I do all that for you?

I'm filled with so much emotion, it makes my stomach feel

heavy. Of course I feel that way, but it doesn't change all the reasons as to why we can't do this.

"Bunky—"

"Please," he whispers, cutting me off once more. He leans up, his watery eyes holding mine. "Please, try for me and try for us. I'll gladly take a ticket to Hell as long as that means I can be with you. I don't need anythin' but you."

I get up quickly, hands fisting my hair as I shake my head. "No."

"Whaley—"

"I said no, Bunk!" My voice comes out cracked and tortured. "Don't do this to me."

He stands and slinks closer, and every step he takes, I step back. We do this dance until I'm pressed up against the wall and he's standing in front of me. "You know you want it. You know you want me."

He raises his hands and runs them down my chest, inching on the tip of his toes so his lips ghost mine. I keep shaking my head but it doesn't escape me that I lean closer. I don't kiss him though, keeping our lips hovering above each other. His little breaths fan my mouth and I find that I'm panting against him. Everything in my body is coiled tight, like a rubber band ready to snap.

"Give us a shot," he begs, pressing himself fully against me. "You don't know how much I need you."

I need him too, so fucking much that it physically pains me to keep my hands to myself. Yet somehow I do. "You like torturin' me? Want to see me in pain? You're fuckin' accomplishin' it."

"It's a sweet torture, ain't it?" he replies, pressing a kiss to the corner of my mouth, and I urge to chase his lips even though I shouldn't. He moves onto the spot right behind my ear. "It's everythin' you ever wanted. That pain you feel? I can make it all go away."

I know he can, but at what cost? What will this do to us? To the gang? To our souls if we rush into Hell together?

"Pain is a part of life," is all I say, still trying to come up with a million excuses.

"Let's feel that pain together." He comes back to my mouth, poking his tongue out to run it across my bottom lip. "I'm not just obsessed with you. I worship you. That strength, that composure, the things you do for people... You're such a good man."

My breath hitches and I find my fingers twitching to grab him. What he's saying is so different from the encounters we've had. It's been all about sex, but this level of vulnerability is so new to me. Before I can stop myself, I'm spilling my truth to him.

"You're honest. So authentically you. Whenever you smile, I realize I want to put that look on your face." I drop my forehead against his. "And you're kind too. Kind to everyone who treats you wrong. Even when you snap, you apologize after like some psycho saint." My hands latch onto his hips, pulling him flush against me. "You're so unique. So unlike anyone I've ever met. I think you could get me in a way no one ever has."

"I can," he confirms, nuzzling his nose in my neck. "We could be those things for each other."

We breathe each other in, our confessions drawing us closer.

My throat works to swallow as my brain and heart battle one another. Then I take his face in my hands, tilting his chin so I can see every beautifully tragic inch. "Bunky, you have to be real sure about this. This will change everythin'. Once you're mine, I'll never let you escape."

"I'm sure," he mutters, voice full of sadness as his hands grip my wrists. "You need to be sure too. You've said all that to me before and it all turned into broken dreams. I don't want you to get my hopes up and break my heart again. It's destroyin' me."

Fuck me.

I lean in, pushing my forehead against his again, all reservations out the window. How can I tell him no anymore? How can I keep hurting him? Denying us what we both want? What we both desperately need?

"I mean it this time, Bunk. A man like me can't do casual. If we're in this, we're fuckin' in this. If we do this, you're mine. No break ups, no misunderstandin's, *nothin'*. We're together and that won't change for as long as we're alive." I can feel his body trembling as a little humming noise leaves his lips. He likes that. A lot. "If you say yes one more time, you're sealin' your fate."

His breath stutters and I feel the whispered response against my lips a half-second later. "Yes."

I close my eyes, the world feeling like it's aligned for the first time in my whole life. I may regret the way everything burns around us one day or the way we're going to consume one another. It's probably going to piss people off, and I'm probably going to be battling over him for the rest of my goddamn life, but I don't care.

Not anymore.

I don't think I'll ever regret finally accepting and taking what's mine.

"You're so fuckin' mine," I tell him, pulling back to stare into his watery eyes. "Can't believe I tried to deny this."

"Wasn't gonna let you." His lip wobbles and he swipes his face quickly with his sleeve. "Would have chased you your entire life. Stalked you until you caved. Carved my name into your skin to show you how serious I was. You'll never be able to escape me."

"Fucking' psycho," I mutter, my lip kicking up on one side.

"*Your* little psycho." He puts a hand against my chest,

pushing me back to lie on my bed. Then he follows me down, thighs caging my hips and hands bracing on either side of my head. "Now, fuck me like you've missed me. Fuck me like you hate me. Fuck me like you can't live without me."

That I can do.

I place my hand on his back, flipping us so he's now underneath me. I sit back, quickly taking off all his clothes and shedding my boxers before coming to rest on top of him again. His legs and arms wrap around me instantly, fingers coming to the back of my head to pull me down for a kiss. I comply easily, groaning when our mouths reconnect for the first time in too long. His tongue sweeps out, pushing inside my mouth and tangling with mine, and I let out a groan before sucking on his barbell, loving how good it feels.

He rolls his hips, hard cock sliding against mine, and the pleasure from that movement alone makes my already closed eyes roll back into my head.

I tear my lips away from his in a gasp, leaning back to riffle through my drawer for some lube, not able to take another agonizing second of not being inside him. "Fuck, you feel so good. Can't wait. I need this."

"Don't wanna wait," he agrees, placing his feet on the mattress and spreading his legs wide. "Want you inside me more than I want my next breath."

I bite down on my lip, pouring way too much lube on my fingers before reaching down and toying with his hole. His eyes flutter shut at my touch and his chest rises and falls in uneven pants. He's a sight, so damn enchanting that I never want to look away.

"You're beautiful, Bunk," I tell him, sliding a finger inside.

He moans, blinking bleary eyes open before giving me a teasing smile. "I know. Feel free to compliment me anytime. I like it."

"I know." I give him a smirk, not wasting any time adding a second and a third finger, enjoying the way he's grinding down against my hand with every forward push. He's desperate, gripping and twisting my sheets as he begs for me to get inside of him.

I don't make him wait, removing my fingers to pour more lube on my cock, making sure my piercings are nice and coated.

"You ready for me?" I mutter, jaw tightening when I press my head against his hole.

"So fuckin' ready. Gonna die if you don't get in me soon. Wanna feel you so badly."

I slide forward, pushing in all the way, my bottom lip locking between my teeth as the feel of him overwhelms me. How in the hell did I think I could live without this for the rest of my life? The feel of his warmth? The sounds he makes when I get inside of him for the first time? The way he begs? I'll never get enough.

"Bunky," I groan, falling forward and crushing him with my weight. He doesn't care though, only lets out a pleased moan as he wraps around me, legs locking my waist as he clings like he never wants to let me go.

I rock in and out of him, moving so fast that I'm pushing us further up the bed with every thrust. I feel desperate, like I've never needed anything so badly in my whole life. I'm pretty sure I never have. I need *him*. He doesn't seem to care about my rough handling, his nails digging into the skin of my back as he holds onto me. He nips my lip with his teeth, using his pierced tongue to soothe the sting after.

"You're mine, Whaley," he rasps, eyes drilling into me. "You're never allowed to leave me." His hands slide from around my back, teasing the skin at my sides, and glide up my chest before coming to wrap around my throat. "I'll kill you before I let you."

A normal person would run the fuck away now, tuck tail and escape, but not me. My eyes fall shut and my hips stutter as the orgasm threatens to burst from my dick.

"Fuck," I moan. When he adds more pressure, I halt my thrusts, the urge to come increasing with every second that passes. "Keep doin' that and I'm gonna come. You're really turnin' me on."

He leans up, slamming his lips against mine, and devours my mouth before pulling away all too quickly. "Remember that, Whaley. No one will ever make you feel the way I do."

Cocky little brat.

I smirk, letting him think he's won before ripping from his hold. Then I sit back, grabbing his thighs to flip him around, dragging his hips up, and shoving my cock back inside.

He lets out a loud grunt, and I fist his hair, pulling his head back, making his body arch more. Wrapping my free arm around, I palm his cock, giving it a harsh tug.

"God, you're so fuckin' wet. You like the way I touch you? Like the way I handle you?"

"Yes! More!"

I chuckle, giving him a few more hard tugs. "You always seem to forget who's in control here." I nuzzle his neck, nipping the skin there, loving all his little noises of pleasure. "That's fine, I'll remind you who runs the show."

Then I let go of his cock and push him back down into the mattress, smacking his ass three times before fucking him like he's never been before.

He's moaning, panting, crying, and I can't get enough of those sounds.

"Yeah, you like that? Like me tearin' apart this tight little hole?" I pant. His skin is red everywhere from where I've handled him, and the monster inside of me beats its chest in victory. He's covered in all of my marks.

"L–love i–it, Whaley," he stutters, pushing back against me. "Ne–never want y–you to sto–stop."

"So greedy," I grit out, jaw clenching as my orgasm threatens to crest once more. I tease my finger around the spot where we're joined, loving the way his ass sucks my cock so hungrily. "You're so fuckin' swollen and red. Wanna shove my fist up there."

"Another time," he whines, hand snaking down to grip his cock. "I wanna come."

"Want me to make you come, little psycho? You need it?"

"So bad." He nods against the sheet, his voice muffled by the fabric. I reach down, taking hold of his balls and giving them a gentle tug. "Whaley!"

"Want me to fill all your fuckin' holes?"

"Yes, please! Oh, God!"

"Picture it. You, tied to the bed, completely at my mercy. A dildo up your ass, my cock in your mouth, ropes diggin' into your skin." I'm panting, those images of Bunky have my body thrumming, and my demon sighs in sick satisfaction.

"Yes!" he cries out, hand knocking against mine as he jacks his cock.

"Want me to paddle that sweet ass? Turn it cherry red?" I taunt, letting go of his balls to get leverage on his hips again.

"I want all of you. Hurt me as much as you want. I love the pain."

Music to my ears.

"Perfect for me in every way, ain't you?" I say, unable to stop the orgasm from rushing over me. "God, coming so deep inside you."

"Whaley! Yes! Oh *fuckfuckfuck*—"

His body goes stiff as his orgasm hits, and I continue to pump into him, letting his ass milk every drop of cum I have.

I can't hold myself up any longer, a boneless feeling rushing through me, and I fall to the side, taking Bunky with me, not wanting to leave his body just yet. The room is silent, the only sounds are our panting breaths as we come down from our high.

I lean in, kiss his shoulder, neck, back, anywhere my lips land, and just hold him. My arms wrap around his middle and his hands come up to rest against my forearms. He lets out a little hum, purring like a satisfied cat as he nestles his body back against mine.

I guess we're cuddling. Is that what this is? Fuck if I know, but it's nice. It's definitely something I've never done, but with Bunky, I'm willing to give him everything.

We're quiet for so long, and Bunky is the first to break the silence. "So we're in this? You ain't gonna back out again? The game's over?"

"No more games," I confirm, kissing his neck again. "You and me... we ain't goin' anywhere."

"Good," he whispers, flipping around in my arms before throwing his leg over my hip. We're gross, both sticky and covered in sweat and cum, but neither of us care. Bunky hums again, clinging to me as he rubs his cheek against my pierced nipple. "I'm so happy, Whaley."

I feel this weird flutter in my chest and my stomach flips at his confession. I kiss his forehead, hands trailing over the skin of his back as the thought occurs to me. "Me too, Bunk."

I realize it's the first time in a truly long time I've ever been happy and it's all because of this pushy, bratty, psycho baby that's tucked beside me.

Which makes me feel really damn lucky.

THIRTEEN

Bunky

Crack.

Squish.

Pop.

"How do you like that, you bitch!"

I'm trembling, cowering in the corner. My knuckles are bloody, and I can't move.

Squish. Squish. Squish.

I watch as he beats her. He's a man I barely recognize.

Squish. Squish. Squish.

Why is he still hitting her? She has to be dead by now, right? That's what the brains mean. Her brains. They squelch under his punches, shards of bone digging into his hands, but he doesn't stop.

Squish. Squish. Squish.

I'll never forget that noise. It'll haunt me forever—what it sounds like when your brain gets beaten to a pulp.

Her face is caved in. It doesn't look like Mama anymore.

I tremble, unmoving, my instincts gone out the window.

Because I know I'm next.

I shoot up with a start, the back of my neck sweaty as I

reach for my pocketknife. When I don't find it on my night-stand, the same place I keep it every night, I start to panic. Someone took it. They must have. They're hiding in the shadows, ready to get me, ready to—

"Bunky?"

I close my eyes and breathe through my nose at the sound of Whaley's sleepy voice. Strong arms wrap around me from behind, tethering me back to reality. I sink into his hold, leaning my head against his shoulder, shivering from the fear that lingers inside me.

"Nightmare?" he asks, his breath hot by my ear. "You good?"

"Not in the slightest."

He hums under his breath, his fingers splayed against my stomach, caressing my skin. "Wanna tell me what it was about?"

"I haven't had one in a while," I whisper, shuddering at the memory. It's actually been a few weeks since I've had to relive that moment in such vivid detail. I think about it often, little glimpses and flashes, but this total immersion into the memory has rocked me. "It's what happened..."

He gives my stomach a squeeze and his lips brush the crown of my head. "Okay. You wanna talk about it?"

I shake my head so quickly that I nearly crash into his nose. "No. Not at all. Let's fuck."

When I turn in his arms, ready to crawl down his body and suck his dick, he stops me with a hand to my chest. "Sex don't solve every problem."

"Not the way you've been doin' it," I try to joke, flicking the barbell through his nipple. "Lemme suck you. I'm hungry for your cum."

He clenches his jaw, dark eyes filled with lust, but of course, Whaley's self-control is legendary. He leans forward, pressing a quick kiss to my lips, then pats my ass. "Get dressed."

"Why?" I pout, wanting to feel connected to him again, wanting him to take away the shadows that have settled over me.

"Well, you ain't gettin' it." He manhandles me so he can get up, then grabs my arm and drags me along with him. "Come on and get dressed. I'm gonna take you somewhere."

Even though I don't want to get dressed and would much rather get dicked down, I relent, interest piqued. I groan and moan the entire time though, letting him know how much effort it takes me to put on my clothes. Thankfully, Whaley had made us shower before we went to sleep because I definitely wouldn't feel like it now.

"Always with the dramatics." He chuckles, clearly finding me amusing.

"You knew what you were gettin' yourself into," I tease, slinking up to him and wrapping my arms around his thick middle. Jesus, he's built. Just want to climb him and rock his—

"Enough stallin'," he rasps, cutting off my dirty train of thought. By the look in his eyes, he knew where my mind was headed.

He takes my hand in his, tugging me out of his room. One glance at the clock in the living room tells me it's past three in the morning, too early to be going anywhere. He doesn't seem to care though. He leads me outside to his truck, unlocks it, and gestures for me to get in.

Once we're on the road and I realize we're headed toward the shop, I frown. "Work? Really?"

"We're takin' the Harley. I managed to fix it after *someone* fucked it up."

My cheeks tinge pink, but I giggle regardless. "Oops?"

"Oops," he mimics, but there's a lightness to his voice as he places his hand on my thigh. "It's alright. I'm over it. My little psycho wanted my attention so badly, didn't he?"

The little flirty tilt to his voice is going to kill me. I've never heard that tone from him before.

"Just wanted you to notice me…" I trail off. "It worked, didn't it?"

He nods, smiling as he squeezes my thigh. "Yeah. It did."

We ride the rest of the way to the shop in silence. We don't linger, going straight to his bike, and I snort when his free hand hides the panel as he types in the new code. I don't know why he tries to hide it, it's not like I won't figure it out at some point.

He grabs us two helmets as he opens the garage door, then mounts his bike, and I follow suit, snuggling into his back, enjoying the way he smells—like cigarettes and peppermint. "Could sniff you all day." I bury my nose against him, still able to smell him through his leather jacket. "Mmm, yummy."

"Hold on tight! We got a ways to go," he shouts over the rumble of his bike. "Don't go fallin' asleep on me."

"Where are we goin'?" I yell back.

"It's a surprise."

"Wait, no! Tell me," I whine, poking his stomach.

He takes off, keeping his mouth shut the entire ride. Even though I'm eager to know where we're going, I settle in. Being able to hold him and not be afraid that he'll pull back is enough to keep me content for now.

It still seems so surreal to me, that after all that frustrating push and pull, we're together now. I know it's not going to be temporary either. We're not the kind of people that do casual, and we're not the type of people that do things half-assed.

Now that we're in, I know we're all in.

I don't have a watch, so I can't be sure, but it feels like a little over an hour until we reach our destination. I hop off the bike first, itching to stretch my legs, and give him a taunting smirk. "You finally gonna kill me, Whaley?"

He chuckles, wrapping his hand around the back of my

neck as he leads us to what looks like an abandoned building. "Come on."

"Really? You're not gonna say anythin'?" I ask, not passing up the chance to tease him a bit. "How you gonna do it? Gonna stab me and watch me bleed out? Gonna tie me up and poison me?"

He looks down at me, thick brows furrowing in confusion. "You shouldn't sound like you're gettin' off on the idea."

"What can I say?" I shrug, giving him a wink. "I'm unique."

"That's one word for it." I don't get the chance to half-heartedly slap him for his comment before we're in front of the warehouse door. He knocks three times, pausing in between each, and after a moment, the door opens. It's still on its chain, but I can make out beady eyes staring at us through the gap. "What do you want?"

Whaley doesn't bristle at the man's annoyed tone, although I can tell he doesn't like it when his hand tenses. "Euphoria."

The man's eyes track us for one second before he nods, closing the door only to open it back up without the chain. He steps to the side as Whaley pushes me in, still keeping a secure grip on my neck. The inside is dark and dingy, little rivulets of water trickling from the wall of the hallway we're walking through, and it smells moist.

Ew.

I'm about to ask him what we're here for until I hear it. At first, it's a low rumble—barely audible—but the closer we get down to the end, the louder it gets. Finally, we reach a set of steel doors, and all I can hear is the roaring of a crowd.

"Whaley?" I ask, turning to him with a quirked brow. "What's goin' on?"

He smirks, rubbing the back of my neck before dropping his hand. "Trust me. I think you'll like it."

He pushes the doors open, and it takes me a second, but when I realize where we're at, I fucking lose it.

He brought me to a fucking fight night.

"Holy shit!" I scream, rising to my toes as I look at the raised platform in front of us. The thick crowd is blocking most of my view, but I can still make out two large guys beating the ever-living shit out of each other. There's blood flying, rough grunts filling the open space, and I swear to God I see a tooth on the ground. "You're kiddin'! You took me to a fight?"

"You like it?" His head tilts in question. He already knows my answer but still seems nervous for whatever reason.

"I love it," I tell him honestly, reaching for his hand and lacing our fingers together. "Aw, is this a date?" I tease, swinging our hands back and forth. "You brought me on a date. Am I your baby?"

He yanks his hand away and glares at me. "I don't date, and I don't say 'baby.'"

"Where are my chocolates? My flowers?" I continue, following him when he turns on his heels and starts to walk away. "You need to step up your game—"

In an instant, he's spinning and hauling me up against his strong body, gripping my shoulders tightly. He bends down to drag his nose across my cheek. "If you want chocolates and flowers, you're gonna be sorely disappointed. I don't do that shit. Now, you want blood and guts? I can give that to you in spades." He lifts his head and nips at my mouth. "So, what do you say? Wanna head back home and grab a milkshake like Silas and Blaine, or you wanna watch someone get the shit beat out of them?"

That's an easy answer.

Even though I love being this close to him, and I'd never pass up the chance to make out, I move around him so I can get a better view of the platform. One of the guys that was fighting is now passed out cold on the ground, his limp body twitching with the aftershocks of a beating. Two guys come and drag him away, and he's quickly replaced with a new guy.

The guy organizing the fight stands in the middle between them, nodding to each one before hooking two fingers in his mouth and whistling. That's the cue for the fight to begin. I wouldn't call these guys amateur but everything they're doing chalks up to sheer bulk and strength.

Even though there's no finesse or technique, it's still entertaining as hell.

"Fuck yes!" I roar, pumping my fist in the air as one of the guys tackles the other to the ground. "Hit him harder!"

"Glad you're enjoyin' yourself." Whaley chuckles, and snakes his other hand around my waist.

"What's not to enjoy? I'm gettin' hard just watchin'," I say, cozying up next to him, the heavy pressure of his hand on me in public intoxicating. Then an idea hits me. "Ooo, can I go in?"

Damn, I'd love to fight right now. It'd be fucking awesome. Blood, gore, maybe even a few broken fingers. It sounds like the best thing in the world. The adrenaline would give me a boost no drug ever could. Just the idea of being so close to death but overcoming it is too tempting.

He squeezes my ass so hard that I yelp. "No."

"Oh come on," I whine, facing him and running my fingers up his chest, toying with his nipple piercing that I'm absolutely obsessed with. "I know I'm not a bodybuilder like that guy, but I've got skills."

"I know. Seen you and Fox fight enough," he gently placates me, like he's facing a wild animal. "That ain't why you're not goin' in."

I wrinkle my nose and pout, damn near close to stomping my foot. "Why's that?"

He tugs me until I'm flush against him, pinching my face between his fingers like he's trying to get his point across.

"Unless you want me to commit murder, you'll keep that tight ass right here next to me."

My heart melts.

"Are you sayin' you'd kill someone for hurtin' me?" I can't help but fish for what I already know. "Tell me."

He stares me dead in the eyes, nothing but conviction in his expression, showcasing how serious he is. "I wouldn't just kill them. I'd chop off all their fingers and feed 'em to them."

I get hard.

The level of commitment... That's not something that everybody gets. Once again, I'm overcome with the rightness of him and I, thankful that he came to his senses and realized we were right for each other.

I hug him, making sure to reach up and peck his cheek before pulling back quickly. Big, mean, scary gang leader. My man has an image to maintain.

We watch the fight a bit more, this one longer than the last, and I wish they sold some popcorn to go along with the show. After a while, the questions I had forgotten about when I saw the violence pop up once more.

"So, not like I'm not lovin' this, but how did you know this place would be here?"

"I used to come here a lot when I was younger. Fought some too."

My eyes widen before I smile. "Really?"

"Before I became leader of the Aces, I was…" he trails off, shaking his head with a huff and pinching the bridge of his nose. He keeps his eyes trained on the fight, but I don't miss the ghosts of the past swirling through them as he speaks. "I got stuff, Bunk. Just like you. Had to fight to keep myself in check. If I didn't, shit in my head got messed up."

"And you're better now?"

His head tips at my question before he looks at me. "What do you mean?"

"You don't fight anymore. I'd know it if you did," I point

out. It's not like Whaley comes home from runs or nights out with bruises and cuts all over him. I think I would have gone mental a long time ago if he did. That begs the question... "If you needed to fight before, what do you do now?"

He rolls his bottom lip in his mouth, considering what I asked. He thinks on it for a few minutes, but I don't dare take my eyes off him as he does, trying to see what he's not saying. Finally, he seems to have gathered his thoughts. "Can't be riskin' myself for nothin' anymore. Over time, I got a handle on things. Don't need to fight it out, you know?"

So many more questions arise from that statement. "Are you ever gonna tell me what *things* you're referring to?"

I know Whaley has skeletons. Everybody knows that, but he's kept his past locked up tight, so tight that I don't think even Badge is aware of what's happened to him.

I'm special though, different. I'm his everything now—or at least I should be—so I should fucking know every single inch of his mind like it's my own.

That's why my heart breaks a little when he shakes his head.

"Not now," he says, but he covers up my frustrated sadness by pecking the top of my head. "Now is about you. I know you got demons too. I know they haunt you. I know they're waiting to break outta your head and eat you alive."

I go to turn away, suddenly filled with a coldness I don't like, but Whaley beats me to it. He seizes my chin between his fingers, tipping my face up, and he looks almost pissed as he speaks. "You don't keep shit from me. Got it?"

Yeah, totally. A little hypocritical, considering he won't dive into his own shit, but I'm too big of a sucker for this guy. "They get so loud sometimes."

He looks at me with nothing but empathy, and I can't describe how much I appreciate that. When most people sense there's something wrong with me, like my friends, they care. They care but they don't get it, and I can read that in their eyes.

In Whaley's though, I see nothing but familiarity, like something within me is reaching out to him. Whether it's the darkness trying to find its newest victim or kindred souls wanting to suffer together, I don't know.

All I know is that it makes me love him that much more.

"I know," he whispers, everything besides his voice, touch, and eyes disappearing into the background. "I'm not sayin' you should fight—don't think I'd even let you—but you have to find something to keep you level."

"I have my Tai Chi," I point out.

To that, he lets out a full belly chuckle. "I'll suck your dick for an hour if you can prove you're doin' it right."

Rude, but also hot.

I open my mouth to tell him I'm a master of my craft but quickly realize he's not wrong. I know I'm not doing it right. It's complicated! I'm trying to be all bendy, but my body doesn't move that way. "Okay, okay. I get you. I'll figure it out."

And I will. I think that he's right. I need something to calm the demons, make the nightmares go away, and take care of my shit. If Tai Chi isn't doing the trick—no matter how much fun it is—then it has to be something else.

A few more minutes of silence between us pass, and there's a lull when the fighters switch over. Whaley's arm finds its way around me again, but I feel his body tense, and I look up at him in question. He looks like he's holding something back, and I don't like it.

"You don't keep shit from me either." I jab a finger into his chest.

"What do you remember about that night?"

I freeze, instinctively trying to get out of his grip, not because I want to, but because my body is conditioned to run from the things it'd rather not think about. Whaley keeps a hold of me, though, and it helps reground me.

Helps remind me that I can trust him with anything.

"Everythin'," I begin. "It's like…"

When I pause, he gives my ass a squeeze, his sole focus on me. "Go on."

"You sure? It's dark," I mumble, fiddling with my tongue piercing.

He only shrugs. "Nothin's too dark for me."

I nod, taking a deep breath before I begin again. "It's like I'm trapped when I get pulled back there. I try my hardest to keep it locked away, but it always comes to the surface when I least expect it. It's like a monster under the bed waiting to eat me alive, and some days, I don't know if I can take it anymore."

The agony starts building and building and building, and I'm stuck in this never-ending cycle of pain. It makes me want to run away, drown myself in drugs and booze just so I'm not tempted to give up. It's why I always live on the point of breaking because I'm just one memory away from being gone.

I make jokes, I fuck, I drink, and I smoke to escape but it's all fruitless in the end.

After a moment, when Whaley is silent beside me, I poke him once more. "Is that bad?"

"It's honest," he says, and I don't know if I like that answer. Isn't he supposed to reassure me? "Everyone handles trauma differently. No one's the same. What you feel ain't what I feel, and what I feel ain't what you feel."

"Do you think that's why I like violence so much? Why there's…" I trail off, not liking where my thoughts are headed.

"Finish your sentence," he presses, giving me another squeeze.

"Why there's somethin' wrong with me?"

I know it. Everyone knows it. I don't like to think about it much. I like to play it off as if it's nothing, but we all know there's more than one screw loose in my brain. For the most part, I'm okay with that. I've embraced who I am, eccentricities and all, but I won't lie and say that I sometimes don't wish I was better. Normal. *Sane.*

His eyes roam over my face as he contemplates what to say. "You want me to lie to you?"

I shake my head rapidly. "Never."

He nods slowly and eyes something over his shoulder. Then his hand settles in on the back of my neck and he leads me away from the crowd to the back of the open room. We hug the grimy wall, only a few people scattered around us, and he backs me up, both arms on either side of my head as he leans down so we're nose to nose.

"You ain't right, Bunk," he starts, and my heart practically stops. He must see the expression on my face because he curses next. "Just listen. That shit you think in your head? It ain't normal, but who fuckin' cares?" He kisses me lightly, trailing his tongue along my bottom lip, causing me to moan into his mouth and my body to relax. Before I can deepen it and feel his tongue against mine, he pulls back. "You're my little psycho, and I don't give a shit about what's right or what's healthy. You ever feel like there's somethin' wrong with that, you come to me and I'll set you straight. Got me?"

My cracked heart swells.

That... That might be the most romantic thing I've ever heard.

Before he can stop me, I'm throwing myself into his arms and wrapping my legs around his middle, my lips finding his. He opens up with a gasp, and I cram my tongue into his mouth. I play with him, brushing my piercing against his teeth, groaning and moaning and whining as I take what he's so freely giving.

His hands cup my ass and his cock swells against me. Like usual, he doesn't let me have control for long. He slams me against the dirty wall, grinding up into me, completely uncaring about the people around us. I move right back against him, desperately whimpering into his mouth, and I only pull back because I need to breathe, but I'd also happily die from his kisses. "You're such a softie."

He narrows his eyes before biting hard on my bottom lip until I taste blood. "Shut up."

"A fuckin' marshmallow," I tease, licking away the droplets of blood. "My hero, you gonna fight for my honor tonight?"

The corner of his lip quirks up. "Nah, don't think so."

"You'd look so hot up there," I tell him, imagining a shirtless Whaley beating the hell out of someone. Blood on his knuckles, bruises on his face...

Jack off material for years.

"I always look hot to you. Could be pissin' and you'd jump my bones."

"You ain't wrong." I am obsessed with him.

"I'm never fightin' again," he continues. "Not for fun."

If he doesn't want to fight, I won't push him, but I am curious. Whaley's built and strong. He'd definitely kick some ass. "Why?"

"Because I fight to kill," he whispers, and I almost don't catch it over the noise.

Holy mother of...

"Bend me over and fuck me right here."

He laughs, tapping my ass as he sets me down and brushes his thumb against my bottom lip. I trap it in between my teeth, giving it a little nip and lick, and I can see the cords along his throat straining with the effort to keep himself in check. "Later, your ass has gotta be sore. Let's watch a couple more fights."

We go to head back to the front of the crowd, but a growl from Whaley stops me. I look up at him in question, watching the way his face has morphed into violent rage. His jaw is clenched, his eyes blazing, and I try to look around to see what caused it. "What?"

"Guy's lookin' at you," he grunts, and I don't miss the way he takes a step closer to me.

I can't see what he's talking about, so I shrug. "So?" But then it hits me, and I smile deviously as I work my fingers up his shirt to brush against his hard abs. "Oh, you're jealous."

I can get used to this.

"Can't be jealous over somethin' that's already mine." He looks in the distance and then back down at me, cocking his head to the side as he thinks. After a second, he shrugs. "Guess I have to make that message clear."

"What—"

I'm cut off when Whaley moves behind me, snaking his hand down my front and holding my now hard cock in his hand. He backs himself up against the wall, and I feel on display to anyone who might turn around and watch us. We've already attracted a few curious eyes, but I would let Whaley stuff me in front of all of them with zero shame. "*Whaley…*"

"Fuck. Love and hate how people look at you," he whispers in my ear, flicking his tongue against my lobe. "Feel like I gotta piss on you to send a message."

I groan when he starts massaging my aching dick. "Hot."

"Not my thing." He grazes his teeth against my throat, and my head automatically rolls to the side to give him better access. "Should add somethin' else right here. Some solid proof."

Even though he can't see me, I nibble on my lower lip. It's no secret I've got tattoos that match Whaley's, the proof is already there for anyone who takes a good long look, but there's something I've been keeping from him that I don't think he's noticed yet. "Wanna see somethin'?"

He doesn't stop his assault on my neck, biting several parts of my throat, making my eyes roll to the back of my head at the fact I'll be covered with them. "Am I gonna like it?"

I manage the strength to push off of him, then turn around slowly, looking up at him through my lashes as I work on my belt. His eyes follow my hands, his Adam's apple bobs, and his chest wavers when I pull down my fly. I don't push my pants all the way down, just hook my thumb in my underwear and lower them enough for him to see.

The tiny little blue whale tattoo on my hip.

I can't tell if he likes it or not. He's just staring at it, completely unmoving. I'll admit that it *might* border on creepy, but I got too drunk one night and went a little wild. I wanted some ink, and this seemed like the perfect thing to add to my collection.

"Whaley, if you don't—"

I'm silenced when he falls to his knees and gives a nice long lick to the tattoo. I can feel his heavy breaths against my skin as he rolls his forehead against my hip. He's growling under his breath, the hands that are holding onto me tightening enough to leave bruises.

"Not that I don't love where this is heading," I groan, carding my fingers through his hair. "But a lotta people are staring now. Am I gonna have reason to use my pocketknife?"

My dick twitches at the thought.

"No," he growls, voice distant. "Shit like this happens all the time here, no-one cares." He slowly gets up, his face hard as he seizes my throat and pulls me to him. "But they ain't getting a show. You're mine."

Seriously, my heart is gonna explode by the end of this.

"Bathroom," he barks. "Now."

I grin. Don't have to tell me twice.

He drags me willingly into a stall, and when he shoves me to my knees to stuff my mouth full of his dick, I get my answer about the tattoo.

He fucking loves it.

FOURTEEN

Bunky

This is depressing.

I'm really going to miss Silas.

Silas, Blaine, Raid, Landon, and I are all sitting in the back room of the bar, shooting the shit and drinking. Well, with the exception of Blaine and Landon. They're drinking cokes and watching as Silas, Raid, and I toke.

"This sucks," I say, coughing after a particularly deep hit and passing the joint to Raid. "Why you gotta leave so soon?"

"What do you mean?" Silas asks, wrapping his arm around Blaine's waist where he sits on his lap. "School starts in two weeks. We gotta get our shit ready up there."

"*Blaine's* school starts in two weeks," I argue. "*You* don't have to go so soon."

"Um, I told him he could stay," Blaine adds, blushing as Silas works his hand up his shirt. He bats his boyfriend's hand away, glaring at him before turning back to me. "He didn't want to though."

"I didn't want to leave you," Silas corrects, taking the joint from Raid. "Not like you were arguin' about it last night, baby."

Blaine's face turns even redder, and the way he glares at Silas again is kind of adorable. A mix between annoyance and love.

Ugh, I miss Whaley.

It hasn't even been five hours since I've last seen him, and my soul is screaming out for his. Dramatic? Yes, but it's absolutely true and I don't give a fuck. I'm obsessed with my boyfriend and don't care what anyone thinks about it

I was going to ditch this last hang out, but Whaley so annoyingly pointed out that I would regret missing a night with my friends. I invited him along, told him some of the older members could join, but he brushed that suggestion aside, saying we needed to come out to everyone in the right way. I know he's right but it doesn't mean I like it.

He had a point though. The three of us needed this time, and I'd have regretted not coming.

Well, three plus Blaine and Landon now.

It's not that I don't like the two jocks. They're cool as hell and okay to hang out with, but it's always been Silas, Raid, and I. It feels like we're breaking up our trio and that makes me really fucking sad. Silas is going off to Connecticut and Raid's going to do whatever the fuck he's going to do. It's like we're all moving on without each other.

Totally not the case but I'm clearly not a rational guy.

I need another hit.

"What did you say you were gonna do up there?" Raid asks Silas, reaching for his beer.

"Whaley's got a contact that's gonna set me up at his shop," he responds with an easy grin. "Get to work on bikes all day while Blaine studies his ass off."

"It's exciting," Blaine tells us, sipping his coke with bright, gray eyes twinkling. "I've already decided which classes I'm going to take. Hopefully, I can get into this one about Russian history that seems interesting."

Silas cocks a brow at him. "Since when the fuck have you been into Russian history?"

"Bolsheviks," is all Raid says, eyes red and glossy as he grabs the joint.

"Bless you?" I throw out, laughing when he rolls his eyes. "Not everyone can be as smart as you, asshole."

"You ever pick up a book?" he throws back, and I flip him off before he turns to Landon. "What about you? When are you headed to Georgia?"

Landon shrugs, picking at his nails as he stares at his can of soda. "I don't know. I may not even go."

I note Raid's confused face before he shifts to pleased. "Oh, really?"

"I just don't know if that's what I want," Landon admits, almost bashful at his words.

"Then just don't go," I chime in, smiling happily and throwing Raid a subtle look.

"You think so?" Landon asks, slack-jawed, as if my suggestion is the craziest thing in the world. "Why would I do that?"

"Because it's not what you want?" Blaine laughs, shoving Landon's shoulder when he gasps.

"It's more complicated than that," Landon mutters under his breath before he turns and looks up at Raid through his lashes. "What do you think?"

Raid grits his teeth, taking a long swig of his beer before passing me the joint. "Think you should do whatever you wanna do."

"Right," Landon mumbles, and I see his face fall a bit before he schools his features. It's so fast that I'm sure no one noticed, but I did, and it has me ready to lean across the table and give Raid a shake. But I don't because it's not my love interest and not my place to intervene. Landon's face morphs into a bright smile, white teeth on full display as he nudges Raid again. "Are you still going to want to talk to me if I do go?"

My eyes nearly bug out of my damn head when Raid gives Landon a smile. A *real* one. Raid never smiles. He smirks. Or grins. Frowns most of the time, really. The look he's giving Landon though?

Fuel for the fan fiction I'm going to write about them.

It's actually perfect because I'll need another couple to focus my attention on now that I don't have to write my own Whaley fantasies anymore. Nope, I get the real thing whenever the fuck I want.

I'm so damn excited I could scream. Hell, I almost do, but Raid starts speaking the next second, cutting me off.

"Who else is gonna make sure you study?" Raid teases, nudging him right back. "Can't get rid of me that easily."

Blaine hums under his breath from across the table, pulling my attention toward him. He's looking between Raid and Landon with a questioning look on his face. He then looks at Silas who gives him a quick nod. We're all getting the same vibes I think. Raid and Landon... Yeah, that's totally gonna fucking happen. I'd be shocked if it didn't.

"So... Anyone want to play a game?" Blaine strums his fingers on the table in front of us.

Raid snaps out of whatever daze he was in and turns to Blaine. "What kind of game?"

"Truth or dare!" I blurt out. Excited by my own idea, I bounce in my seat. "Fuck yeah! Let's play truth or dare!"

"You're never fun to play with," Silas grumbles, taking the joint from me. "You always pick dare and there's never anythin' you won't do."

"Isn't that the entertaining part?" Landon asks, cocking his head. "Wouldn't you want everyone to choose dare?"

"Not the way Bunk does it," Raid explains. "Somehow, he always makes *us* look like the idiots."

"I want to play," Blaine says, squirming in Silas' lap when Silas' hand migrates to what I can only assume is Blaine's nipple.

"So it's decided," I cheer, clapping my hands as I adjust myself to sit on my knees. "That way, Silas will stop gropin' his guy in front of us."

"Shut the fuck up," Silas barks, but nonetheless, snakes his hand out from under Blaine's shirt. He sighs, leaning forward and killing the joint. "Alright, who's goin' first?"

"I'll go." Landon rubs his hands together as he looks at Raid. "Truth or dare?"

Raid thinks about it for a moment. "Truth."

"Weirdest place you've ever had sex?"

Raid freezes, hands tightening around his beer bottle as he swallows harshly. "Next."

"You can't say next," I remind him. "Unless you wanna streak through the trailer park."

Blaine furrows his brows. "Are those the rules?"

"It is when we play." Silas smirks. "Come on, man. That's an easy one. Blaine and I fucked in the school bathroom once."

"They don't need to know that," Blaine snaps, slapping Silas' chest. "Shut up."

Raid locks up, cheeks puffing out a bit as he exhales. "I don't wanna answer."

"Why?" Landon scooches closer to him, waggling his brows. "Is it because you're secretly vanilla?"

"Or because you finish in two seconds?" I throw in, unable to fight the urge to pick at him. "Do you cry after sex? Oh, do you—"

"I've never fucked before, alright!" he barks out in frustration. "Now, fuckin' drop it!"

Silence rings out in the room, and my jaw drops in surprise. I mean, it's totally okay to be a virgin. It's really no big deal. People have sex at their own pace, and some people don't need it at all to be happy and fulfilled. I never imagined that Raid was a virgin though. You'd think being my best friend and all, I'd know this about him.

Clearly, he's keeping more from me than I realized.

"Oh." Well, now I feel like a dick. "Sorry, man. I wasn't tryin' to—"

"I've never had sex either," Landon blurts out, cutting me off, scratching the back of his neck nervously. "I don't know."

There's a tense silence between them as they stare at one another, and it feels entirely uncomfortable, like something none of us should be witnessing.

I clear my throat, ready to move the fuck on from this awkward shit. "Silas, truth or dare?"

"Dare." Silas smiles, full of cockiness as he strokes Blaine's hip.

"I dare you to keep your hands off your boyfriend for at least five minutes," I taunt, sticking my tongue out when he growls at me.

"Fuck you," he spits, sliding Blaine off his lap. "Your turn, Bunk. Truth or dare?"

"Truth," I say, opting for the element of surprise. "Hit me."

"How are you and Whaley doin'?"

If Silas thought that would stump me, he was wrong. I'll happily write a whole-ass novel about my man. Hell, I'll walk down the streets singing his name if he'd let me. "Great. He's everythin' I thought he'd be. God, the way he fucks me—"

"That's enough truth," Blaine interjects, letting out a little cough as he chokes on his coke. Then he turns to Landon, a look of determination on his face. "Truth or dare?"

Landon puffs out his chest. "Dare."

"I dare you to kiss Raid."

Yes!

Blaine for the win, baby. I can't resist the show, so I turn completely, basically hovering over Raid's shoulder as I take in Landon's stunned expression.

Raid opens and closes his mouth, not exactly opposed, but confused. "Why?"

"Because he dared you to," Silas throws back. "You gonna streak or you gonna do it?"

Raid shakes his head. "I don't think—"

He's cut off when Landon grabs both his cheeks and plants a fat kiss on his lips. I think it was supposed to be quick, but the way Raid's hands snap up and latch around Landon's neck prevents that from happening. In a split second, they're full-on making out, trying to devour each other's mouths, and the rest of us are left gaping. Landon makes some sort of choked noise and Raid growls—holy shit that's hot.

My eyes sweep to find Blaine and Silas are also staring, slack-jawed as they take them in. Yeah, safe to say none of us were expecting that.

It's a solid minute. I know because I started counting as the time ticked on. Got to fifty-five before they both broke away with a gasp.

"Jesus Christ," I mutter, wishing Whaley was here now more than ever. "I need to fuck after that."

"It was no big deal." Landon chuckles, wiping some of Raid's saliva off the corner of his lip.

"Yeah," Raid mumbles, looking kind of dazed as he grabs his beer. "No big deal."

"You're a great kisser, man," Landon jokes. "Gotta give me some tips."

Raid clenches and unclenches his fists before he gets up, nearly knocking me off the couch in the process. "I gotta go. Be right back."

Blaine frowns. "Where are you going?"

Raid doesn't stop, just leaves the back room in a rush. Blaine looks at Landon, and the jock shrugs, equally perplexed. "Think I should apologize? I didn't really give him a choice. I don't think he liked it."

"Really?" Silas deadpans. "You don't think he liked it? Are you— Ow! Fuck!"

"I'm sure he's fine," Blaine adds quickly, glaring at Silas after elbowing his ribs. "But if you want to apologize, it couldn't hurt."

Landon nods, getting up quickly and following behind Raid. Once it's the three of us, I let it all out. "What is goin' on with them?"

"I..." Blaine starts, shaking his head at me before turning to Silas. "Does Raid like Landon?"

"Well, you saw the proof, baby."

"And Landon doesn't know," I guess, looking in the direction they ran off to. "I mean, he has to now though, right?"

Blaine releases a little wince. "I love Landon, but he doesn't take hints well."

"Raid gave him the biggest hint on the planet. I have no fucking idea how he could miss that."

Blaine shrugs at me. "Do you think Raid will do anything about it?"

Honestly, I have no idea. Raid always keeps everything close to his chest. He's my best friend, but there's still things I don't know about him. He's loyal to a fault, and that's all that's ever mattered. Raid better get his head out of his ass and make a move before it's too late.

I go to tell Blaine that but see Silas has already broken his dare and has his tongue down Blaine's throat. It's cute—the fact that they can't keep their hands off each other—and I'm no longer filled with jealousy at that.

"So, I'm goin' to go," I tell them, scoffing when they ignore me. "Alright, I'll go fuck myself. Have a nice life, Silas."

Silas flips me the finger, never stopping his kiss, but I

know it's all in good fun. Once he's all done fucking Blaine, I'll call him to meet up so we can say a proper goodbye.

I head out of the back room, and nod to various Aces as I go. I already feel the sweat starting to bloom on my neck from the Georgia heat when I'm outside and itch to take off my leather jacket, but I won't. I love my patch and wear it proudly.

I spot Landon and Raid behind the bar when I'm almost to my car, and I pretend I don't see the heated conversation they're having, opting to run as sneakily as possible to my ride. He'll tell me what's going on when he's ready. I'm sure of it. For now, I'll be the supportive friend from a distance and help when I can.

I'm about to reach my car when I hear the shuffling of feet come up behind me. Acting on my instincts, I whirl around quickly, knife out and ready. When I see that it's Gunnar, I relax a little, a wicked smile tipping up my lips. "Gunnar!"

He snarls when he sees me. "Fucker."

"What are you doin' here, friend?" I ask, always taking the chance to fuck with him when I can. "Itchin' for a fight? Oh, *please* tell me you want one."

His fists clench at his sides, anger lacing his expression, but he doesn't make a move. "Where are your friends at?"

"Why the fuck do you wanna know?" I snap. I know that Raid and Landon are still out here somewhere, and while I have no problem getting into a fight with Gunnar, I don't want my friends to be in the crossfire.

He takes a step toward me, reaching into his pocket, but it's at that moment when Raid appears beside me. I don't know where Landon went, but Raid's sole focus is now on the dick in front of us. "The fuck do you want?"

Gunnar stops in his tracks, biting the inside of his cheek as he looks around. "Nothin'. Just comin' to find a fuck."

"You can do that somewhere else," Raid snarls. "Better get

out of here before I bring out Silas. Three against one is an easy score."

"Fuck you," Gunnar spits out. He takes a step back though, his stare penetrating me with a promise of a threat. "You ain't gonna have your friends with you all the time, freak, and I won't always be alone."

"Oooo, keep talkin' dirty to me," I singsong, reveling when he winces at my comment. "It's a date."

Gunnar flips me off before stalking back to his car, and Raid turns to me with a worried expression. "You good, Bunk?"

"That? That was nothin'. Gunnar's all bark and no bite."

"Just be careful around him," he warns, clapping my back. "Won't always be like it was tonight."

I nod, but I'm not worried. I simply shrug and then wag my brows at Raid. "Where's Landon? You fuck yet?"

He narrows his eyes at me. "Fuck you, Bunk. Go home."

Raid walks back to the bar and I get in my car and head straight to Whaley's trailer. I considered earlier whether Badge might know about us, seeing as though I haven't slept steadily in my own bed in over a week. Well, it's not like I necessarily ever had a curfew or any strict rules. Most of the time in the past, I'd crash somewhere else or sleep at the bar, so he's probably not phased in the slightest.

I tighten my hands nervously around the steering wheel. The thought of telling Badge is both exciting and nerve-racking because I have no idea how he's going to react. One would think he'd be happy for me, right? But I remember vividly what Badge is capable of when he's pissed enough. Not that he'd ever kill Whaley, but he's Whaley's right-hand man. I'd hate to be the reason they have a falling out.

I have to tell him soon, don't I? He's my dad after all.

I ignore that pressing thought as I park my car and head into Whaley's trailer. I can worry about Badge later. Maybe Whaley can help me come up with a game plan.

I let myself in with the key he gave me, immediately stripping as I head toward his room. I'm a lot higher than I thought I was, and I nearly float as I stumble against the wall.

But all of my high thoughts vanish when I see Whaley.

He's naked, lying in bed with his sheets draped half over his delicious ass. His tattoos are bright, even in the dark, and the strong muscles of his back call to me. He's sleeping on one side of the bed, arm stretched out to the other side, as if searching for something.

Someone.

I smile like a love-drunk fool and strip the rest of the way before crawling into bed, automatically burrowing myself in his arms. He groans and opens his eyes for a second before rolling over onto his back and tugging me to him, placing a kiss on my bare shoulder. "How'd it go?"

"Good," I whisper, brushing some of his hair away from his face. "Your night?"

"Fine. Missed you, little psycho," he mumbles, eyes closing as he fights sleep.

Yeah, he's half dead to the world right now because I doubt he'd ever admit that in the light of day. I don't taunt him, however, not about this. Instead, I wiggle so that I'm facing him and hook my leg over his hip before pressing a quick kiss to his lips, savoring the tobacco and the mint flavor. "Missed you too."

Then I nestle against him, resting my head against his chest and let the pounding thuds of his heartbeat lull me to sleep.

FIFTEEN

Whaley

It's that time again.

When I drown myself in booze and drugs to keep memories from my past at bay. I don't know how it always manages to sneak up on me, and yet every year, it's always the same. I'm seemingly fine, going through the motions, then everything comes to a screeching halt. It's like my internal clock starts ticking, never letting me forget the worst period of my life.

Usually, I'd take my R&R trip, but I can't do that this year.

I have Bunky now, and as much as I know he'd let me take out every bit of pain and suffering I harbor inside on his body, that's not a side of me I ever want him to see. He likes it rough, likes the bits of pain I give him, but he doesn't know how twisted and fucked-up things get.

My urge and desire for control that I not only crave but need when I'm on this spiral come out to play in the ugliest of ways. There's a reason I used to pay women to satisfy these needs, someone who understood and was well-acquainted with the kind of treatment I wanted to give them. Bunky isn't one of those women and doesn't deserve to be the punching bag for all my pent-up wrath, even if I know he wouldn't mind.

I can't do that to him.

So I'm trying my best to hold it all together, pretending I'm fine, and like things aren't twisting and crumbling inside my head.

Only I'm doing a shit job and everyone can tell. I fucked up two car repairs, and I also ordered an entire list of the wrong parts, and let's not forget about the fact everyone is now walking on eggshells because I flipped out on Pike and Raid for no damn reason.

I haven't slept in a few days because the second I close my eyes, I'm plagued with flashes of blood and screams, and it's making me lose my mind. Realizing there is no way around the fucked-up shit in my head, I send everyone home early. They all agree, but I don't wait to see them go. I need something to take the edge off.

I storm to my office, plopping down in my seat and riffling around in my desk drawer for the provisions. I have them in case the voices in my head become too loud and the ability to hold it all back grows too weak.

Tugging out the bag of coke and unopened bottle of Jack, I set it on my desk, eyeing it with a mix of growing hatred and looming desire. I want to upend the whole bag and snort it all. I want to turn the bottle up and gulp it down like water. Both would be so easy, a little relief, a second away from all of this.

But I hold myself back because I can't let myself dive into these habits.

Bunky. Bunky. Bunky.

Like usual, his name rings through my mind like the beating of a war drum, but even he can't keep the memories at bay. Clenching my fists, I sit back in my chair, palms pressing into my eyes as I count down from ten. That's what most people do when they're in a shit storm, right?

It's not working for me though, of course not. When I start counting, I feel like I'm being sucked into the past more quickly, each number symbolizing shit I'd rather not think about.

Ten... "Charlie, hide. I need you to hide, baby."

Nine... My legs running, sprinting through the house trying to find a spot.

Eight... Crawling. Need to hide.

Seven... Shaking... it's cold in the basement.

Six... "He's over here."

Five... A wail, a punch... both from me.

Four... The bitch is dead.

Three... "Mommy. Mommy, please, wake up."

Two... Blood. So much blood.

One... A gunshot.

I jump from my seat so rapidly that I knock my chair over in the process. My heart's pounding so hard inside my chest, and I fight the urge to vomit. Bile coats my tongue and I start to sweat. I can't... No... I don't want—

"What's your name, kiddo?"

"Charles Whalen."

"Stop!" I yell, sweeping almost everything off my desk in one swoop. The contents scatter to the ground in a crash, but it does nothing to satisfy me.

I'm slipping.

Slipping into the past, slipping into the chaos, slipping into the memories.

Red, blue, red, blue.

"He has no other family."

"Shut up!" My hands cover my ears, trying to block out the noise, wishing away the buzzing that's coursing through my brain.

"He's not doing well in foster care. He's been through eight families already."

"There's only one more option."

I grab the bottle of whiskey that's still on the corner of my desk, chucking it against the wall with everything I have. It shatters into pieces, broken glass scattering around my office.

"Get the fuck outta my head!" Fisting my hair, I crouch, rocking slightly as the world around me begins to fade. The only thing I can focus on is the boy from my past. "Stop!"

"He'll do well there. It's for troubled kids. The ones who don't fit in anywhere. They know how to handle them."

"Don't want to go there! Don't make me!"

"Whaley…"

Someone calls my name, and I want to answer, but my voice is lost amongst the spiraling memories. I try to swallow, but there's a lump in my throat. I try to breathe, but there's a weight on my chest. "Go away."

"Whaley!"

My hands are jerked off my ears and I try to focus through my blurry eyes.

"Whaley," they say again, calmer this time. "You need to breathe. You're freakin' me the fuck out."

That voice. I know that voice.

My vision begins to settle and Bunky becomes my whole world. He's all I can see through the haze, big green eyes staring at me with fear and concern. He looks so young right now, innocent as a lamb that's being soiled by my filth. My tattooed hands that come up to cup his face ruin him. But I can't let him go. His hands latch onto my wrists, and I look at our connection, trying to let his touch ground me back to the reality that's slipping through my fingers.

Bunky. Bunky. Bunky.

"Bunky?" I question, blinking rapidly to clear the tears away. "I… I don't know what happened."

"Whaley." He whispers and I can't make myself hold his

gaze. I'm worried about what I'll show him, scared of what he'll see. "What do you need? How can I help?"

Help?

There's no help for me. I'm way too broken and my mind is too fucked. I can't tell him that. I can't open that door or spill truths that he won't be ready for, that I don't think he'll ever be ready for.

"Can you take me home?" I mutter, still not meeting his eyes. Standing on shaking legs, I fish around in my pocket for my truck keys, dangling them out for him to take.

He hesitates for a moment before grabbing them, and I know he must have a thousand thoughts in that head of his, but I'm grateful he doesn't voice them. He only grabs my arm and maneuvers me out of my office.

The ride to my trailer is full of tension. He may not say shit, but the silent words are practically screaming in the cab between us. I run away from them, snatching the door to the truck and barreling out before he even parks. I hear him curse as he scrambles to catch up with me, but I move quickly, unlocking the door and heading inside with him hot on my heels.

"Whaley—"

"I think you should go home tonight," I blurt, needing him to be as far away from my fucked-up head as possible. I can do this. I can push through. I've done it by myself before, and this won't be any different.

Bunky will leave. He'll be safe. I'll get over this blip in my sanity and everything will be okay when the sun comes up.

His face pinches and he shoots me a glare. "The fuck? Hell no. I ain't leavin'."

"Bunky—"

"You ain't changin' my mind. I don't know what the fuck happened, but I do know that it was serious, and I'm not goin' to leave you alone," he argues as he grabs my hand and starts pulling me toward the back of my trailer. "Now, come on."

"We ain't fuckin'," I tell him seriously. No way I can do that when I'm in this headspace. I'd rip him to shreds and eat up all the pieces, and there'll be nothing left of him when I'm done.

He doesn't sense the danger he's in as he grumbles while opening the bathroom door and pulling me inside. "Didn't say we were. You need to shower, and I'm goin' to help you." I open my mouth to protest but he reaches up, pressing a finger to my lips, eyes softening as he takes me in. "No. Stop. Just let me take care of you."

I want to argue, but how can I when he looks at me with a mix of precious concern and fiery stubbornness? It's like he's reaching deep inside of me, begging me with those fucking eyes, and I can do nothing but cave to his will. I'll do this one thing he wants, then I'm going to send him home so I can chase the memories away on my own.

Nodding, I begin stripping my clothes, ignoring the way his eyes flare and how he bites down on his bottom lip when I'm done.

"Stop it," I growl, trying to stop my dick from taking interest. Only it's fucking Bunky, so he's very much interested in anything he has to offer.

He shrugs, flipping on the water. "Just admirin' the view. It's one of my favorites."

I grumble my way into the shower, wincing when cold water hits me. It takes a second for it to warm up, and when it does, Bunky joins me.

"You sure I can't tempt you?" he whispers, his chest flush against me.

"Stupid little bastard. I'll kill you." She raises her fist, about to hit, and I close my eyes, preparing to feel the—

"I'm sure," I say with a gulp, both to him and to my mind as I dig my hand through my wet hair.

Bunky's hand runs up and down my back. "Hey, Whaley, are you okay?"

No, I'm the furthest thing from okay right now. He really needs to leave before I say or do something I regret. "Bunk, just go."

I can hear him petulantly huff behind me. When he doesn't speak again, I think he might have stepped out, but the soapy hand that starts running up and down my arms tells me otherwise. "Bunky—"

"No sex, I get it," he says, moving in front of me so he can get my chest. "But you smell like a damn bar, so I'll do this instead."

I let him clean me off, something inside me falling into heady complacency as he washes me. Every now and then I glance at him, and it's like he's stuck in a trance. His pierced tongue is poking out as he focuses on my arms, and his eyes are concentrated as he kneels down and washes my thighs. He takes his time, making sure every inch of me is clean before shutting the water off. I get out before him, snatching a towel and heading to my room.

In this momentary state of sanity, I have to make it clear that he's not wanted here tonight. At any moment, it could all come rushing back to me, dragging me down, and taking poor Bunky with me.

I throw him some of my clothes, a T-shirt and a pair of sweats. "Put these on and leave."

"What ain't you gettin'?" he asks, although he does fucking listen to me for once as he starts getting dressed. "I'm not goin' anywhere."

"I already told you we ain't fuckin'." I shove myself into a shirt, nearly tearing the damn thing as my frustration starts to rise.

He scoffs, an annoyed glint in his eyes. "And that's the most important part of our relationship? Me takin' your cock?"

"Shit," I growl, shaking my head. I can feel it getting all blocked up again, the edges starting to fray, the walls I built starting to rattle. "I didn't mean that—"

"Sounded like it. So, what? If none of my holes are filled I'm no use to you, huh?"

"What?" I snap, turning to him as soon as I have my pants on. "What the fuck did you say?"

"You can talk to me," he yells, frustrated, throwing his hands up in the air. "We can *talk*! You know, mouths moving, noises coming out, *communication*."

I can shoulder Bunky's demons for him. I can take all his pain and protect it from ever hurting him, but I can't say the same about Bunky when it comes to mine. They'd take the first chance to eat him alive, going through me to get the job done.

If I told him everything, spilled my truths, then I'd become someone else in his eyes. He would see a side of me that would scare him, and not in the way either of us would like. While I like all the things that we get up to, all the darkness we share, there's a line I don't want to cross.

I don't want him to ever *actually* fear me.

I go to my nightstand and grab a pack of smokes, keeping my back to him as I speak. "Now's not the time to be stubborn. I got a lot of stuff goin' on and I don't want you to be on the receiving end of that. You don't deserve my shit right now."

"Are you fuckin' serious?" he hisses. "That's what I'm here for. I'm here for you any way you need me. You got stuff, Whaley? I want to know about it."

"No, you don't."

"Please stop. I'm sorry. I won't do it again."

"Did you think I wouldn't notice?" my foster mother growls, hand gripping my hair and snatching me out of my chair at the kitchen table, the roll I had tucked under my shirt falling to the

floor. *"Since you don't understand, I'll have to show you a different way."*

Bunky takes hold of my arm, trying to make me see reason, but I'm slipping the more he presses. "Yes, I do."

Why can't he see that I need him to go? Why is he pushing? Why won't he fucking stop?! I need him to stop before it all cracks. Before everything inside my head breaks and I'm no longer in control.

My heart thuds inside my chest as she drags me toward the basement.

"No! Please, I'm sorry. I won't do it again. I'll listen!"

"Too late for that."

I beg and beg but she doesn't relent, dragging me down the stairs that look so much like the ones from my first house.

I don't like the basement. I don't want to be put in that little cage. It's cold and small and… and… and… it's cold…

I'm hungry.

"Charlie, hide. I need you to hide, baby."

"Bunky, I can't. It's what's best—"

He smacks the cigarette out of my hand, lighting every nerve inside my body, and my fight-or-flight instinct takes over. "I don't give a damn about what's best! Tell me—"

But it all swirls to black.

She shoves me into the small confinement under the basement stairs. It's more like a dog cage, and I draw my legs up, rubbing my dripping nose across my knees.

"I'll leave you here to think about your actions. When I say no food, I mean it. Maybe if you start behaving you'll get to keep all your privileges."

"Please, I'm sorry," I whisper brokenly, hoping she'll let me out just this once. "I won't do it again. I'll listen from now on. I promise."

She doesn't say anything else, only shoving my extended hand out the way before slamming the cage door and sliding a lock in place.

I cry for hours, begging her to come back, and she doesn't until my tears are long gone, my body hurts from being smooshed, and my stomach's no longer hungry.

Help me, please. I don't want to be down here anymore. I don't want—

"Charlie, hide. I need you to hide, baby."

"The bitch is dead."

Gunshot.

"What's your name, kiddo?"

Sirens.

"Welcome to your new family."

Hunger.

Cold.

Starving.

Pain.

Pain.

Pain.

"No!" I push my attacker, using too much force and knocking them on the ground. I hover above, chest heaving, fists clenched by my sides. The monster is rattling at the cage, begging me to take everything out on them, sensing that we have our prey exactly where we want them.

Blood. Blood. Blood.

No!

Hurt them.

Stop!

But my pleas mean nothing. I'm not myself anymore. My body is trembling as chaos takes over my mind. All logic and reason fly out the window. My vision turns red and the noise in my head is an ominous pounding.

Who am I now?

Where am I?

It's dark but bright all at once. The noise, the rattling... I can't focus, can't—

They jump to their feet, shoving me right back, but I'm too big to move.

Don't let them touch you.

Something in my blood heats, and I move, crowding them, pinching their cheeks in my hands, so tempted to squeeze until their jaw cracks. I back them up into the wall and they fight me the entire time.

You have to fight. You can't let them win. No more cages. No more dark places. No more beatings. No fucking more!

"You thought you could get away with this forever," I bellow, hands wrapping around their neck and squeezing tightly.

"Whaley!"

Squeeze, smother, suck their life away like they've been doing to you for years.

I squeeze and squeeze, listening to that voice inside my head, basking in the chaos and power that thrums through me.

They will not win. They never will again.

"Whaley, stop! Please!"

An unexpected jab to my face has me blinking rapidly and my hands loosening. *Wait.* This isn't how it's supposed to go. I'm hit one more time, and my eyes begin to focus. I drop my hands completely, taking a step back.

What the fuck is happening?

I'm so confused and lost until that voice rings through my spiraling haze.

"Whaley? What the hell was that?" Bunky coughs and I jerk my gaze to where he's heaving, lips tinged in a frosty color, cheeks so red they almost look purple, and the worst of it all is his eyes, slightly red and confused.

My fingers tremble as he takes in sharp quick breaths before crumbling to the ground.

Oh, God. Was I…? No, no, no…

I'd never hurt him. I need him to know that. I bend down

to help him up with shaking hands. "Why didn't you leave? I told you to leave!"

I do a slow spin, trying to wrap my head around this but I can't. It's all too much. "I could have killed you," I yell, reaching up and fisting my hair. Plopping down on the edge of the bed, I bend forward, resting my elbows on my knees as I try to clear the fog. "Fuck, why didn't you leave?"

He should go. This is exactly what I didn't want to happen. I didn't want him to suffer because I couldn't control myself, but he can't leave now. Fear courses through me at the thought that this could be over, my paranoia all-consuming. What if this is it? What if he leaves me? What if he finally realizes that I'm no good for him? I can't let any of that happen, I can't have a life without Bunky.

If I don't have Bunky, there's nothing left to live for.

"What are you talkin' about? Why would I leave?" he questions, but when I look up at his face, he's still painted with what I've done to him. "It's not a big deal."

"Not a big deal?" I growl, shooting up. "I tried to fuckin' kill you."

"So? It'd be a good way to die," he says, giving me a teasing smirk. "Your crazy is stuck with my crazy, Whaley."

"I didn't mean it. I didn't mean it. I didn't—"

Bunky stops me in my mad rambling when he wraps his arms around my waist. "Whaley, relax. I'm okay."

"I'm so sorry, Bunky. I would never hurt you like that. I couldn't stop it from happenin'. Jesus Christ, I'd rather kill myself than ever harm you in a way you didn't want." I find the strength to bring him against my chest, my hands still trembling with the itch to kill, something that brings shame to my gut. "It just took control."

He looks up at me with confusion. "What took control?"

"There are things you don't know about me…" I start, trying to use his fucking scent to keep everything at bay. "Dark things. Things I never wanted you to know."

"I can handle dark," he tells me, and it sounds so similar to what I once told him. "Whaley. I'm right here, let me help you."

I shake my head, wanting to press my fists into my eyes to stop these fucking tears. "You won't leave?"

"Never," he says, stroking the side of my face.

"It's so fucked, Bunk."

"I don't care." He kisses me, hands rubbing my shoulder comfortingly. "I don't care if it's fucked or not. All I care about is you."

My reasons for keeping my past to myself begin to crumble with every kiss to my face and every touch of his hand. My selfish soul wants to share this pain with someone, make them feel the burden of suffering, and Bunky's offering himself right up.

"Are you sure you want to know?" I question, my fingers gripping his hips as I try to ground myself further.

He moves me to the bed, sitting beside me, his face serious as he nods. "Tell me."

I sigh, leaning forward and cupping my hands together between my spread thighs, not wanting to look at him as I tell the story of my past, hoping he'll still be here when I'm done.

SIXTEEN

Whaley

"We are the same in a lot of ways, you and me," I start, thinking about the boy I used to be. "My mother was obsessed with the idea of love. She was so easily manipulated that nothin' mattered but finding the right one. Always glidin' from one guy to the next like a revolvin' door." I pause, thinking about that time and all the men she was with. Some tall, some fat, some nice, some… "She never seemed to have a type, hopped on the first one to give her that attention she was seekin'. They'd date, he'd eventually leave, and the cycle would start over again."

Bunky doesn't say anything and I'm grateful for his silence because I don't think I'd be able to do this if he did.

"It all changed when I was seven. She met someone that she thought would change our world." A little laugh bubbles from my throat as I picture the scene perfectly. Her long brown hair braided, face full of makeup, and the blue flower dress she was wearing as she sat me down to tell me all about Pat. *He's the best, Charlie. He's going to make it all better for us, baby.* Little did she know that he was a wolf in sheep's skin. I do my best to push through the memory. "Pat was fine until he wasn't. It was little things at first, like he'd make her change her clothes, or pick what food she ate. That quickly turned to isolating her and controlling who she saw and what she did. Then it got even worse."

I sigh, remembering the first time he hit her. We were sitting on the couch watching a movie and he didn't like the choice of film. He told her to change it to some wrestling thing, but she didn't want to scare me.

"Don't you think that's too rough for Charlie?" She reaches over, rubbing my head. "I think maybe—"

Pop.

Her head snaps to the side and her eyes widen as she cups her cheek.

My stomach feels sick as I scoot back into the couch.

"Do as you're told."

"He was an abusive piece of shit. Hittin' her for no reason, lockin' her in her room." I shake my head. "I remember the first time he hit *me*. She went out of her mind. I thought for sure he'd kill her then, but he only managed to break a few ribs and blacken her face." I felt helpless as I watched her jump to my aid, and then felt like a waste when I did nothing to help her as he beat her.

"Whaley—"

"She wanted to leave him, had it all planned out. He was workin' nights at this paper company and wouldn't be back until the followin' morning." I can see it all vividly. My black and red *Mickey Mouse* suitcase lying on my bed filled with my clothes, and how fast she moved as she tossed some of her things into a bag. We were so close. "Pat came home early though. Apparently, he was fired for showin' up drunk. He stumbled through the front door with one of his buddies and caught us in the living room with our bags."

"Where the fuck do you think you're going?"

"Oh, nowhere." Mom scrambles, hand reaching out to run through my hair. *"Charlie wanted to stay the night with his friend."*

What friend?

"So why do you need a bag too?" he questions, taking a step toward her, and she steps back, pulling me along.

"I remember the first blow to her face. How it sounded, the way she crumbled to the floor."

She whines, clutching her face as he drags her up by her hair.

"Did you think you could leave me?"

He hits her more before dropping her to the ground again. She comes up on her knees, hands grabbing my shoulders as she looks into my eyes with so much sadness. "Charlie, hide. I need you to hide, baby."

"I didn't hesitate. I ran. Left my mother there with that... monster."

"You were a child," Bunky interjects, hand coming to squeeze my shoulder soothingly. "You were scared."

"I should have done somethin'. Anythin'. Ran out the back door of the house, went and got the neighbor, used their phone to call the police. Instead, I went to the basement and hid while he was drainin' her life away." I shudder, reaching up and fisting my hair. "I don't know how long I was down there. I just know it was cold and my stomach hurt by the time they came for me."

"He's over here." Pat's friend grabs me, draggin' me from my hidin' spot.

"Don't touch me!" I wail, kicking, screaming, trying to get him off.

"Pat didn't know what to do with me, I think. That's the only explanation I have for why he didn't kill me. After I was dragged back upstairs, he locked me in the room with my mom. I crawled to her, the feelin' of relief at bein' near her again until I realized she wasn't breathin'."

"Mommy. Mommy, please, wake up." My lip wobbles as I shake and shake and shake her.

Blood. Why is there so much blood?

"I don't know how much time passed. It was long enough for her body to grow cold and pale. For my stomach hunger to turn into brutal starvation before I wasn't hungry at all."

Twinkle, twinkle, little star. How I wonder what you are...

It's nighttime again. How many nights is that now?

I don't leave the room. Only huddling against the wall, near the window.

I can hear Pat in the living room but he never bothers me. The door only rattled once before the person on the other side gave up.

He must have forgotten I was here.

Will I die here too?

I'm tired. Ready to sleep. Maybe if I close my eyes, all this pain will go away.

Bang! Bang! Bang!

I'm jostled from my sleep, eyes bouncing around the room as the wood is kicked in. I scream, hands pressing to my ears as I block out the sound.

Twinkle, twinkle, little star.

"Hey, kiddo. You okay?"

"The cops showed up. Apparently, my mom's boss reported her missing after she didn't show up for several days. The police stopped by to do a well-check and you can guess the rest." Bunky's hand squeezes harder, and I feel the bed shift as he scoots closer toward me. "The police were nice though. I remember being so grateful that I didn't die there too."

"Fuck, Whaley. I'm sorry. That's terrible."

I turn to look at him, taking in his flushed cheeks and sad eyes. "That's only the start of it all."

"The start?" His brows lift as he shakes his head in confusion. "What do you mean?"

I inhale deeply, trying to think of where to begin. "I was placed in foster care for a while, the families there were nice but I struggled to fit in. I was really messed up after everythin' with my mom and no one wanted to deal with the emotionally fucked-up mess that I was. After bein' bounced around to several homes, I was placed in a group home."

"Ready to meet your new family?"

"Mrs. Simmons was nice on paper, known as the fixer for broken children with a laundry list of issues. I remember when my social worker walked me inside her home for the first time, how clean it looked." No, not clean, fake, like it was plucked straight from a magazine. "Even the children that were there seemed great. All smiled and welcomed me easily. That was all face value. I could sense it even then. Could see the things the kids weren't sayin'..."

"And what was that?"

"They were scared." It was so clear that I really don't understand how the social worker didn't see through the facade or the haunting looks in the kids' eyes.

"Fuck, Whaley," he growls. "She hurt you?"

"A lot and all the time. She had these rules and crazy chore charts. She would time you on stuff like moppin', laundry, and cleanin' out the dog crate. If you went over the time, you'd be punished. If you didn't complete a task, you'd be punished."

My throat works as I think about the cage in the basement. As I think about all the meals I never had. All the beatings and smacks for not moving fast enough when my name was called.

"She'd time our showers. Five minutes, or it'd make the bill too high." I can practically see her standing there outside the bathroom with a stopwatch, beating down the door if we were even a second over. "If we went over five minutes, the rest of our showers for the week were cold. No heat as a punishment."

"Maybe a week in the cold will jog your memory next time."

"God, and the food. She used food as the biggest punishment of all. Starvin' us for days until we would do anythin' for a slice of bread." *"You didn't finish your homework and got a C? I don't allow Cs in this household. No dinner for the night."* "The bad thing is she'd make us sit at the table even if we weren't eatin' that day, wantin' us to watch."

"What the fuck?" Bunky barks, hand sliding from my shoulder to my forearm. "I want to kill this bitch. Please tell me she's locked up."

"That is only the tip of the iceberg. The cold showers and starvin' nights…"

"What do you think you're doing?"

I hold the food close to my chest, trembling with how weak I am. "I'm so hungry. Please."

She stares at me, her icy glare chilling my spine. "Let me show you what happens to boys that don't listen."

And it's all a blur from there.

The whip. The blood. The pain.

I need to make it stop. I can't take it anymore. It's too much.

"Stop!"

"She whipped you?" he asks, breathless with disbelief.

"I snapped after that. It's all kind of a haze. I had just turned ten, been dealing with this shit for almost three years and I was done." I don't know what came over me. Don't remember the initial switch being flipped. I remember coming to, hands covered in blood as I stood over her mutilated body. "When I think back on it, it's as if I'm watchin' it through a camera, like I was there for it but I wasn't the one in control. One moment, I was bein' hit, and the next, I just… I came to clutching the knife, standin' over her body in the kitchen."

"Whaley, that was not your fault. That bitch had it comin'. You responded in a way that anyone would after bein' pushed too far."

I smirk, throwing him a look despite the war raging inside me. I stabbed someone to death and here Bunky is making excuses for it. "Your outlook on me has you blind."

He huffs and reaches out to cup my cheek, and I close my

eyes, soaking in his warmth. "You did what you had to in a shitty situation. I know you, you wouldn't have done that had she not had it comin', and from what you're describin', she did. Wish I could bring her back and kill her myself."

I grab his hand, giving his wrist a kiss, taking a moment to breathe before jumping back into the past.

"There was another abused boy standin' in the corner of the kitchen, watchin' me with huge eyes."

Bunky's eyes widen and his jaw drops at that. "Oh shit. Did he call the police?"

"Charles, you have to run. Run far away and hide. The police will be lookin' for you." He shoves a bag into my hand full of items that aren't mine. Clothes, a flashlight, money.

"Why are you trying to help me?"

He gives me a sad smile. "Because you just saved all of our lives."

"No, he helped me. Thanked me even. Let me get a head start before calling the police."

"Oh wow. I wasn't expectin' that," Bunky mutters in surprise. "That was nice."

I laugh, shaking my head. "It was more than that. He saved me too. Who knows where I'd have ended up had I not run away." I think about those other kids often and wish I'd done more to keep up with them. Maybe one day I can find that boy and thank him.

"What happened next?"

I lift my shoulder in a half shrug. "I was homeless. On the run being a kid, I learned quickly that I had to blend in so people wouldn't notice me."

"What do you mean?"

"A good samaritan sees a kid on the side of the road, what's the first thing they do?"

His eyes shift to knowing and he nods in understanding. "They call the cops."

"They call the cops…" I confirm. I can see myself in

tattered clothes, covered in dirt, digging around the back of a fast food's garbage can, practically starving. "They always thought they were tryin' to help and I don't blame them. It just wasn't what I needed. I kept to the shadows, hidin' in alleyways, avoiding people. I sometimes ran into other homeless people but they were all fine."

I wasn't though. I was dying. I was withering away one passing day at a time, but anything was better than being locked in that prison of a home.

"I didn't think I would survive until the leader of the Aces branch in Vegas found me." Almost dead, unresponsive, and in their territory.

Bunky's eyes light up as everything clicks into place. "And that's how you became an Aces?"

"Hinge, the leader, took me under his wing. He was basically my Badge. The dad I always wanted." I say, recalling those days fondly. "He raised me. Taught me everything I know, helped me grow into the person I am today. It's how I became the head of the Aces so young."

"Well, what happened?"

"This branch needed help and Hinge sent me," I tell him. "I worked hard and proved myself over the years. I learned a lot from Badge during that time. He was supposed to be the next in line here after the other leader died here, but he didn't want it. So he entrusted me with the position instead."

"That's impressive," he says, a proud smile on his face.

"It was hard work. I poured my blood, sweat, and tears into this gang, but just because I grew and learned doesn't mean the demon went away."

"I get that." He snags my hand once more. "Mine's not goin' away either."

I nod. "I turned to fightin', which you already know. Drugs, partyin', all kinda like you did. Hinge set me straight before I came here, told me I needed another outlet. So I buried that shit because I couldn't think of anythin' else to do."

"That ain't workin' now," he points out.

"No, it's not." My brows furrow and I shake my head. "You think I'm so great? I'm just tryin' to make up for all the shit I've done in my past, lead by the example that was set for me, but I'm weak, Bunk. Sometimes I need more."

He leans in closer, resting his head on my shoulder, thumb stroking across my hand. "So, what do you need now?"

I feel vulnerable, weak, so small while Bunky comforts me. This is the opposite of how we usually work, and while it's really hard to relinquish all my control, I'll admit it's nice to be able to fall into him and let my inhibitions down for once.

I think about everything I've gone through. I think about the way I used to cope. None of those things can help me now. The pain is too much, it's all too much, and I need something to make it all go away. I need Bunky.

I bury myself in his arms, breathing him in. I lucked out with this one. He's here for me, he loves me, and I think he's the key to all of this. I don't know if what I want is the healthiest way to deal with this but fuck that. We've never claimed to be perfect, never said we weren't destined to be fucked-up together. So, I'm going to take everything he's offering. If he can give me a reprieve, I won't let that go.

"My little psycho," I whisper, kissing the parts of his arm I can reach. "Take the pain away."

SEVENTEEN

Bunky

I hold him in my trembling arms, because I didn't see this coming. Whaley is always so strong, so daunting, so unbreakable, but he feels fragile right now. Telling me about his past must have been hard, impossible even, but my heart warms at the level of trust he's given me.

I'll hold his secret in my hands, keeping it close to my chest where it's safe and treasured, away from all of those who would look to exploit it.

My soul calls to his. We're both fucked-up for similar reasons, no chance of redemption, not that we're asking for it. Everything about our past twines together to form a beautifully twisted web. He and I are the same.

"What do you need?" I ask, brushing his hair away from his face, seeing the turmoil and pain in his dark gaze.

He closes his eyes, pressing his forehead against mine as his hands wander down my body. "My little psycho..."

My heart does a happy flip at his admission.

That's all I need to hear.

I push him gently until he's lying on his back. It's my turn to take care of him, like he's taken care of me.

"How do you want me?" I question, slinking up his body, pressing my chest against his as I peck his nose. "How do you need it?"

"I need to hurt you," he manages through gritted teeth, looking like he's holding himself back. I glance at his knuckles and see that they've turned white with how hard he's clenching his fists. "I need to make you bleed."

I nod. I'll do whatever and be whatever he needs me to be. I'll be his willing victim. I'll be his solace.

I'll be the outlet for all his wickedness.

I'll give him everything—

Including my soul.

I strip wordlessly, tossing my clothes over my back until I'm completely naked before hopping off the bed and standing there, waiting for him to make a move. He rises slowly before circling me, like he's stalking his prey. Like I'm a baby deer standing in the face of a mountain lion that wants to eat me alive.

"You're such a beautiful psycho," he murmurs, stopping in front of me to run a finger down my chest. "Tell me what's in that head of yours."

He doesn't have to say what type of thoughts he wants to hear. It's written in his hungry, lust-filled eyes. "I want to feel weak."

He hums, moving his fingers down to my belly button. "Why?"

"So you can feel strong." I let out a shuddering breath when he reaches behind me and strokes my ass. "I want to feel like your victim."

"Why?" he asks again, this time dragging that same finger through my crease.

I stare him dead in the eyes, my heart skipping a beat as I

hesitantly raise my hand and place them on his chest. "So you can be my monster."

He lets out a choked moan, gripping me and spinning me around so my back is pressed against his front. The rough friction of his clothes scratching against my bare skin is enough to have my toes curling. He holds my throat roughly, owning me, and he squeezes hard until I struggle for air. "You better be sure about what you just said," he whispers slowly, the threat evident in his voice. "You want me to be your monster? I'll fuckin' eat you alive."

"Do it," I beg, tears springing in my eyes from the pressure of his hand and my own overwhelming emotions. "I only exist for you."

He chuckles darkly by my ear. "That's too much power for a man like me."

"It's true," I insist, grinding my ass against his jean-covered cock. "Lemme make it better. Lemme take your pain. Gimme all of it."

"Every single bit?" His voice trembles as he waits for me to answer.

"Everythin' you have," I choke out when his hand tightens a little more.

He looks almost angry as he takes my balls in his hand and gives them a harsh squeeze, the slight sting of pain making me jolt. "You're playin' with fire, Bunk. You wanna get burned that badly?"

"I love you enough to fuckin' die for you."

Silence meets my confession. I mean, is it really out of the realm of possibility to hear that? He has to know how consumed I am with him and has to know it's more than simple *like*.

Obsession bloomed inside me and sprouted love in its wake.

He doesn't respond with words. Instead, he turns me again, backing me up until my knees hit the edge of the bed. I fall willingly, watching as he towers over me and begins to strip. I'm mesmerized by the sight of all the tattoos covering his broad chest. There's so much I want to do. I want to play, take my time, make him feel every ounce of my love for him, but that's not what he needs.

"What are you goin' to do?" My breaths are coming out in choppy little bursts, filled with anticipation.

"I'm goin' to make you wish you never offered yourself to me," he says, something dark in his eyes that I've never seen before. "Stay right there."

I nod, and he walks over to his closet, digging through it until he comes back with a large box. He sets it on the bed, using a keypad to unlock it before showing me what's inside.

My blood sings when he pulls out a long thread of red rope and a—

Holy shit, is that a whip?

"Turn over," he demands, wrapping one end of the rope around his hand. "Get your ass in the air."

I turn immediately, getting on all fours, a gasp escaping me when I feel the rope being tied around my legs, locking them together. From the corner of my eye, I see him take out another rope before he walks up to my front and seizes my wrists. He ties them together too, using the end and hooking it to his bed frame.

I shiver when he takes the whip and runs it down my back, the teasing edge making me moan.

"What's your word?" he asks, voice down an octave and a growl in his tone. "I won't stop unless you say it."

"A–Alfredo," I stutter as I test how tight the ropes are, growing pleased when I see they don't have any give. I look over my shoulder and find his chest heaving, his fists clenched at his sides, and a feral gleam in his eyes. "Give me all of it. I can take it for you."

"This ain't a regular whip. It won't leave any scars or long-term damage, but it's gonna hurt." He slaps the whip against his hand, and the sound has me jolting forward on instinct. "I'm doin' this because I care about you, because you want me to. If at any point you want to stop, say the word and it ends."

I shake my head. I'm going to love every second of this. Pain is something I crave, but I crave helping him even more. There's nothing I wouldn't take for him. "You can start now." I close my eyes, taking steady deep breaths, but I'm not prepared when he brings the whip down on my ass.

I *scream*.

"You like that, huh?" he taunts, hitting me again with the whip, the frayed edges stinging my skin. "Such a fuckin' slut, moaning like a whore for it."

"Yes!" I cry out, screaming again when the whip comes down on my back. "Please! More!"

He chuckles, almost mockingly, whipping me again, but on the backs of my thighs this time. It hurts so much more than the other places, yet it makes my poor cock drip onto the bedspread.

"You look so beautiful like this," he growls, running his hand down my hot skin as the sound of the whip being tossed aside reverberates around us. "You're doin' this because you love me?"

"More than anythin'." I crane my head as much as I can so he can see the look in my eyes. "More than life." He takes the lube, uncapping it and pouring some onto three of his fingers before shoving them into me. I gasp at the thick intrusion but wiggle my hips to chase more. "Add another one. Gimme your whole fist. Do it."

He smacks my ass with his free hand, making me lurch forward. "You don't get to tell me what the fuck to do. You're a toy right now, my tight cocksleeve, and I'll do whatever the fuck I want to you. You'll take it, won't you? You'll let me destroy you?"

As long as you're there to put me back together again.

I moan loudly when he plunges his cock in all at once. He doesn't take it easy on me, pressing his hand against the back of my neck, cutting off my airwaves as he gives my ass everything he's got. He's grunting, growling, groaning; mumbled degradations leaving his lips as I lay there and take it.

"You fuck me so good," I pant, spurring him on and crying out when he slaps my ass again. "Yes! Bruise me. Show me you want me."

"I more than want you," he groans, hitting me again and again until my skin is white-hot and a mess of raw nerves. "I want to consume you, want me in every part of you, want you to be nothin' without me."

I nod because I'm already there. I'm completely lost without him. You can't untangle me from him any more than you can drain me of my blood and keep me alive. The pain, the feeling of him inside me, the way he's simultaneously hurting and giving me the best experience of my life is perfection.

He covers me with his body, every thrust moving me and making the ropes dig deeper into my skin. "Wanna hear somethin' fucked-up?"

I smile manically, a crazed laugh leaving my lips. "Always."

"I like chokin' you," he confesses, biting down on my ear. "I didn't mean to hurt you before, but fuck, I want my hands wrapped around your throat. I want to take your breath away. I want purple, finger-shaped marks around your neck."

"Do it," I beg, knowing that I'd die happily if it were by Whaley's hand. "Fuckin' hurt me. I love you so much. I wanna die for you."

Something happens at that moment. It's like he's overcome by the monster he tries to hide. Everything becomes more passionate, more brutal, more primal. He's panting behind me, animalistic growls leaving his lips, and I feel possessed by him. "I own you, Bunk," he breathes against my ear, biting down on the skin again until I cry out in delicious pain. "This ass, your heart, every part of you belongs to me, and it always fucking will."

He pulls out and quickly unties me, making sure to bite the back of my thighs where the rope was, giving the same treatment to my sore wrists.

"Whaley?" I arch a confused brow.

"Get on your fucking back," he demands, slapping my ass roughly.

"Why?"

"I'm gonna show you, Bunk." When I don't move, still confused by what he wants, he moves me himself. He practically tosses me onto my back. "Just like you want."

He takes my leg, hitching it up around his waist, and I throw my head back with a cry when he slams into me in one sharp go. I hold onto his shoulders as he takes me on the ride of my life, all while snarling dirty promises against my lips.

"You fuckin' love me?" he roars, one hand migrating to wrap around my neck. "You love this?"

I can barely breathe with the pressure he's putting on my throat once more, but I still manage to speak. "Yes, harder, more!"

Like a wild beast, he uses his other hand and pulls me to meet every one of his brutal thrusts. "You'll die before you leave me. I'll chase you to Hell to keep you with me. You're my every thought and my every desire. You're *mine*, little psycho."

"All yours," I agree, coughing as my vision starts to blur. "Whaley…"

He releases my throat quickly but cups my cheeks between his hands. "Tell me more. I wanna hear it."

"You're the love of my life," I mumble, feeling the tears in my eyes. I won't cry, I refuse to, but I'm so overcome with emotion that I can't help it. "I was made for you. Your strength, your kindness, your loyalty. The way you take care of me. The way you say my name. I'll always belong to you."

"Bunky, fuck," he snarls, hands dragging down to my shoulders, his nails leaving violent marks on my skin. "Every breath I take is you. You've consumed me. Gonna show you just how much."

His confession makes me snap but in a good way. I bury my face in his neck as he fucks me like he can't control how much he wants me.

"Gonna come inside you," he tells me, holding onto my leg, hitching it higher up his waist. "Gonna show you…"

"Show me what?" I gasp when the new angle makes my cock brush up against his stomach.

"Gonna show you…" he repeats, and I feel it when his cock swells while he unloads inside me. Before I can come, because I'm so fucking close even untouched, he pulls out and lays me on my back.

He leaves kisses down my chest, stopping to give little licks to my nipples before exploring me further. My eyes widen when he takes my cock in his mouth, staring up at me the entire time. It's desperate, hungry, like he's going to die if he doesn't taste my cum. When he roughly toys with my hole, entering me so he can play with his cum, I can't take it anymore.

"I'm gonna…"

He pulls off, heated eyes blazing as he nods. "Do it. Let me have a part of you inside of me. Let me taste how much you love me."

So I give him everything I have. Every ounce of my soul, every bit of my obsession. Once I'm done, so out of breath from the intensity of our… Can you call it lovemaking? It must have been, just Whaley's own way of showing it. He brings my legs over his shoulder and licks his cum out of me. I can feel the way he swallows, and he's greedy as he takes all of him from me. As soon as he's done, he slides up my body, his cum mixed with mine on his lips, and kisses me deeply.

"What just happened?" I ask once we break apart.

He chuckles softly, hands squeezing my sides. "I showed you."

Then he takes care of me, rubbing some lotion on my back, soothing away the lingering sting. We fall asleep quickly after that, holding each other, sticky skin meeting sticky skin with the smell of us in the air.

I wake up later that night and sit on his cock, and he lets me ride him. He stares up at me the entire time in wonder, teasingly flicking my nipples and lazily stroking my cock. I rock my hips with sensual movements, keeping everything slow and meaningful, trying to convey what I feel.

"Can you tell?" I'm on the cusp of shattering, but I need to know he understands. "Whaley, tell me you know."

Know how much I love you. Know how much I want you. Know how much I need you.

He sits up, bracing a hand on my back as he urges me on, his mouth enveloping my nipple where he plays with my piercing. Then he lets go with a pop, his eyes smoldering darkness as he nods. "I do."

When I come again, it's with his name on my lips, and when he comes again, it's with a whispered 'little psycho,' the words meaning so much more now. I tell him I love him again and again, but he stays silent. He pulls me closer, nuzzling his nose against the top of my head, and that's enough. He might not have said the words back, told me he loved me, but I know he feels it too.

Even if he might not believe it.

EIGHTEEN

Whaley

I strum my fingers on my desk, trying to focus on the numerous invoices in front of me. With the roller-coaster that was the last few days, and with how I've been drowning myself in Bunky, I've let too much get away from me. I'm taking an admin day to do bills, balance, and make sure shit is running the way it's supposed to.

Well, that's what the plan was anyway, but my brain does not want to focus on the pressing issues. It keeps going back to last night, how he let me handle him, take over his whole body. *Own him.* Then more specifically, the confession Bunky made.

I love you enough to fuckin' die for you.

Does he really feel that way? Things were really heavy last night. It could be that he let himself get carried away. That's all it was, right?

Though deep down in my gut, I know that's not the case. Bunky may never be rational or think before he acts, but he doesn't lie and he doesn't spout bullshit for the sake of it—

heat of the moment or not. That's probably one of my favorite things about him.

He's real.

He doesn't sugarcoat or keep his words to himself. If he wants something, he gets it, and if he feels something, he expresses it. All those myriad of emotions within him come to the surface for everyone to see.

It's a problem though because his bomb drop about his feelings means I'm once again unable to concentrate on the work that needs to get done. He's dug his way into my skull, making himself my sole focus. He's rattling away in there, demanding my attention, his words on a fucking loop in my head.

Nope. I can't let that happen today. I refuse. I need to push through and work on all my stuff, then take out my frustrations on his tight ass later.

Which works for about five minutes.

I love you enough to fuckin' die for you.

"Goddamn it." I slam my fist down on my desk, annoyance filling me. "Stop fuckin' goin' off topic and focus."

"Well, I was comin' to ask how the invoices were goin' but I'm guessin' not well?"

I look up, spotting Badge leaning against the doorframe of my office. His arms are crossed, brows pinched together as he looks me over.

"Yeah, it's goin' like shit," I grumble, about ready to fight myself. "I can't concentrate."

"Noticed you've been strugglin' with that quite a bit lately." He comes inside, plopping down on the chair across from me. "Somethin' on your mind?"

"You could say that."

He hums thoughtfully, fingers running through his beard as he waits for me to continue, but after a few moments, he must realize I'm not saying shit because he presses a little. "Care to share?"

I sigh, lifting a shoulder. "Don't really have nothin' to say."

That's a lie, a big fucking one, and with the way his eyes narrow a little, he knows it too. He won't call me out on it though. That's not who he is. He'll sit here and stare as he waits for me to either change the subject or come clean about whatever's on my mind. His gaze is laser-focused, thick arms folded across his chest, displaying all his tattoos. My eyes trail over them, pausing at the Kings of Aces skull on his forearm, and I'm slammed with guilt over what I've been keeping from him.

It's like all the shit from the past week, everything I've been hiding for months is bubbling up, threatening to spill over. No, fuck that, it's about to explode—combust and blast everything nearby.

I'm not impulsive. I'm calculated. Always. I never jump the gun, choosing to keep my wits about me. It's something I've spent years working on, training myself to be the best leader I can, knowing that's what everyone needs from me.

That was until Bunky, and now I'm doing dumb shit.

Like…

"I'm fuckin' Bunky."

…That.

Badge doesn't react at first. It's like the words I just vomited are still lingering in the air, not making it to his ears because he does *nothing*.

I look down at my desk, trying to figure out what to say. My brain, mouth, and heart are feeling all kinds of fucked-up. Why the hell did I blurt it out like that? Why am I acting like I've got no sense of self-control?

This is stupid. I'm acting like a dumbass, but I can't seem to stop.

"I mean, it's not only fuckin'," I start, trying to gather my words. "It started that way, but it's not now. It's become so much more than that and—"

Pop.

My face blooms in pain and the next second I'm falling, my chair flipping backwards, all the air is knocked from my lungs as I hit the ground with a thud.

Stars explode in my vision and I'm left in limbo for a solid ten seconds as I gasp for my next breath. Oh fuck, it feels like I'm going to die, but then sweet air rushes through me and my stunned lungs kick back on. I inhale on a gasp, sputtering and coughing as the pain radiates from my chest. It's been a long time since someone's hit me, let alone knocked the wind out of me, and I'm kicking myself for letting my guard down. I should have expected Badge would flip, hell, I did, but I still looked away from him anyway.

I blink, jaw pulsing as I stare up at Badge. He's standing over me, chest heaving, jaw clenched, fists balled at his sides, and eyes filled with murder.

Yeah, I really shouldn't have let my guard down.

It takes me too long to get up, but I do, all the while never taking my eyes off Badge. He doesn't do anything else though. He just stands there, drilling me with his hate as he waits for me to right myself.

"Whaley." The way he says my name is like nothing I've ever heard from him before. It's kind of a growl, but not in anger, more like betrayal, and that shit guts me. I never wanted it to be like this. I knew it would come down to this and that's why I've been avoiding this conversation.

"Yeah?" I prepare for another punch, knowing he needs to get it out before we can hopefully move on.

"I feel like I could kill you right now," he bites out sharply. "Strangle you with my bare fuckin' hands."

"I know," is all I can say.

I'm willing to be his punching bag as long as we come to the consensus that Bunky is mine. I feel like shit over hiding things from Badge, but I don't feel bad about it being Bunky.

I can't find it in me. That little shit means too much, and if Badge tries to take him away, we're going to have a problem.

He lets out a humorless laugh, shaking his head before looking at me with disgust. "Out of all the fuckin' people…"

"I know."

"It's my fuckin' kid!" His fist slams against his chest as he takes a small step toward me.

I don't retreat, holding my stance and his gaze, letting him know I'm not cowering. "I know."

"Can you say somethin' else?" he spits out. "How the fuck did this happen? For how long?"

How long? That's a loaded question. I'm not even sure how long it's been myself. Should I count the first time we fucked during the bonfire party? Or do I start from a few weeks ago when I finally claimed Bunky as mine? Or maybe it's deeper than that and we've been together since my mind decided he was my perfect match.

"Whaley!" Badge snaps, making me realize once again that my brain was spiraling.

Pull your shit together.

"I don't know how to answer that," I say truthfully. "It's been a while, I guess."

"You guess?" He huffs, shaking his head as he paces in front of me. "So Bunky is so damn unimportant, you don't even know when everythin' started?"

Now that pisses me off. I can handle anything he wants to throw at me, but trying to say I don't care about Bunky crosses a damn line.

"Bunky's the most fuckin' important person in my life," I snap back, unable to control myself. "Don't go spewin' bull-shit because you're angry. You wanna hit me? Fine. Go for it. I'll happily take every blow, but I ain't gonna let you stand there and say shit you know nothin' about."

He scoffs. "I know nothin' about it because you've kept it

a secret. You knew it was fucked or else you would have told me about it already."

He's not wrong. That's how it started, but after a while, that changed. It had to or I ran the risk of losing Bunky, and that wasn't going to happen.

"Well, I'm tellin' you now."

He inhales deeply, looking up at the ceiling as if he'll find the answers there before looking back at me. "What a fuckin' way to drop that bomb, Whaley." He reaches up, brushing his fallen hair back. "I mean, you announce that you're fuckin' my kid but don't elaborate. Don't say shit else. What am I supposed to think?"

"I was tryin' to tell you all of it before you clocked me in the jaw."

"Yeah, well, you had that shit comin'. I mean, what the hell? I can't believe you did that. God, I still want to fuckin' beat you to death."

He doesn't seem as mad now, which is good, but my guard is still up. I'm not lying. I'll let him whoop my ass if it's what he needs, but I'd rather be prepared for it this time.

"Well, let me explain it all first, then if you still wanna hit me, I'll let you."

This makes him laugh maniacally. "You better be prepared to get your ass beat then. I can't imagine there's anythin' you could say that will stop me from knocking your teeth out."

I fix my chair, gesturing for Badge to sit as well while I try to come up with what to say to give justice to what's been happening between Bunky and me.

"I care about him…" I start, biting my bottom lip as my mind races. "It began months ago. We hooked up one night—"

Badge waves a hand through the air and nails me with a glare. "Spare me those details. I don't wanna know that shit."

I narrow my eyes, annoyed that he thought I would. "Give me a little credit, I wasn't gonna tell you specifics."

"Thank fuck," he grumbles, running his hand down his face. "I wanna know, but I don't *want* to know."

"So yeah, it started with a one-off. Didn't mean anything—"

"This is supposed to stop me from wantin' to beat your ass?" He looks appalled, and his fists tighten at his sides.

"Stop fuckin' interruptin'," I growl, growing impatient. Badge or not, Bunky or not, he's got to let me fucking speak. "I'm tryin' to explain' but you ain't lettin' me."

"You're doin' a real shit job at gettin' to the damn point." His hand comes down to smack my desk as his irritation rises.

"Oh, for fuck's sake. Badge, I care about Bunky, alright? A whole fuckin' lot. I won't lie, this shit was not expected, and it wasn't what I wanted either. I'm not a romance guy. Not one to do relationships, you know this about me. I'll bet it's the main reason you want to tear my head off right now, but with Bunky it's different. I can't explain it. There aren't words. We're a beautiful fucking disaster waitin' to happen, I know it. I know it and yet I can't find it in me to stop what we've started. I won't."

I pause, trying to explain this the best way I know how. "It's like the chaos, the bullshit, every bad thing that makes us who we are just fits together somehow. Like all his frayed edges match my jagged ones so seamlessly. He's like my imperfect perfect missing piece. I know it doesn't make sense, and I don't expect you to understand, but it's the truth. He's dug himself beneath all my layers, forced his way in, and now that I know what it's like to have him, I'm never gonna let him go."

Badge is staring at me, brows pinched and mouth turned down. Okay, maybe I shouldn't have said the last part, but I need him to know how serious this is for me. How 'mine' Bunky is and that no one is taking him away. "I know it sounds crazy—"

He cuts me off, shaking his head in disbelief. "It sounds like fuckin' doomsday, and very unhealthy, which isn't somethin' I want for Bunky."

"Respectfully, it doesn't matter what you want."

"Considerin' he's my fuckin' kid, it does matter," he seethes, jaw ticking and his eyes burning with reawakened fire.

"He's not a kid anymore. Even so, with all of Bunky's quirks, he wasn't ever goin' to have a 'normal' relationship. You have to know that."

"Maybe not but at least it wouldn't be toxic," Badge argues, tossing his hands up in the air. "You're gonna ruin him, Whaley. You want him to be like you?"

I shake my head. "Of course not, I want him to be better than me—"

"Then you should know this won't ever work—"

"But I'm also being realistic about the whole thing. He's got so much fucked-up shit in his head. So much stuff he's battling every day. It's only a matter of time before he does end up like me, hell, worse than me even." I take a deep breath, trying to collect myself.

There's so much I could say, so much about Bunky I could confess, but I'm not sure he's ready for that, let alone myself. I can't even wrap my damn head around the fact that he loves me, so how am I going to explain that to Badge?

"I know I ain't perfect but I've got my shit under control. I've come a long damn way. Dug myself up from Hell, kickin', screamin', and fightin' the whole way. You know Bunky can't do that on his own. Look at how badly he was spiralin' before this past year. All the drinkin', drugs, the fightin', going AWOL for days. He hasn't done that in so long, and you know why? Because of *me*." I beat my chest in pride, voice rising with every word that passes my lips. "So yeah, maybe I'm not the best one for him, but I'm the one he needs, and if you can't get behind that, then I'm fuckin' sorry because I refuse to let Bunky go now."

I'm panting by the time I finish my spiel, locked in some weird stare off with Badge. His face hasn't changed at all. He still looks like he wants to climb across the table and wring my neck.

I wait for what feels like ever for him to say something, for his expression to change, for him to give me fucking anything, and when he finally does, it's nothing like I was expecting. "Do you love him?" His tone is soft, despite the little edge there, and his face, while no longer murderous, is wary.

I'm speechless. Out of all the things to ask, that's what he chose? "Excuse me?"

"You heard me," he says, reaching up and strumming his beard. "Are you in love with my son?"

"I..." I take a deep breath, conjuring up the honest truth. It's the same damn thing I was racking my brain about earlier, and I only have one answer. "I dunno."

"That's not good enough, Whaley." His eyes are assessing, and I swear he's gonna crack a tooth if he doesn't stop clenching his jaw so hard.

"That's all I can give you right now," I tell him, not liking the pressure I feel to come up with an answer I don't have.

"It's still not enough."

Oh, for fuck's sake.

"You don't repeat this shit, Badge, but..." I inhale deeply, trying to get my thoughts in order. "He's my life. I won't say I love him because I won't lie, but that don't mean I wouldn't take a knife to the heart for him. I know our relationship is hard to justify but don't ever fuckin' doubt the extent of my feelin's. There are no lines I wouldn't cross for him, even if that means pissin' you off."

He's still rigid, but he softens with each word I say. After a moment, he shakes his head and pinches the bridge of his nose. "I don't like it."

"Like I said, respectfully, you don't have to." My tone is calm, not wanting to rile him up again. "This ain't goin' anywhere. Nothin' you say or do will change that."

He stands and places both hands on the desk, leaning forward. The determination there would make any other man cower, but not me. "If you fuck this up, I'll kill you myself."

"I won't." I hold my hands up placatingly. "We're all sorts of wrong, but we're permanent. I give you my word."

"Your fuckin' word?" he mutters, as if it's a runaway thought.

"Has that ever not been enough?" I throw back in challenge.

That gets him. He knows me and he knows how serious I am about this kind of thing. My word is my bond. It's a part of my code. If I give him it, there's no going back.

"Fine. I'll adapt, I guess." He winces, as if a thought just hit him, then looks like he's about to pass out as he sits back down, blood draining from his face. "But I can't promise that I won't punch you again if I see you guys all over each other."

Yeah, that shit's bound to happen. Bunky and I can't keep our hands off each other if we're in the same room. "Can't guarantee that won't happen."

"Goddamn it," he groans, throwing his head back with a sigh so dramatic, he looks like Bunky. We sit there for a few moments, neither of us saying anything before he finally gestures to my desk. "Need help with these?"

He's obviously still irritated, but I take the white flag for what it is, thankful I didn't get another clock to the jaw. "Yeah, actually. I could use it."

He grumbles under his breath but helps me nonetheless. We spend the rest of the day working, getting everything sorted, but he can tell I'm itching to leave when closing time comes around. He doesn't have to ask because I'm sure he knows I've got Bunky on the brain. Even though things got rough, we part ways with an understanding. I won't fuck up with Bunky and he won't interfere with our relationship, which is better than I expected.

Now I'm free to claim my guy whenever I want in front of whoever I want, and I can't wait to make it clear who the fuck Bunky belongs to.

NINETEEN

Bunky

I suck on my lollipop, staring down Whaley from across the trailer park, making sure to do that thing he likes with my tongue around my treat. I can see the way his features darken, almost like a warning to cut my shit out before I get it.

I want to get it though. He's always feral as fuck in the bed when he's annoyed. But I know he isn't going to do anything. He won't stalk over here like I want him to and put me over his knee. He won't drag me away to his trailer to pound my brains out. It's early in the morning, and Whaley decided to throw a breakfast hang out in honor of this special day.

It's my birthday, bitches!

Fox makes a noise, drawing my attention to how he's eating like a madman. You'd think he'd never had pancakes a day in his life with the way he's scarfing them down. I nudge him with my boot, something that finally makes his head snap up in irritation.

"What?" he questions, voice muffled by a helping of pancakes.

"What were you and Whaley talkin' about this morning?"

He rolls his eyes, continuing to stuff his face. "Not tellin'."

"Oh, come *on*," I whine, shaking his shoulders. "You're really not gonna tell me? Is it about my present? Is he plannin' somethin' special?"

"Guess you'll find out later." He shrugs.

I open my mouth to ask him more questions, but a broad body steps in front of us, so big that it blocks the sun. "Bunky, let's go."

I don't even miss a beat. I spring from my seat, giving Fox one more curious stare before jumping in front of Whaley. I wish I could kiss him the way I want to, but we're keeping things on the down-low for now.

"Where are we goin'?"

"Not tellin'. It's a surprise."

I'm giddy with excitement at the word *surprise*. I'm a bundle of energy as Whaley leads me to his Harley, asking him question after question that he refuses to answer.

After a minute, and once we're on his bike and ready to go, he turns to me, voice sharp. "Bunky, shut it."

"But I'm so excited!" I argue, wiggling in my seat. "Is it a pony? Did you get me a pony? I've always wanted one, but Badge said ain't no pony livin' in the trailer park."

"Badge is right. Why the fuck do you want a pony anyway?"

"I dunno." I shrug. "They're cute."

"I guarantee that you'll like this more than a damn pony you can't even ride," he tells me, revving up his bike. "This'll take a few hours, so I hope you're settled in."

"A few hours? What—"

Before I can finish my sentence, we're off. The scenery we pass is gorgeous, everything lush and green despite the blistering heat. Mountains fly by us after the first hour, and I wonder if Whaley's surprise has something to do with a secluded cabin where he can have his devious ways with me.

Wouldn't that be a treat?

After another hour of winding mountain roads, we slow down and finally make it to our destination. I frown when I see that it's nothing more than an empty field. "What are we doin' here?"

"Just down that way," he says, hopping off his bike and helping me do the same. "Get your ass over here."

I rush to his side, letting him slide his big hand into my back pocket as he leads us down a trail. He isn't carrying anything, so this isn't some sort of romantic picnic. Not that Whaley would ever do something like that, but fucking in the woods does sound exciting, minus the fact that twigs might go where twigs are never meant to go.

"How much farther?" I whine, purposefully dragging my feet with dramatic heavy footsteps. "I think I'm dyin'."

"Damn smoker's lungs," he sighs before giving my ass a squeeze. "You're fine. It's right around the corner."

I open my mouth, ready to be even *more* dramatic and demand he carry me on his back, but no words leave me when I see what my surprise really is.

"Well, Bunk..." He tosses an arm over my shoulder, looking down at me with a proud smirk. "Ready to go bungee jumping?"

Am I fucking ever!

"Whaley!" I shout, hopping up and down as I shake him. "This is awesome! How did you even think of this?"

"Fox," he explains with a shrug.

When I turned eighteen, Fox went all out for my birthday. He had a big party and we did the drinks, the drugs, the whole shebang with all my friends, but I wanted to do something more. I made that fact very known to everyone, and the next day, Fox had the brilliant idea to take me bungee jumping.

Of course, I rushed at the chance to do it. It seemed so fucking cool. Who doesn't want to jump off a tall cliff and glide through the air, just one strap away from bashing your brains out against the side of the mountain edge? Fox, even though he was the one that took me, refused to do it. He made it clear that in no way, shape, or form was he stupid enough to risk his life for three seconds of weightlessness.

Then there's me…

The idea hits me, making me hold on to Whaley's arm as he leads us toward the platform. "Wait, are you doin' it too? I don't wanna do it alone."

He stops in his tracks, cupping my face in his hands, then kisses my forehead and the tip of my nose before settling on my lips. "You'll never have to do anythin' alone for the rest of your life, little psycho. Anythin' you do, I do too."

"My fuckin' *heart*." My knees are close to collapsing at his admission. "Fuck, I love you."

He chuckles, kissing me once more before slapping my ass. "Let's do this."

I nod my agreement as we approach the entrance. We go through the whole process of paying, the safety instructions, and gearing up. The guy goes on and on about rules and procedures and risks, which is so fucking boring.

When he's finally done yapping away, he looks between the two of us. "Couple?"

"Hell yeah," I beam, pride in my voice, and can't help but tease him. "This is my *daddy*."

"Bunky," Whaley hisses, eyes narrowing, but I see the way one side of his lips wants to quirk up.

To the guy's credit, he doesn't react, just holds up two different harnesses. "Are you doing this together or individually?"

"Wait, we can do it together?" I ask, hope blossoming in my gut as I look at Whaley. "Can we?"

He thinks it over for a moment before reaching out and squeezing my hand. "Wouldn't want it any other way."

I can't stay still as the guy gets both of us suited up,

putting on our own harnesses and helmets before connecting us. Then he walks us over to the edge of the platform, giving us one last talk before asking if we're ready.

"Every fuckin' day," I singsong, clapping my hands.

When he looks at Whaley, Whaley nods, albeit with less enthusiasm than me. "Can we go now?"

The guy shrugs. "Knock yourself out."

"Okay, okay, okay…" I repeat, psyching myself up by bouncing on my toes, which proves difficult with the way Whaley and I are connected chest to chest. "I can do this. We can do this. It's gonna be fuckin' amazin'. Whaley, are you—"

Then we free fall.

His lips capture mine as he tips us over the platform, and there's nothing but weightlessness and thrill coursing through me. The way our lips connect combined with the rush of air that flies by us is incredible. I know I've done this once, but it pales in comparison to this experience.

Because I'm with Whaley and this is what loving him feels like.

It feels like standing on the edge of a cliff, not knowing whether I'm going to soar or crash. It feels like I'm constantly on the verge of being struck down and hurt. It feels like things could go terribly wrong at any moment.

But it also feels entirely captivating.

Like my blood is soaring because even though I might get hurt, I know the euphoria is worth it. Like my heart is pounding because they're the ones that can give me both pain and pleasure. Like my soul is yearning and breaking because every moment is special. Like my heart is going to stop. Like my lungs are going to breathe his last breath. Like my eyes will never see him again.

Loving Whaley is dangerous, but I wouldn't want it any other way.

TWENTY

Bunky

I scream, throwing my head back as the spray of water runs down my throat and chokes me.

"Such a fuckin' tease," Whaley growls. "You knew exactly what you were doin', didn't you?"

I nod.

Messing with Whaley is my favorite pastime, and I couldn't resist the urge to make him lose his shit again. When he told me we weren't having sex this morning, I severely disagreed. After trying my hardest to get his hand down my pants and failing, I took matters into my own hands.

Literally.

I know he hates it when I touch myself in front of him. Sure, it gets him all hot and bothered, but I know he'd rather be the one in control of my pleasure. And that's exactly what he's doing right now as he fucks me in his shower, pounding into me, purposefully hitting that spot that makes me see stars.

I reach back and wrap a wet arm around his neck. "Fuck, your piercin's feel so good."

"Thinkin' about gettin' another one," he mumbles in my ear, hands sliding up my chest to play with my nipples. "Right at the tip. You'd like that, wouldn't you? Give you somethin' else to play with while you choke on my cock."

Damn, that's hot. I want to get my name tattooed on his dick too, to make it clear he belongs to me. Maybe I'll broach that subject later. I was serious about getting his name somewhere on my body, somewhere obvious where everyone could see it though. That way—

"Fuck!" I shout, toes curling when his hand finds my balls. "Jesus Christ, Whaley. You're gonna make me come so fast."

"Good," he rasps against my ear, speeding up his strokes and his thrusts, intent on making this quick. "Got shit to do, Bunk. Hurry up and come so I can breed that tiny hole. Fill you up so good you'll smell like me for days."

I have no control over my orgasm. When he twists his wrist and gives my balls a harsh tug, I coat the bathroom wall with my cum.

"Yes," he growls, moving to bruise my hips with his grip as he fucks me like it's the last time he'll get my ass. "Take it, little psycho. Take every fuckin' drop."

His cock thickens before warmth fills me as he comes with a moan and my name on his lips. He stays locked in there, reluctant to leave until the water starts to get cold. Then he slides out, giving my ass a rough slap before spinning me around. He claims my mouth in a brutal kiss, his tongue brushing against my piercing that I know drives him wild.

"Made me late," he mumbles against my lips, biting down so hard until I can taste blood. When he sees what he's done, he smirks and licks the crimson away. "You taste so good."

"Cut me then," I tease, walking my fingers up his abs, tempted to lick him dry. "Make me bleed for you."

He's considering it, but then curses under his breath and shuts off the shower. He takes my hand and drags me out with him, handing me a towel. "Meant it when I said I got shit to do. You already distracted me enough as it is."

I pout as I towel off, throwing it on the ground once I'm dry, and follow him into his room. "How long are you gonna be gone?"

He shrugs, riffling through his drawers for something to wear. "Dunno. It's supposed to be quick. Pike and I are goin' to check on the recent shipment we got. Maybe a few hours?"

"Take me with you," I whine, moving behind him and wrapping my arms around his middle. "Don't wanna be without you."

He chuckles and turns in my arms, then looks down and thumbs my whale tattoo. A starved look is in his eyes as he licks his lips, and I can see the tremble of his body as he tries to hold himself back, but he shakes his head and takes a step back to get dressed. "Can't."

"And why not?"

"Because if you're with me, I ain't gettin' shit done. Hard enough to leave you."

I sigh dreamily. I still want to go with him, but I get his reasoning. Some would call how consumed we are by each other unhealthy, but I think it's romantic. I'm so dependent on him now, and I know he feels the same way, but still, he needs to attend to the business. I wouldn't want to interfere, no matter how much I want to tie him to the bed and force him to stay.

"I'm gonna miss you," I whine, reaching around him to grab one of his shirts. "Gonna take this with me."

When I tug it over my head, his eyes darken with lust, and he bites his bottom lip, looking me up and down. "Look so good in my clothes. Should burn the rest of yours."

I shrug. "Doesn't sound like the worst idea. I could—"

I'm silenced when he takes my face in his hands and shoves his tongue down my throat. We fuck each other's mouths, and I don't realize we're on our way to the bed until

I'm falling back into it. He mounts me, grinding his clothed cock against mine, and my eyes flutter shut when his fingers find my hole.

"I wanna take a look." He pushes my legs up until they're pressed against my chest, growling at what he sees before sucking on two fingers and then pushing them into me. "So puffy. So wet. You sore?"

"Extremely," I tell him honestly. Every step I take aches, and I know we should take a break for my own good... "Good thing I like the pain though."

"I'll use my mouth on you next time," he says, pulling his fingers out as he bends down and licks my hole. "Maybe I'll eat you out. Suck on this pretty pink pucker until you're screamin' my name."

I nod dumbly, too consumed with the way he continues to give me teasing licks and nips. "You could do that now."

He reluctantly stands, snagging his leather jacket off the dresser before grabbing his pack of smokes. "Gotta go, Bunk. I'm serious this time."

"You gonna pine for me while you're gone?" I joke, spreading out on the bed. "Gonna be thinkin' of me the entire time?"

"Yes." His answer is quick and short as he cocks his head to the side while lighting up. He's about to leave, but he turns around at the last second. "What are you gonna do today?"

"I dunno." I shrug. "I think Raid and Landon are hangin' out. Blaine and Silas are gone. Might fuck around with Fox if he ain't busy."

"Fox is out too." After a moment, and with something akin to nerves in his eyes, he speaks. "You should hang out with Badge."

Something twists in my stomach because I'm still pissed at Badge. When Whaley told me that Badge had punched him after he found out about us, I had understood his rage, but I still didn't like the fact that he put his hands on Whaley. It made me feel all stabby, and he should be grateful he's my dad, or else it wouldn't have been pretty. I haven't talked to him since, but I guess this is as good of a time as any. "Okay. Gonna be awkward as hell though."

"He's your dad. It'll be fine. We're sorted now."

Sadness hits me again when he turns to leave. "No goodbye kiss?"

"Can't do that, or else I'd never leave." Right when he's at the door, he turns again. There's a hesitation in his movement, and I cock my head to the side in silent question. "Tell me again."

I know exactly what he's referring to, and I indulge him happily and easily. "I love you, Whaley."

He hums under his breath. The words are easy for me to get out, but now that I know about his past, I can understand why they're not for him. That's fine by me. I know exactly how he feels, even if he can't say it, so I let his silence slide. "Keep your phone on you, alright? I'll be back later."

"Okay," I say. When he still doesn't move, I throw my head back and laugh. "I thought you had to go?"

He growls under his breath, looking like he wants to join me on the bed, but then thinks better of it. Without another word, he spins on his heels and marches out of the room.

Fuck, I miss him already.

Codependency is hot as hell.

I lay on his bed for a little longer, considering taking a nap, but when my stomach starts to rumble, I get up and find some pants. Once I'm fully dressed, I grab my own smokes and my pocketknife before heading out. I know Badge is probably at the shop, so that's where I go.

During the drive, I crank up the music to try and settle my nerves. I consider smoking the joint I keep in my compartment, but I don't. I haven't really needed to do that now that I have Whaley. Sure, the promise of getting high as hell and munching is strong. It's not like I'll never smoke again, but my cravings for it have diminished the past couple of weeks.

Once I get to the shop, I'm feeling a bit better, that is until I see Badge.

Damn it.

I decide to take the casual approach since I haven't talked to him in a while, and I know that makes me a shit son. "Hey."

Badge looks up from his clipboard, and there's a moment of hesitation before he smiles at me. It's unsure and a bit tentative, but it's a smile nonetheless. "Hey, kid."

We stand in awkward silence as I rock on my heels. "What are you doin'?"

He cocks his head to the side and raises his clipboard. "Workin'?"

"Right," I mumble. I get the feeling I'm going to have to be the one to initiate anything. "Do you think you could get someone else to watch the shop? Thought we could hang out today."

That brightens him up. His smile is sincere now as he sets the clipboard down. "I think we can close up for the day since there's no pickups coming. Want me to call Fox?"

I love my brother, but I think this should just be Badge and me, at least until I get a feel of where we're at. "He's out, but the two of us can hit up that diner you like. The one a town over?"

We'd usually go to Kelly's, but I have to admit their pie sucks, and I know that Badge goes crazy over the banana pudding at Ralf's. Sure, it's a bit of a drive, but it'll be worth it. Maybe it'll butter him up some too.

He nods. "Yeah. Wanna ride?"

"Can we take your truck?"

"Just gimme a second to settle this and I'll meet you at the trailer?"

I agree and head out, thankful that the conversation

wasn't as painful as I had expected. I get his truck started once I'm home, cleaning it a bit while I wait, and he meets me only after a few minutes.

"Ready?"

"Yeah." I lean back in my seat. When he gives me a pointed look, I tilt my head to the side. "What?"

"Seat belt?"

"Seriously?"

"You know I don't like when you don't wear one."

I groan dramatically but do what he says. In truth, it's not a hardship, I always forget, but it's nice to be reminded that Badge is still looking out for me.

The ride to the diner takes about thirty minutes, but it feels good to be out with him again. Passing the fields is peaceful, and I smirk when I see a herd of cows grazing to my right. Silas and Blaine have a thing for cows apparently, but Blaine always gets flustered when Silas tries to tell the story. Wonder what their deal is.

We get to the diner and park the truck around the back, both of us groaning as we stretch our legs. There aren't any cars around and that's good. Badge and I don't like leaving our rides around crowds. It's gross back here, but this way we know nobody is going to fuck with it.

We head inside and sit at a booth in the back. Even though it's not our diner, we've been here enough to know what we're going to order.

In the past, Badge and I have taken these little trips together, so it's almost nostalgic to be here again. Anytime I went off the deep end or found myself all dark and depressy, this is what he did to cheer me up. It's probably the best place to have the conversation we need to have.

Our waitress spies us immediately and takes our order. Everything is normal until it's only the two of us again and that awkwardness settles over us. I wait for Badge to say something first, but he doesn't. I really don't want to start this shit off, but Whaley's voice in the back of my head encourages me.

"Whaley and I are fuckin'."

Graceful, Bunk.

Badge stiffens before he closes his eyes and lets out a withering sigh. "Did you have to say it like that? He said the same shit when he dropped the bomb on me. Are you two tryin' to kill me?"

I'm usually straight to the point but he's right. A more gentle approach might be needed.

Like a therapist, I prop my elbows on the table and set my chin on my hands. "How does that make you feel?"

"Honestly?" he questions, rage filling his eyes. "I don't fuckin' like it."

I nod, figuring as much, but still, I need to make him see that Whaley and I are so right together and to push aside any reservations he has. "I get it. Wanna tell me why?"

He's been Whaley's right-hand man for so long, and I'm sure he doesn't want to talk shit about him. However, being a dad trumps that, so he doesn't hold back. "You're nineteen, Bunk. He's thirty-five."

"So?" I argue, annoyed that our ages are his first point. "That don't matter to me."

He shakes his head. "What if you eventually want someone else?"

"That'll never fuckin' happen," I snap, a little panicked at the thought. "He's my entire life. My fuckin' soul. I'd fuckin' die for him."

"Don't you see the problem with that?" he asks, face morphed in disbelief.

"Not at all."

"Kid…"

"I ain't a kid," I growl, not caring that some of the people in the diner turn to look at me. "And I ain't stupid. Whaley and I were meant for each other. Everythin' about him is mine, and everythin' about me is his. Who wouldn't want a love like that?"

"And does he love you?"

"I know he does."

"Has he said it?" He presses.

"Not with words," I tell him. Truthfully, I don't know if Whaley's ever going to tell me he loves me, but I don't think that's a problem. But we're committed. This is somethin' that's gonna be permanent.

"Whaley is…" he trails off, once again looking hesitant. "I know bits and pieces of his past, not the full picture, but enough to know he's no good for you. You deserve someone better than that."

I know what he's talking about. The darkness Whaley carries, the scars on his back, they all scream of a past that's haunted, but Badge doesn't see that the point he's making proves mine.

"Don't you see? He gets me. You think anyone else could handle me? You think anyone else would embrace every part of me like he does?" I sigh, knowing that I'm working myself up when I feel tears welling in my eyes. "You know he calls me his little psycho?"

"He actually said that? I'm gonna punch him again—"

"But he don't mean it like that," I say quickly, cutting him off when he goes to stand as if to deliver on his threat. "My point is, I'm *his* psycho. He wants me for everythin' I am. He ain't tryin' to change me. He knows I'm not perfect, but that don't matter to him."

He stares at me like my face will somehow have the answer to this problem of his. More time passes as I squirm in my seat, waiting for him to say something, and I finally relax when he sighs. "This really ain't goin' away."

"No." I cross my arms over my chest. "I'll be with him until the day I die."

"There you go bein' dramatic again," he murmurs before

looking up at me. He's still frowning, but there's more understanding now than there was before. "Okay."

My brow lifts and I look him over with apprehension. "Okay?"

"I'm gonna have to get used to it." He shrugs. "Not much I can do about it now that you have your mind set. All I can say is that he better treat you right, or else I'll have his ass."

"You don't have to worry about that." I laugh, once again getting all lovey-dovey at the thought of Whaley. "He's everythin' I ever wanted."

"Good." He stops when our waitress comes by with our food. "Alright, let's dig in and talk about somethin' else."

From there, we talk about everything, even trivial things, and it feels nice to have a sense of normalcy. I tell him that I need to pick up parts for my bike, and he offers to go with me to the junkyard later to find them. He tells me about a date he went on, and I suggest he bring her by sometime soon. Once we're done, we leave some cash on the table and head out, deciding to drive around a bit more before going back to Brookshire to really take advantage of the day.

This is the first time we've spoken in what feels like weeks, since the whole Whaley thing came out. I really do love my dad. I love everything about him, from the way he's so honest and loyal to the understanding in his eyes whenever he looks at me. He's the real deal, a great fucking man, and spending the day riding around with him sounds like the best thing I can think of.

We're about to get into the truck when a sharp, angry voice stops us in our tracks, causing our heads to snap around to the sound of the threat.

"Bunky!"

Badge and I turn, coming face-to-face with Gunnar and two other Vipers. This isn't their territory, but it's close enough to their town for them to be sniffing around and trying to make a profit. From the look on Gunnar's face though, he's not looking to make a sale.

Gunnar's furious, his fists balled by his sides as he approaches us. He might be a short guy, but he's bulky, easily a heavyweight, and the last time I fought with him I got a run for my money.

He nearly beat the crap out of me.

Well, I did fuck his sister.

"Oh for fuck's sake," Badge mumbles, turning a glare toward Gunnar, knowing exactly why he's pissed. "You need to fuck off right now."

Badge looks like he wants to do the whole let's-avoid-the-problem-here, but I'm all about let's-break-the-problem. Gunnar's a straight-up dick, and I'm not going to miss a chance to fuck with him.

"Gunnar!" I say cheerfully, leaving Badge behind even though he tries to stop me. "How you been, buddy?"

He takes a step toward me, jaw clenched, seething with fury. "You don't wanna push me right now. I still owe you for what you did."

I roll my eyes. "It's been almost a year. You're tellin' me you're still salty about it?"

"Bunky, watch it," Badge warns, coming to stand behind me, being the overprotective dad he is. "We're leavin'."

Gunnar looks behind me to where Badge stands, and whatever he sees pleases him because his lips split into a sinister smile. "You ain't got much backup this time, freak. Just you and your daddy. There's nothin' stoppin' me now."

Instantly, adrenaline and thrill rushes through my blood. Because of Whaley, it's been a while since I've had a proper fight, and I'm itching to shed some crimson. I pull out my pocketknife quickly, holding it to Gunnar's throat before he or the guys with him can react.

"Ooo, we gonna have some fun?" I taunt, pressing down.

"Jesus, you're makin' me happy. Let's fuckin' do this, Gunnar. You gonna make the first move, or am I?"

"You ain't doin' shit." This comes from Badge as he takes hold of my jacket, snatching me back. I glance at him questioningly, a pout on my lips as I continue to point my knife at Gunnar. "But, Badge—"

"No," he snaps, trying to drag me away, but my feet are glued to the ground and my eyes trail back to Gunnar and his stooges. "Think about your actions, kid. Think about Whaley."

He's right. Whaley didn't want me fighting for a reason, and I'm sure he'll be pissed if he finds out I broke our agreement. No matter what, Whaley will always trump any crazy I feel. Every decision in my life revolves around him now, so if he doesn't want me doing this, I won't.

I sigh reluctantly, and with one last look at Gunnar, I turn and tuck my knife back into my pocket.

"Whaley?" Gunnar asks, laughing cruelly. "Whaley's not here to save you."

"I don't need anyone to save me," I grit out, fighting against Badge's grip. This asshole is taunting me. I want to have some fun and put Gunnar in his place, but Badge is being such a buzzkill. "Badge, lemme at him."

Before Badge can respond though, I'm knocked on my ass, hitting the concrete with a loud thud and something digging into my back. The breath has been knocked out of me, and I try to scramble up to my feet, but Gunnar's there with a booted foot pressed to my chest.

"Get off him!" Badge shouts, but he's being held back by the two Vipers, fighting against their grip. "Fuckin' touch him and see what happens."

"Daddy can't save you either." Gunnar whips out his knife. "Time for payback, you dick."

That's the last thing I hear before he starts hitting me. All I can feel is the rough kicks being delivered to my sides, the fists that come across my face and split my lip. I recover quickly though, getting up and giving as good as I got. I'm punching everywhere I can reach, using my size and speed to my advantage, just like Fox taught me. I have Gunnar in a good place, nearly down on his knees, but when Badge shouts, I tear my gaze away for a second.

That's the second Gunnar needs to get me back on the ground.

Gunnar leans down and presses the knife against my face, but I don't even blink. I'm not scared of this piece of shit. I lean in, bringing us closer together. "You gonna cut me? You got the balls, Gunnar?"

Gunnar growls, pressing the knife down on my cheek, cutting a thin slice across my face. "Gonna do more than that. Gonna show you that no one fucks with me and gets away from it."

I don't fear for my life when he raises his knife. It's twisted and fucked-up, but I'm biding my time until I can get the upper hand.

Only Badge knocks Gunnar off of me before he makes contact. They roll and tussle as Badge tries to fight him for the knife. Then the word seems to slow, and I watch in horror as Gunnar jabs the knife in Badge's middle. My heart feels like it stops and my stomach feels like it's inside out, and then... All I see is fucking *red*.

Crash.

Squish.

Pop.

"Bunky!"

The world blacks out around me as anger takes over. Badge's now lying on the concrete, blood seeping from his wound and his face is growing pale. I don't even recognize the yowl that escapes me, and the next second, I'm quickly overpowering Gunnar, straddling him and reaching for my knife before plunging it into his fucking chest.

"Stop! Please!"
Brains scattered on the bathroom tile.
Blood on his hands.

I don't stop there. Every time Badge wheezes, I bring the knife down again. Blood is splattering on my hands, my shirt, my face, but I laugh. Someone tries to pull me off, but I'm in a frenzy. The demon is ringing in my head, happy, and urging me on.

It wants to see Gunnar's guts spilled on the pavement. It wants to see the life drain out of his eyes. It wants to see itself win. The second Gunnar's eyes dim, the second his chest ceases to rise, and the second he lets out that final gasp the demon is satisfied.

I killed someone.

And I feel fucking fantastic.

I move to stand as the two other Vipers freak the fuck out. I don't care about them though, I'm still hyper-focused on Gunnar's slack face and all the blood that's gathering around him. I go to do more damage, cause more destruction until a voice snaps me out of it.

"Bunky…"

I don't know how long Badge has been calling out my name, but when I see him, I once again panic. He doesn't look good, all pale, lips blue, and eyes fading. He's reaching for me with a bloody hand, crawling on the pavement in his desperation to get to me.

"Dad!"

I rush to him, barely registering when the other Vipers begin to take Gunnar's lifeless body away. I don't know what to do. I don't know what to think. My blood is pounding inside my ears and everything is getting fuzzy and hazy, but not like before. I look around frantically, spotting the truck, and act completely on instinct.

With all the strength I can muster, I drag a bloodied Badge to the vehicle. I make sure to buckle him in as best as I can, then take off without a second thought, not knowing where I'm going but knowing I have to get there quickly.

"Dad, you're gonna be fine," I tell him, desperately going over the speed limit. Do I take him to the fucking hospital? To Donna? I'm panicking, my breaths coming out in uneven little puffs. What should I—

"You called me dad." He chuckles lightly, wincing when the action causes him pain. "Whaley. Call Whaley and tell him what happened. Take me to the shop."

"But—"

"Do it, Bunk."

I scramble for my phone, nearly driving us off the road as I call Whaley. It rings only once before he answers. *"Bunky, better be important. Don't got time for—"*

"Badge is hurt," I rush to say, seeing that Badge's face is turning even paler, his eyes drifting shut. "Dad, come on! Stay awake! Please!"

"What happened?"

"I— We— I couldn't— And then Gunnar." I let out a choked cry, everything rushing past me in a blur, everything blending together. I can't fucking think. All I know is one thing. "We need you, Whaley."

"Go to the shop. I'll be right there."

I put my hope in Whaley like I always do and pray he can stop the past from repeating itself.

TWENTY-ONE

Whaley

I pull into the shop but don't see Badge's truck, which means they aren't here yet.

What the fuck? I dig out my phone, calling to see where he is, but he doesn't answer, only making my worry flare. I reach up, dragging a shaky hand through my hair as my thoughts wander.

Bunky was such a mess when he called that I could barely make out what he was saying. Hearing him like that—completely freaked and crying—will forever be engraved in my brain. It'll replace the nightmares I have, playing every time he isn't in my sight. That shit has me twisted up in knots, and now he's not answering. He was driving, so I can't help but worry that something else happened. What if he got in a wreck? What if the Vipers chased them down?

What if…

No, stop it. You need to focus.

This is one of those times where I have to be strong, put on my brave face, and handle all the bullshit that other people can't.

Hopping off my bike, I head inside, thankful there aren't any customers when I push my way through the front door. Raid's sitting behind the desk, doing something on the computer, but he stops when he looks up and takes me in.

"Get towels, call Donna, and grab Pike," I shout, adrenaline pumping through me. "It's an emergency."

Raid doesn't hesitate, jumping from the stool and rushing to the back. I go outside, pacing the length of the shop as I call Bunky two more times, still getting no fucking answer. I'm about to call again just as Badge's truck comes barreling into the shop parking lot, almost running me over in the process.

"Fuck!" I curse, jumping back and out of the way as the tires screech and the truck jerks to a stop. Raid and Pike burst outside at the same time, confusion mixed with worry on both of their faces. I look at Bunky briefly through the windshield and immediately rush to him. "Bunk…"

He stares straight ahead, a grotesque mess of blood and cuts on his face and it makes me want to rage. I take a quick look at him, thankful the wounds I see are superficial, but as much as I want to make sure he's okay, I know I can't right now.

Keeping Badge alive has to be my number one priority.

I turn to Raid, taking the towels from him before motioning to Bunky. "I need you to take care of Bunk. Get him to my trailer and clean him up. Keep him there until I say otherwise. I need him out of the way for now."

Raid still looks confused but nods, stepping in front of me and helping Bunky out of the car. Bunk goes easily, blinking like he's in a daze, but something snaps the second Raid starts to drag him away from the scene.

"Dad!" he screeches, thrashing when Raid grabs him by the middle. "Fuck! Badge! No!"

He's struggling so hard, probably furthering any injuries I can't see, and my heart breaks. I want to hold him, kiss him, make sure he knows that everything's going to be fine, but I can't, which is agonizing. I have to turn my back on them as Raid drags him toward his car.

Fuck, why is being a leader so goddamn hard?

"Pike, I need you to drive us to the hospital."

He nods, already going to the spot where Bunky just was. "Got it."

I toss my smoke to the ground and run to the passenger side door, snatching it open to look at Badge. His cheeks are pale, the hand clutched to his stomach doing absolute fuck all as blood seeps through his shirt.

"Shit." I climb on his lap, shutting the door as Pike shifts gears and takes off.

"Badge?" I bark out, giving his face a smack, rousing him a bit.

He blinks, looking up at me with confusion as I lift his shirt. The gash in his stomach is oozing so much and so fast that I can't tell how deep it is. The only thing I know is that it's bad, so bad I can't believe he's still alive. I take the towels, using all my force to smash them against the wound, making him groan loudly.

"Sorry, I gotta stop the bleedin'," I say, apologizing again when he gurgles and lets out a cough.

"It's fine. Whaley, can't say I ever expected to have you on my lap like this," he teases, eyes blinking closed and chest stuttering as he tries to catch his breath. "Bunky's gonna be pissed when he finds out."

That makes me laugh. "Yeah, well, you can tell him all about it later at the hospital."

He shakes his head, hand reaching out to touch the wound I'm currently covering, bloody fingers slipping unco-ordinatedly over mine. "Ain't gonna make it to the hospital."

"Hey, fuck that." I press down even harder, gulping when I see that the bleeding isn't stopping and is seeping quickly through the white towels. "Don't say shit like that. You are. We're almost there now."

We're not. We still have about ten minutes, and I won't pretend like I'm not freaking the fuck out over us making it there in time. He doesn't need to know that though. All he's got to focus on is staying awake and staying alive.

"Whaley, you gonna take care of him for me, right?" he mumbles, head lulling forward. "Make sure he don't go to prison for Gunnar."

I can't deal with any of that shit right now. "No, you stop talkin' like that. You're gonna be fine and you're gonna keep him outta prison, you hear me?"

"He killed him, Whaley," he continues, coughing and crying out when he does. "Stabbed him about ten times. Vipers took the body, so we don't gotta worry about that."

"We're not talkin' about this shit," I demand, watching as Badge begins to slump a bit more. "Pike! How much farther?"

Pike looks over his shoulder, eyes widening when he sees the condition Badge is in. "Five minutes."

"Why the fuck didn't Bunky take you to the hospital?" I growl, more to myself than Badge.

"Because we gotta talk about this. You needed to know the details so you can handle it. Just in case I…" He coughs again, eyes unfocused as his words begin to trail off. "I… Bunky… He's…"

"Drive faster!" I don't recognize the sound of my own voice, it's too high-pitched, too frantic, but it matches how I feel on the inside. "Badge!"

I take hold of his face, forcing him to look at me. "So tired, Whaley. Just wanna sleep."

"You listen to me. You got two kids that need you, and people who can't live without you, alright? So I need you to stay the fuck awake! No closing your eyes, no sayin' these goodbyes. We are fuckin' Aces and we don't give up." I feel my lip wobble, but I fight it because I'm not fucking crying. That isn't my style, but it's *Badge* and there's a pang in my chest at the thought of him being gone forever…

Yeah, I can't go there. I need to stay in my right headspace or I'll lose control, and that is the last thing I need.

"Badge?" I give his face another smack, determined to keep him awake. "Wake the fuck up!"

He blinks rapidly, trying to fight the urge to close his eyes again. "I–I'm try–trying…" he stutters, coughing again, and I notice a tinge of blood coating his teeth.

No, no, no.

I spin to look out the window, trying to gauge where we are, and see the red hospital sign in the distance.

So close. So damn close. We're going to make it.

"Hey, Badge, you know Bunky has a whale tattoo on his hip?" He makes a little grunting sound, eyes still blinking. "Yeah, it's cute. I like to kiss it."

"The fuck, Whaley?" Pike questions, but I ignore him, focusing on Badge only.

"He likes that, you know? My mouth on him there."

"Please fuckin' st–stop." Badge glares, eyes finally focusing on me. "Just because I'm d–dyin' don't mean I wanna know about this shit."

"Well, if making you angry will keep you awake, I'll take it. I'll give you every detail," I tell him, relieved he's still talking.

"Prick." He smirks, giving his head a little shake. "Swear, you were r–right about one th–thing."

"What's that?"

"You and Bunky really are cut f–from the same cloth." His lip kicks up and he takes hold of my wrists, his expression morphing to complete seriousness. "Whaley, p–please take care of my kids. Fox too. Fuck. Please."

"Badge—"

"I'm serious," he cuts me off, eyes falling shut again. "P–promise."

I'm shaking my head, tears welling in my eyes because I

know what's happening. "I'll promise after we get you to the hospital."

"Pulling in now," Pike yells, swerving into the parking lot.

"See, we're almost there." Badge doesn't answer and I give his face a smack, but it doesn't rouse him this time. "Badge!" I shout, trembling fingers pushing against his neck. "I swear to God, don't fuckin' die on me. You can't. What the fuck am I gonna tell Bunky?"

He still doesn't answer as the truck comes to a halt and Pike jumps out, running inside to flag for help.

The whole time I'm sitting here, babbling, talking to Badge, shaking him, trying to get him to wake up, but he doesn't. He's—

No.

The door is snatched open and I'm shoved off Badge, watching as several people get him from the truck and onto a gurney. I'm frozen, limbs feeling heavy as I do nothing. The doctors and nurses are talking, but it's like they're speaking in another language. I don't understand anything. They take off in a run, wheeling Badge through the ER doors, but I'm frozen in place, unable to move, my mind running a thousand miles a minute…

Pike comes to me, eyes filled with worry. He tries to say something too, but again, I don't hear it. It's like the world is muted. I fall back into the side of the truck, my knees giving out.

What the hell is happening? I feel weird, wrong, like I did too many drugs and the world is dimming. I reach up to swipe my face when I'm slammed with several realizations all at once.

I have tears leaking from my eyes.

I have Badge's blood staining my hands.

I didn't feel his pulse when I searched.

TWENTY-TWO

Bunky

Crack.

Squish.

Pop.

"*Bunky!*"

I can't speak. I want to call out for Mama, but my words are gone.

Face caved in, eyes bulging out, hanging on to the sliver of life as she reaches for me.

The life drains out of her eyes.

It leaves her with one more brutal punch, and she's dead.

It was so immediate. So permanent.

I'm next. My life is now in the hands of a madman, but I feel no fear.

Death is just—

"Bunky?"

I snap my head up, looking at Raid. Shit. When did he get here?

Here? Where exactly am I?

"Bunk," he repeats, "We're at Whaley's trailer."

Oh, I said that out loud. Didn't even feel my lips moving. What happened? What's going on?

"You don't..." He gulps, kneeling in front of me. "You don't remember what happened?"

Why can't I speak? I open my mouth, but my words come out short and stuttered. "Badge. Stabbed. Where?"

Raid sighs with relief, head dropping briefly before looking back at me. "Yeah, Whaley took him to the hospital. He'll be back in a bit. Donna's gonna come by and take a look at you."

"Me?" I question dumbly, already trying to get up. I'm sitting? "Badge—"

"Whaley's got him." He forces me back down. "I know all you wanna do is go see your dad, but we've got to take care of you too. Plus, Whaley told me to keep you here, and he'll have my ass if I let you leave."

I want to fight against him, but his grip is too strong and I'm... I'm too weak? I ache. I feel that now. My cheek is sore and my ribs are screaming. I lift my hand up to my face, fingers running over what I'm guessing is dried blood. "What happened?"

Raid opens and closes his mouth before saying, "I really don't know, but we should get you cleaned up."

I nod dumbly, letting Raid move me however he sees fit. We go through Whaley's trailer, but my movements are robotic and foreign to me.

He takes me to the bathroom, turning on the shower and testing the water. "Okay, Bunk," he says slowly. "Time to get in the shower. Got to get the blood off you."

I nod again but don't move. I don't think I can.

Badge.

"How's Badge?"

Raid frowns, furrowing his brows. "He's at the hospital. Whaley will update us when he can." He points behind him. "Bunk, you need to shower."

I know I should, but my limbs won't move. Raid must realize this because he lets out a deep breath, cursing before his fingers find the hem of my shirt. "Whaley better not kill me for this."

Ever so slowly, and with gentle care, he starts to undress me. I let him take my clothes off, shivering for no reason, despite the fact that steam quickly fills the room. He keeps his eyes up, very clinical in his movements. When I'm naked, he takes my shoulder and turns me to the stall.

I don't do anything but stand there, dropping my head and bracing my hands on the tiled walls.

"Bunk, goddamn it." Then he steps in behind me, fully clothed, and reaches around me for a bar of soap. "Gonna help you out. Stop me if you get uncomfortable."

When he starts to wash my chest, my arms, my hands, I don't feel uncomfortable at all. I don't feel anything really. Once he's satisfied that I'm clean, he turns me around, working on my face. He's careful, but it still stings, and he gives me an apologetic look when he reaches my cheek. "Might have to get stitches for this. Good thing Donna's got a steady hand. Almost done, Bunk."

He's still working on my face when Whaley enters a moment later. His eyes widen in surprise, but he doesn't comment on why Raid's soaked and in the shower with me.

Instead, he rips off his bloody shirt, throwing it behind him. "I got this, Raid. Thank you."

Raid looks reluctant to leave, but with a parting squeeze to my shoulder, he does. I want to thank him, but I still can't speak.

Badge.

"Badge..." I eye Whaley as he strips and steps into the shower with me. His hands are coated with dried blood. "Whaley..."

"We'll talk about that in a bit," he tells me, taking the soap from where Raid put it in my hand. "Let's get this blood off us."

I feel so numb. Nothing sparks in me when Whaley takes over the job of cleaning my face. His touch isn't as warm as it usually is. There's no electricity or sharp sizzle. He's also curt and to the point. Once he feels like he's done with me, he takes the bar of soap to himself. I look down and see the red-tinted water flowing down the drain, making me gulp. Normally, I love the sight of red, love the blood, but this makes me sick to my stomach.

Literally.

I double over, barely avoiding vomiting on Whaley. He rubs my back soothingly, washing me again once I'm done heaving. After that, he brings me in his arms and holds me. We stay like that for far too long, until the water turns cold and he decides we need to get out.

We leave the shower, and I still can't do anything but stand there. He takes over drying us, first myself and then him before leading me out of the bathroom with a hand on my back. He sits me down on the bed and steps away to rifle through his drawers, pulling out two pairs of boxers and two shirts.

Moving my arms up, he puts the shirt on me before kneeling and lifting my foot so I can step into the boxers. He dresses quickly and takes me back to the bed, but instead of sitting next to me, he puts me on his lap.

We sit there in silence until I find my words again.

Badge.

"Badge."

"It's…" he trails off, brushing his thumb against my split lip. "It was touch and go, but he's gonna be fine. We made it to the hospital in time." Relief courses through me and tears spring to my eyes. A part of me doesn't believe him, but the other part feels overwhelming joy. "It's gonna be a long road to recovery, but he'll be okay."

"I wanna see him," I say, trying to get off his lap. "Take me to him."

He shakes his head, anchoring me to him once more. "Can't do that. He's in the ICU and can't have any visitors."

"What about Fox? He should be here. We need to call him—"

"Already took care of it," he assures me. "He's a day out, but I'm sure he'll be ridin' through the night."

"Okay," I breathe out before inhaling deeply. Badge is okay. He's going to be fine, but the look on Whaley's face unsettles me. Deep down in my gut, I know something else happened, but I can't quite place it. "Whaley… Did I do something wrong?"

He winces before dropping his face to my shoulder and breathes me in. "We don't have to talk about that now."

"Whatever is it, I can handle it," I insist, clutching at his shoulders. "Just tell me."

"I can't believe you don't remember." He sighs, shaking his head. "Shit, I do, actually. You probably blacked out when you did it."

"When I did what?" I growl out, growing frustrated. "I need to know."

"You killed Gunnar," he whispers, holding onto me tightly.

The words make me freeze, my jaw dropping as I look at him in shock. "No, I didn't. I couldn't have—"

"Badge couldn't tell me a lot, I'm figurin' it was self-defense, but you went feral. Stabbed him over ten times."

Then it flashes through my mind.

Blood. So much blood. The feel of it squishing under my fingers. The way my arms strained with every stab. The smell of copper in the air. The life fading from Gunnar's eyes. It slams into me, and before I know it, I'm doubling over, the urge to throw up again consuming me.

Whaley consoles me through it, murmuring soothingly

into my ear the entire time. "Let it out, Bunk. I know it's rough. Been there before."

"But I…" I stand, trying to filter through my thoughts and memories. "Whaley, I'm scared."

He nods. "You don't have to be. I'm here. Nobody's gonna hurt you—"

"That's not why I'm scared," I cut in. "I'm scared because I don't…"

"Don't what?"

"Don't care."

I truly don't. I think about it, really *think*, but I don't feel anything at all. I should be hit with regret, with disgust, with mortification. Throwing up was a bodily reaction, but my mind isn't following along.

Shouldn't I feel bad? Shouldn't I be horrified? Shouldn't I *care*?

I don't though. Gunnar had it coming. He attacked me and Badge—he nearly killed him—and I did what I had to do. Maybe the reaction was extreme, at least from what Whaley told me, but does that mean it was wrong?

"I see," Whaley mumbles, furrowing his brows. "You don't care?"

"Not in the slightest," I whisper back, shaking my head. "What does that mean?"

"It don't got to mean anythin'." That's cryptic as fuck. He's got curiosity in his eyes as he asks his next question. "How did it feel when you did it?"

"I felt…" Jesus Christ. I shouldn't say this. It's so wrong, so twisted, so demented. "…good," I finish, letting out a half-hearted laugh and smiling like a madman. "Fuck, Whaley. It felt amazin'. Once I got past all the shit I was thinkin', I felt such a rush. That bastard deserved it."

He looks at me for a beat, entirely interested in my response, but he doesn't flinch or even react. "What were you thinkin' about when it happened?"

"My Mama," I say truthfully, only now feeling a pang of fear. "The night she was murdered. I thought about how she looked, how she screamed, how she died. I think that's why I lost it. Does any of that make sense?"

"If it makes sense to you, it makes sense to me," he mutters, pausing as his eyes zero in on my cheek. "That's gonna scar."

"Gonna be badass, right?" I tease, ready for a subject change and to move on. "Wanna get a matchin' one?"

He shakes his head, trying to suppress an inappropriate chuckle. "Bunk, we really gotta focus."

"I am focused," I whine, all of a sudden feeling too hot. I squirm on his lap, fingering the barbell through his nipple under his shirt. "Wanna be focused on that dick."

Want to indulge in this sick desire I feel. Want to not care about how fucked-up I am.

"Cut it out," he snaps, slapping my hand away, but I can feel him growing hard underneath me. "Got to make sure you get what happened. You *killed* a man."

He says this like I don't get it. I do get it. I just don't care. "I know."

He cocks a brow, and I can see the wheels turning in his head as he tries to read me. "You really straight?"

I take a deep breath, think it through, and come up with the only logical answer.

Well, logical for me.

"Yep." When he curses under his breath, I cock my head to the side, feeling uneasy. "Wait, does that bother you? I—"

His lips slam against mine before I can finish my sentence. In the jumble of confusing information, fear for Badge, and rush of my confession, it all fades. I moan into his mouth and move until I'm straddling his lap. He nips at my lips, growling the entire time as his hands migrate to my ass. He squeezes *hard*, and he greedily eats the whimper I let out.

I want so much more. I reach for his underwear, but he pulls back before I can. "Whaley..."

"You're so fuckin' hot," he rasps, palming my crotch. "So perfect for me."

"I know," I whisper confidently.

"You don't get it," he insists, shaking his head as he fumbles with my boxers. "I like it too."

"Like what?" I ask, eyes fluttering shut when he gets my cock out. "Jesus, *yes*."

"I love feelin' in control, love playin' God." He leans into my neck and groans before biting down on the skin and stroking me at the same time. "The way you felt when you killed him, that's a feelin' I chase."

"You like bein' in control? Shockin'," I tease, but my words are cut short and my greedy eyes bulge when I see he's using his other hand to fish out his own cock. "Fuck, yes. Grind your dick against mine."

He takes us both in his hands, and I throw my head back at the pleasure. Whaley doesn't do his normal dirty talk, instead, continues his deep dark confession.

"No matter what it is, I relish it. Whether it's beatin' or killin', it's the feeling I chase." He tips my chin down with one hand, angling it toward our cocks. "Spit."

I keep my eyes on him as I let spit dribble from my mouth to coat us, easing the glide of his hand. He closes his eyes momentarily before they snap open again, searing and boring into my very soul. "You and I are different from everyone else, little psycho. We got our own moral code. Our own law. Nobody will fuckin' get it, but I do."

"It's so wrong," I whimper, so close to coming but holding back because I want this moment to last forever. "So fucked-up."

I fucking love it.

"What did I tell you?" he asks, his tongue tracing the cut on my cheek. "Who cares about right and wrong? You liked killin' him, I get you. You get off on it, I'm here with you. It's us against the world, Bunk."

Those words are what does it. My entire body tightens, tension coiling in my gut as I spill all over his hand, the universal truth leaving my lips. "I love you so fuckin' much."

My words are what triggers him, and after one more thrust into his fists, he's cresting along with me. "*Bunky.*"

I drop my forehead against his shoulder, reality crashing back down after a few moments as I come down from my high. "You sure Badge is okay?"

He palms the back of my head to kiss my temple before nodding. "Promise. He'll be fine."

"Thank fuck," I breathe out, suddenly flooded with guilt. "Feel like a terrible son. Fuckin' you when I should have been worried about him."

Whaley bobs his head, then presses his forehead against mine. "Told you we'd screw each other up." He looks at me with a crooked smirk on his lips. "Any regrets?"

I wrap my arms around his neck, not feeling a single one. "None. You?"

"Absolutely not."

We stay like that, lingering in silence before a thought occurs to me and I pull back to look at him better. "Raid said Donna was comin' by to look at me?"

"Might be here already but is givin' us some privacy." He taps my hip to signal for me to get up so we can get cleaned and dressed.

Afterwards, he keeps one hand firmly planted on my ass as we head to the door, but I stop him before he can open it, a sudden realization making me gasp. "Whaley..."

He looks down at me, nose wrinkled in confusion. "What?"

"The Vipers," I start, nibbling on my bottom lip. "I killed Gunnar. I just started a war. Shit. What are we gonna do?"

He nods, solemn and stoic, like a true leader. He considers

his words before brushing me off. "You let me deal with that. We need to get you checked out first."

"Me first?" I snort, rolling my eyes. "Priorities, Whaley."

He backs me up against the door, grinding his crotch against mine as he drops his lips to my ear. "You fucked me up, Bunk. I got shit I need to take care of. I got loyalties to reward. I got a gang to lead, but *you're* my priority. Always. Nothin' comes before you."

I swoon, tilting my head so I can capture his lips with mine. He moans, reaching for my arms and trapping them up against the door. I can feel him growing thick against me again, so I arch my back, ready to—

"Sorry to interrupt, boys, but you better let me look at Bunky to make sure he's okay."

Whaley and I rip apart, eyes widening. Damn, we got caught. Whaley sighs, giving me one last peck before stepping back. "Let her patch you up. Gotta sort some shit out anyway."

When he opens the door, we come face-to-face with a concerned Donna. She looks at us and shakes her head, not in disapproval, but probably disbelief. I think she might have put two and two together.

Whaley nods at her before leaving us, and Donna raises a brow at me. "You got a lot of explainin' to do, honey." She *tsks*. "Now, you're gonna tell me the whole story while I get you patched up."

I agree and follow her to the living room. She patches me up efficiently and quickly, all the while prying into Whaley and mine's relationship. I let her ask her questions and respond with what I can, but now that the adrenaline has settled, I feel the fear rushing over me. Not the fear of what I did, but the fear for Badge. Whaley said he was okay though, and I trust him with my life.

Now I'm counting down the seconds until I can confirm that myself.

TWENTY-THREE

Bunky

The steady beat from the heart monitor soothes me. With every rhythmic beep, I'm reminded that Badge is alive, in serious condition, but alive nonetheless.

Fox and I sit by his bed in the hospital. He's woken up a few times in the last couple of days, but the nurses say it's best if he gets his rest. Fox has been here every single day, not going far from his side. When he needs a break, other members rotate so Badge isn't left vulnerable and alone. I would be here every day too, but Whaley's had me glued to his side. With everything going on, I don't want to be apart from him either, but I love my dad and I need to see him.

Fox's fingers twitch and he looks like he's desperate for a cigarette. "You can go smoke," I tell him, gesturing at our sleeping dad. "Don't think he's gonna wake up any time soon. Take a break."

Fox's jaw is set in a tight line and there's something akin to anger in his eyes. "No. I'm not lettin' shit slide again."

"Again?" I can't help but wrinkle my nose. "What do you mean?"

"He got stabbed," he states, waving his hands at Badge and the bandages that cover his torso. "Fuckin' almost died and where was I? Fuckin' around when I should have been here."

"You were on a run," I say, but as the words leave my lips, Fox's face falls. He was on a run, *right*? "Fox—"

"I can't leave him, Bunk," he cuts me off, shutting his eyes for a brief second before turning to me. "Can't let him down again."

"You didn't let anyone down," I insist, grabbing his arm. "If it was anyone's fault, it was mine. I wanted to start shit with Gunnar, and Badge was protectin' me."

"It ain't your fault," he snaps, almost like he's angry at me for even suggesting that. "You ain't the one that stabbed him. Either way, you paid that motherfucker back tenfold. Glad he's dead."

"Me too." I'm still not not really feeling anything now when it comes to Gunnar's death. Excitement, maybe? But even that's wearing off into a dull buzz. It's like when I snort a bump. I hit that high, bask in it, but then come crashing down until it's nothing but a memory. I shake my head, focusing back on the matter at hand. "When do you think we can take him home?"

He shrugs. "Doctor said it might be a week or two. He's clear, but they wanna make sure of that before they release him."

I nod along, snagging a pen from the chart hanging on the foot of the bed and start to doodle on a hospital magazine. I don't realize what I'm making until Fox nudges my shoulder. "You gonna get that?"

I blink at him, then look down, eyes widening when I realize I've drawn an ornate badge. I'm tempted to let the tears welling in my eyes fall, but I don't. Instead, I blink them away and shrug. "I mean, why not?"

"You should put our initials in it," he suggests. "Maybe a skull. I'll get it too."

"Really?" I ask, excited at the prospect of Fox and I having something shared between us. "That'd be pretty awesome."

"It's a deal," he agrees

"Better include me in that deal."

"Dad!" Fox and I say at the same time, straightening in our seats as Badge blinks his eyes open. "How you feelin'?"

"Like shit." He chuckles, wincing and holding onto his side as he tries to sit up.

"Don't be stubborn, Dad," Fox chastises, forcing Badge to stay lying down. "Water? Ice chips? Need to take a piss?"

Badge's eyes grow more aware as each second passes. "Don't tell me you've been here all day? Thought you were gonna stop by this mornin'?"

"Is that how you thank your dutiful sons for sitting at your bedside?" Fox jokes, squeezing Badge's ankle. "Real nice, old man."

Badge rolls his eyes. "You must have better shit to do."

"Not really." I fiddle with the pen in my hand. "Besides visitin' you, we've kinda been on lockdown."

Badge raises his brow at that, but he doesn't look surprised. "Tell me more."

"Well—"

"Whaley's handlin' it," Fox cuts me off. "All you have to focus on is gettin' better so we can get you the fuck out of here and home."

I don't agree with Fox's decision to keep our dad in the dark. I know he's recovering, but I think he has a right to be aware of what's going on outside the hospital and with the Aces. I don't argue or intervene though. I'm doing the little brother thing and following his lead, letting him take charge of the conversation.

Badge, however, is a stubborn motherfucker. "How's Whaley handlin' it?"

Fox frowns, but since Badge asked again, it'd be rude not to tell him the truth. "Just a curfew for now. Don't go anywhere alone. That kind of stuff. He's waitin' to see what the Vipers' first move is gonna be."

"Smart," Badge grunts, then he squints at me, eyes assessing before he speaks again. "You should go, Bunk."

I'm hit with a pang of fear and worry. What does he mean by that? Does he not want me here? Why doesn't he want me here? Has he finally realized that he's lying in this hospital bed because of me and my lack of control? What if—

"Cut it out, kid." He reaches for the pen in my hand to stop my incessant clicking. "Didn't mean it in a bad way. Whaley's probably all wound tight that you're gone. Sure you are too. Go back to him and stay there."

"But what about you?" I ask. Although what he's saying sounds entirely appealing, I'm trying not to lose myself to that craving. I really do want to be here for Badge, no matter how much it hurts being away from Whaley.

He waves my concern away with an easy smile. "Nah, I'm fine. Strong as hell, right? I know you love me, son. That's all that matters. But what you need is Whaley, and I'm sure as hell he needs you too. Can't get through this without each other."

"So you're…" Fox trails off, eyes bouncing between me and Badge. "…cool with them? Whaley and Bunk? Heard you beat the hell out of Whaley when you found out."

"It was one punch. Just a love tap. He's bein' a big baby if he's sayin' that shit," Badge defends. He turns to me again and nods. "Go, Bunk. Take Fox with you. He smells like ass."

"Hey!"

I ignore Fox's offense and think about what Badge is giving me. It's deeper than his permission. It's his understanding. I think, maybe, he finally gets it. At least, he's acting like he does. He's reaching into me, reading me, and looking at what's best.

He's so strong, so loyal, so clever. He sacrifices his own wants and needs for others, and I think he's one of the greatest men I've ever known.

"Wanna hug you," I blurt out but stop myself from doing just that. I think it through before giving his foot a squeeze instead. "Love you, Dad."

"Bunky, don't do that shit," Fox scolds, knocking my hand away.

Badge laughs, wiggling his foot away from me before tossing me a wink. "Love you too, son. Now, both of you fuck off. You can visit another time."

"Let's at least wait until other people get here." Fox worries his lip, reaching for his phone. "Then we'll leave."

Badge nods his agreement, then looks around the room and frowns. "Where's my fuckin' jello?"

I throw my head back with a laugh, getting up and harassing the nurses until I get him not one, but *two* green jello cups.

TWENTY-FOUR

Whaley

Things are too calm.

I can't explain it. It's like before a storm where the air is warm and still. How it's eerily quiet and nothing seems real. That's the only way I can describe how it's been for me the last week. *Fine.* It's all been fine, and that doesn't sit well.

I'm waiting for the other shoe to drop. Maybe for Bunky to flip a switch and go apeshit, to be flooded with guilt over what he did, or to become overwhelmed with the desire to do something just as insane again.

Then there's the other gang. I haven't heard a peep, and none of my guys have seen them out and about. It's like they've disappeared into thin air. No—scattered like roaches, lurking in the shadowy depths while preparing to make their move.

Or maybe I'm being paranoid, which I highly doubt. Gunnar may have stabbed Badge, but Bunky killed one of theirs. They're completely different outcomes of a shitty situation. Not to mention Gunnar was Thorn's son. I have no doubt the leader of the Crown of Vipers will be seeking revenge soon. I know I would be if I were him, which is why I've been extremely cautious.

I've had Fox stay at the hospital with Badge, not trusting him to be alone. I told all my guys to go everywhere in pairs, not wanting them to be picked off or ganged up on. It's been working fine, but I'm still concerned.

Thankfully, Bunky is listening to me for once and is taking things seriously. Aside from today with him visiting his dad, he's been glued to my side. It was hard enough to let him go off with Fox, but I knew he needed to. That doesn't mean my skin isn't itching with the need to see with my own eyes that he's really okay.

The Vipers are going to want him the most. With him killing Thorn's son, Bunky's put a massive target on his back. It's open season on my little psycho, and the Vipers are likely preparing for the hunt. If anything were to happen to him...

Stop it.

When I said we'd burn the world to the ground if we were together, I should have mentioned it'd be tenfold if we were ripped apart. While I know we're equal parts insane and a disaster, I also know we are two coexisting halves of the same whole, and separating us would be our undoing. It'll push us past the point of no return, and I have no doubt that'd be the truest devastation. The demise of everything.

There's no longer a me without him.

A loud crash has me jerking away from the car I was working on, and I spin around, preparing to whip out my knife but stop when I see one of the members knocked over a toolbox. He shoots me an apologetic look and I wave him off, trying to appear unbothered even though my heart feels like it's going to pound out of my chest.

Fuck. I need a beer or a bump, but I can't afford for my inhibitions to be down right now, so I've been steering clear of all recreational activities. Not that I ever really partake anyway, but I like to at least have the option.

"You good?" Pike questions, coming to stand beside me, his face pinched with concern.

"Yeah." I sigh, crossing my arms and leaning against the car I was supposed to be working on. "A lot on my mind."

"Can't blame you." He pauses, reaching up to rub the back of his neck. "It's been a lot."

"That's one way of puttin' it." I smirk, fingers instinctively going to my pocket, itching to pull out my pack of smokes. "Just tryin' to keep everyone alive."

"I speak for the whole gang when I say we all got your back." He gives my shoulder a squeeze, a half smile on his lips as he tries to reassure me. "I know it's hard with Badge bein' gone, but we're all here. Tell us what you need and we're on it. "

"Keep your ear to the ground, make sure everyone's on high alert. Don't want Thorn comin' out balls to the wall and us not bein' ready for that shit."

"You think it's gonna happen?" he asks curiously.

"Yeah, I mean, I can't speak for him, obviously, but I know if it were one of mine, I'd want someone to pay."

Especially since the cops haven't shown up to arrest Bunky. I'm assuming Thorn's going a different route which only puts me more on alert. Only a dumbass would think there wouldn't be some kind of retaliation.

"Have you thought about goin' to him? Maybe seein' if he's willing to come up with some kind of truce?" he asks.

"I've thought about it, but I always circle back to revenge. That's what he's gonna want. Eye for an eye. Trouble is, the only eye he's gonna want, he ain't fuckin' gettin'. I'd sooner kill Thorn before I let him take what's mine."

"Whaley…" Pike's tone is apprehensive. He's eyeing me, his bottom lip trapped between his teeth, and I can tell he wants to say something.

"What?"

He takes a small step back, arms unfolding so he can hold

out his hands. "Listen, I mean no offense, and I hope it doesn't piss you off, but everyone's been wonderin'. You see, we've noticed things. Again, you don't have to tell me. Actually, you know what, forget—"

What the fuck is happening right now? Why is he rambling?

"Out with it," I snap, annoyance rising because he won't get to the damn point. "What is it?"

"Well, you see, we were wonderin' if something's goin' on with you and Bunky?" He winces as he says it, taking a big step back and nervously glancing around.

I figured people would be curious. I was assuming that once Badge knew, the rest would soon after. I mean, I don't owe anyone an explanation, but it'd make sense that people want some clarity.

I open my mouth to tell him the extent of my relationship with Bunky when it dawns on me how quiet the shop is suddenly. I look around too, expecting the place to be empty, but am shocked when I realize the entire place is frozen. *Literally frozen.* People are hunched over, hands glued to whatever the fuck they're working on, but no one moves an inch. It's as if Pike pressed the universal pause button.

I can't help it. I laugh loudly as I bend over and clutch my knees because I've never seen something like this before. Sure, in a movie, but never in real life. It takes me too long to stop laughing, and when I do, I reach up to swipe my eyes, trying to pull myself together. There are several looks being passed between my guys. Some are smiling with me while some look downright horrified, Pike being a part of the latter. I'm about to confirm what he suspects, let everyone know that it's true, that Bunky is mine, when the object of my desires comes barreling through the side door with Raid on his tail. They're talking about some parts Bunky needs for his bike, completely unaware of what they walked into.

We're all watching them, every single person in the shop, and it doesn't take them long to realize it either.

"The fuck?" Raid barks out, adjusting his glasses. "What?"

No one says a word and it only causes Bunky to raise his brow in question. "Did we walk in on somethin'?"

Yeah, little psycho, you walked in on something alright.

Instead of answering with words, a thought occurs to me, and I beckon him to me with a finger. His smile turns to a confused one, that much is obvious, but comes to me without a blip of hesitation anyway.

"What's up?" he asks, brows furrowed as he closes the gap between us. "Did I fuck somethin' up? I promise I didn't mean to—"

I snag his waist, pulling him to me, and slant my lips over his. He lets out a surprised grunt before his hands snake up to cup my neck as he kisses me back. It's meant to be a quick peck to show everyone he's mine, but it quickly turns into more the second our lips connect. Bunky shoves his tongue into my mouth, flicking his piercing against my tongue as he tries to eat me alive. I let him dominate for only a few flicks before taking back control by cutting him off with a nip to his bottom lip.

He whines and rocks his hips against me. "Aw, Whaley. That was a tease."

His eyes are glazed, lips shining from my saliva, and his hands are twisting the hair at the nape of my neck.

"None of that, little psycho. Can't give everyone a show." I reach up, swiping his lip.

"Oh, you think I care about that? I'd let you destroy my ass right here in front of everyone." He gestures to the car beside me. "Would drop my pants and bend over right now."

My hand shoots up, caging his throat as possessiveness burns in my gut. "Ain't nobody seein' what's fuckin' mine. You got me?" I bite out, annoyed at the idea.

He blinks, lust shining through those green depths as his

tongue licks out to wet his lips. "Oh fuck, you're claimin' me in front of everyone. It's gonna make me nut without even touchin' myself. Your growly voice with all this—" He waves his hand at me before motioning to all the guys who I'm sure are staring. "It's the hottest thing ever ."

I give his neck a little squeeze in warning before looking at my guys and confirming that they are indeed all looking at us.

"Does this answer everyone's question?" Everyone nods, but no one says a word. "Good. Now, if you'll excuse us, I have to handle somethin'."

Then I drag Bunky by his neck to my office, barely locking the door before pushing him over my desk and showing him just how much *mine* he is.

TWENTY-FIVE

Bunky

I'm in a mood.

I've always been prone to fits of unstable temperaments. It's not something I can easily control, it just *is*, and some days, the pressure in my head gets too tight and I feel like causing chaos. Like I need to expel all the pent up energy inside me by being as erratic as possible.

Today is one of those days.

I huff, tossing the wrench behind me, not caring where it lands.

"You gettin' fucked out here, Bunk?" Whaley asks, appearing from his office, eyes narrowed as he looks at me. "The fuck are you gruntin' about?"

"It's nothin'." I cross my arms over my chest and shoot him a glare. "Just feelin' a certain type of way today."

Which I know I shouldn't be. It's been a few days since Whaley claimed me as his, and by all accounts, I should be fucking soaring. That's what makes it especially irritating that I'm not.

He cocks a brow before realization fills his eyes. "Feelin' reckless?"

"Stabby," I correct, turning my nose up at him. "Can't help it."

He chuckles. "Right. Normally, I like it when you get stabby, but you're just bein' a brat right now. Pike told me you threatened to cut him if he talked to you today."

I stick my bottom lip out and shrug. "So? Pike's annoying."

He ignores that and instead suggests something that piques my interest. "Wanna get out of here?"

I eye him warily, even though I really want to say yes. "Where?"

"Come on." He grabs my arm and urges me to follow him to his Harley. "Let's go somewhere."

"We goin' to another fight?" I ask, excitement racing through me at the thought. "Please, tell me we're goin' to a fight."

"It's too early in the day for that, but I got another idea." He grabs his extra helmet and secures it on my head. "Get on the damn bike."

I nod my agreement, doing as he says and clinging to him like a little spider monkey. I make sure to grope him because —*duh*—how can I not? Whaley only grunts, hardening under my palm as he starts the bike and we take off.

We don't go far, and end up at a little strip mall by the high school, and I eye the yoga place with too much enthusiasm as we dismount.

"Finally gonna let me show you my doggy style?"

He snorts, throwing his arm over my shoulders. "Been inside you when you've shown me. Now look to the left."

I furrow my brow as I scan the strip mall, jaw dropping when I see what he's talking about. Immediately, I perk up, jumping on my toes as I clap. "A tattoo parlor?"

He smiles, leading me toward the entrance. "Figured you

needed to redirect all that crazy to somethin' else. Wanted us to come here, anyway, and today seemed like a good time."

"Why?"

He spins me on my heels to cradle my face in his hands. "Because I want somethin' on you that makes it clear you're mine."

I grin. "And for you?"

"I'm gettin' one too," he says, taking my hand. "That way we'll both have somethin' permanent on us for each other."

"I love it, Whaley," I gush, cuddling up to his side. "So romantic."

"Yeah, yeah." He rolls his eyes, opening the door and ushering me inside. "Romantic? I dunno about that, but self-ish? One hundred percent."

I prefer *possessive*.

The shop is pretty empty, not unusual for this early in the afternoon, and Whaley and I walk right up to the reception desk without any delay. There's a guy covered in tattoos at the front who looks like he could be Whaley's age. When he looks up, he shows recognition, smiling at us as we approach.

"Whaley!" He steps from around the counter to shake Whaley's hand. "How's it been? Long time since you came in."

Whaley nods, giving him an equally fond smile. "Good to see you, Randy."

"Who's this?" Randy questions, turning to me and also reaching for my hand.

"Bunky," I tell him. "Whaley's boyfriend." I can't help the possessive edge to my tone. I don't know this guy, but he clearly knows *my* guy and that shit is unsettling to me.

"Nice to meet you. Whaley and I go way back." Randy chuckles, not at all bothered by me, and I don't know how I feel about that. He then motions between the two of us. "You here for some ink?"

"If you got time. I should have called but..." He gives me a knowing look. "Wanted to surprise him."

Randy nods in understanding. "I have some time before my next client if you want something small."

Whaley thinks it over before agreeing. "Small should be fine."

"Sounds good. Come on back, you know the way."

We follow Randy to his station, decked out in anime posters and cool designs. "What are we gettin' today?" he asks as he sits on the rolling stool by his machine.

I have no idea. This was all Whaley wanting to get matching tattoos, so I'm sure I'm going to like anything he comes up with. Just to help, I offer some suggestions. "Our names?"

Randy tips his head from side to side as he thinks. "If you want somethin' unique, I wouldn't go for that. What do y'all have in common? What's special to you two?"

I think about it. I mean, I have my whale tattoo, but I can't think of anything that would represent me besides my actual name. "Maybe we can get matchin' knives? That'd be cool. Or—"

"Bite marks," Whaley cuts me off, tone dropping an octave as his eyes fill with something primal. Okay, that definitely wasn't where I was going, but I can't lie, that's hot.

When Randy nods and starts to prep his tools, it dawns on me why I like that idea so much. Bite marks—besides being super sexual—represent not only our obsession for each other but also our inner demons as well. The violence, the savageness, the primalness all call to the parts of us that everyone shuns but we embrace.

I smile up at Whaley, tempted to kiss the smirk off his face. "I love it."

"Knew you would," he teases, brushing his thumb against my bottom lip before pulling it down so he can examine my teeth. "You're gonna look good with my mark."

"Where are you getting them?" Randy chimes in, pulling our attention back to him.

"He's gettin' his on his ass," Whaley throws out before I have a chance to blink.

Damn, that was fucking quick. It's like he's been planning this.

My eyes widen. It's hard to make me blush, but my cheeks are on fire right now. My jaw drops as I look at Whaley, a bit flustered. "I am?"

"Wanna be able to see it when I'm fuckin' you," he tells me, squeezing my ass as if to prove his point.

"And where are you gettin' yours?" I choke out, trying to ignore the fact that this shit turns me on.

"Wherever you want."

Oh, he shouldn't have said that. "Your dick."

His brow arches and I see a slight moment of regret before he sighs. "That appealin' to you?"

I bite my bottom lip as I scroll through all the images of a naked Whaley I have in my mind. He's already covered, more than I am, so there isn't much room. His hands, his arms, his chest, they're all full of beautiful, black and white patterns that I admire so much.

"Nah, I want it right here," I say after a moment, reaching up on the tip of my toes so I can brush the spot right under his ear. "Out in the open."

That devilish smirk of his makes my knees weak, and he leans in, planting a quick kiss to my lips. "Done."

Randy reaches for some black gloves once he's ready, eyes flicking between us both. "So, who's going first?"

"I'll go!" I practically yell, eager to get started.

"Alright." Randy reaches for some alcohol, nudging his head toward the seat. "You can keep your pants on, just pull them down for me."

I unbuckle my belt and wriggle my pants over the bottom

of my ass, making sure to keep my dick locked up as I lay stomach first on the table.

"Where?" Randy questions Whaley.

I feel Whaley's finger as he points to the fullest part of my butt. "There."

"Okay, so for the outline, I'm gonna need—"

He doesn't get to finish his sentence as a sharp pain courses through me and I release a startled gasp. I look over my shoulder but don't get a chance to say anything as Whaley digs his teeth into my cheek, hard enough to dent the skin but not to draw blood. Then he licks the mark, smiling as he pulls back, and my eyes darken at the tent in his pants.

"*Okay*," Randy draws out, clicking his tongue at Whaley and shooting him a look. "I have to sanitize the area anyway."

Whaley doesn't seem bothered, only looking at my ass. "That work?"

"You know that's not how it's done, but it'll do," Randy playfully scolds before looking at me.

My lip kicks up and I nod as Randy starts tracing over Whaley's bite mark. Randy's a tattoo artist, so we can't be the most out-there people he's ever met, but I bet we're giving him a run for his money on the crazy side of things.

"Be as heavy-handed as you want," I tell him when I hear the whir of the machine start. "I fuckin' love it."

"So do I. That's why I have so many. This won't take long, then we'll move on to Whaley."

Randy gets started a second later, and I close my eyes, enjoying the sound of the buzzing from the tattoo gun, the smell of rubbing alcohol in the shop, and the feel of the needle digging into my skin. This is one of my favorite things. My vice. The perfect way to zone out and just be.

It's over all too quickly, minutes feeling like seconds when he's shutting off his machine and tapping my hip.

"All done." He pulls off his gloves and gestures to the mirror. "Check it out and tell me what you think."

When I walk over to the mirror, I nearly jump Whaley after looking at the finished product. I'm sure Whaley feels the same way as he stares at my ass, more specifically the large, black bite mark now on it.

"It's perfect," I say, looking at Randy. "How'd you do it so quickly?"

"Practice," is all Randy says as he motions for me to spin so he can clean and wrap the area. "After twenty years of tattooing, you get really good at it."

"That's how long you've been doin' this?" I ask as I pull up my pants once he's done. "That's so cool."

"It was always my dream." He turns to Whaley and smiles. "Alright, your turn."

I spin on my heels and start my march toward Whaley, teeth already bared. "Come here—"

"Nope!" Randy shouts, jumping between us and holding up a piece of paper. "We're doing it my way this time. Take this, bite down hard, and hold it for a second."

I pout but defer to the professional. While I follow his instructions, Randy wipes down the bench, changes his supplies, and resets before motioning for Whaley to sit once he's done. He sanitizes the part of his skin Whaley's getting his on and takes the paper from me.

I wander around his area while he's working on tracing my bite mark to another stencil, looking at all the intricate tattoo designs he has hung up next to his anime. I'm not an expert on tattoos, far from it, but he looks like he's skilled in multiple different styles. There are some American Traditional, a few Neo-Traditional, and I spy one Trash Polka.

"You like what you see?"

I turn to Randy who's already started tattooing Whaley's neck. I nod as I let myself examine his tools, maybe standing a bit too close to him. "How do you know how far down to press?"

"There's a certain amount it needs to be below the surface of the skin, but it really just depends on the canvas and the placement," he explains. "The skin on the neck is thinner than the skin on your ass. I don't have to go as deep here or else I'll fuck it up."

"And the shading? Do you have to change instruments for that?"

"Yeah, but I won't be using any for this. It's just an outline."

"What about for color? Is there a different needle for that or can you use the same one for black and white or grayscale?" Words are spewing past my lips because I find this so fascinating.

Randy pauses to look at me and smirks. "You seem really interested in tattooing."

I shrug as he turns and gets back to work. "I dunno. Seems cool. I love tattoos, and I think the idea of givin' people somethin' they'll carry for the rest of their life is awesome. It's like they take a part of you with them when they leave."

"I agree, I feel the same way about it," Randy tells me. He's close to being done with my bite mark and wipes Whaley's skin before continuing. "You do any drawing?"

"I guess, but I don't know if they're any good." I think of the doodles I sometimes do when I'm bored when the fan fiction doesn't come to me. It's something that helps me get out of my head.

He hums under his breath. "What do you draw?"

"Just things I'm interested in or that I think look cool," I say. A thought crosses my mind, and maybe it's a little ridiculous, but I decide to shoot my shot. "Um, how does apprenticing work?"

Whaley gives me a questioning look, but Randy just smiles. "You want to become a tattoo artist?"

It's not something I've ever really thought about, but the more I sit on it, the more I like it. It's not that I don't like the work I do for the gang, but I think maybe I'm ready for a change. I've never been good at dealing, and cars are nice and all, but this seems like something new and exciting. "This is probably gonna sound bad since I didn't really think of it until today, but I'm liking the idea."

"That's okay," he assures me. "People aren't born with knowing what they want to do in life. That comes to everyone at different times."

I never thought of it that way, but I see what Randy's saying. Everyone finds their own path. "What would I need to do?"

"You can come by the shop and show me some of your work." He wipes down Whaley's tattoo one more time before preparing to clean and cover it up. "Can't promise you anything, though."

"I understand," I say, nearly bouncing on my heels in excitement. "So, I can just come by whenever?"

He gestures behind him at his station as he hands Whaley a mirror. "Grab one of my cards and give me a heads-up first."

I don't need Whaley's permission, but I look at him anyway, more to gauge his reaction than anything else. What I see is a knowing smile directed right at me. He's probably thinking the same thing I am. He once talked to me about finding my thing, my passion, something that was just for me, and this could be it.

Maybe I'll be shit at it, or maybe I'll get bored, but I'm young enough to seize the opportunity and figure it out.

"Will do," I say, a wide smile splitting my face.

Whaley stands in front of me, leaning down a tad so I can see behind his ear. "What do you think? You got a big mouth for such a small thing."

I can't see it a hundred percent with the film Randy put on

the tattoo, but I'm in love with it already. I'm sure it's not hygienic, and Randy might call me out for it, but I lean up to press a kiss to it. "I love it. Thank you for today, Whaley. I really needed it."

"I know," is all he says, brushing my hair away from my face. "Just want you happy, little psycho."

"*You* make me happy." I wink at him. "But this was also great."

We follow Randy up to the front of the shop to pay. He doesn't charge us much, but Whaley makes sure to leave him a nice big tip for what he did.

"Thanks for coming in, guys. Hit me up if you want any more ink."

"Definitely," I say, shaking his hand when he offers it.

"Thanks for fittin' us in."

They go back and forth for a second, exchanging good-byes before Whaley thanks him one more time, and I don't miss the way he slips him an extra twenty. We walk out happily tatted up, buzzing from our day. We were only here for an hour or two, but it feels like we were in our own little bubble, away from all the external shit that we've had to worry about lately.

But our happy, domestic, perfect day is quickly ruined when we get back to the shop and see what's waiting for us.

TWENTY-SIX

Whaley

I can't believe I let this happen.

I look around my torn-up shop, trying to wrap my mind around the damage that's been done, not only to my place but to my guys that were here working as well. I should have been here. I knew the Vipers were going to strike, and I still left anyway. I let my desire to make Bunky happy take priority over the issue at hand.

I'm so fucking glad nobody died though. That'd be one more thing to add on to the guilt that's already flooding me at the fact I wasn't here to help them. I should have been. I should have made sure everyone was safe.

Anger bubbles up inside of me and I rear back, kicking a busted-up jug of oil, not feeling an inkling of satisfaction afterward.

"You good, Whaley?" Donna yells from across the garage.

Pike called Donna to come clean up a few guys who had minimal injuries from the brawl while he took the ones who needed more serious treatment to the hospital. I'm glad he used his head and took control of things since I wasn't here to do that.

Hunt Thorn down and make him pay.

I want to. Fuck, do I want to, but I can't right now. I have too much shit to fix first. My garage, my guys, my rapidly crumbling sanity. I need to tackle each issue one by one before I go out and pay Thorn back for what he did.

"Whaley?" Donna questions again, her voice sounding more concerned now. "Are you okay?"

I inhale deeply, noting the random specks of blood on the floor, and release a frustrated groan. My gaze sweeps across my shop, taking in all the damage again, and I reach up to pinch the bridge of my nose as I fight the urge to rampage. There's glass scattered around from where bullets shot out several windows, most of my inventory is fucked—tires slashed, oil busted open, shit all pulled down and destroyed, and I won't be able to salvage most of my equipment. This is easily thousands of dollars worth of damage and it's going to take so much time to get everything in order.

So, am I okay?

"Not really," I grumble, going to where she's now attempting to clean up the mess that is my shop. "I appreciate the effort, Donna, but it's no use. I'm gonna have to hire some people to sort this all out."

She gives me a sympathetic smile before giving my shoulder a quick squeeze. "You know I'll help with whatever you need."

"You've done a lot already. Thanks for getting here so fast. I was unavailable." The words leave my lips a little harsher than necessary, but I can't help it. I'm so damn pissed at myself for not seeing the big picture when all I saw was Bunky.

"Hey, no need to beat yourself up over it. Shit happens." She shrugs, and I try to not let it bother me that she's being so nonchalant, even though I know it's probably for my own benefit. "You can't expect to live here twenty-four seven."

I shake my head. "I'd have to disagree because of my role."

She folds her arms over her chest, giving me a thoughtful look. "So leaders don't get days off?"

"Not when they know their enemies are lurkin' in the background. What I did was stupid. I fucked up, and now my shop, my guys, everyone fuckin' paid the price for it."

"What would you have done though?"

I cock a brow, not understanding the question. "What do you mean?"

"If you were here, what could you have done to stop it?" She pauses briefly, not giving me a chance to answer. "Nothin'. You bein' here wouldn't have changed anythin'. You and Bunky not bein' here kept you two from gettin' hurt."

My lip kicks up despite the war raging inside of me. "I don't believe in that fate shit, Donna. I should have been here."

"Well, we can agree to disagree," she says as she bends down to grab her filled trash bag. "I'm gonna throw this away. Do you need anythin' else?"

A gun. Thorn. A fucking bump or two would be nice.

I rub my temple to quiet the noise. "No, I'm good. Gonna try to sort my shit out, figure out who can come and fix the windows ASAP. Don't need to add robbery to the list."

Not that there's anything to rob now, aside from the safe in my office, but no one is getting through that level of security.

"I can call around too if you want. See if anyone has any deals or a clear schedule?"

"Yeah, that'd be good." I appreciate the fact that she wants to help, even though she doesn't have to. That's one of the many things I've always respected about her. "Thanks, Donna."

"Got it. I'll see you tomorrow."

She spins to leave, but I stop her when a thought occurs to me. "Wait, I'll take you home."

She shakes her head, motioning to where Raid and Bunky are leaning against the far wall of the shop while talking. Damn, I forgot they were here. "Raid's my ride."

That makes me feel better. At least I know she won't be heading home alone.

"You ready to go?" Raid perks up and comes over with Bunky following behind him, obviously hearing his name, then snags the bag from Donna. "I got this."

"I can get it," she protests, trying to take the bag back.

He dodges her and lets out a scoff, already heading toward the exit. "No way am I lettin' you carry this out. I can handle it."

I follow, needing to make sure they get into the car safely and am thankful when they do. I doubt anything else is going to happen today, but I can't be too sure. I wouldn't put it past the Vipers to try more shit, especially not after this sneak attack.

Rolling my neck, I release a sigh before spinning around to look at all the damage again. I should probably go home and sleep, but I know that'll be pointless. My brain is working overtime, plotting revenge, feeling guilty, and worrying over how the fuck I'm going to make everything right.

Truthfully, I don't even know where to start, but throwing some of the messed up shit away sounds like the way to go. So that's what I do. I get to work, cleaning up the broken pieces of my shop and separating items into stacks of things that can potentially be saved.

Bunky tries to help, but he mostly gets in the way. He keeps trying to talk to me too, following me around the shop to pick up the things I've missed, which only irritates me more.

"Whaley?" He calls me yet again for what feels like the

tenth time in five minutes, and I'm over it. I need some fucking quiet.

"What?" I bark out, standing from my hunched down position and shooting him a glare. "I'm fuckin' busy."

"Whoa." He holds a hand up, eyes widening with surprise at my outburst. "The hell? I was tryin' to see if these were salvageable." He holds up two oil containers in his other hand. "The tops are busted but they're still half full. I noticed you were keepin' some but not all, so I wanted to check before I threw them out."

"They should be fine," I grumble before turning back to my task.

"Yeah, but do you need to look at them? See if any—"

I turn on my heels, tossing the shit I was handling onto the floor. "I said they're fine! Damn it, if you don't know, just leave the shit where you find it and I'll check later!"

His face sours as he levels me with a glare. "I'm tryin' to help. Why are you bein' such a dick?"

A loud laugh tears past my throat before I have a chance to stop it. I shake my head, unable to believe he's asking me that. He of all people should understand what's going on in my brain. He should get that I'm barely hanging on, trying to sort stuff, and feeling guilty about all of it.

"Why am I bein' such a dick? I don't know, Bunky. Have you looked around?" I spread my arms out wide, motioning to the havoc around me. "See my shop? See all the shit I gotta deal with?"

"Of course, I see it. I ain't blind," he throws back. "I know it's shitty, but why are you snappin' at me? I didn't do anythin'. I just wanna help."

"You've been helpin' me enough, don't you think?" I bite out through clenched teeth.

His brows furrow in confusion. "What are you talkin' about?"

"Distractin' me. Keepin' me from doin' my fuckin' job." I

drag a hand through my long hair, not caring when I tear a few strands in the process. "It's all so fucked."

"Wait, wait." He sets down the oil jugs he's holding, eyes full of disbelief and hurt. "You're mad at *me* for this?"

I know what happened today isn't his fault, but I'm not thinking logically. I'm really pissed off, and I need him to leave me alone and let me work through my thoughts.

"I'm angry in general." My jaw tenses as I bend down to put more shit aside, hoping it'll be the end of it, but of course it's not. Bunky always has to have the last word.

"Okay, and that's fine. I get it, I'd be mad too. Hell, I am." His tone is earnest, and I hear him take a step toward me. "But my anger ain't misplaced."

"You don't get it." I don't know why I'm still talking. I need to keep my mouth shut before I say something I don't mean. "This is about me failin' in my role. I'm supposed to put my people first. Look out for their best interests."

It's the code I live by. My people give me everything— their loyalty, their safety, their trust—and in return, I keep them safe. I feed them if they don't have food, and I give them jobs when they need money. They're my family, and being an Ace trumps blood, and it used to trump everything else in my life.

Bunky obviously doesn't get why I'm so upset as he takes a hesitant step toward me, reaching out for my arm. "You do that every day."

"Clearly," I grunt, taking a step away before he can touch me. "Just let me deal with this, Bunk." I should have stayed here, not taken him out, and definitely not let my fucking phone die. Why in the hell did I do that? So fucking stupid. I knew better. I knew it. "I knew it was a bad idea," I say, grabbing an already busted tub of oil and flinging it across the garage. It smacks the ground with a plop, sending oil flying everywhere.

"What the hell does that mean?" Bunky asks in a tone I've

never heard before. "What was a bad idea? *Me*?"

Wait, what?

I look at him, taking in his red-rimmed eyes, clenched jaw, and fisted hands. He looks like he's about to burst into tears or fly forward and beat the shit out of me. Neither are things I want, and I'm suddenly flooded with even more guilt.

"Bunky—"

"You regret me, Whaley? Is that what you're sayin'?"

I step toward him, shaking my head desperately. "No—"

"You knew it was a bad idea? You never should have let this happen? You mean me, huh?" His fist comes up to smack his chest, voice cracking as the words leave his lips. "I was the bad idea?" He lets out a humorless laugh, shaking his head and swiping his arm across his face. "Well, fuck you!"

Then he whirls around, kicking shit out of the way as he storms off. I stare after him for a blink, trying to understand what the fuck just happened when everything sinks in.

He thinks that I'm blaming him for all of this. Maybe it came off that way, but I didn't mean that.

When we started this, I told him in no uncertain terms that there were no breakups, no misunderstandings, nothing. I'm sure as shit not letting him leave without explaining myself. I run, chasing after him, and barely grab him before he escapes out the door. He fights me, trying to shake me off and smacking my hands away. I don't let him though. The urge to have my hands on him increases the more he fights me.

"Stop," I beg as he kicks his legs out. "I didn't mean—"

"No," he barks, body thrashing and elbows jabbing me as I wrestle him to the ground. "Get off. You don't want me anymore, do you? You don't fuckin' want me." He's screaming in this guttural tone, literally destroying my heart with every sobbed word.

"Bunky, little psycho—"

"Don't call me that," he growls as he tries to roll us, but I'm faster. I use my weight to pin his hips to the ground and shackle his arms above his head with one hand. "You don't get to call me that."

"The fuck I don't. Stop and listen," I bark out, fighting him tooth and nail to get the upper hand, using my free hand to snag his jaw, forcing him to look at me because I need him to see how serious I am. His eyes are full of pain, shimmery with unshed tears and it makes my heart crack wide open.

"Fuck, I wasn't talkin' about you. Dammit, Bunky, don't you get it by now? *I'm* the fuckin' issue. I knew that I shouldn't have left. We could have spent the day together here, but I chose to escape instead of stayin'. Sure, I did that because I'm so completely consumed by you, but you ain't the problem."

"Would have been happy to just be with you." His lip wobbles. "Just bein' with you is enough."

"I screwed up so damn bad." I inhale deeply before letting it out slowly, watching as his eyes go from a hard edge to a softer one. "You're the only thing that matters to me, but *I* have to remember that there's sometimes more. I messed up."

"You couldn't have known this would happen."

"Maybe not this exactly, but I suspected somethin'. The worst is that I let my phone die. So reckless and stupid. I wanted to have a moment with you that didn't feel so full of bullshit, and I let poor judgment win. I acted impulsively, and now…"

"Whaley…" He sighs, leaning up and nipping my bottom lip, comforting me the best way he can. "First off, don't ever fuckin' yell at me like that again. We're a team, and if you're strugglin', I want to be there to help you. Lean on me, but don't take it out on me." A teasing smile covers his lips. "Well, I take that back, you can take anythin' out on me in the bedroom. I'd be okay with *that*."

I lean down as a little chuckle leaves my lips, nuzzling the scar on his cheek with my nose, grateful that he understands, but also… "You never stop."

"Never. I'm serious though." He breaks the hold on his wrist to cradle my face in his hands. "We're a team. Don't shut me out and don't keep things from me. You're upset? I wanna know so I can make it better."

"Just… be patient with me," I tell him, twirling his hair through my fingers. "I'm goin' to have to go dark for a little while. Make shit happen. Do things I haven't in a long time."

His eyes dance at that. "I like dark, Whaley."

"He almost killed you." I remind him.

He laughs as if it's such a pleasant memory. My little psycho. "Well, show him to me again. I want all versions of you, no matter how messed up you think they are."

I lean down, knocking his hands away so I can kiss him deeply. I snake my tongue past his lips, flicking his piercing, and everything feels right again. He always knows what to say, even when I'm fucking everything up. No matter what I do, he'll always come back to me, and that steadying presence means the world to me. There should be limits to the things we'll take from each other, but I don't give a damn about that.

"I'm sorry," I whisper, pulling back to look at him once more. "Sorry I lost my temper. Sorry I hurt you. I didn't mean to."

He nips my chin, arching his back and pressing into me. It's only now that I feel his hard cock rubbing against me. I have to chuckle because even in the most inappropriate times, he's fucking hard. "Guess you'll have to make it up to me." He then does some move I didn't even know he was capable of, flipping us so I'm now on my back with him straddling me.

"The hell…" I mutter, staring up at him in awe, my hands already working on his shirt.

"You're gonna lay here and take it," he purrs, rocking his ass over my cock.

And I do, again and again until I can't even remember my own name.

TWENTY-SEVEN

Bunky

Whaley's avoiding me.

Okay, that's not exactly true. He warned me this would happen. We had a long talk about the fact that he needs to be more focused now, needs to give his sole focus to the Aces and getting us through this hurdle, but that doesn't mean I have to be happy about it.

I miss him.

He's constantly in his office or at the shop, not having time to spend with me, and I don't fall asleep in his arms anymore since he's gone all hours of the night. He's also been keeping me away from the action, and that's what's pissing me off the most.

He's snatching Vipers, making his point known, and he's not letting me be a part of it which is driving me crazy. Every time I see Pike or Fox bring one in and take them to the soundproof room in the shop, I chomp at the bit to join. I get the same response every time though. Fox shakes his head, Whaley gives me a look, or Pike ignores me.

I'm trying to follow his wishes but I'm getting antsy.

So I fiddle with the pen in front of me. It's a slow day, Whaley not taking as many customers with everything that's going on, and I'm bored. Randy said I could start as his apprentice next week, so I can't even hang around the tattoo parlor while I wait for something to do.

"Want a tattoo?" I ask Raid, looking at his inkless arms. Ah, virgin skin—no pun intended. I'm eager to get my hands on it. "I could do somethin' you'd like."

He snorts, tilting his head at me. "You think I'd let you put somethin' permanent on my skin?"

"Why not?" I pout, feeling a little offended. "I wouldn't do it *now* but eventually. I'm gonna need people to practice on. I barely got enough room on me."

"I won't be one of your test subjects." He quirks a brow. "You excited about it?"

I nod rapidly, smiling with an enthusiasm that I'm sure is apparent. "Super. I'm itchin' to get started. Think I might have found my thing."

"I'm happy for you, Bunk," he tells me, giving me one of his barely there Raid grins. "Things have been tough for you, but you're pushin' through. I'm glad you've found somethin' you're passionate about."

"Whaley is too," I add, rolling my eyes. "Gave me a whole speech about how I need to find my passion." I pause and squint at him. "Speaking of passions, what's yours?"

He stares blankly, almost like he thinks I'm stupid. "I ain't got a passion, Bunk, and who says I need one?"

"Whaley probably would." No, Whaley *definitely* would. "Come on, what gets you up in the mornin'?"

"Life…" he drones, not giving me an inch.

"Not funny," I tell him. Then I get an idea. "Maybe I can help you? We can think of things you might wanna do?"

He looks skeptical, glancing at his phone before sighing and putting it into his pocket. "Sure. Why the fuck not?"

His answer isn't really convincing, but he agreed, so he

can't back out now. I go to ask him some questions to help me narrow down my ideas but stop short when Whaley and Fox walk in.

Whaley marches to the back room while Fox flips the closed sign and starts to lower the garage door. Just before it's shut, a few older members come in, dragging a man who's got a canvas bag over his head and restraints on his wrists.

I smell blood.

Raid notices me staring as they take the man to the back room, and he nudges me. "You know he ain't gonna let you back there."

"Why do you think that's the case?" I question, chomping down on my bottom lip for a moment. "It's not like I wouldn't enjoy it."

"Maybe that's the point. Maybe you'd enjoy it a little too much."

I hadn't considered that, but Raid might be right. The rush of killing Gunnar still pumps through my veins, the satisfaction of taking justice in my own hands filling me with pride. Yeah, it's fucked but true. Now, if I got my hands dirty, played with some fresh meat, I don't know how I'd react. That doesn't mean I don't want to find out.

When I see the older members filter out from the back room after several minutes, all it does is pique my curiosity further.

"I'm gonna go," I state, standing up and cracking my neck, unable to sit on the sidelines anymore. "They ain't gonna stop me this time."

"Whaley's not gonna be happy," Raid so accurately states, snagging my arm.

I cackle, waving his concern away. "You let me worry about Whaley. There ain't nothin' my ass can't fix."

He cringes, nose wrinkling in discomfort. "Details, Bunk. Whatever, you wanna go, be my guest. You're the one that has to deal with Whaley."

I can't help but smile at that thought because I want Whaley to deal with me.

"I'm goin'," I tell him, and he lets go of my arm before going back to his usual sulking self.

I head to the back of the shop and stop in front of the metal door. It takes me longer than I care to admit, but I manage to break into the back room in the end, thankfully not alerting Fox or Whaley in the process.

The back room is laid out a little weird. The metal doors don't directly open to the main part of the room, but to something that resembles an entryway with a sink, cleaning supplies, tarps, and aprons. I press my ear against the next door, giddy with excitement when I hear a scream tear from someone's lips.

This is going to be so much fucking fun.

With one final check that I really want to do this and one final fuck it, I burst through the door in the most dramatic way possible, putting my hands up and giving them a little shake. "Ta-dah! It's me!"

Whaley and Fox snap their heads up, and turn to face me. Fox looks surprised, but Whaley looks pissed. I shrug sheepishly, giving him my best puppy dog eyes. "Oops?"

"Bunk, you can't be in here," he growls, dropping a thin surgeon's blade on the metal table beside him. "You need to leave."

I know he's talking to me, but I'm too caught up staring at their victim to care.

Damn…

He's a fucking mess. He's got blood coating his entire face, and when he opens his mouth, I notice that he's got some teeth missing. I look to the side and see them on the table.

"You took his teeth out? Fuckin' awesome!" I feel my face split in a smile, because holy shit, my guy is fucking awesome.

"This ain't a game," Fox snaps, looking to Whaley to make

sure that he didn't cross a line before continuing. "We're workin', tryin' to get information. We can't have you goin' all…"

"Psycho?" I offer the word he was thinking but refused to say. I know Fox isn't going to budge, he's stubborn like that. Now that I'm here, however, I'm sure I can make Whaley cave whether he likes it or not.

"Fox, can you give us a second?" I ask him, and the dude doesn't immediately leave, instead, looks to Whaley. It takes a beat before he gives a curt nod, and Fox leaves.

Once he's gone I slink closer to Whaley, running my hands down his chest as I reach him. "You made me angry."

He quirks a brow, his own annoyance mirroring my own. "Yeah, and you've pissed me off."

"Why'd you leave me out of this?" My brows scrunch and I drop my hands, unable to hold back my slight irritation. "Do you think I can't handle this kind of stuff? Didn't think I'd be able to get what you needed? That I'm so crazy I'd push aside the objective to have fun?"

His gaze is hard, jaw ticking as he assesses me. "You sayin' that's not true?"

"I would keep myself in control for *you*." I should be offended that he thought I couldn't be what he needed, but I'm not. I haven't exactly given him any reason to think that I'm capable of keeping myself in check, but I am. I want the gang to get over this hurdle. I want to prove that I'm Whaley's match, not just with our crazy and with our sex, but in all the ways. "Just let me show you."

I can tell by his face that he doesn't really believe me, and I half expect him to say no before he releases a long sigh and motions toward the man who is looking at us. "Okay. Let's see what you've got."

My heart is beating so fast and my hands tremble. Whaley is testing me, and I refuse to fail him.

Walking over to the table lined with tools, I run my fingers along the edges before settling on an ice pick. I pick it up and wicked adrenaline rushes through me. I spin to the guy as he looks up at me through bloodied, busted eyes, but he doesn't look fearful. If anything, he looks… unimpressed.

Well, that just doesn't fucking work for me.

I twist the ice pick in my hand before strumming my fingers on it. "Looking awfully confident for a guy tied to a chair," I say, squatting down in front of him. "You don't feel like talkin', huh?" The man doesn't say anything, only watching me with that same look, and I cock my head to the side, letting out a *tsk*. "You sure you wanna go this route?"

He still doesn't respond, and it pisses me off. So I shrug, standing once more. "Have it your way then." I move before he has time to react, rearing back and jabbing the ice pick into his thigh, giving it a little twist but not pulling it out. I can't have him bleeding out too quickly.

His loud screams ring throughout the space, body jolting as I continue to dig. I close my eyes, the sounds he's making having the effect of a bump as endorphins run through me. "Oh, I like that sound. Can you do it some more?" He stops instantly, mouth slamming shut as he looks at me with hatred. Now we're talking. Give me some reactions. "Pity. Guess, we'll just have to keep goin'."

Leaving the ice pick, I go back to the table, pursing my lips as I look over the choices. "Hey, Whaley? Do you think a blowtorch would be more effective than a chainsaw?"

"Chainsaw would make him bleed too much," Whaley calls back, voice sounding full of pride.

Yes! This is what I want. Let me show you I can do this.

"What do you think, Viper? Are you feelin' a blowtorch?"

"You guys are fuckin' nuts," the Viper spits out, body struggling as he tries to escape his restraints.

I let out a manic laugh, grabbing the blowtorch and flipping it on briefly for effect. "Ready to talk now?"

He's hesitant, eyes bouncing between me and the fire

before he lets out a little grunt. "I can't tell you where Thorn is."

"Well, see, that just doesn't work for me."

"What's it matter if I tell you? You're goin' to kill me anyway. Even if you don't and I tell you where Thorn is, him and his followers will kill you if I get out. So I have nothin' to lose. It's die here or die there."

Damn, that's true. I look at Whaley once more, but he's not looking at the Viper, he's looking at me, waiting for me to make my next move. "I guess the next question is, do you wanna die quickly or slowly?" I face the Viper once more, and this time, his eyes are stubborn, lips in a line as he accepts his fate. Flipping on the blowtorch again, I nod my head. "Slowly it is."

I go ahead and deliver on my threat, delighting in the process. I keep asking questions but get no answers, and I reach a point where I think he really doesn't know anything. I stop, looking back at Whaley to see him giving me a small nod.

"Welp," I say, stepping back and smacking my hand against my thighs as the Viper's head falls forward. "Seems that's all he's going to give us. Can we have fun now?"

Whaley stares at me, searching for something with an unreadable expression on his face. "We?"

I nod, licking my lips as I approach him and stand on the tips of my toes. "You forget, I was *made* for you. Every sick, twisted thought you have, I can sense it."

"Enlighten me," he says, crossing his arms over his chest as he takes a step back. "Tell me my secrets."

"You want to watch me lose it," I begin, taunting him with a devious grin. "You don't want to admit it, but the thought of seeing' me let go... You want me to be your little psycho. You want to see just how crazy I can be."

He cocks a brow at that. "I've seen you let go before."

"That doesn't mean you don't want me to see it again." I

turn and fiddle with the various instruments on the tray beside us once more. "Wouldn't that be cute? Couples that torture together last forever."

"That ain't a sayin'," he says dryly, but his lips kick up despite his tone.

"Well, I'm countin' it either way."

Whaley lets me pick up an instrument of torture, and I choose a knife that's very similar to my own. Keeping my eyes locked on his, I lazily walk behind the passed out, barely alive man, then hold the knife to the top of his ear, blowing Whaley a kiss before bringing it down. The guy's ear falls with a sticky plop onto the floor as he shoots awake, releasing a bloodcurdling scream. He writhes around in the chair, pain consuming him before he passes out again.

"How'd that feel?" I ask Whaley, cocking my head to the side as I play with the bloody knife. "Did that get you hot? Are the demons in your head screamin' at you to join me in the fun? Are they happy they've found a kindred soul to share this filth with?"

He swallows, his fists clenching at his sides and nostrils flaring. He's not pissed though. The opposite. That beautiful spark of lust and darkness I always crave from him flares in his eyes, a sign that everything I've said is true.

I need to push a little further.

"Healthy shit is borin'," I tell him, walking around the guy and up to Whaley. I stop right in front of his chest, using my bloody hand to cup the back of his neck. "Let's give in to our darkest impulse. Let's be ourselves the way we can only be with each other."

He doesn't answer me with his words but his lips instead. I moan in victory, scrambling to climb him like a tree. His hands are under my ass as he carries me over to the metal table, setting me down roughly as he digs his hands into my hair. He tips my head back, nibbling down my neck before coming back up to lick across the healing cut on my cheek.

"You wanna go to Hell together?" he rasps against my ear. "You wanna prove how fucked we really are?"

"Always."

He growls, swooping down to kiss me once more before taking a step back. Then he taps my thigh, motioning for me to move around him and approach the tied-up man.

From there, it's all a blur when I let my demons out and they take the reins. All I recall is blood splattering everywhere, begging and pitiful cries for me to stop, for me to have mercy. I remember Whaley's hands on me, moving up my sides, lips ghosting my temple as I have my fun.

When it's all over with and the reality of what we've done settles in, I don't feel a shred of guilt. Just like I didn't when I killed Gunnar and like I don't when I think about killing again.

"What do we do with the body?" I wipe the blood off my cheek with the back of my hand, feeling my mind start to settle. "We made a mess."

"You don't worry about that. Fox and Pike will take care of it. Let's go home and clean up."

I nod, taking his hand as we leave the back room. The drive to the trailer park isn't far, and we usually take the back roads anyway, so there's no fear of getting stopped. Even if some of our neighbors were out and about this early in the day, they wouldn't bat an eye at the fact that we're covered in blood.

This is Aces' territory, and they know shit's got to get done.

Once we're in his trailer, we go straight to the shower. The air is hot and heavy, cloaked in lust as we soap each other off. Our hands can't stop wandering, eyes locked on the other, the tension building and building, bound to snap.

I immediately sprawl across the bed after we get out and dry off, arms raised over my head and back arched with a needy lust I haven't felt before. I always want Whaley, but today is more pressing, more urgent.

"You look beautiful, little psycho," he whispers, running a light finger up my ankle and across my calf. "Want to taint you."

I bite my bottom lip, blinking up at him with a sultry promise. "Get my knife."

He doesn't miss a beat, digging through my pants to produce my pocketknife, flicking it open before going to the bathroom, and when I smell the deep stench of alcohol, I know he's cleaning it off. He comes back with a piece of toilet paper that also reeks, bringing it to my thigh and wiping it across my skin.

"I want to be a part of you," I start, head lolling from side to side as he teases the handle of the knife against me. "Want you to cut me, want you to make me bleed, and want you to clean it afterward."

He licks his lips as he flips the knife over, pressing the tip against my skin, and I whimper when he digs it into my thigh. It's not deep enough to cause any damage, but deep enough that I know it'll scar. I'm mesmerized as I watch the blood trickle down my pale skin. When our gazes collide again, I take in his smoldering eyes as he bends down and licks it all up.

"*Yes*," I hiss, eyes fluttering shut when he cuts me again and I feel his soothing tongue moments later. "How do I taste?"

"Like fuckin' Heaven and Hell," he mumbles against my skin, hand wandering to fondle my hard cock. "Like fuckin' sin. Best thing I've ever tasted."

When he moves down, my eyes spring open, wanting to watch him. He hovers above my cock, and a breathless gasp leaves me when he takes me into his mouth. His eyes watch mine as he runs his tongue up, twirling it at the head, all the while he slices me again.

"So good," he mumbles, more to himself than me as he twists his neck to drink up the blood. He sucks one of my balls into his mouth and hums around it before popping off. "Could do this forever."

It's a torturous, repetitive process of blood and sucks. I'm a pure mess, littered with superficial cuts and so close to coming. He keeps playing with me, giving me little licks, but when he takes me into the back of his throat, I shake my head.

"I want you," I beg, reaching for him. "Need you inside me."

He crawls up my body, wet, puffy lips curled into a smile as he places the knife in my hand and reaches for the lube on the nightstand. "Gonna claim you. Gonna show you that I love every piece of you, no matter how twisted it is."

My eyes snap open and I push at his chest. I need to know what I'm hearing isn't just my lust-drunk imagination. I sit up, lip trembling. "You... You love me?"

"How can I not?" he breathes out, running a finger across the cut on my cheek. "I think I have for a while, Bunk. Just couldn't... couldn't say it." He leans forward, pressing a kiss to both my eyelids before his lips travel to mine. "But today made it so clear if it wasn't already."

"All because I tortured a guy?"

"All because you knew what I was thinkin', what I wanted, what I couldn't say myself." He smiles and my heart melts. "Because you didn't judge me, because you didn't hesitate, because you danced with my demons and came out alive."

"Will you tell me again?" I loop my hands around his neck as I lay back down, dragging him on top of me again. "I wanna hear it."

"You'll hear it every day for the rest of your life. I love you, my little psycho. More than myself, more than my life, more than anythin'."

I capture his mouth in a sloppy kiss, tongues brushing

against each other, lips moving lazily as I sink further into the mattress. He lubes up his finger next and gently stretches me, making my toes curl with every brush against my prostate. When he enters me, it's with the same care, same tenderness, but the sweet moment doesn't last long, not when we both need something else right now, something only the other can deliver.

He urges my wrist up, angling the knife in my hand to his shoulder. "Make me bleed for you, Bunk. Make me yours. Take every piece of me and twist it until it's at your mercy."

I bring the knife down without a second thought, and his blood trickles down his shoulder and onto my chest. When I latch my mouth around the wound, he tastes like copper, tangy but sweet, and I moan as I take everything he's offering.

He fucks me harder, throwing his head back with a growl as I bite down exactly where he has my mark tattooed on his skin.

"I love you, I love you, I love you," I bellow, clawing at his back when he wraps his hand around my throat. "Whaley, please!"

He takes my cock in his hand, jacking me roughly, the cords in his neck straining from holding back his own orgasm. "You're gonna come for me, Bunk. You're gonna come hard. Want you to be a filthy mess when I'm done with you."

I nod rapidly, tears springing in my eyes as he presses down harder, strokes me quicker, rails me deeper.

I come on a scream, squirming underneath him, and right when he's about to unload inside of me, he pulls out and tugs on his cock. He's growling, pupils blown as he aims at my thigh and his cum drenches my cut skin.

He smirks like a madman after, rubbing his cum and mixing it with my blood, and when he bends down, mouth on the mixture, he moans, making me cry out as he takes our combined essence.

When he pulls back, it's with blood and cum on his lips, and I pull him toward me with greedy hands. Our mouths meet, and it's the most euphoric thing I've ever felt. "Your cum tastes so good mixed with my blood."

He gives me a smile, running his tongue along my bottom lip. "We better get ourselves cleaned up and wiped down. Don't want this shit to get infected."

"Always thinkin' of everythin', ain't you?" I giggle, on cloud-fucking-nine. I lean forward and tongue his nipple piercing, causing him to grunt. "Can we stay like this a little longer?"

He bites his bottom lip before nodding, flopping onto his back as he moves me across his chest. His fingers wander to my ass, squeezing my globes tenderly as he kisses every inch of my face. We're a mess of blood, sweat, and cum, but it's the most delicious thing on the planet.

"Tell me again," I urge after a while, brushing my nose against his hard chest.

He kisses the crown of my head. "I love you."

"Until the day we die?"

"Until the day we die."

I hope when we go, we go together, because I can't imagine ever living without this.

TWENTY-EIGHT

Bunky

"Raid, are you payin' attention to me?"

Raid sighs, looking up from his phone and realizing that he's about to walk straight into a pole, dodging it at the last second. "Damn, Bunk. Don't be so fuckin' needy."

"We're supposed to be pickin' up parts for the shop," I tell him, the urge to bat his phone out of his hands strong. "Whatever you and Landon are talkin' about can wait."

He glares at me briefly before looking back at the screen. "Ain't talkin' to Landon."

"Really?" I tease, poking at his side as I try to look over his shoulder at his phone, but Raid is freakishly tall and doesn't even let me get a glimpse. "My mama."

Raid's relationship with his mom is not the best. His old man was locked up when Raid was just a baby, no parole in sight, and his mom kind of went off the deep end because of it. If she's not getting high as a kite and having ragers in their trailer, she's gone for weeks at a time without a word. Sometimes, she gets blackout drunk at bars and Raid has to pick her up and take care of her.

I know it bothers Raid more than he lets on, but he's so tight-lipped about all of it. He's not the type of person who'll ever ask for help or even accept it when it's offered. That doesn't stop me from doing just that though.

"Is everythin' fine?" I ask. "Do we need to grab her?"

Raid chews his bottom lip, looking furious as he shoves his phone into his pocket. "Nah. She can deal with her own shit today. Let's get these parts and head back to the shop."

I give him a moment to change his mind. If his mom needs him, I'm more than happy to help carry her out of wherever she is, but Raid's a stubborn bastard. He pushes past me without a word, entering the auto store. I sigh as I follow him in, wondering why he can't let someone in to help him ease his burdens. I swear he'd be a lot happier if he did.

"You got the list?" he questions, thumbing through the air fresheners by the entrance.

I fish the paper out of my pocket and hand it to him. "Yeah, plus the cash to pay for it."

He hums, grabbing a cart before we make our way to the engine filters. "Surprised Whaley had us make this run. Couldn't he wait for the parts to get delivered?"

"Didn't want more people there than necessary." To make room for the torture and such, but I don't say that out loud, not when we're out of Aces' territory and around normies. "And this way we're ready for when he decides to open it again."

He nods. "It's nice to have a normal day," he says, grabbing a couple of filters and tossing them in the cart. "I got work comin' out of my ass too. Gotta sort through those invoices later."

His phone pings loudly in his pocket, but he ignores it, going toward the next aisle. We pick up other stuff Whaley wanted—mufflers, a couple of batteries, a camshaft—all the while his phone won't stop going off. When the pings stop, that's when the calls start, and every ring further adds a tick to Raid's jaw.

"You gonna get that?" I ask after the seventh time, taking the cart from him. When he shakes his head and continues to shop, I stop him. "Seriously, man. She ain't gonna stop."

He lets out a groan, angrily grabbing his phone and accepting the call. "What? I'm busy. I don't care if you're lonely, I'm workin' right now—No, Ma. Can't you just…" He turns away from me, back tense, clutching his phone so hard it's about to break. "Seriously, I can't—Wait, don't do that. I'm —Fuckin' fine. I'll be right there!" He hangs up and slams his fist against the rack beside us, rattling the contents of the shelf in the process. He whirls around, fury in his gaze as he angrily takes the cart back from me. "Gotta make this quick 'cause I gotta pick up my ma."

"I'll go with you." I give him my best supportive smile. "You don't got to deal with that shit on your own. Let's split up, grab everythin', and then we can swing by and grab her on the way to the shop."

He looks like he wants to disagree, but when his phone dings again, he relents. We each go to one end of the store so we can cut the shopping trip short. Once we're done, we pay and are in the car, heading toward wherever Raid's mom said she was at.

We pull up at one of the local dives a town over. I go to unbuckle my seat belt, but Raid shakes his head. "I got it. Just wait here."

"I wanna help," I argue. "Come on."

"You don't get it, Bunk. Sometimes it's…" he trails off, looking over his shoulder at the bar before sighing in defeat. "Sometimes it's hard to get her out. Just let me deal with her, we'll drop her off at the trailer, and then we can go back to the shop."

Raid grumbles as he steps out of the car, slamming the door shut with so much force I'm surprised his window didn't shatter. I sulk, slumping in my seat as I take out my phone. When my phone dings, I take a look and immediately smile at who's texting me.

WHALEY:

How long does it take to pick up some parts?

I laugh, my thumbs flying across my keys.

ME:

You miss me?

WHALEY:

Don't be a brat, you know I do. Get your ass back here.

I sigh dreamily, tucking my phone away as I reach for a cigarette from Raid's console. Whaley hasn't been letting me leave his side, but he knows I get a little restless when I can't go out and do things. So we compromised. As long as I was out with Raid or Fox it was okay, but I have to check in. Looks like he's the one checking in now though.

God, I'm going to attack Whaley when I see him. It's only been two hours, but my heart and soul are calling out to him. I swear, if there's such a thing as fated mates like in romance books, then we're it.

I wait a few more minutes and grow impatient when Raid doesn't appear. I guess he was right about his mom being hard to rein in. I decide to veto what he said. He's my friend and I'm going to help him. I get out of the car, cigarette pinched between my teeth, and I'm about to turn when something cool and metallic presses against my temple.

"Lucky me, catching you alone like this. Ready to pay?"

Shit.

TWENTY-NINE

Whaley

I pull out my phone, but there's still nothing from Bunky.

He hasn't responded to my last message and that was over an hour ago, which makes me frown. Although I don't respond half the time because I don't like texting, Bunky always messages me back. I'm about to call Raid when the bell chiming above the shop door has my head snapping up, taking in Fox.

"How's Badge?" I note his slightly damp red hair and tired eyes.

With everything that's been going on lately, I haven't been able to stop by and see him like I want to.

"He's good. I went home to shower and change, figured I'd stop in to see if you needed anythin' before I went back up there," Fox tells me, lip lifting slightly.

I look around, taking in the half-put-together space, and shrug. "Not really much to do. Pike's in the back goin' over a few repair quotes with the window guy. I'm lookin' over invoices."

"Well, don't hesitate to let me know…" he trails off.

I can tell he doesn't want to leave yet, probably bored out of his mind at the hospital. "So, Badge really okay? Healin' up good."

"Oh, yeah, he's chompin' at the bit to get out of there. Those poor workers though…" He sighs. "He's givin' the nurses' hell."

I chuckle, having no doubt that's true. "I'll bet. He never was one for sittin' still."

"Never and he hates it. I tried to tell him to look at it like a vacation but he's relentless. Tryin' to get me to sneak him in a beer when I come back." He pauses, shaking his head. "He's a mess."

"That he is."

"He feels bad for not being here to help you." His tone is a little more serious now, as if he's fishing. Badge must have told him to ask but he shouldn't worry about that.

I scoff, images of Badge almost dying flashing in my head. "I'll have to call him and jump his ass over that. He almost died, and he's worryin' about this place? He needs to focus on his recovery."

"That's what I told him, but you know he don't listen." He shrugs, tinkering with the pen on the reception desk. "He's stubborn."

I round the counter, leaning back against it as I give him a nod. "Yeah, like you and your brother."

"Hey, hey." His hand flies to his chest in defense. "I'm not stubborn. If anything, I'm the only one who thinks with their head most of the time."

"You may be the most sane," I confirm. "Doesn't mean you ain't stubborn."

"Well then, pot meet kettle." His hand extends for me to take, and I eye it with confusion. "It's nice to meet you."

I smack it away, chomping the inside of my cheek to stop my smile. "I ain't stubborn."

Now it's his turn to scoff. "You can't be serious? You literally live by the whole my-way-or-the-highway mentality."

"What do you expect? I run the Kings of Aces. It's my job."

"Fair, but job or not, you're still stubborn." He takes a step back, humor dancing in his eyes. "Like an old mule."

The laughter I was trying to hold in escapes me. He's so much like Bunky, especially their mannerisms. How their eyes gleam with mischief, how they smirk when they're about to taunt, and even the evil glint they get when where they're about to fuck some shit up.

"An old mule that can still whoop your ass." I take a step toward him, ready to show him just that, and he jumps back, holding his hands up as he trips over his own feet and falls back into the wall by the door.

"I have no doubt." His tone is teasing but his hands are still raised, which is good. Means he knows I'll follow through with my threat.

"Good." I pull back, thinking of the phone burning a hole into my pocket. "Speaking of stubborn, have you talked to your brother?"

"Aw, trouble in paradise?" My fist instinctively juts out to nail his shoulder. "Ow, fuck, damn," he winces, rubbing the spot. "You almost knocked my shoulder out of the socket."

"Stop fuckin' with me or I'll do it again."

"Fine, fine. I get it." He stands upright again, rolling his assaulted arm. "No, I haven't talked to Bunky since earlier. Yesterday, maybe? Don't know since he ain't sleepin' at home anymore."

I smirk at that because he's been at my place, in my bed, right where he belongs, getting thoroughly fucked.

"Alright," I say, pulling out my phone again, wondering where he is. When I see that there are still no messages, I get irritated. There's no reason he shouldn't be responding, especially to me.

"In all seriousness though, is everythin' good?" Fox asks, and I look up, taking in his concerned expression.

Waving him off, I shrug and tuck my phone away. "Yeah, he went out with Raid, needed to pick up some supplies."

"Surprised you let him out of your sight."

I really didn't want to, but the little shit wouldn't stop bothering me. Not that I didn't like the incessant way he was trying to get into my pants, but I noticed that his attempts were more out of anxiety than anything else. I felt bad, so I told him he could go as long as Raid went with him.

I sigh. "I'll be alright once he's in my sight again."

"Ah, Whaley, you done got bit by the love bug too." He places a hand to his heart, eyes blinking rapidly at me as he does some weird swaying shit. "Never thought I'd see the day, and with Bunky no less."

Fuck's sake. "You really gotta death wish today, huh?" His face pales and his Adam's apple bobs. His smile is long gone as he carefully inches away from me, like a prey trying to outsmart a predator. "And on that note, I'm headin' back to my dad."

I smile in triumph, happy I can still scare the living shit out of people. I think about Badge and realize I really do need to go see him. Maybe once Bunky's back I'll take him with me. "Tell him I'll come see him soon."

"Will do," he calls out before nodding and heading outside. "Call if you need me."

I nod too, even though he can't see, pulling out my phone once more. I call Bunky but he doesn't answer. Then I try Raid, who also doesn't answer. My heart starts to speed up, hands becoming clammy as I start to pace. There are a ton of rational reasons why they wouldn't be answering. Maybe they lost track of time or left their phones in the car? I can't spiral like this. He's fine. They both are, and I need to chill the fuck out.

I head to the back, wanting to see how things are going

with Pike and the repair guy when the shop door bursts open so hard and fast that the damn thing smacks the wall with a loud *pop*. I spin around, prepared to lose my shit on whoever the hell it is, and stop dead in my tracks.

It's Raid, but he looks like a mess. His glasses are busted, lips caked in blood, and his clothes are all torn up.

"What the fuck happened?" I bark out, pushing past him and running out into the parking lot, eyes frantically searching for Bunky. I don't see him though. I don't even see Raid's car. "Where's Bunky?"

"I don't know," he says, coming to stand beside me.

I spin around, heart pounding so harshly I wouldn't be surprised if Raid could hear it. I feel sweat break out across my back as chills erupt on my skin. "What the hell do you mean?"

His eyes are dazed and panicked as he shakes his head in confusion. "I just… My mom was on another bender and I got the call to come get her. Pointless because by the time I even got to the bar she left already, probably stumbled to the next bar like she sometimes does." He bites his busted bottom lip, grimacing slightly at the pain. "I swear, I wasn't in there long, only a few minutes, tops. I was lookin' everywhere for her in the bar, checked the bathrooms, and the—"

"Where the fuck is Bunky, Raid?" I yell, cutting him off, crowding his space. "I don't need all those bullshit details. I need to know where the hell he is!"

"That's what I'm sayin'. When I was leavin' the bar, I saw Bunky bein' dragged away. I tried to stop them but was caught off guard when someone nailed me from behind." He reaches up, rubbing his head and wincing a bit. "When I came to Bunky was gone…"

I don't hear the rest of what he says. It's like I'm suddenly underwater. My thoughts feel gargled and acid burns in my gut. I feel hot. So fucking hot, like my skin is about to boil off my bones.

Someone took Bunky.

No, not someone. *Thorn.* I know it was him. Stupid son of a bitch.

My temples are pounding and the long-forgotten buzzing starts inside my head. It's small at first, but turns into a swarm before long, getting louder and louder until I feel like it's drilling into my brain.

Do it. Let me out.

I close my eyes, fist rubbing my head as the noise shifts from buzzing to roaring, and then the rattling begins. The monster inside is wrestling with his cage, eager to burst free, wanting to come out and play. I have one second, only one brief hesitation where I think to hold him back, where I think about all the work I've done to keep his blood-hungry ass tucked away, but that disappears in an instant.

Bunky. Bunky. Bunky.

All I can see is my little psycho being hurt, the love of my fucking life being ripped from me forever, and every bit of restraint I have snaps as easily as a single thread.

I picture my monster, that vengeful demon as he bares his bloodstained teeth and snarls.

I smile internally, opening my arms, calling out to him like an old friend, ready for him to wrap his arms around me and take control.

And he does.

It's easy and quick, every nerve, cell, and fiber of my being ignited. It glides through me like a water ripple, and I let out a little hum at the feeling of no longer being in control. This is the version of myself only Bunky knows, the same one who hurt him, and one I hoped would never show its face again. Too bad for Thorn. He had to go and fuck it all up.

Well, joke's on him. I'm fucking starving for meat, ready to feed as I rip him apart limb from fucking limb.

THIRTY

Bunky

It's hard to remember that I used to like pain.

It's funny how something you love so much can be twisted and manipulated until you hate it, turned unrecognizable to where you don't even remember why you cared for it in the first place.

The first two days were laughable. Guys trying to have their fun, thinking they could break me, believing that a couple of punches and a few cuts would get to my head. When that didn't work, things got more creative. Now I don't know what day it is, how much time has passed, or how long I've been trapped in this dark room. I haven't eaten this whole time, yet I'm still alive, so I can't have been here that long. They shove water down my throat every now and then, forcing me to almost choke on the thing that's supposed to give me life.

I've been getting hit with questions—where's Whaley's warehouse, how many shipments do we get a month, what's the code to the safe in the shop—and I've kept my mouth shut. If not, every sarcastic reply was met with violence.

I used to like pain, but I've found there's only so much I can take.

I'll never crack though.

My head falls forward when I'm granted a reprieve, watching as thick blood lands on my bare chest. I eye where they pulled my nipple ring right out of my skin, the wound looking like it's growing infected and swollen. My pants are wet from where I've had to piss myself, more mental torture than anything, I'm sure. I try to rotate my wrists and ankles to give them a break, the metal cuffs that keep me confined to the chair digging into my broken skin, sure to leave scars and fuck up my tatts.

"See you got him all ready for me."

I bring my head up slowly, not purposefully, but because it feels so heavy. I can only see out of one eye—barely—and I try to bring back every ounce of Bunky spunk as I'm met with the face of Thorn, Gunnar's dad and the head of the Vipers.

"I've been ready," I taunt, but speaking after so long reminds me that one of my back teeth got knocked out, and my tongue subconsciously plays with the gap where it used to be.

Thorn's an ugly son of a bitch, like Gunnar was. He's heavyset and short with a pockmarked face and wide-set eyes.

Thorn raises one untamed bushy brow and smirks. "Don't think you're in the position to be making jokes."

"Wanna hear a joke? Knock, knock—"

My ears ring as I'm punched across the face, another tooth flying out and clattering to the ground. Damn it, there goes my pretty smile. All my aspirations of being on the cover of a magazine are…

No. Sorry. I can't. I'm so fucking tired, even more so now that I'm trying to keep my chin up and my mind sharp. Getting beat to hell by low-level grunts was one thing, but now I'm face-to-face with the man in charge. I try to push through all the pain and think about what I need to do to survive, but there's no point. I know what's going to happen next.

"You killed my son," Thorn starts, slowly circling the chair before stopping in front of the table that's decked out with weapons of all sorts. "Should've had my guy kill you on the spot, but then I guess I wouldn't be able to have my fun."

I don't move, don't breathe, don't even react to his words. There's no argument coming from me, nothing I can say that'll change my fate. I had this coming. I don't regret killing Gunnar, but this is the way life is. There are consequences for my actions, no matter how justified I might have been.

"Not gonna say anything?" Thorn asks, humor laced in his voice as he chuckles. "Thought you were supposed to be some freak. You telling me you've really had enough?"

I won't say that, even if I'm thinking it. I may be resigned, but I still have my dignity.

"Whaley's probably wonderin' where you are, isn't he?"

That gets my attention. "Whaley?"

Through all the pain, all the cuts, all the bruises, I've only thought of him. His handsome face smiling down at me like he loves me has kept me sane. The memories we've shared have given me something to hold onto. I had a moment, briefly, when Thorn's thugs were threatening to cut off my dick, that I wondered when Whaley was going to save me.

I don't blame him for not being here though. I know he's looking, he has to be, and the reminder that he's out there somewhere, desperate to stop the pain gives me the spark of hope I lost.

"He's not gonna save you," Thorn mocks, shaking his head with disgust. "Bitch let me shoot up his shop because my guys tell me he was too busy fucking around with you. Now, what kind of leader is that? Let me show you what a real one looks like."

He jabs his fists against the corner of my jaw, forcing me to bite my already swollen tongue, and I fight back a wince. Blood seeps through the wound, coating my teeth, but I smile when he pulls back.

Whaley. Whaley. Whaley.

"He's gonna kill you when he finds me," I say, voice cracking when he punches my stomach, knocking the wind out of me. I wheeze but push through the pain. "When he sees what you've done, he's gonna eat you alive."

"That's the thing, freak, he ain't findin' you." His grin is wicked. "Pieces, maybe, but there won't be any of you left to fuck." He takes a step back, moving to the instrument tray. "My guys felt like they had to ask questions, get some information, but that ain't why you're here. Do you know why I took you?"

I try to roll my eyes but only manage the one that isn't swollen shut and crusted. "I can take a guess."

"My son," he growls, beating his fist against his chest. "My blood. You fuckin' took him from me, so now I'm gonna take somethin' from you. Whaley gettin' the raw end of this deal is just a perk."

He grips the back of my head, craning my neck so far back I feel a sharp sting of discomfort. Then he reaches into his pocket for his phone and holds it in front of my face, the flash blinding me momentarily before I'm let go.

"Jack off material?" I joke. "I'm flattered."

"Gonna send this to him." he quips, not paying any attention to me as he looks at the picture. "Can't believe I won't get to see his face when he opens this." He turns to me slowly, pliers in hand. "Or the little present I'm gonna send him."

Present? What does he—

I hold back a muffled scream when he takes hold of one of my fingers, hooks the pliers onto me, and yanks out a fingernail.

"What? Nothin'?" he mocks, carefully placing my bloody

nail on the table. "Thought that would get somethin' out of you."

Tears blur my vision as my body tries to catch up with what happened. I won't let him win. I said I had my dignity, and now that he's brought Whaley into it, it's a matter of pride for the both of us.

I'm Whaley's equal, his partner, his soulmate, and I won't cower in the face of a bastard like Thorn or beg him to stop.

He doesn't. He takes a couple more nails, each one increasingly more painful as he does, but I keep my lips sealed shut. I won't cry, I won't beg, I won't scream.

"I see. Maybe we need to do somethin' a little more drastic then."

I'm not prepared for the knife that comes down on the tip of my finger, cutting it to the bone. I shut my eyes, not wanting to look, but I can hear Thorn's disappointed hum when I continue to keep quiet.

"Oh, thought that would do it. Lemme try again."

This time I can't hold back. My mouth opens on a yowl as he starts slicing my fingertip off, taking his time so I can feel every nerve in my body awaken.

"Finally got what I wanted." Thorn laughs, and I open my eyes in time to see him waving my fingertip in front of my face. "Think I wanna take a couple more now. See how much you can take before you pass out."

Unfortunately for me, I take and feel every single slice, losing track of how many pieces of me he cuts from my body, all the while taunting me with reminders that I'll never see Whaley again. He threatens things that I've dreamt of in my wildest imaginations but would never actually do to a person, promising that he'll do them to me.

"I wanna take my time with you, freak," he explains, holding up a tip of my finger to my lips. "He's gonna have to wait a long time to get each piece of you back."

When he gets bored with my hands, he moves to other

parts of me. He compliments my tattoos and then proceeds to start slicing through my skin. He asks if my ear piercing hurt when they did it and then rips it out.

It's too much pain, too much brutal torture, too much of the one thing I thought I couldn't get enough of.

My mind starts to drift as he plays with me, growing more creative with each bloody second that passes. I shut my eyes, breathing harshly as my head lolls and I'm taken somewhere else.

Crack.

Squish.

Pop.

I don't get a reprieve from the brutality. Instead, I'm brought to another one just as tortuous.

I poke my tongue out as I draw on my arm, the red sharpie making my monster look pretty cool. I grab the green pen because I want his eyes to glow. I'll call him Benny or something. Benny, my tentacled monster friend.

"Bunky!"

Mama's calling me again. It's the fifth time tonight. I haven't wanted to leave my room because I didn't know if her friends were over. I don't like them. They always say mean stuff to me and treat Mama badly.

The only one who doesn't is that one guy I haven't met. Patch? I think that's his name. Or maybe not. I just know she goes out with him sometimes, and those times are my favorite. I never get to go but she always comes home happy, and doesn't do her weird slurring thing for a few days after.

I go to her because I know she won't quit, and I'm not surprised to see her lying on the couch, eyes a little red as she looks at me.

"Yeah, Mama?" I ask, going to her when she reaches for me.

She smiles, but it's a bit wobbly. "Aren't you so handsome, baby?"

My cheeks flush. Mama's not okay right now because she'd know that was a lie. She forgets sometimes that I need to eat and shower, so I'm a mess. My hair's grown out because I haven't had it cut in a while, and our washer broke so my clothes are dirty and torn.

Either way, when Mama says it, I believe it. "Thanks, Mama."

"S–Sit here w–with me," she slurs, patting the spot beside her. "L–let's watch a m–movie."

I brighten at that. Mama and I don't really do much together. I know she loves me because she tells me a lot, but she's normally too busy to spend time with me. Nights like tonight are special. I wonder if she bought any popcorn. "What movie?"

Her eyes are unfocused as she looks at me. "Whichever you want."

I think that's code for 'I'm going to pass out as soon as you put it on,' but I don't argue with her. I go to take the remote, but I'm interrupted by a loud knock on the door.

"Bunky, can you grab that?" Mama closes her eyes like it'll cost her to get up and do it herself.

I sigh in defeat. It's probably her friends I don't like. I hate it because they're ruining our movie night.

I'm too short to look through the peephole, so I keep the chain on the door as I open it. When I see who it is, my blood runs cold. "Mama, it's—"

Dad pushes past me, ripping the flimsy chain clean off the door as he storms inside.

"Bitch!"

Dad's always coming by every now and then, and I don't like it. I don't like him either. If Mama's friends are mean to her, he's just cruel. Whenever he leaves, Mama's always left with bruises and we're always left scrambling for food for weeks. I know tonight is no different.

I cover my ears and run to my room as an argument breaks out, like I always do. I don't like when they fight.

It scares me.

They're screaming at each other, and even though I should stay in my room, I can't help but want to look back out there. I think things are being thrown everywhere because the shattering is loud even through the closed door. When Mama calls out my name, I slowly inch out of my room, looking around and finding that they're no longer in the living room. I follow the sound of shouts, bangs, and curses, leading me to Mama's room.

She's there, trying to fight off my dad as he grabs her arms and yanks her hair back.

"You fuckin' bitch!" he seethes, slapping her across the face. "Give me my fuckin' money!"

She squirms in his arms, trying to break from his hold. "I don't have any."

I must gasp or make some kind of noise because he whips his head to look at me. The minute he sees me, his lips curl into a snarl and he lets go of Mama. "You!"

I bolt before he can grab me, running around the room, jumping over Mama's bed, anything to get away from him. The entire time, she's trying to hold him back.

"You're what she's spendin' all my goddamn money on, you little fucker."

"Stop," I cry out, scared at the angry look in his eyes, unsure of what he'll do next. "Dad!"

"Ain't your fuckin' father!" he spits out, chasing me into the bathroom and backing me against the tub. "Gonna wring your —"

He doesn't get to finish his sentence because Mama hits him on the back of his head with her hairbrush. Dad doesn't like that. He turns and takes her in his arms, slamming his fist against the side of her head and she collapses.

And he doesn't stop hitting her.

He does it again and again and again. Her blood is splattering everywhere and getting all over me. It looks like Mama's reaching for me, extending her hand out, but I don't know how she can do that when her eye is popped out of the socket.

Crack.

Squish.

Pop.

Her skull.

Her brain.

Her eyes.

Am I screaming? Is that why my throat hurts so much? I don't understand the sounds coming out of my mouth.

He hits and hits and hits until she's unrecognizable and there's nothing left of her. He's out of breath and shaking with rage, the skin of his knuckles broken from her bones, and I know I'm next.

That is until we hear the front door being busted open. He bolts up, giving me a look that tells me not to move, but I don't think I could even if I wanted to. I'm trapped staring at my mama.

That's all I can focus on. I hear a commotion outside the bathroom, but I don't bother paying any attention. After a while, I finally crawl toward Mama, grabbing her hand, but it's cold and still.

So very still.

"Think you've had enough, freak?"

Yeah, actually. I think I have.

THIRTY-ONE

Whaley

I'm going out of my mind, or what's left of it anyway.

This is day three of my search to find Bunky and he's still
nowhere to be found. It doesn't make sense. I've scaled every
damn inch of Viper territory and *nothing*. I'm lost in my haze
and torture, snatching any Viper I can get my hands on. I
need one to crack, just *one*, but they aren't breaking. The
bodies are piling up, and my thirst for vengeance and desperation to have Bunky in my arms again is growing with every
fading heartbeat that pounds inside my chest.

My monster took over but much like me, he is falling into
despair. *We* are fading, withering away into nothing but a
shell. I don't even know who I am anymore.

No, I do. I'm nothing without him.

"Where the fuck is he?" I scream, rearing back and nailing
my brass knuckle-covered fist into the tied-up Viper's face.
I've been going at this for hours, burning, beating, and water-
boarding this motherfucker, but he's not saying shit. Thorn
has a damn army of martyrs ready to die for him. That's fine

though. I'll kill every single one, rip this fucking world apart, and make them all bleed if it means I find Bunky.

The guy gurgles something unintelligible, blood, spit, and snot pouring from his mouth and nose like a running faucet. I can't tell if he's even awake because his eyes are swollen from my assault. Though that doesn't stop me from hitting him again.

And again.

And again.

"Whaley," someone calls out, but I don't stop.

I can't stop.

Not when Bunky is somewhere out there probably being tortured. Are they doing to him what I'm currently doing? Hitting? Burning? Cutting him up?

"Fuck," I roar, but it sounds more like a cry as images of Bunky in a similar torture chair come to my mind.

"Whaley!"

"Tell me where he is!" I grab the remaining tethers of the guy's shirt, giving him a shake, trying to force the information from him.

"Whaley!" I'm suddenly swarmed from behind, arms locking around my waist as I'm pulled back. I fight it, beating my fists down on whoever the fuck dares to stop me.

"Let me go, I need to find Bunky!" It's a wail, a desperate cry, something I feel so deep inside that it makes my bones ache and my organs scream. "Please, I just— I can't— I need—"

I drop to my knees because everything is too loud, everything hurts too bad, and everything feels hopeless. I scream, leaning forward to press my head on the concrete floor, agony and pain ripping from my lips as loss washes over me. Bunky's gone and I can't find him. He's gone and it's my fault because I didn't protect him well enough. He needed me, still fucking needs me, and I'm useless.

"Whaley." The voice is calm, hands rubbing my back in soothing circles. "Whaley, it's okay. It's goin' to be okay."

A hiccuped sob leaves me as I shake my head, drilling my forehead into the floor. I don't believe that. I think about the package I got from Thorn, the one with a picture of my perfect little psycho beat to hell, and I wail again. I think of the fucking *fingertips* that were also in the box, knowing they were Bunky's. If that's what Thorn did to him after only a few days, I can only imagine what Bunky's been through by now. It's been too long. He's going to be destroyed when I get him back. *If* I even get him back.

"I need to find him," I mutter, my body shaking as adrenaline rushes through me. "Please, God, I have to find him."

"We will, I promise. I've never let you down, and I don't plan to now," they say, and the slight hitch in their tone has me focusing as they speak, and I realize it's Badge.

He's here and I have so many questions, but my brain can't process any of that now. I just stay there, immobile and hopeless as he holds me, tethering me to a reality that I'm sure no longer exists.

He speaks for a long time, telling me all kinds of things, reassuring me, rubbing me, and I close my eyes, trying to take that comfort and project it to the deepest parts of my mind. My head and body are at war, one trying to force me to get up and do something while the other wants me to close my eyes and never wake up again.

"I don't know what to do," I croak, voice scratchy and full of hopeless insecurity. "I want him back. I have to have him back. I need him, Badge. *I need him.*" My lip wobbles and I bite down on it, trying to stop the sobs from breaking free once more.

"I know. We all do and we will. Whaley, we *will* get him back."

I need to pull myself out of this. Need to get up off this floor and come up with a plan. Something. *Anything.*

It takes every ounce of energy and willpower I can muster, but I get up, legs shaking and heart feeling like it's broken into a million pieces. Bunky needs me to find him, and I have to remember that. My eyes move to Badge, where he now stands too, and I note the dark circles under his red-rimmed eyes. He looks as bad as what I'm sure I do. I also have to remember that he's Bunky's dad, and it must be taking everything in him to comfort me instead of the other way around.

"You look like shit," he tells me, lips tilting up in a smirk.

"I feel like it," I mutter, trying to smile back but failing miserably. "Sorry about…" I wave my hand to the floor. "I should have kept it together—"

"Fuck that," he barks out, cutting me off and shaking his head in astonishment. "Don't apologize for havin' feelins. You're a person too, regardless of your position."

"Bunky needs me to find him, not to be an emotional little bitch," I huff in frustration.

"I know your head's a fucked-up place right now, but you can't think like that." He places his hand on my shoulder, squeezing tightly. "Bunky won't hold this against you. He knows you're tryin', knows you'd do whatever it takes to get him back."

"That all feels pointless. I don't know what to do now, where to even look…" I trail off, reaching my hand up to drag through my hair, realizing I'm still clutching my brass knuckles. I stare down at them, smeared with dried blood, and it gives me a fleeting moment of calm. "I love him, Badge. We can't give up."

"Never," Badge assures me, his voice filled with anger, pulling my attention back to him. "When we find him, Thorn's goin' to pay."

I nod, a million ideas dancing inside my head. "He will, and I can't wait."

———

It's two more sleepless nights before I finally catch a break.

I'm at the shop, racking my brain to figure out a plan when Raid comes bursting into my office.

"My contact came through," he says, thumbing over his shoulder as if I can't see Milo with my own eyes. He's wearing his Vipers' vest, and I fight my instant reaction to shoot him on the spot. Hell, I still might for taking his sweet-ass time to get back to me.

Milo is my inside guy. He came to me in the past, telling me about his dissatisfaction with the Vipers. I was wary at first, would be stupid not to be. He's a Viper after all and I'm not fucking stupid. It took a lot of convincing, a lot of digging, but I eventually came around. He has his reasons for wanting out and I have mine for wanting a mole. I had Raid as his primary contact in case shit went south, that way he wouldn't be connected to me. It's worked out well aside from the fact that he's been MIA for the last few days.

"Where the fuck have you been?" I seethe, shooting up from my chair. "I've had Raid callin' you for days."

"Do you know how damn hard it's been? You know Thorn's been suspicious of me for a while," he throws back, looking at me like I'm an asshole. "I don't need anyone runnin' back to him to fuck up my cover. Was hard enough gettin' over here today."

"Tell me somethin' I don't know," I snap, once again resisting the urge to beat the hell out of him. I want Bunky back.

"Thorn's been MIA. Haven't seen him once. I had to keep my ear to the ground to find out anythin' about Bunky." He sits down in the chair, face looking sullen but also annoyed. "Him and his closest were like sealed vaults. I had to do a lot of fuckin' snoopin' and diggin', but I finally found your guy and he's alive."

My whole body vibrates like I touched a live wire. So many emotions flood me with just those simple words.

He's alive.

I can get him back. I can save him, hold him, make him forget whatever hell he's been through. I don't know what he'll be like when I get him, but at least he'll be alive.

"Get to the point. Tell me where Bunky is." I grab my jacket, ready to pull it on and head to get my guy. "Come on, we can go now. I'm ready. Raid, go get the guys."

"Wait!" Milo snags Raid's arm to stop him. "We can't go in there balls blazin'."

"The fuck we can't," I growl, placing my hands on the desk and leaning forward. "You expect me to sit here? I'm crawling out of my fuckin' skin."

"I know, but we have to think rationally. Let's line up all our ducks or whatever before we go in there."

"He's right, Whaley," Badge chimes in from where he's now leaning against the doorframe. "We act rash, Bunky gets hurt. We need to figure out what we're doin'."

Nah, fuck that. I'm not waiting.

I round my desk, about to pull my knife and threaten Milo or beat him until he tells me, but Badge is faster, cutting me off and gripping my shoulders.

"Whaley, look at me." His tone is firm, but his eyes are full of conflict when I finally meet his gaze. "I get it, okay? I do. He's my damn kid, you know how much I want him back, but we have to know what we're gettin' into. What if we act irrational and end up gettin' him killed? We have to be smart about this, and deep down you know that."

He's right, I do, but it doesn't mean I like it. I fist my hair before pulling away from Badge and sweeping the contents of my desk onto the floor. Then I close my eyes, warring with my demon.

It takes me a minute but I calm down enough to look at Milo again.

"What do we do?"

He leans forward, bracing his elbows on his knees as he levels me with a hard look. "I have a plan, but you're gonna have to trust me."

I nod, going back to sit at my desk. "Tell me what we need to do."

THIRTY-TWO

Whaley

My body is humming with anticipation as I fight the urge to throw my carefully constructed plan out the window.

I'm biting my fists, drawing blood from my knuckles. My guys and I are parked on a hidden path in the woods, behind the abandoned building I didn't even know existed until mere hours ago.

The building Bunky is in.

I know he's close, can practically feel his soul calling out to mine, and it has me fighting every instinct I have not to storm in and get him out. Every second that ticks by is like my own personal form of Hell.

Jesus Christ, I just want him back.

"You good?" Badge asks from beside me, his nails in a state of disaster from where he's bitten them down to the quick.

"I dunno if *good* is the right word," I mutter, still staring at the building, almost as if somehow I'll manage to get X-ray vision and see Bunky in there. "Ready? Absolutely."

"Me too," he agrees, fingers strumming against his thigh.

"Ready to get my hands on Thorn and see my kid with my own eyes."

"He's gonna be fine," I say, not even sure I believe it but having to say it anyway. All we can do is hope to God it's not as bad as we think it is.

Badge grunts, hand fiddling with the gun on his hip. "Yeah, he has to be."

We sit in silence for far too long, my mind churning with every possibility, thinking the absolute worst. I'm about to jump from the car and say fuck it when I get the text from Milo. It's my sign to get my ass in there.

Thank fucking God.

"Let's go," I tell Badge, pushing open my door and barreling out the truck. I hear several doors open behind me as my guys follow suit, but I don't wait for them. My time for waiting is over. Right now, I want blood. I untuck my gun from my pants, armed and ready for whatever happens next.

Milo is waiting for us at the entrance as planned, and he gives me a nod when I approach, taking one last drag off his smoke before tossing it away. His eyes scan me and my guys before his hand reaches for his own gun. "The guard is takin' a break, but it won't be long, five minutes, tops. Are you ready?"

"Born ready," I growl, cracking my neck from side to side, blood already roaring with what's to come. "Let's fuckin' go."

"Alright. Try not to shoot anyone until after we have Thorn." He gives me a look that tells me he's reading my mind. "You don't want to alarm him."

"That's why I have a silencer." Badge gives the end of his gun a little flick, eyes gleaming with manic delight. "Works like a charm."

"Then by all means, shoot them all." Milo gives him an equally unhinged smile, obviously loving the idea. He snags the handle, eyeing us one more time before opening the door.

The building is small, mostly a maze of hallways. I have

my gun ready, heart pounding so hard and fast that I can practically hear it in my ears.

"Where is everyone?" Badge asks Milo, looking around and seeing that there's nobody here. "If this is some sort of fuckin' trap—"

"Like I said earlier, only so many people know about this place," he grits out, narrowing his eyes at Badge. "I'm a mole, not a goddamn triple agent. Thorn has a heavy guard on Bunky but that's about it."

The sound of my guy's name and the implication that several people are keeping him locked up makes me want to blow this whole fucking building to smithereens. Who knows? Maybe I'll come back with a grenade when it's all said and done and do just that. Bunky would probably like that too. He likes chaos and wreaking havoc. It could be a present to him from me.

"Stupid on his part, good on ours." Badge nods, jutting his chin toward another narrow hallway in front of us. "Let's go find my son."

"I'm so ready to be done with this shit, you have no idea," Milo mutters, a hard look on his face before he shakes his head. "It's been a long time comin'."

"Well, that time is almost over," I confirm, pausing when we get to the end of the hall.

Anticipation is coursing through me, knowing Bunky is near and that Thorn is about to get what's coming to him. It's silent, so silent as we all wait with bated breath for Milo to make the next move. Milo pauses, giving me one more questioning look, then his hand goes to the knob when I nod. He doesn't have to ask if I'm ready, I was ready the second I knew where Bunky was.

Lifting my chin, I motion to him with my gun to hurry the fuck up. His eyes hold understanding before he raises his own gun, determination settling over his features. "Alright, here goes nothin'."

This is one of those moments that feel fast yet slow all at once. I rush inside but am hyper-aware of everything that's happening around me. My gun is raised, eyes bouncing around the room as I look for my prize.

Thorn.

He shoots up from the desk and his hand goes to his gun.

"I wouldn't do that if I was you," I bite out, my gun pointed at his face. "I'll shoot your fuckin' hand off before you're even in breath's distance of touchin' the handle."

I watch as he contemplates his next move, hand still frozen midair as his eyes look around and note my guys. He must quickly realize he's outnumbered, but his face still blooms into a smile before he releases a laugh like this is some game. "Can't blame a man for tryin', right? So you here for the boy?"

"Amongst other things." My gaze stays on him, never breaking eye contact as my finger rests on the trigger. It would be so easy to end his miserable existence right here, but I want to keep him alive for now. Once I have Bunky in my hands, however, then all bets are off.

"Shame. Why don't you sit? We can have a chat," he offers, motioning to the chair beside me.

"You think this is some fuckin' game?" I snarl, taking a step toward him as I spot his right-hand man moving in my peripheral. He whips out his own gun and points it at me.

"You got a death wish?" Badge questions the right-hand, voice low. "You got about six guns pointed at you right now. You wanna take that chance?"

"I'm a dead man either way," the guy fires back. "May as well go out with a bang."

"Want me to disarm him?" This comes from Fox. "Just give me the word."

"No, I will. Shoot him if he shoots me," Badge tells him, and I hear the shuffling as they move, but I'm solely focused on Thorn. "I'll be takin' that."

The whole room is silent for a beat as Badge disarms Thorn's right-hand man. I watch as Thorn's face fills with amusement before he lets out a long sigh.

"Ah, now, none of that," Thorn says, reaching up and running a hand down his shirt. "We can negotiate some terms. Make this work for everyone."

"Terms?" I bark out, unable to stop myself, my finger heavy on the trigger. "The only term I'm about to give is my nine mil to your fucking skull if you don't tell me where Bunky is."

"Love." He *tsks*, folding his arms over his chest as he looks at me with wonderment. "Never thought I'd see the day. You should know better, Whaley. This is the kind of shit that puts you in situations like these. Weakness can be used against you, don't you know that by now?"

Weakness? Bunky is *not* my weakness. Once upon a time, I thought that was the case, but I'm realizing with every day that passes how untrue that was.

He's my fucking strength.

He's turned into my daily motivation, the reason I want to be better. It used to be all about making up for my past, wanting to help people because I felt like I owed the world something after all the fucked-up shit I'd done. Bunky showed me a whole new outlook. Now all the things that I did for redemption, I started to do for him. He gives me everything, and to call him a weakness only pisses me off.

"Where the fuck is he? Tell me now!"

Thorn ignores me, shaking his head. "This was always going to happen. The second he killed Gunnar—"

"Gunnar stabbed me first. Gunnar started the whole fight with Bunky," Badge cuts him off, and Thorn swivels to look at him. "Bunky was defending me. Your piece of shit son is the one who had it comin'."

"It doesn't matter who started it," Thorn snaps, face now red with anger and loss as he slams his hand down on the table. "Blood was drawn and lines were made. It was an eye for an eye."

"I was stabbed and almost died. That *is* the fuckin' eye," Badge snarls.

"No, that wasn't enough! My kid is dead!"

"You're about to be too," I grit out, done with all this bullshit as I advance on him. Using his distraction to gain complete control, I grab the back of his neck and slam his face down onto the desk.

"Fuck," he shouts, scrambling under my hold and stupidly flailing for his gun. I disarm him easily and then bitch-smack him with his own weapon.

"Where the fuck is he?" I growl. "I'm done with the talk, I'm done with the fuckin' games, and I'm done with your bullshit. Take me to Bunky or I'll rip your throat out."

He looks past me to his right-hand man, who I'm sure is restrained by Fox or Badge. It's as if, finally realizing the seriousness of his situation, he tries to backpedal.

"Hey, no need to get serious. It was just a lesson that needed to be taught. Let's talk reason."

"You wanna talk reason?" He nods, a flicker of relief flashing in his eyes. "I'll show you reason."

I look to where his right-hand man is, making sure my guys aren't in the way before aiming my gun and pulling the trigger, bullet planting between the fucker's eyes. He goes down like a sack of bricks, blood leaving a beautiful arch across the white wall.

A masterpiece. My demon lets out a little hum of satisfaction.

More. More. More.

The room is silent for a beat before my attention is back on Thorn. "Now, take me to my fuckin' guy before you're next."

"Come on," Milo interjects, coming behind Thorn and manhandling him. "Let's go."

Thorn's eyes widen in surprise before they narrow in hate.

"You piece of shit. You set me up. I'll kill you. You won't have nothin' without me. I fuckin' made you—"

Milo cocks his gun, jabbing the barrel into Thorn's temple. "Yeah, yeah, enough of your shit. Just fuckin' walk. Tell your guards to stand down so we can get in and out."

"You're a fool."

"And you're a dead man. Now go," he growls, forcing Thorn to walk and us to follow.

"Don't even know why you need me." Thorn tries to reason with Milo as we walk down the long corridor. "Let me go and you can kill the others."

"You're a real piece of shit," Milo grunts. "All those men are faithful to you and you don't give a fuck about them. You'd piss all over them and their loyalty to save your own ass. You're trash."

"How much further?" I grit out, not giving a fuck about anything else.

"Just around this next hall. Have your guns ready," Milo tells us.

I hear Fox let out a snort somewhere behind me before he speaks. "Like we don't have our shit out already."

"Can never be too prepared," Milo fires back, punching the back of Thorn's head when he tries to get out of his grip. "Fuckin' move!"

As expected, three Vipers by the door jump to alert the second they see their leader being handled. One moves, advancing quickly, knife extended, but Milo shoots him before he even makes it a foot. The other guys look shocked, eyes moving from each other before looking at us.

"Tell them to open the fuckin' door," I growl, ready to see Bunky.

"Open it," Thorn tells them. They don't move though, as if they're in some kind of confused trance.

Well, fuck all this.

I aim and shoot, ripping the remaining two open through

their middle. They fall to the ground like lead weights, and I move around Milo to get to the door.

It's locked with some kind of key code, and I spin around to glare at Thorn. "What is it?"

His stubborn jaw is set, and I cock my gun when Milo releases him and aim at Thorn's foot, pulling the trigger. He yells out in pain, his body doubling over. Grabbing him by his hair and ripping it back, I drill my barrel into his temple. "There's a lot of body parts you don't need to live. Give me the fuckin' code before I shoot your other foot."

"1482."

I don't think I've ever moved so fast in my fucking life. I enter the code and push the door open, running into the room. There are four guys inside, smoking and laughing at something on one of their phones. Badge, Fox, and the other guys handle them, but I don't even bother. My heart feels like it's going to explode inside my chest when I finally rest my eyes on Bunky.

My heart. My soul. My fucking life.

I feel numb as I stagger to where he's tied to a chair. His head is bent forward, and I barely make out the rise and fall of his chest. I'm in front of him in an instant, and everything else ceases to exist, my entire world flipping when I take in the blood that's saturated his body. I flip the safety on and tuck my gun away before dropping to my knees, gently cupping his bruised and beaten face.

He's covered in so many bruises and so much blood that I can barely tell it's him. My stomach twists and I fight the urge to vomit when I see his fingers, the tips missing with jagged, uneven cuts. I scan the rest of him and try to hold back the bile that's still threatening to spill. Both his ear piercing and nipple ring have been ripped out of the skin, and there are slices of skin missing on his arms, the wounds bright red. The thought of how much he's been through almost sends me on a spiral, but I hold myself back because Bunky needs me right now. I need to hold him in my arms and take care of him, to show him that he's safe and that nothing like this will ever happen again.

"Bunk," I call out, but he doesn't rouse and I'm actually thankful because I don't want to hurt him when I pick him up. I look down, noting the cuffs, and growl. I glare at Thorn, ready to rip him apart. "Give me the fuckin' key."

Milo is holding Thorn once more and digs into his pocket for the key, tossing it to me once he has it. As gingerly as I possibly can, I unfasten Bunky's restraints, tempted to kiss the place where the cuffs cut into his skin. I take extra care of him when he slumps forward into my arms, letting out a little sigh of relief, holding him to me as I stand and cradle his body.

I don't give a shit about the other Vipers in the room, not even noticing if they're dead or alive. My eyes can only find Milo where he's clutching Thorn, despite the way the bastard is thrashing in his hold, trying to break free. It takes great effort not to put Bunky down and beat Thorn to death with my bare hands.

"Knock him out, don't kill him," I command, hefting Bunky in my arms and pausing to nuzzle my nose in his blood-caked hair. "Take him to the shop room."

"You want us to leave him alive?" Fox questions from across the room, murderous eyes staring at his brother. "Look at what he did."

"I fuckin' see it," I bite out. "Like I said, leave him alive. He's for Bunky to deal with." A look of understanding crosses Fox's face and the room breaks in murmurs of agreement. "As for the rest of them? Do what you want, but I want them dead. The *how* is completely up to you."

"Happily," Badge snarls, whipping out his knife, and picking up a Viper to hold against his chest, slashing his knife across his throat. "Fuck, that feels good."

I let my guys have their fun and look down at Bunk, heart

breaking when my eyes roam over his perfect face that's a bloody and bruised-up mess. I want to see those emerald eyes I've missed so much, want him to smile at me and tell me that everything is okay. I have a feeling he won't be doing any of those things for a long time though.

"You're safe now, little psycho," I murmur, heading out the door, my guys parting like the Red Sea to let us by, each bowing their heads as we pass. "I promise nothin' like this will ever happen again."

I try to give him comfort the whole way to the truck, telling him how much I missed him and how much I love him, but he doesn't stir.

It's not until I have him settled in the seat, about to leave to take him to the hospital, that he rouses. He lets out a little grunt, wincing as he tries to move.

"Bunky," I whisper, reaching over to glide a finger down his arm, wanting to give him the reassurance that I'm here. Only the second my finger touches his skin he goes apeshit. Screaming, flailing, thrashing about, completely falling apart.

"Hey, it's okay." I try to grab him to tell him it's me, but he's not having any of it. He clocks me in the cheek and I jerk back, trying to get out of the way before he nails me again.

Something about that first punch calms him though. It's as if he's just now realizing he's no longer confined. He draws his legs up, arms wrapping around them as he begins to slowly rock back and forth, and I'm stuck with recollection from a time many years ago.

A broken boy, rocking on the bathroom floor next to his mother's dead body.

THIRTY-THREE

Whaley

I don't know what to do.

It's been hours since I brought Bunky home, and he hasn't said much. He won't look at me or let me touch him. I asked if he wanted to go to the hospital but he only whispered one word.

"Donna."

So I called her over. She was able to persuade Bunky to take a shower and clean up his chest, and now she's tending to his other wounds, but he has yet to say anything. She's made small talk, being careful to not touch anything aside from his gashes, and I can't help but be slapped with a sense of déjà vu. Well, more like a repeat because this is all eerily similar to all those years ago.

"You sure you won't let me take you to the hospital, Bunk?" Donna asks, gingerly taking his hands and cleaning them the best she can before wrapping his poor fingers in ointment and gauze.

"No. Don't want to," he mutters in a crackly tone.

"Okay. That's fine. I'm gonna see about gettin' you some

medicine though. Need to get you some antibiotics, maybe some saline. You're probably dehydrated." She reaches up to touch his forehead but he jerks back, guarded eyes flying to hers, and she holds her hands up in surrender. "Hey, sorry, I just wanted to check your temperature. Make sure you don't have a fever, but I should have asked first. I didn't mean to startle you. Is it okay if I check?"

He bobs his head, fearful eyes staring through her as she reaches up to cup his forehead. After a moment, she drops her hand, giving him a sweet smile. "Good news, no fever. Let me grab you some water."

She gets up from the couch to go to my fridge when a thought occurs to me.

"Are you hungry?" I tilt my head so I can catch his eyes. "Want me to make you somethin'?"

He avoids my gaze but gives me a sharp nod. "Starvin'."

My heart aches for a real conversation. I want him to talk to me, want to hear his voice, want so many things that I've missed, but I have to take this slow. This is about doing what he needs at his pace, and I'll do everything in my power to help him.

Donna gets his water and goes to sit beside him again while I head to the cupboard, grabbing out a pack of Ramen Noodles. It's not the best, but it'll do in a pinch. I make them quickly, trying like hell to eavesdrop as Donna talks to him, but I can't make out what she's saying.

I take the bowl of noodles over to Bunky, setting them down on the coffee table in front of him. "Be careful, they're ho—"

He grabs the bowl awkwardly with his bandaged left hand, practically shoveling some noodles into his mouth despite the fact that they must be burning the hell out of his taste buds. He doesn't relent, finishing off the bowl in under a minute before placing it back down on the table.

"More?" he mumbles, but doesn't look at me. God, I just

want him to look at me. I need to see those beautiful green eyes and that little manic smile that I love so much.

"Of course." I'll make him every damn pack I have in this house if it'll make him happy.

"Maybe that's not the best," Donna suggests, giving me a subtle look. "Give it a little time. Your stomach needs to adjust."

Damn, why didn't I think of that?

"You tired?" Donna asks him, and he gives her a slow, dazed blink. "You can close your eyes," she assures him, leaning back and sinking into the couch too. "I'll be right here the whole time, I swear. I won't leave you."

His gaze darts to me before looking back at Donna. "You swear? Won't leave?"

She gives him a reassuring smile. "I promise, I'll be right here."

His gaze flicks to me again, and I'm suddenly slammed with the realization that he's scared. That's the reason why he's barely looking at me, why he won't speak to me, and why he keeps looking at Donna for reassurance, almost like he's afraid to be alone with me.

The thought has me nearly doubling over in pain. I never want to make him fearful, and I want to voice that, but how can I? Especially now?

Clearing my throat, I do my best to keep my tone even, not wanting to raise any alarms. "I'm gonna run over to check on the shop. I'll leave you to it," I tell Donna, knowing good and well that I won't be leaving the front porch, but also knowing I'll do anything to make Bunky comfortable.

Even if that means being without me.

Bunky's eyes move to me and I see a little flash there, something that looks like sadness before it's gone and he looks at his lap.

"Donna, call me…"

"I will." Her tone is filled with sympathy, no doubt knowing this is breaking me apart.

I turn to leave, unable to stop myself from looking at Bunky once more before pulling the door open and walking out onto the porch. I plop down on the first step, fighting with my shaking fingers to pull out my pack of smokes.

He doesn't want me.

I fumble with my lighter, flicking it a dozen times before finally getting my cigarette lit. I inhale deeply, reaching up and rubbing my chest, trying to soothe the aching, barely-beating organ that lies there. Things are bad, far worse than I ever could have imagined. I always know how to help Bunky, always have ideas or things to say to make situations better, but they all escape me now.

How do I make it better for him?

He's not only dealing with a ton of physical pain from the torture but so much mentally too. I know what he went through was traumatizing, but I don't know to what extent. I don't know where his head is at, or if he even really understands he's no longer in that place.

I sigh, running my hand through my hair. I just want to hold him, to whisper over and over that he's going to be okay, and that I'll be here to help him with whatever he needs every step of the way.

But my touch isn't welcome, my presence isn't wanted, so I'll do what I can and love him from a distance, be there for him from a distance, no matter how much I hate it.

Badge and Fox finally arrive at my trailer hours later after dealing with the clean up crew. I'm so grateful that even though I know they were anxious to get here, they handled that for me. There's no way I'd have been able to deal with that on top of trying to figure out how to help Bunky.

I'm still sitting outside, the daylight trickling to nighttime now, but I can't make myself go inside yet. I've been texting Donna, wondering if I should go in, but she keeps assuring me they're fine, so I'm letting things be. Maybe if I give Bunky some space, it'll be what he needs. That's all I can do right now. Just sit back and wait.

"How is he?" Badge asks, eyes bouncing from me to the trailer door. "Surprised you ain't glued to his side."

I pull out another smoke, lighting up and taking a long drag. "Yeah, I tried earlier, but he freaked out. Didn't want me to touch him."

Fox's brows furrow in confusion. "Did he realize it was you?"

"I don't think so." I sigh, reaching up and pinching the bridge of my nose for a second. "It's been a rough few hours. In the truck, he flipped out, then went completely blank. Locked inside his head and stared off at nothing. Then when we got here, he didn't want anyone but Donna…"

"It's like when he was a kid," Badge finishes for me, eyes filled with sadness. "That's how it was after we brought him home here in the beginning. He wouldn't leave Donna's side for weeks." He does a slow circle, kicking at the grass. "Fuck. This ain't good."

"I know," I mutter, that hopeless feeling doubling. "But we have to be there for him. Have to help him in every way we can."

He nods, sad eyes holding mine. "I'll do anythin' for that boy. You know it."

"Can I see him?" Fox jumps in, practically vibrating next to Badge. "Just need to see that he's okay. Won't do anythin' to scare him. Just need confirmation that he's here and safe, you know?"

"Yeah, go ahead. I'll come in with you." I stand, tossing my smoke to the ground and Badge stomps it out. "Fox, be calm, okay? He's skittish."

"I will."

They follow me up the porch, and I knock on the door as gently as possible before opening it. Bunky is still sitting on the couch, legs drawn up as he rocks from side to side while Donna sits beside him, whispering calming words to him.

"It's okay." She tries to help, but he's shaking his head, panicked eyes darting around.

"Don't want them," he mumbles, voice hoarse as he starts to back up into the couch. "Out."

"Bunky—"

His hands shoot up to cover his ears as he continues to rock. I barely move, Badge and Fox crowding me from behind as we watch our guy break apart in front of us, knowing there isn't a single thing we can do to help.

"Please don't," he whimpers, and I shut my eyes briefly as the room becomes suffocating.

"Bunky, it's okay. There's no one here to hurt you," Donna soothes. I see her hand reach out before she snatches it away, not wanting to touch him. "I promise, no one will hurt you."

"Always hurt. Always come back. Always fightin'. Tired. *So tired*," he whispers, fists coming up to drill into his temples. "Please stop."

"That's all in the past, no one here will hurt you."

He looks like he doesn't believe her, eyes flicking to where we're all standing. "Won't?"

Donna shakes her head, hand cautiously reaching out to give Bunky's leg a squeeze, which he surprisingly welcomes, bandaged hand shooting out to cover hers. "Of course not, they're your family."

He frowns, shoulders trembling as he tries to understand. "Family?"

"Yeah, Bunky. It's Whaley, Badge, and Fox."

"Whaley, Badge, and Fox," he repeats, voice sounding far away.

"That's right. Your boyfriend, dad, and brother. You remember?"

His face twists and his busted lip juts out as he works out the pieces, and my heart begins to fill with hope.

"My family…" The word comes out in a broken cry, and he swivels to look at us. Nobody moves, no one does anything as we wait to see what Bunky wants. It's like a fog's lifted from his mind, maybe only temporarily, but enough where I can actually see recognition in his eyes.

"I—" he starts, going to stand before shaking his head and plopping down again. He's warring with himself as his whole face contorts in pure torture. "I'm sorry."

Then he bursts into a fit of sobs that almost have me dropping to my knees. There is truly no greater agony than watching the love of your life break apart and hit rock bottom, knowing there's nothing you can do to save them.

THIRTY-FOUR

Bunky

How is it possible that everything still hurts?

I think it's been a week, maybe more since Whaley rescued me. I'm not sure because I can't keep track of time anymore. Every moment outside of my nightmares is blurring together, carrying over to reality, leaving me immobile and useless.

I get up to piss and nibble on the food and drink the water that Whaley or Donna bring me, but I can't manage more than a few grunts before I'm crawling back into bed.

Because everything still hurts.

The parts of my fingers that were cut off ache, almost like they're taunting me by reminding me that they used to be whole. In the grand scheme of things, they're four measly tips, but their lack of presence rings loud. Whaley told me he could get some money to fix my teeth, the ones that nobody would be able to see anyway, but I said no.

It feels like nothing can erase the damage that's been done.

Something happened to me inside that torture room. It took something from me. I've been trapped in torturous daydreams, surrounded and pounded by nothing but memories and pain.

I don't know what it's like to *not* feel pain anymore.

I burrow deeper under the covers, stuffing my face into the pillow, and when I feel dampness under me, I realize that I'm crying.

I cry now all the time for no apparent reason. It seems to be the only thing my body is willing to do besides sleep. Even though I know that I'm free, alive, and back home, I still feel like I'm trapped in that room, waiting for my next beating.

I don't know if I'll ever stop feeling this way.

The bed shifts beside me and a hand comes up, attempting to stroke my face, but I flinch before it can touch me.

"Bunky," Whaley begins, speaking in that soothing voice that brings me little comfort now. "You should try gettin' up today."

I don't answer him, only bring the covers higher over my shoulders and under my chin. I don't want to do anything but this. I don't even want to do *this*, quite frankly, but I have no other options.

Whaley's tried so hard to get me back to being okay. He has to be frustrated that I won't let him touch me, even to pet my hair or squeeze my shoulders, and he's been infinitely patient. That's another reason I feel like the worst human being alive. Guilt eats me from the inside out because he's only trying to help and I'm making it difficult.

We've talked about our demons before, the things that we hid from others to portray a semblance of sanity. Whaley and my demons danced together, interlocked in a passionate embrace that consumed us, but I don't think that's the case anymore. His demons are different from mine now, and I don't know what to make of that.

I'm broken, tainted, miserable, and he deserves better.

Because I'm not the Bunky he fell in love with.

"My little psycho," he whispers, scooting closer to me,

which only causes me to shift away. I don't want to look up and see the hurt in his eyes, so I turn around to face the wall. "I need you to try. Not only for me but for everyone that cares about you. Badge, Fox, Raid, Silas, we're all worried. I understand what you're feelin'—"

"How?" I snap, speaking before I can think, almost as if it were a gut reaction. "How the fuck do you know what I'm feelin'?"

"I only meant—"

"Meant what?" I ask, sitting up to face him. He's worried, apprehensive, looking miserable, but that doesn't stop the venom in my voice as I speak. "They took *pieces* of me, Whaley. I'm no longer whole. Thorn fuckin' broke me."

"At least I got you talkin'." The corner of his lips tilt in a sad smile. "You need to come with me."

"No," I say quickly, shaking my head. "I... I can't. Lemme stay here. Please. I can't..."

I can't be myself again. I can't face the people I love who once loved me. I can't do anything but stay stuck in the past that wants to manipulate, torture, and shatter me.

It's doing its job.

He shifts so he's fully facing me, crawling up on the bed as he sits back on his heels. Then he holds his hand out like you would to a feral cat, eyes guarded but pleading as he reaches out. "Let me touch you."

"No..." I breathe out harshly, shaking my head as I back away from him. "You can't. *I* can't."

I don't know if his touch will feel the way it did before. Whaley always made me feel so free, like I could do anything, like I was someone that mattered. My biggest fear isn't that it won't be like that anymore, but that the pain will replace all the good memories. Those memories are the only thing I cling to. The only thing that's kept me from a complete meltdown.

The only thing that's keeping me alive in a world I no longer want to be a part of.

A world I don't belong in anymore.

A world that would be better off without the ghost of myself.

"Please let me help you," he begs, and I see tears shimmering in his eyes. Whaley doesn't cry. I've *never* seen him cry, and his crying for me only furthers my point. To make him suffer? I'd rather have death.

"I don't think I can be helped," I answer honestly, heart cracking as he lets out a pained groan. "Whaley, I can't do this."

His eyes look panicked as he gauges me with worry. "Do what? We'll do whatever you need."

"*This,*" I say, gesturing around to the room, to myself, catching the sight of my bandaged fingers and bursting into tears. "I don't want to feel any of this anymore. I want the pain to be over. I want to be done."

His eyes widen and he shakes his head. "You don't mean that."

"But I do. I'm no good to anyone anymore. I'm no good to you. I should just—"

He cuts me off. "I'm sorry. Forgive me."

I cock my head to the side, wondering what he needs forgiveness for, but am tackled onto the bed before I can even ask. It's not violent, not in the slightest. It's like he's cocooning me with his body, wrapping me in his embrace, and trying to protect me from the world itself. I brace myself for the pain, but nothing comes. It's just Whaley. Whaley and his peppermint tobacco smell. Whaley and his muscular frame. Whaley pressing kisses to my tear-stricken cheeks.

"Don't you ever fuckin' say that again," he growls in my ear, his breaths coming out choppy and uneven. "Don't even fuckin' think it. I can't lose you, Bunky. There's no me without you. If you're gone, you better take me with you because I would die either way."

I bury my face in his chest and wrap my arms around his

back as I breathe him in, letting the familiarity ground me—thankful that it still can. "I don't know how to do this anymore. I don't know how to live. I don't fuckin' know what's wrong with me."

"There's nothin' wrong with you." He pulls back so he can look at me. "My beautiful psycho, it's gonna take time."

"How long?" I whimper, hating that I do.

"I don't know." He sighs and looks regretful as those words leave his lips. "But I'll wait until the end of the world for you. No matter what it takes."

I still feel an uneasiness in my gut, a lack of belief that what he's saying is true because I think I might be broken beyond repair, stuck in Hell, and not even Whaley may be able to drag me out.

"Let me take you somewhere. Please."

"Where?" I mumble into his chest.

"If I tell you, I don't think you'd wanna go." He pets the back of my head, dropping a kiss to my forehead before tipping my chin up. "Do you trust me?"

I know I've been struggling with everything lately, but that is one thing I do know, despite all the fucked-up shit inside my head. "I do."

"Then how about you shower and change? Can you do that for me?" He leans forward, kissing my forehead again.

"I'm so tired, Whaley," I mutter, shaking my head. Just the thought of getting up is hard enough, add showering to that? It seems like such an impossible task.

Whaley must sense that because he slowly helps me sit up, gently dragging me off the bed as he starts to work on my shirt.

"I'll help you. I'll always be here," he whispers, scowling when he reveals the cuts and bruises on my torso. His jaw clenches when he sees what used to be my nipple, ugly and still healing. He runs his fingers across it, leaning down to kiss it. It's not a sexual touch, it's one of comfort, and when he pulls back, he rests his forehead against mine, making me feel less ashamed of how I look now. "Through thick and thin, right? Good times and bad?"

"This is the bad," I confirm, palming the back of his head with trembling fingers.

"And I'm here to help you every step of the way." He taps my hip lightly as he guides me to the bathroom. "Let's go."

I let him strip me the rest of the way down, and when we get into the shower, he holds me as I cry. He reminds me that his presence in my life is unwavering and that I'll always have his love. And maybe, just maybe, I'm starting to believe that.

"A graveyard? Is this really the best place you could think of to cheer me up?"

I look around at our surroundings. We drove for a bit in his truck, going through several towns before ending up here. When we first entered, I thought it was a joke, that maybe he was cutting through this place to save time, but when he parked, I realized he was serious.

"I ain't tryin' to cheer you up, Bunk. I'm tryin' to remind you of somethin'."

"What?" I ask as he leads me toward one particular headstone, and my jaw drops when I see the name scrawled on the top. "Is this..."

"Your mama's grave," he confirms, looking down at me with apprehension.

"Why are we here?" I take a step back but knock straight into his body. "Whaley."

He deflects the question, massaging my shoulders as he brings me closer. "Have you ever wanted to pay your respects?"

"I haven't really wanted to think about it. Never thought about askin' where it was."

Honestly, I never even considered this as something I wanted to do. For all these years, all I've wanted was to put that night behind me, no matter how much my mind wouldn't let that happen. Being out here and facing the reality of her death, I don't know how to feel.

"Wanna go home?" he prompts after a minute of silence. He looks like he's regretting his decision, but Whaley's smart. I meant it when I said I trusted him. If he thinks this will help, I'm willing to do anything he asks.

I shake my head and bite my bottom lip. "No, we can stay."

We stand here for what feels like hours, staring at the headstone. I'm sure I'm supposed to be the one to say something, but I don't. I'm at a loss for words. How exactly does someone pay their respects? Is there some sort of script I don't know about?

When he sees that I'm not going to say anything, he starts talking.

"Your mama's dead, Bunky. The life she lived is over," he says, walking up to touch her headstone, and then he looks back at me, sadness in his eyes. "She never got to see you grow up, never got to see the amazin' person you turned into."

I scoff. "Is this supposed to make me feel better?"

"When have I ever done anythin' just to make people feel better?" His face is incredulous. "I do things because they're honest and for people's own good. I want you to sit here and talk to her."

"Why?"

He comes up to me and cups my face in his large hands. Those beautiful brown eyes dig deep into my soul, reaching for the parts of me I thought I'd lost. Something stirs inside me, almost a nostalgic sort of feeling for a time that's passed.

"Because while she's dead, you're not. You're alive, Bunky. Despite what happened to you, you survived. Not because I saved you but because you held on. You were holdin' on for a reason."

I know exactly why I held on. "You were the reason."

He nods as if he knew that already. "If that's the case, I still should be."

Insecurity bubbles up inside of me again, and the doubt creeps in, nearly suffocating. "How can you want me anymore?"

The hands that are holding my face tightens, and his eyes are furious as he leans in close. "I'll always want you. Old and wrinkly. Batshit and impulsive. Depressed and catatonic. There ain't ever gonna be a time when that's not true," he growls, then his eyes soften as he rolls his forehead against mine, minty tobacco breath ghosting my lips. "Like I said, Bunk, if you're goin', you're takin' me with you."

I can't hold back my amused snort. It feels weird but nice all at the same time. "That's so fucked-up."

He brushes my hair away from my face. "Have we ever claimed to be normal?" I smile because that's so completely true. When I do, his breath hitches and he runs his thumb along my bottom lip. "Look at that. I've missed that."

I wrap my arms around his middle, resting my head on his chest as my eyes mist and my body trembles. "Things will really be okay again?"

"One day they will be. You know why? Because you get the chance to *make* them better," he tells me, hands running up and down my back. "You wanna fight out the pain? I'll take you to the ring. Wanna see a therapist, I'll set it all up. Together we'll get through this. Always us together."

I pull back, looking at the honesty on his face, the love. I had thought that maybe it wouldn't be there anymore, that maybe the broken pieces of me would turn him off, but I see it written plainly in his eyes. He's not going anywhere, he still wants me, and I start to believe that things really will be okay again.

For the first time in weeks, I kiss him. It's not just a brushing of our lips, but a full-blown kiss to let him know that I heard him loud and clear. My tongue snakes into his mouth, and he lets out a groan as he plays with my piercing. His hands migrate up to my neck, pulling me deeper and tighter into his embrace. I lick into him slowly, passionately, and he returns that same emotion.

It's all filled with love and tenderness, swelling up inside me until I can't breathe. It tells him the story I'm sure he knows, that I'll be his until the day we die. "I love you," I whisper when I pull back, panting for breath.

"I love you too, little psycho." He smiles, dipping down once more, as if he couldn't resist it. Once again, we're trapped within each other, lost in the magnitude of our emotions, victims to what we feel for each other.

I'm hesitant to pull back, but I do. Then I jut my chin at the grave. "Should I talk to her?"

"Only if you want," he says with a shrug. "I thought it might help."

I nibble on my bottom lip, contemplating my choice. After a second, I nod. "Could you give me a minute?"

He nods as well, kissing me once more before stepping away. "Take all the time you need. I'll be over there."

When he walks away, I turn to the grave, cracking my neck and shaking my hands before sitting down in front of it. "So… This is weird, right? I'm not too sure what I'm supposed to be sayin' to you. My life ain't that interestin'."

Okay, that's probably a lie. Between my own personality, the gang, and everything that happened with Thorn, one could argue that it's a cinema-worthy life.

"Badge took care of me after what happened. You picked a good one, Mama. He loves me like a son, did everythin' he could to help me heal."

I didn't know Badge when she was dating him, knew *of* him, but that was it. Although, I couldn't miss the way Mama used to smile when getting one of his calls. I know that if she had lived and they had stayed together, Badge would have worked to make her happy every day. I hate that she didn't get to experience it.

That neither of them did.

"Somethin' happened to me. I'll spare you the gory details, but I thought I was done after that. Still feel that way, honestly. Mama, I think you would have hated Whaley." I shake my head as I reach forward and finger her name. "You'd probably want your little boy to be with someone a bit more traditional, but I love him. Probably in a way that ain't healthy, but love is love, right? You wanna hear about it?"

So, as I sit there and tell her the story of our love, I can't help but smile the entire time. When I'm done, I say my good-byes before rejoining Whaley, thanking him with a kiss for what he's done for me today. Although I still think it's a little weird, I do feel a sense of closure and finality. I've talked to Mama, something I never thought I'd do again, and she listened. Through her lingering spirit, we connected.

When I'm home that night, wrapped in Whaley's arms, the nightmares don't come.

THIRTY-FIVE

Whaley

The days that followed visiting his mama's grave were a little shaky.

He's trying to find his way back to his old self, but it's the navigating to get there that's hard. He's made a couple of strides, but not nearly as much as I hoped he would. His progress has shown me that Thorn hadn't won by taking Bunky away from himself completely, and I'm grateful for that.

He's sitting in the chair on the other side of my desk, doodling away on a piece of paper while I work on invoices. The Georgia heat is stifling today, and even my AC isn't doing much to curb the humidity. I'm sweating through my thin T-shirt while Bunky's wearing a long-sleeve shirt and gloves.

He hasn't outwardly said it, but I know he can't stand looking at the damage Thorn caused. Hell, it takes him ten minutes to work up the courage to strip before showering. Some parts of his skin that used to be decorated in eccentric colorful tattoos are now scabs that must be sensitive to the touch. The only reason he's not wearing bandages is because Donna says those parts of his skin need to breathe. Thorn didn't take all of his fingertips, but he might as well have.

Bunky's afraid. All the time he's living in fear, and it makes my heart crack in two to see the expression on his face when he is. Now that we're back to touching, he's been glued to my side at all times. It's the way I wanted it, and a sick, twisted part of me loves it.

He has nightmares too. While his old nightmares were about what happened when he was younger, they've never affected him the way his most recent ones have. He wakes up in the middle of the night screaming, thrashing in my arms, and crying out my name. It takes me ages to console him and remind him that he's alive and with me, but even then he devolves into a crumbling mess.

I don't know what to do. I know it's going to take time to get things back to the way they were, and fuck, they might never be again. Regardless, I'll love Bunky through it, but I don't want him to feel this way anymore. I feel so useless when his red-rimmed eyes stare up at me at night. I feel like a piece of shit when he jumps every time a guy slams the hood of a car. I feel like I want to burn the world when he looks over his shoulder like Thorn will pop up any minute and drag him back to that shack.

"Do you like this one?"

I'm pulled from my trance when Bunky stands to come over and show me his tablet. I made sure to get him something more high-tech for his new apprenticeship. I couldn't have my guy doodling on paper when most artists nowadays use tech. I have to squint to make out what he drew since he's not used to the design program I installed for him.

"What is it?" I finally ask when I give up.

He frowns at me, big green eyes almost irritated as he points to the screen. "It's a fox."

That's a fox? I don't dare say that though.

Now that he's pointed it out, I guess I can see it. It's not a traditional drawing, more Trash Polka than anything else, with big red blocks cutting across it.

"Maybe Fox will like it." He half shrugs. "He doesn't have many tattoos. I thought he might wanna get this one once he's over his fear of needles."

"I think he'll love it," I tell him, knowing that even if Fox doesn't, he'll still get it because Bunky made it. "Have you texted Randy? Let him know you're not forgettin' about the job?"

He nods. "I did. Told him I caught somethin' and wouldn't be able to work for a while. He said it was alright and to hit him up when I feel better."

I choose my next words carefully. "Maybe you'll be able to start sooner than you think."

"What do you mean?"

Once again, I hesitate. "I'm just sayin', I think maybe it's time."

His eyes widen with fear as he starts shaking his head. "N–No, I can't… I don't…Whaley, I—"

I wish I had kept my fucking mouth shut as he starts to panic. His chest rises and falls rapidly, his hands start trembling, and his face goes pale. I grab him quickly and have him straddle my lap, where he buries his face in my neck and starts to cry.

"I'm sorry. I didn't mean anythin' by it."

"I don't want to leave you," he sobs, still shaking his head as his gloved-fingers clutch at my shirt. "I'm not ready…"

I kiss his sweaty temple, rubbing my hand up and down his back as I rock him from side to side. "You don't have to be yet. It was only a suggestion."

"You're not annoyed with me?" he questions once his breathing evens out.

"Of course not," I assure him. "Shit, I'd have you tied to

me every day for the rest of my life if I could. I thought it might help you move on."

"I can't..." he trails off, almost as if he's ashamed to admit his next words. "I can't move on with *him* still out there."

I'm sure he feels the way I flinch at the mention of Thorn. He doesn't know the bastard has been locked up in the back room of the shop since we rescued him. He never asked, so I never brought it up. I didn't want to make anything worse by saying his name or telling Bunky how close he was.

But I think maybe it's time he knows.

"He's not out there. We've got him."

His head snaps up and his mouth drops. "You... You have Thorn?"

I can't quite tell what the expression on his face means. There's a hint of surprise mixed with what I'm guessing is anger. Is he mad I didn't tell him? Shit, I didn't know how to broach the subject, didn't know if it would do more harm than good. Under all those layers, I can also see fear. A fear that he no longer needs now that he knows his tormentor is incapacitated.

"Yeah."

He chomps on his bottom lip before sliding off my lap, wringing his gloved hands as he thinks before letting out a deep breath. "I want to see him."

"You sure?" I ask, brow cocked with apprehension. "He can't hurt you, but maybe seein' him will—"

"I want to see him," he shouts, fists balled at his sides. "I'm pissed off, Whaley! How could you keep this from me?"

"I didn't want to make things worse, Bunk. I didn't know how you'd react seein' him."

"I don't know either," he admits, face switching from anger to nervousness again, gulping audibly as he takes a step toward me. "I *do* feel like this is somethin' I need to do."

I stand, cupping his face in my hands and brushing my thumb against the scar on his cheek. "You sure?"

"I am." Although he's shaking, I know he means it. "Take me to him."

With lingering hesitation, I take his hand and lead him out of my office. We pass by a couple of guys who react the same way to Bunky's presence like they have since he got back. They all take a step away, lowering their eyes as we pass, almost as if they're afraid they're going to set him off.

God, I'd love to see that. I want to see the fire reignite in Bunky's eyes that he's missing, not for my own personal entertainment, but because it's something so *Bunky*. But I remind myself that no matter what, he's alive. I'll love him for everything he is, just like I loved him for everything he was, and everything he will become.

I take him to the back where the locked door is and type in the code. When we get to the first entrance, I look back down at him. He's still sweating, nervously hopping on his toes, gloved-fingers twitching at his sides. "You really *don't* have to do this."

"I…" He shakes his head before taking in a deep breath and holding his chin up. "Let's do it."

I commend his bravery with a quick kiss to his temple before letting us into the next room.

Bunky gasps.

Thorn is tied to a chair in the center. He's completely naked, allowing Bunky to see every inch of his tortured skin. In retaliation for what he did to my guy, we decided to return the favor by cutting off some parts of our own, but we didn't stop at the fingers.

Suffice to say, we gave just as good if not better than Bunky got.

I hold my breath as I look down at Bunky once more, and my heart somersaults when I see the look on his face.

He's fucking *smiling*, but it's not any smile.

It's that insane, psychotic, batshit smile that I became obsessed with.

"Bunk…" I start, giving his shoulder a little nudge. "Gonna say somethin'?"

He ignores me completely, letting go of my hand and stalking toward Thorn. "Is he dead?" he grits out bitterly.

"Don't think so," I answer, still a bit baffled by his response but pleased all the same.

"Why is he still alive? How?"

"Wasn't ready for him to die yet," I tell him, blood boiling briefly at the memory of what he did to my little psycho. "Decided to keep him alive for a bit."

Bunky nods, fiddling with his tongue piercing as he stops in front of Thorn. "Wake him up."

What my little psycho wants, my little psycho gets.

I go to the table in the corner of the room where we keep the smelling salts. I move around Bunky and place the container under Thorn's nose before cracking it open. It only takes a second for Thorn's head to snap up, swollen eyes as wide as they can be in their condition as he lets out a scream.

He's screaming because every time he's woken up, it's been Hell on Earth.

Without breaking eye contact with Thorn, Bunky reaches into his pants to produce his pocketknife. "You see me?"

Thorn mumbles nonsense that neither me nor Bunky understands but that seems to satisfy Bunk. He takes a step forward, laughing under his breath as he cocks his head to the side. "Shit, they really did a number on you, didn't they? Didn't leave anythin' for me to play with."

All I can do is stand back and watch as Bunky does his thing. This is a far cry from the trembling mess that sat in my lap ten minutes ago. I'll take it. Maybe I should have shown him Thorn sooner, or maybe this is what Bunky needed at this exact time.

"I'm goin' to say what I need to say and then I'm goin' to kill you myself," Bunky seethes, pressing the tip of his knife against Thorn's stomach. "Let's have some fun while I do it, yeah?"

Thorn lets out a muffled scream as Bunky sinks his knife into his gut.

"Oh, come on!" Bunky shouts, jumping up and down on his toes. "That was a love stab. Didn't even go too deep. How about this one?"

He does it again, a bit deeper this time, but not enough to kill him.

"You fuckin' took somethin' from me," Bunky growls, pulling out his knife only to dig it right back into Thorn's stomach. "You fuckin' *destroyed* me."

Thorn's actively crying now, tears falling from his face and—

"Jesus Christ, did you piss yourself?" Bunky throws his head back with an evil cackle, eyes gleaming with wickedness. "Fuck yeah. Now you know how it feels, don't you? Don't worry, you'll get used to the smell. I mean, I did."

Bunky retracts the knife only to wave it in front of Thorn's face like a taunt. "You made me want to end my life. You made me want anythin' but my miserable existence, but lookin' at you now? All covered in piss, blood, and snot? Don't know why I was afraid of you in the first place."

He stabs him again and again and again, all the while smiling like a madman and giggling like a schoolgirl. Bunky's smart and doesn't hit any major areas or go too deep, so Thorn's gonna feel every single one of his brutal attacks until Bunky decides to put him out of his misery.

"Whaley, he shit himself." Bunky yells, clapping his hands together, blood splattering on his black shirt.

I smile, propping up against the wall, letting him have his fun. "I see that, Bunk."

"You're nothin', Thorn," Bunky tells him, holding the knife right above his heart. "I thought my life was over. I thought I was goin' to have to spend the rest of it lookin' over my shoulder for you, but I realized somethin'..."

With a roar and a quick flick of his wrist, he brings the knife down straight into Thorn's heart.

"I'm the real monster here."

Thorn lets out a final gasp, choking on his own blood before his body falls forward with finality.

Bunky's chest is heaving, his shirt completely soaked in blood, some of it even in his overgrown black roots. He turns to me slowly, the realization of what he's done hitting him, and that's when I feel it.

And I pray to whoever's listening that I don't lose him again.

It's at this moment that his darkness reaches out to me. I feel it tugging at my soul, curling around my heart, and letting me know that everything is going to be okay. Without any words spoken, he drops the knife and rushes toward me, wrapping himself around my body. I'm prepared and catch him, hands sliding under his ass. Then I spin and back him out of the room to cage him against the wall outside.

Our lips clash in a desperate mess, tongues seeking each other out, hands wandering greedily, souls being repaired. We drag each other down into the depths of Hell, curling around the fire and reveling in the bliss of this unholy reunion.

I have my Bunky back. Maybe a little different than before, but he's with me.

Until the day we die.

EPILOGUE

Whaley
Two Months Later

The shop's back to the state it used to be. Our customers who had to wait for all the repairs are finally filtering back in and money's good again. When I walk into the shop nowadays, it's no longer with a seething rage or a sense of loss. The shop's always been like a second home, and that feeling of pride and comfort is finally back.

I haven't heard anything about the remaining Vipers. After killing Thorn and their right-hand man, I figured there'd be some type of retribution, but there wasn't any. I think they've all gone underground, whether to save themselves or plan their return, I don't know. I can only hope it's the former, but if it isn't, I'll be prepared regardless.

Badge is all healed up too. He tells me that sometimes his torso still hurts where he took the knife, but he's back to being the bastard who always calls me out on my shit. I know

Fox and Bunky are happy that he's finally back and that their dad seems to have recovered with minimal complications.

Bunky.

I look over at my little psycho, watching as he sketches a new design on the part of his skin Thorn sliced away. The jagged and marred surface is still healing, as well as his fingers. Thankfully, neither has kept him back from his new job.

Bunk's been apprenticing at that shop we went to months ago. He leaves every morning looking forward to the day and comes home at night to talk my ear off. He doesn't have much room for new tattoos, but he's found a way to squeeze a couple in. He says the best practice subject is himself, *and me.*

I look down at my middle finger and smile fondly at Bunky's name scrawled in terrible script, looking like a kid drew it. It's an absolutely shitty tattoo, but I love him enough to let him practice on me.

I glance back up and see his tongue poking out in concentration, eyes narrowed and focused as he finishes up his design. Then he snaps his head up when he's done, swinging his arm in the air. "Wanna see?"

I nod, getting up out of my office chair to walk over to where he's sitting. I take his wrist, looking at the squid he drew that I'm sure has one too many tentacles. My eyes catch the brutal scar on his wrists, left over from the metal cuffs he wore for days. I rub my thumb against them, making eye contact as I do. For a brief second, his eyes flash with insecurity. He has moments like that, where he doesn't quite believe that I still want him, and I always make sure to reassure him the best way I can.

Keeping our eyes locked, I raise his wrist up to my lips, tracing my tongue along the scarred edges, and he smiles warmly at me. That smile, those big green eyes, the fact that he's alive—I get hard. I don't act on it, however, just like I haven't in three months.

Yeah, I haven't fucked my little psycho in three *fucking* months.

It's not like I haven't tried. At first, I gave him his space, knowing that it would probably take a bit for him to get in the mood. When I thought that maybe enough time had passed, I kissed him in a way that made my intentions known, and he quickly stated that he was tired and wanted to go to bed. I tried once more after that, to see if that was a one-time thing, and he made an excuse about going to hang out with Raid.

So I haven't tried again, not wanting him to feel pressured.

I'm not pissed, not in the slightest. I won't lie and say it hasn't been rough though. Sex has always been the best way for Bunky and I to connect. It's not the most important part of our relationship, but I feel its loss now that it's been so long.

I'll wait for him to be ready though, and if he's never ready then call me a monk because there's no way in Hell I'm ever touching anybody but him.

Even though we haven't been fucking, we've been finding different ways to connect. He took me to a drive-in film where he learned that I'm definitely not a fan of horror movies. We went axe throwing, bungee jumping, basically any activity we could find to help remind him that he's alive —my little adrenaline junky.

He's growing more and more like the Bunky pre-torture every day. That wild spirit of his is coming back. His wit and sass never went away, but now it comes in sporadic little bursts. I don't think Bunky will ever be the same man he was before everything he went through, but he'll be a stronger version of himself because of it.

"You're starin'," he mumbles, flicking his tongue out to lick his bottom lip, and I growl. Sure, he hasn't let me get in his pants, but he loves being a fucking tease—drives me wild. "What are you thinkin' about, Whaley?"

"Honest truth?" I ask, waiting a beat for him to agree like I knew he would. "Thinkin' about that bite mark on your ass. Want to give you another one."

He bats his eyelashes, lounging back on the seat. "You want me, Whaley?"

"Don't fuckin' act like you don't know I do," I rumble, too sexually frustrated to watch my tone. When he raises his brows and smirks, I know he's gotten the exact response he wanted.

He stands slowly, wrapping his arms around my neck and brushes his nose against mine, mouth open and breathing my air as I pant. Fuck, he feels so good. Warm, solid, smelling delicious.

"How bad do you want to fuck me?" He drags his hand through my hair. "What would you do for a chance to get in my tight hole, Whaley?"

I groan at his dirty words. This is the closest we've gotten to anything remotely sexual, and I don't want to mess it up by coming on too strong, but screw it. I'm horny as shit. "I'd do anythin'."

"Anythin'?" he taunts, giggling a little as he starts showering my neck with kisses before sucking on his bite mark. "Be more specific."

I risk moving my hands from his hips to that pert ass I love so much, my eyes rolling to the back of my head at the feel of it. God, don't know how I've gone three months without even touching him like this. "Walk on shattered glass, sell my fuckin' kidney. Fuck, Bunk, I'd kill someone for it."

"I like that," he says, squirming in my arms. "Love that you're still crazy over me."

"Crazy because of you," I correct him. "The best way to be."

"How about..." he trails off, gulping as he looks up at me through his lashes and nibbles on his bottom lip. "Whaley, I think..."

I hold my breath, eyes widening, but I quickly school my

features. Despite how desperate I am, I don't want to show it. This has to be on his terms. "Yeah? Tell me what you need."

He presses his forehead against my chest, digging his nails into my bicep. "I think I'm ready for you to fuck me."

Thank God.

"You sure?"

"Yeah." He nods. "I want—"

He doesn't get the chance to say anything else because I haul his body against mine and devour him. He lets out a little squeak of surprise, although he shouldn't be. He should know by now how ravenous I am. I'm like a starving fucking lion, and I'm going to gorge myself on my prey.

I force him up, his legs coming to wrap around my waist, then push him up against the wall before stopping. I shake my head, cursing myself for how aggressive I'm being. Shit, I didn't even think. "Bunk, I'm sorry. I didn't mean—"

He cups my cheeks between his hands, green eyes flaming with that familiar boiling fire I fell in love with. "You've been patient, but I'm ready. I'm not fuckin' breakable, Whaley." Then he smirks like an evil maniac. "But you can give it your best shot."

I was trying to be a gentleman. I was trying to be considerate, but Bunky issued a challenge I won't back down from. I claim his lips again and bite down hard enough to taste his blood. Fuck, I love it, love getting a part of him inside of me.

"Gonna destroy you," I moan as I lap at his mouth. "Gonna take it all out on your ass."

He nods quickly, eagerly, tightening his legs around my middle. "Please. Now? I can't wait anymore."

I can't either, but we're not doing this here. Not after three months.

Without any regard for a single-fucking-thing besides getting my dick in his ass, I kick open the door to my office and march right out. I don't let my lips leave his the entire time, only peeking my eyes open to make sure I don't trip over shit. I can see the guys eyeing us, Fox wolf whistling, and Badge looking like he's ready to throttle me.

I. Don't. Fucking. Care.

I barely manage to get us in my truck, laying him on the bench seat and climbing on top of him. I grind down, practically roaring when I feel his hard cock pressing against my hip. It gives me a rush of power I didn't realize I was missing. I wrap my hands around his throat, feral with the need to have him. "Bunk. I love you so damn much."

"I love you too," he wheezes, clawing at my wrists, not to escape but in a desperate attempt to stay close to me. "Take me home."

I hate tearing myself away, but if we're going to do what I have planned then we have to be in our room. I sit up, watching him out of the corner of my eye as I start the truck and take off. The short drive feels like infinity, especially when Bunky reaches into his pants to play with his dick. He throws his head back against the headrest, exposing that gorgeous neck I'm going to grip with my hands. He's panting these sweet little breaths, wiggling around, and I barely contain the urge to pull over and finger fuck him until he comes.

When we finally make it home, I haul him out of the truck and into the trailer. We're stumbling together, crashing into all the furniture, but that doesn't stop us or our frantic need to tear each other's clothes off. By the time we get to our room, we're fully naked, and I push him onto the bed. It's when I take a step back to admire him that the mood shifts. It's as if a flip switches. The confident, sexy, alluring Bunky that taunted me until I cracked is gone. In his place is someone softer, more vulnerable, with tears in his eyes.

"Bunky," I rush out, scrambling to get him in my arms once more. "What's wrong?"

"I— I—" he hiccups, reaching up to cover his face. "I'm s–sorry."

"Talk to me," I tell him, moving so that I'm on top of him, running my hands up and down his sides. "What's goin' on?"

"N–Nothin'. You've waited s–so long. Let's just— Let's—"

"We're not doin' anythin'," I say firmly, rocking him back and forth as he bursts into tears. "I'm sorry. It's too soon, isn't it?"

"It's not that," he sobs, still shaking his head. "I'm not... Whaley, I'm not good enough anymore."

My eyes widen as I lean back to look at him. "What? You're kiddin', right? Why would you think somethin' like that?"

"Just look at me," he wails, gesturing toward his naked body. "You're gettin' damaged goods."

I do take a good look, and I don't see anything wrong. Even without four fingertips, slices of his skin scarred from where Thorn went at his tattoos, and a barely there left nipple, he's still the most perfect thing on the planet.

"Bunky," I begin softly. "You're beautiful. I love every part of you."

He scoffs. "You're sayin' that because you want to get laid."

"Hey, don't put words in my mouth that ain't fuckin' true," I growl, not liking where his head is at. "You wanna know what I see when I look at you?"

His lip juts out and he bobs his head. "What?"

I move him so he's on his back, watery eyes staring up at me with a mix of rage and sadness. I kiss him, tasting the tears on his lips before I start on the rest of him.

My little psycho is everything I've ever wanted, and I'm going to prove it.

"You're so sexy," I mumble, sucking his barely there nipple into my mouth, licking what I assume is sensitive scar tissue. He whimpers, eyes locked onto me as I lave my tongue over him. I let him go with a wet *pop* and move to his right arm. "You're so irresistible." I nibble at the violent scar where his biker tattoo used to be, feeling the warped skin under my teeth. "Fuckin' hell, Bunk. There's never a moment where I don't think about how lucky I am to have you." He gasps when I take his left hand and suck his finger into my mouth, taking my time with each one before I drag his hand down to my hard cock. "Jesus, you're perfect to me. I wanna spend my entire life lookin' at you."

His bottom lip wobbles. "You really mean that?"

"Of course I fuckin' do," I tell him sincerely, wishing he could see himself through my eyes. "I'll wait forever. I'll wait until we're old and wrinkly, and if it never happens again, I'll still love you with the same fuckin' burn that I feel now."

He searches my eyes for the truth, and he must find it. "Take me away, Whaley. I don't want to think. I don't want to breathe. I want to feel."

"I can do that," I promise, knowing that it's finally time. "Do you remember your word?"

"Alfredo."

"Perfect. You just lay here, okay? I'm in charge. Let me take care of everythin'."

He lets out a heavy breath and closes his eyes, melting into the comforter. I take a second to gaze at his body, loving every inch of it and feeling grateful that he's trusting me enough to do this for him.

I walk over to my closet and reach in the back for the box. I slowly take out the cuffs, testing the inside to make sure they're soft enough for his sensitive skin, then return to him and gently grasp one of his wrists, hesitating for only a moment before securing it. He lets out a sharp little gasp but doesn't try to fight it. This gives me the confidence to extend the cord between the cuffs and restrain his other wrist. I hook the tie that connects the two cuffs onto the headboard next, tugging to make sure he has enough room to move if he needs to.

"How are we?"

He nods, eyes still closed as he breathes out slowly through his nose. "Good. Keep goin'."

I grab the silk blindfold and a small paddle next, tying the blindfold over his eyes before grabbing his hips. "Turn over."

He's able to move onto his stomach, and I help him hike up a bit. I'm salivating over his body, eyes immediately latching onto my bite mark on his ass. I let him lay there for a second as I get the lube, placing everything on the bed beside him.

"Just breathe," I remind him, grabbing the paddle to tease his crease. "We're goin' to loosen you up a bit."

"I want to love pain again," he begs, arching his back. "Please, help me."

I suck in a sharp breath. That darkness that called us to each other is still in there like I knew it was. It's brimming under the surface, tamed and scared, but now it's coming out. "Trust me. You'll feel pain."

And that's the only warning I give before bringing the paddle down *hard*.

He lets out a yelp, lurching forward with the force of the blow. "Yes!"

"Are you okay?" I ask, rubbing his ass, loving the way his skin is already turning pink under my touch. "Want another one?"

His head lolls from side to side. "Please."

"Four more." I know there's a limit to how much he can take before I do harm. "You're goin' to take every hit, ain't you?"

"Yes," he says breathlessly.

"And you're gonna thank me after."

"Whaley! Hit me again!"

I smirk at the edge of frustration in his biting words. Impatient little shit. He's wagging his ass in the air and I love it. "Okay. If you say so."

So I do. I hit him four more times, each spank earning me

a beautiful, toe-curling scream, which only makes me harder. I set the paddle aside once I'm done and fall to my knees, dragging my tongue across his red skin.

He moans. "That feels…"

"Good," I finish for him, moving my tongue down to play with his crease, ghosting over his tight hole. "Enough?"

"Never," he breathes out, tugging at his restraints. "I'm ready to be fucked. Stuff me, Whaley. Fuckin' fill me."

I had so many plans. I could use the pinwheel, get the prickling needles to tease his skin. I could even bring out the feather duster, see how he likes that. I have other ropes in my box. I could bend and mold him into whatever shape I want while I fuck him.

But he's needy for me. He's finally ready for this next step, and I don't need any toys to do what we do best.

I fumble for the lube, getting my fingers nice and wet before toying with him. He growls, so animalistic that it makes me groan. "Do it. I'm tired of waitin'. What did I tell you? I'm not breakable— *Fuck!*"

I shove three fingers into him at once, cutting off whatever his smart mouth was going to say next. "You wanna be fucked hard? Used up? Be filthy for me?"

"Always," he whines, fucking himself on my fingers, hands fighting against his restraints. "Want to feel alive, Whaley. Screw me like you want. I know how much you've missed me stranglin' your cock. Know how many times you've wanted to bend me over. Do it. Please!"

Jesus Christ, he's going to kill me.

I pull my fingers out quickly, knowing that he could be prepped a little more, but neither of us can wait. I get my dick wet, making sure to squirt some extra lube on there before lining myself up to him. I prod at his hole, but instead of taking mercy on him, I find the restraint to go inch by inch.

"No!" he cries out, trying to impale himself on my cock,

but I keep him in place with an iron grip on his hips. "That's not how I want it."

"You wanted me to take charge? This is what it looks like," I growl, slapping his ass for good measure. "You're gonna feel every bit of me and my piercin's, little psycho. Gonna feel me stretchin' you until you can't take it anymore. Then and only then I'll give you what you want."

It's a tortuously slow process that I've inflicted on myself, but it's worth it to see every single one of his body's reactions. First, his mouth drops open in a silent shout. Then his toes curl. When I'm more than halfway in, his arms start to tremble. It's only when I'm fully seated inside him that his back arches and sweat blossoms on his back.

"Holy hell," I mumble, fingers digging into his pretty pale skin, sure to leave dents. "Bunky, you feel so good."

"I've missed this so much." His entire body is shaking as I hold myself still inside him. "Let me go. I want to hold you."

I don't hesitate to do as he asks. God, we went from toys to dirty words to this. It's such a feeling of whiplash, but I don't care. It's chaotic, messy, all over the place, but it's just so *us*. I uncuff him so he can flip onto his back, his hands reaching out to me instantly, and I come down willingly. I enter him slowly again, hooking my arms under his back and over his shoulders.

"I love you so much," I tell him, thrusting at a gentle pace, catching every one of his sweet whines and whimpers. "Fuck, nothin's ever gonna change that."

"Until we die, right?" His eyes get teary once more, but this time for an entirely different reason. "When I go, you go?"

"Exactly." I groan when he clenches that sweet hole around me. "Jesus. Do that again."

He does, and I'm so close to coming it's ridiculous. I can't be blamed for being a quick trigger after three months without sex. I think Bunky must be feeling that way too by the way he starts panting and the way he reaches down to grab his leaking cock.

"You close?" I mumble against his lips, speeding up so I can pound into him. "Gonna spill all over that pretty hand? Gonna let go?"

He nods, eyes fluttering shut. "Yes, God, please. Whaley, want to feel you fill me. Need it."

Christ, I need it too.

It takes only a few more snaps of my hips before he's crying out my name, and I'm quick to follow him.

I don't know how long we go for after that. Hours and rounds blur together as we try to quench our need. We're a mess of sweat and drying cum, but I've never felt so satisfied. I look down to where Bunk is passed out across my chest, and I reach up to draw a line down his face. His brows furrow and his lip juts out, making me smirk.

My demon lets out a little hum, tucking himself away in his cage, finally feeling some reprieve now that his match is sated. Yeah, it sounds crazy, but it is what it is. Neither Bunky nor myself ever claimed to be normal. We're a little wild, unhinged for sure, but that's us.

It's messy, it's fucked, but it's ours and that's the real beauty of it all.

I wouldn't change a fucking second of it...

BONUS EPILOGUE

Want a sneak peek of Raid's book? Subscribe to our newsletters to read the prologue for *Sinful Love*!

Subscribe Now!

ACKNOWLEDGMENTS

We would like to give a huge thank you to all the amazing people who made this book possible.

To Ari from Chaotic Creative: you are a wonderful PA and thank you for all the things you do for us.

To our betas, Spicy, Colleen, Eryn, and Monique: thank you for all your amazing feedback and how much you grew to care for Bunky and Whaley.

To Polly: thank you for the incredible edits and showing us everything we never knew we needed.

WHAT'S NEXT FOR ADDISON & T. ASHLEIGH

Kings of Aces Series

This was never intended to be a collaboration or a series, but when we first started writing Silas & Blaine's story, we fell for their world immediately. After writing Bunky and Whaley's, we were hooked!

We have plans for two more books in this series—including Raid's story.

We'll just see where these boys take us.

Thank you again for reading, we're so excited for what's to come!

While Bunky and Whaley's story was centered around dark themes, Sinful Love will be a lighter read. If you're itching for Raid and Landon, preorder now!

WHAT'S NEXT FOR ADDISON BECK?

While I absolutely *adore* the Kings of Aces series, I'm in the middle of writing my next solo release!

While I can't share all the details with you, if you're interested in forbidden romances with two people who should *definitely* not be together, subscribe to my newsletter to get all the information once I'm ready to announce!

Visit www.addisonbeckromance.com to subscribe!

WHAT'S NEXT FOR T. ASHLEIGH

<u>All Roads Series</u>

Book 2 - Bryan's story
Book 3 - Cooper's story

STALK MUCH?

Thanks for reading. I'm Addison Beck and I love all things sweet, smutty, and sinful. I'm a bit of an awkward turtle that can be found in her little shell eating sushi and binging horror movies with her two cats.

Stalk much?

- Go to my website to subscribe to my newsletter!
- www.patreon.com/addisonbeckromance is where you can find all the great bonus scenes and art!
- My reader group—Addison Beck MM Romance—showcases all my crazy thoughts!
- Follow me on Instagram @addisonbeckromance

Thanks for reading! I'm T. Ashleigh and I love all things K-drama and K-pop related. I have multiple biases and refuse to choose just one... IYKYK.

Stalk much?

- Join my newsletter to get ALL the updates!

- Be a part of my Facebook Group—T. Ashleigh's Reader Group—where my crazy thoughts are shared!
- Follow me on Instagram and tag me in your reviews or posts!.
- Check out my Goodreads page!
- Here's my Amazon profile!
- Want to see some awesome mood boards? Find my Pinterest!
- Like my author page on Facebook!

ALSO BY ADDISON BECK

The One Lie Series

One Lovely Lie

One Manic Lie

One Twisted Lie

Standalones (for now)

Their Ball Boy

Dusk Secrets

Kings of Aces

Hateful Love

Painful Love

Sinful Love

ALSO BY T ASHLEIGH